To N. S.

# JOHN HENRY DAYS

COLSON WHITEHEAD

# JOHN HENRY DAYS

Colson Whitehead is the *New York Times* bestselling author
of *The Underground Railroad,* winner of the Pultizer Prize
and the National Book Award, *The Noble Hustle, Zone One,
Sag Harbor, The Intuitionist, John Henry Days, Apex Hides the
Hurt,* and one collection of essays, *The Colossus of New York.*
A recipient of MacArthur and Guggenheim Fellowships,
he lives in New York City.

Colson Whitehead is available for select
speaking engagements. To inquire about a
possible appearance, please contact Penguin
Random House Speakers Bureau at
speakers@penguinrandomhouse.com
or visit www.prhspeakers.com.

www.colsonwhitehead.com

*The Underground Railroad*

*The Noble Hustle*

*Zone One*

*Sag Harbor*

*Apex Hides the Hurt*

*The Colossus of New York*

*John Henry Days*

*The Intuitionist*

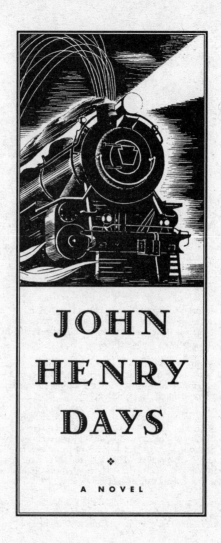

# JOHN HENRY DAYS

❖

A NOVEL

**COLSON WHITEHEAD**

ANCHOR BOOKS • A DIVISION OF PENGUIN RANDOM HOUSE LLC • NEW YORK

FIRST ANCHOR BOOKS EDITION, MARCH 2002

All rights reserved. Published in the United States by Anchor Books, a division of Penguin Random House LLC, New York, and distributed in Canada by Random House of Canada, a division of Penguin Random House Canada Limited, Toronto. Originally published in hardcover in the United States by Doubleday, a division of Penguin Random House LLC, New York, in 2001.

Anchor Books and colophon are registered trademarks of Penguin Random House LLC.

The author has sought to obtain any necessary permissions for quotations included in this book, but has not always been able to locate their authors. If an author of a quotation wishes to contact the author of this book, he or she should contact him through the publisher.

The following sections of the prologue are reprinted from previously published material: Sections 2, 5, 6, 9, and 11 from *John Henry: Tracking Down a Negro Legend* by Guy B. Johnson (Chapel Hill: University of North Carolina Press, 1929); Sections 3, 7, 10, 12, 13, and 14 from *John Henry: A Folk-Lore Study*, by Louis W. Chappell (Port Washington, NY: Kennikat Press, 1968); Section 4 from "John Hardy," by John Harrington Cox, published in the *Journal of American Folk-Lore* (October-December 1919).

The Library of Congress has cataloged the Doubleday edition as follows:
Whitehead, Colson.
John Henry Days: a novel / Colson Whitehead—1st ed.
p. cm.
I. Title.
PS3573.H4768 J64 2001
813'.54—dc21          00-043143

Anchor Books Trade Paperback ISBN: 978-0-385-49820-3
eBook ISBN: 978-0-307-48667-7

Book design by Gretchen Achilles

www.anchorbooks.com

Printed in the United States of America
20  19  18  17  16  15  14  13  12

# PROLOGUE

❖

About 45 years ago I was in Morgan County, Kentucky. There was a bunch of darkeys came from Miss. to assist in driving a tunnel at the head of Big Caney Creek for the O&K railroad. There is where I first heard this song, as they would sing it to keep time with their hammers.

HAVING SEEN YOUR advertisement in the Chicago Defender, I am answering your request for information, concerning the Old-Time Hero of the Big Bend Tunnel Days—or Mr. John Henry.

I have succeeded in recalling and piecing together 13 verses, dedicated to such a splendid and deserving character of by gone days. It was necessary to interview a number of Old-Timers of the Penitentiary to get some of the missing words and verify my recollections; so I only hope it will please you, and be what you wish.

In regards to the reality of John Henry, I would say he was a real live and powerful man, some 50 years ago, and actually died after beating a steam drill. His wife was a very small woman who loved John Henry with all her heart.

My Grand Father, on my mother's side, was a steel driver, and worked on all them big jobs through out the country, in them days, when steam drills were not so popular. He was always boasting about his prowess with a hammer, claiming none could beat him but John Henry. He used to sing of John Henry, and tell of the old days when hammers and hammer men could do the work of the steam drills.

Being pretty young at the time, I can not now recall all the stories I heard, but I know John Henry, died some time in the eighties about 1881 or 1882, I'm sure which was a few years before I was born.

I am setting a price on this information; I am a prisoner here in the Ohio Penitentiary and without funds, so I will be pleased to expect what ever you care to offer.

———

IN 1890 PEOPLE around town here were singing the song of John Henry, a hammering man. I was working in an oyster house here in Norfolk, Va. for Fenerstein and Company, and I am 66 years old and still working for them people.

JOHN HENRY WAS a steel driver and was famous in the beginning of the building of the C&O Railroad. He was also a steel driver in the extension of the N&W Railroad. It was about 1872 that he was in this section. This was before the day of the steam drills and drill work was done by two powerful men who were special steel drillers. They struck the steel from each side and as they struck the steel they sang a song which they improvised as they worked. John Henry was the most famous steel driver ever known in southern West Virginia. He was a magnificent specimen of genus homo, was reported to be six feet two, and weighed two hundred and twenty-five or thirty pounds, was a straight as an arrow and was one of the handsomest men in the country—and, as one informant told me, was a black as a kittle in hell.

Whenever there was a spectacular performance along the line of drilling, John Henry was put on the job, and it is said he could drill more steel than any two men of his day. He was a great gambler and was notorious all through the country for his luck at gambling. To the dusky sex all through the country he was "the greatest ever," and he was admired and beloved by all the negro women from the southern West Virginia line to the C&O. In addition to this he could drink more whiskey, sit up all night and drive steel all day to a greater extent than any man at that time. A man of kind heart, very strong, pleasant address, yet a gambler, a roué, a drunkard and a fierce fighter.

MY NAME IS Harvey Hicks and I live in Evington, Virginia. I am writing in reference to your ad in the Chicago Defender. John Henry was a white man they say. He was a prisoner when he was driving steel in the Big Ben tunnel at the time, and he said he could beat the steam drill down. They told him if he did they would set him free. It is said he beat the steam drill about two minutes and a half and fell dead. He drove with a hammer in each hand, nine pound sledge.

MY UNCLE GUS (the man who raised my father) worked on the Cursey Mountain Tunnel and knew the man. He said he was Jamaican, yellow-complected, tall, and weighed about 200 pounds.

———

I AM A steam shovel operator or "runner" and have heard steel drivers sing "John Henry" all my life and there are probably lots of verses I never heard as it used to be that every new steel driving "nigger" had a new verse to "John Henry."

I never personally knew John Henry, but I have talked to many old-timers who did. He actually worked on the Chesapeake & Ohio Ry. for Langhorn & Langhorn and was able to drive 9 feet of steel faster than the steam drill could in Big Bend Tunnel. Then later he was hanged in Welch, Va., for murdering a man. After sifting out the "chaff" I think I can assure you above is correct.

I have heard three versions of the song, mostly in the same section of the country, that is West Virginia, Virginia, Kentucky, Tennessee and North Carolina, seldom elsewhere except by men from one of the above states. I have worked all over the South, South West, and I have heard the John Henry song almost ever since I could remember, and it is the song I ever first remember of.

I THINK THIS John Henry stuff is just a tale someone started. My father worked for the Burleigh Drill Company and told me for a fact that no steam drill was ever used in the Big Bend Tunnel. He was a salesman for Burleigh.

JOHN HENRY WAS a native of Holly Springs, Mississippi, and was shipped to the Curzee mountain tunnel, Alabama, to work on the AGS Railway in 1880. I have been told that he did indeed beat the steam drill, but did not die that day. He was killed some time later during a cave-in.

HAVING BEEN BORN and raised in the state of Tennessee and, therefore, in sufficiently close contact with the negro element there, it happens I have heard these songs practically all my life, until I left that section of the country six years ago.

I have been informed that John Henry was a true character all right, a nigger whose vocation was driving steel during the construction of a tunnel on one of the Southern railways.

THE BALLAD, BY special right, belongs to the railroad builders. John Henry was a railroad builder. It belongs to the pick-and-shovel men—to the skinners—to the steel drivers—to the men of the construction camps. It is sung by Negro laborers everywhere, and none can sing it as they sing it, because none honor and revere the memory of John Henry as much as do they. I have been a "Rambler" all my life—ever since I ran away from the "white folks" when twelve years old—and have worked with my people in railroad grading camps from the Great Lakes to Florida and from the Atlantic to the Missouri River, and wherever I have worked, I have always found someone who could and would sing of John Henry.

JOHN HENRY THE steel driving champion was a native of Alabama and from near Bessemer or Blackton. The steel driver was between the ages of 45 and 50 and weighed about 155 pounds. He was not a real black man, but more of a chocolate color. He was straight and well muscled.

THE LAST TIME I saw John Henry, who was called Big John Henry, was when a blast fell on him and another Negro. They were covered with blankets and carried out of the tunnel. I don't think John Henry was killed in the accident because I didn't hear of him being buried, and the bosses were always careful in looking after the injured and dead. I don't know a thing about John Henry driving steel in a contest with a steam drill, and I don't think I ever saw one at the tunnel. Hand drills were used in the tunnel. They were using an engine at shaft number one to raise the bucket up when we moved to the tunnel, but they didn't have any steam engine or steam drill in the tunnel.

I'VE HEARD THE song in a thousand different places, nigger extra gangs, hoboes of all kinds, coal miners and furnace men, river and wharf rats, beach combers and sailors, harvest hands and timber men. Some of them drunk and some of them sober. It is scattered over all the states and some places on the outside. I have heard any number of verses cribbed bodily from some other song or improvised to suit the occasion.

The opinion among hoboes, section men and others who sing the song is that John Henry was a Negro, "a coal black man" a partly forgotten verse says, "a big fellow," an old hobo once said. He claimed to have known him but he was drunk on Dago Red, so I'm discounting everything he said. I have met very few who claimed to have known him. The negroes of forty years ago regarded him as a hero of their race.

PART ONE

# TERMINAL CITY

❖

Now he blesses the certainty of airports. His blessings, when he has occasion to perform them, are swift and minimal, thoroughly secular, consisting of a slight nod to no one present, a chin dip that no witness will mark. He nods to luck mostly, to express gratitude for whatever sliver of good fortune drops before his shoes. The day's first blessing is occasioned by a solemn white rind, a little feather, that J. Sutter notices a few yards away on the carpet and immediately recognizes, without a shade of doubt, to be a receipt.

He looks left and he looks right. He waits for one of those dull marchers to open a fanny pack, turn rigid in horror, and retrace steps to rescue the lost receipt as the wheels of their plastic luggage carve evanescent grooves in the purple carpet behind them. It could belong to any one of these folks. The anxious dislocation of travel causes them to compulsively pat pockets for wallets and passports, to stroke telltale ridges in canvas bags that most definitely must be the ticket and boarding pass, but not so definitely that the ridge must not be checked again, the bag unzipped and inspected for the hundredth time that day. In this queasy awareness of their trifling, they might notice the disappearance of a receipt more readily and start searching for it. He factors this consideration into his calculation of how long it will take him to salvage the receipt from its immediate peril in the walkway.

It taunts him, vibrates flirtatiously. What does it record? There are all sorts of things you can buy at an airport, they are becoming more and more like cities every day, one lumbering transcontinental metropolis. Double-A batteries, a teddy bear, a toothbrush to replace the one forgotten back home on the sink. A nourishing lunch—he hopes for lunch because he is hungry and the next best thing to an actual sandwich right now is the paper trail of a sandwich. Something nonspecific, even better, just a fat total at the bottom, he can tell them it records anything he wants it to. Within the elastic confines of reimbursable expenses, of course.

The receipt flutters and taunts. He is at Gate 22, at the mouth of Terminal B, and any one of the laden and harried pilgrims might be searching for the receipt at this very moment and contest his ownership should he in fact make his move. Witnesses at the counter. J. dislikes scenes. As if airport security would take his word over some middle-aged mom from Paramus. Pharmacy bin sunglasses hooked askew into the neck of her striped outlet T-shirt, her faded Cancun souvenir baseball cap, those taxpayer details, he'd have no chance.

This little boy in bright green robot gear, merchandise from whatever kids' show is big now, contemplates the stray receipt just as intently as J. from across the walkway in the opposing camp of Gate 21, Flight 702 to Houston. He reckons the boy is waiting for one of the travelers to step on it, to relish that dinosaur foot carnage, and when this image occurs to J.—the receipt mangled by designer sneaker tread or so smudged that it would be useless to him—he immediately evacuates the plastic bucket seat, strides confidently out into the walkway with nary a guilty twitch, and after one quick glance back to make sure that no one is stealing his stuff, he bends down and grips the lonesome shaving between his thumb and index finger as gingerly as an entomologist stooping for a rare moth. No one raises a ruckus. The little boy sneers at him and performs a baroque martial arts move.

J.'s neck eases, his chin dips and he makes his blessing as he sits back down. For this is pure luck, a pristine receipt newly plucked from the great oak of consumption, and deserves a blessing. Airports bloom receipts as certainly as standing water bubbles up mosquitoes. He chides himself for waiting so long to pick it up. Why would anyone want it besides him? It is litter. Early afternoon in terminal city: most of these people are civilians, off visiting relatives or wherever normal people go, Disneyland. Not executives who will log every transaction on their corporate expense forms, and definitely not junketeers like him. No one was going to fight him over a receipt lost on the floor, tumbleweeding from gate to gate as footfall gusts urged it to some far corner. He feels foolish, but glad nonetheless that he still has his instincts. There is sure to be some hectic receipt wrangling over the next few days.

J. inspects his bounty. He brushes purple carpet fiber and a curlicue hair from the paper, runs his finger over the serration at its head. He makes a wish and scrutinizes. The printer of register #03 at Hiram's News could use some new toner; only twenty minutes old and the receipt is already affecting a world-weary languor. Not a great haul, it won't rank up there with the great found-receipt frauds he's perpetrated over the years, certainly not another

Planet Hollywood Paris or Prague '92, but still useful: one magazine and one item of candy, both identified only by strings of scanner numbers. J. makes the candy for chewing gum, puts the purchaser as a smoker in for a gnashing ride wherever he is going, but the magazine. Looking at three bucks and ninety-five cents, he puts his money on a perfume-packed lifestyle glossy: I'll take something in a Condé Nast, please. DeAngelo Brothers Distribution has most of the Northeastern airports locked up and an agreement stipulates that Nast gets strong point-of-purchase display. He figures that on the expense form he'll write down the magazine as research and slip the gum in as food. J. tucks the receipt in with the rest of the morning's take, the cab and hotel receipts, and resumes listening to the airport announcements. He feels serene. He is a citizen of terminal city and he keeps every receipt in a chosen nook of his wallet and wayward receipts catch his eye from time to time.

It is safe in here. He watches his fellow shufflers queue before the gate attendants, who carve up the airplane cabin into certified tracts. This seems to him an orderly system, one of many in this concrete aviary. The giant brackets lulling the prefab sections of the terminal into peaceful aggregation, the charged and soothing simulated air, automatic flush urinals. He likes the new sound of cash registers, no more chimes: Instead this novel theater of validating purchases, the electronic scrying of purple ink across paper, that tiny pulse that reaches out to the network testing the credibility of credit cards. True, each foray through the metal detector still feels like a prison break and there is no stopping the animal jostling when boarding is announced or when the plane sidles up to the destination gate and all those grubby moist-toileted damp hands grope for the overhead compartment latches, but these are expressions of human weakness, no fault of the design of airports. J. locks his carry-on bag (he is allowed only one on this flight) between his heels. Even the cramped chaos of embarkation and debarkation can be overcome with the right attitude. People movers and white courtesy phones. Food in convenient trays. What the meals lack in taste, they compensate for in thoughtful packaging. He's never found a human hair in airplane food. What else are plastic shells for. Iceberg lettuce contains important minerals. New advances in legroom, he's noticed this in the last few months he has been a resident here. J. is confident that they (an air carrier coalition, squabbles checked at the door, this agenda before them) are dedicated to attacking certain essential problems and have platoons of ergonomists sequestered on a suburban campus working on the problem of legroom, circulation, the facts of biology versus the exigencies of cabin space, and that is why, even though the fruit of this work is difficult for the eye to discern, he has fewer leg cramps these days.

A gate attendant announces boarding and he waits for them to call his row. A gate attendant rips a large section from his boarding pass and he slips the remainder into his pocket as he walks down the chilly declivity to the loading door.

He forces his bag into the trim space beneath the seat in front of him as instructed. He is an aisle man, has been for years. Middle seat is a ham sandwich, and there is nothing to see out the reinforced windows, just the undigested blur of the nation. J. feels he works more efficiently if he does not think of his audience, where they live. He likes to keep his obligations to meeting the word count, a number readily verified by a feature on a pulldown menu of his word processing program.

People carefully push items into the overhead compartment only to have their thoughtful arrangements undone and encroached upon by other passengers. The flight attendants check the overhead compartments and latch them.

A plump white woman in a slim turquoise pantsuit informs him that she has been assigned the window seat. As he allows her room to pass, he composes in his mind an ad for her perfume that describes a versatile essence appropriate for both the office and evenings out. Then he places the scented ad on a page toward the front of the book, between the contributors' notes and letters to the editor. She slides her leather briefcase beneath the seat in front of her and pulls down the shade. Her feathered red hair is as leveled as an ancient pagoda. In unison they fasten their seat belts.

It is a time of checking and rechecking of clasps and buckles and latches throughout the body of the plane, an assembly of minutiae that might make a liftoff.

He is always up in the air.

The woman in the window seat wins the first round by lifting the armrest that divides her seat and the middle seat into discreet pens. She folds her jacket in half and pats it down in the empty seat. Beats him to it. J. tells himself to wake up. He is going to need all of his skills this weekend; this woman is a civilian, a minnow compared to all those other pilot fish he'll be competing with over the next few days.

J. watches the flight attendant nudge the metal cart up the aisle in the dot dot dash of cabin food dispensation. A snack flight, just a little jump south and east. He unlatches the food tray and slides his palms across its unblemished factory surface. The flight attendant smiles at this and deposits a square foil packet of snacks and a nonalcoholic beverage. He turns the package so that it is parallel to the edges of the tray and contemplates his lunch. Pretzel logs dusted with orange cheese flavor. The hotel this morning gave away doughnuts and coffee on a table near the registration desk, so that was one free meal he could easily categorize—even by the standards of normal people—as breakfast, and this is the second free meal of the day because another party had purchased his ticket, and then tonight there is some kind of opening-night banquet, free meal *numero tres*. He'll count this package of pretzels as lunch and gorge himself on the buffet, it is sure to be a buffet, it always is, J. figures he can hold out that long. He can always hold out for a free meal. J. sucks the cheese dust and salt from the pretzels, dissolving these substances by rubbing them against the roof of his mouth before biting down into the pretzel proper. He sees the benevolent and nurturing crimson light of the heat lamp over prime rib, the cheerful blue fire of the sterno cans beneath the metal trays containing local produce. He wipes the orange residue into the cushion of his seat, which doubles as a flotation device if certain situations arise.

The woman in the window unlatches the tray of the middle seat, where she places her empty snack package and plastic glass. Round two, J. observes, flexing her might. Sending the gunboats to Cuba. She refastens her tray and after slow survey of her domain resigns herself to the unalloyed distraction of the airplane periodical.

The magazine contains, scattered among global itineraries and capsule descriptions of inflight movies, informative articles of sundry nature. A few years back J. landed a piece in there, an endorsement of new Zairian hotels; President Mobutu had been trying to rustle up some tourist traffic for that oft-overlooked country. J. observed no rivers of blood while there. It was a junketeer's ball. Every slob on the List roused themselves for that one. Their credentials were never verified. Hepatitis a regular topic of conversation. Only J. was naive enough to actually write an article about the trip. He was green then, nervous about repercussions, clinging valiantly to an abstraction of journalistic ethics. The government flew in crates of liquor from Europe. He got two dollars a word and bought some new pants.

J. looks over the woman's shoulder and notices Tiny's byline on an article about the French Quarter of New Orleans. Fourth or fifth time the fucker has sold that story. At least—there are too many outlets these days for him to keep track of his own stories, let alone his comrades'. You have to admire Tiny's nerve. A junketeer among junketeers. J. wonders if he bothered to change the lede this time. The woman notices J.'s attentions, scowls, and gestures toward him as if to remind J. that every seatback is stocked with the latest volume of the airline journal. His stomach gurgles in hunger.

After a time the flight attendant moseys up the aisle bearing a white plastic bag with a red drawstring slotted into its lip. Same kind he has at home, a convenient model that flatters his farsightedness whenever he purchases a box. J. deposits his trash and the trash from the middle tray into the bag. He returns his tray to the upright position. He almost shuts the middle tray too but then realizes that he may have trespassed by disposing of her trash. She had extended her zone to cover the empty seat fair and square. At least his armrests are uncontested. Just to make sure he grips them tightly. When the plane comes to rest at the gate, the woman grabs her briefcase and coat and shuffles toward him. His only revenge for her excellent gamesmanship during the flight is to sit still and patient as she fidgets beside him, her hand rapping her thigh and eyes prying open the overhead from afar. She is not going to move through him. J. stands when he is good and ready, when it is their row's turn out of the bottleneck. I take it where I can get it, he says to himself.

Forget the South. The South will kill you. He possesses the standard amount of black Yankee scorn for the South, a studied disdain that attempts to make a callus of history. It manifests itself in various guises: sophisticated contempt, a healthy stock of white trash jokes, things of that nature, an instinctual stiffening to the words County Sheriff. One look at the cannibals massing at the arrival gate and his revulsion rubs its paws together and hisses. The faces are different: He always feels this fact keenly when he touches down in a place he has never been before. But on this occasion his dread expresses itself so forcefully that he has half a mind to scurry back up the ramp for the protection of his aisle seat. He has arrived at a different America he does not live in. The undiagnosed press toward the gate waiting for kin. Placed hip-to-hip, the rivulets and shadings of their acid-washed jeans describe a relief map of blighted confederacy. Powerline kids suck fingers. Between the hems of oversized shorts and lips of polyknit athletic socks sally bright red lobster flesh and craggy knees, dumb and unashamed things, sea-bottom tubers uncataloged by any known system of biological taxonomy. (None of this is true, of course, but perception is all; to and from each his own dark continent.) One man had fashioned his beard into a slim rattail, they all draw from the same tainted well, it is simply disturbing.

An image of the impending buffet shimmers in the air before him and his seizure subsides. He's been to Atlanta a few times, but Atlanta is a chocolate city and he was never permitted to stray from the record companies' publicity circuits. Covered Mardi Gras for the travel section of a daily in Des Moines, but felt protected in the prevailing madness of celebration, which creates pockets of safety and violence in equal measure. Stopovers in Texas but damned if he left the borders of terminal city. It is not difficult to indulge his preferences; media events tend to emerge near media centers and that means the coasts. He's been very conscientious about staying away from the forge of his race's history. And now here he is in Charleston, West Virginia, at the behest of the United States Postal Service and a smudge town called Talcott to cover the unveiling of a postage stamp, inertial, grubbing, hoarding receipts, because he is on a three-month junket jag he is too unwilling or too scared to break. He thinks, these people are liable to eat me.

J. searches for his name in crayon on a slab of cardboard but cannot find his driver at the gate or at baggage claim. Nice summer day: the man is probably down at the fishing hole. Or rocking in a frayed hammock. He decides to wait outside.

Hubbub of vehicles at the curb. He doesn't have much choice other than to wait. He has no idea where he is going. Yeager Airport, named after Brigadier General Charles E. "Chuck" Yeager, or so he reads on a well-polished bronze plaque. Chuck Yeager is a native son. No wonder he took flight. J. waits for his driver to pull up in a red pickup with a bunch of chickens in the back spitting feathers.

In the passenger loading and unloading zone the carbon monoxide, so terrible after the careful atmosphere of the terminal, hangs low around his heels, heavier than air. A gang of dirty clouds loiters over there. J. says, "What a dump," and for the second time that day he blesses the certainty of airports because he can always turn around and go someplace else.

**United States Postal Service—Postal News**
*For Immediate Release*

**June 6, 1996**

### American Folk Hero Comes to Life in Stamp Series

WASHINGTON—One of America's best-loved folk heroes will come to life this summer when the town of Talcott, West Virginia, holds the first annual "John Henry Days" festival, which will coincide with release of the U.S. Postal Service's Folk Heroes stamp series. Since the 1870s, John Henry has been extolled as a strongman born with a hammer in his hands and the ability to drive steel for ten continuous hours. It is said that while working for the Chesapeake & Ohio Railroad on the Big Bend Tunnel just outside Talcott, John Henry challenged a steam drill to a race and swung his hammers so hard that he beat the machine. Railroad workers who arduously labored during the building of the nation's rail system literally sang the praises of this hero.

The town of Talcott is pleased to honor one of its famous residents. On the weekend of July 12, 1996, the town will host the inaugural "John Henry Days" festival, a three-day celebration of railroad history and local culture. Representatives of the United States Postal Service will be on hand for the official unveiling of the Folk Heroes stamp series, and many surprise guests and activities have been scheduled. "Folk heroes like John Henry represent the best of American values," said Postmaster General Marvin Runyon. "The U.S. Postal Service is proud to continue their tales through our commemorative stamp series."

Joining John Henry on the Folk Heroes series are Paul Bunyan, Mighty Casey and Pecos Bill. Paul Bunyan, according to lore, was a giant lumberjack who journeyed the country with Babe, the Blue Ox, clearing trees. Bunyan was a hero to legions of lumberjacks, who spun yarns about Bunyan clearing acres of outsized trees and employing legions of loggers from across the continent. Generations of children have heard the classic "Casey at the Bat," which first appeared in the *San Francisco Examiner* in 1888. Written by Ernest Lawrence Thayer and popularized by William DeWolf Hopper, that ballad relates the story of an arrogant young baseball player who strikes out at bat, causing his team to lose an important game. Since his original tale appeared in *Century Magazine* in 1923, Pecos Bill and his mastery of the American frontier have been a part of our national lore. Legend contends that this folk hero was raised by a coyote and was rugged enough to ride a mountain lion and commandeer a rattlesnake as a lasso.

The stamps were designed by artist Dave La Fleur of Derby, Kansas, and will be available nationwide beginning July 15. "The folk heroes are illustrated exactly as in at least one written version of their tales," said stamp artist La Fleur. "Each hero's most memorable moment is depicted: Casey just before he swings his bat, John Henry wielding his hammer, Paul Bunyan his ax, and Pecos Bill his rattlesnake."

The Postal Service will issue 113 million Folk Heroes series stamps in panes of twenty stamps. Each pane will sell for $6.40.

A special reception for members of the media will be held on Friday, July 12, at the historic Millhouse Inn. Accommodations will be arranged. If you plan to attend this event, please contact Arlene at the Summers County Visitors Center.

J sits in the backseat of an American car of recent vintage. Jesus Christ hangs from the rearview mirror and shakes at every turn as if trying to wiggle His crucifix from the ground. Arnie apologizes again for being late to pick up J. at the airport.

J. says no problem. He looks out the back window and returns to his activity of the past ten minutes, a cool contemplation of the eighteen-wheeler chasing their rear bumper. A plastic sheet detailing the Confederate flag dominates the truck's front grille. He can't see the driver but he waves hello to the black window and turns. Around him the outlands of the city of Charleston, clumps of industrial parks and jumbo shopping centers and entire new species of parking lot, recede into the countryside. There is the problem of horizontal space. In the distance J. sees mountains, insurgent green lids peering over the rim of the world, whenever the smaller peaks the road cleaves through allow him to see that far. Did the settlers ever think they'd get past these slopes, J. asks himself. Cross an ocean, they make it this far into the land and worry that the whole place is like this: a concatenation of cliffs and banks, as if some hobgoblin roosting on the other side of the hills had shoved up the earth. Like a giant kicking a bunch of green carpet. Hearty folk, the mountain people.

"Do you mind if I take the back roads?" Arnie asks. He gestures at the lane ahead, the congealing traffic. "They close it up to one lane a couple of miles ahead. For construction. It might take the same time, but it won't take longer."

"You know the way," J. answers. With a little luck, the monster vehicle behind them won't follow. J. puts Arnie in his forties, paying alimony and owning his cab after years of scrimping, part of the far-flung fleet of New River Gorge Taxi. Fleet, as in two or three rheumy vehicles. Arnie's straw hair thins and golden stubble sprouts from his chin. Eats what he catches. The interior of the car smells, not unpleasantly, of the better class of urinal cake.

"So," Arnie clears his throat, "what are you, with the Post Office?"

"I'm a journalist."

"Writing an article about the festival?"

"That's right."

Arnie asks him if he writes for newspapers and magazines and J. says yeah, even though this particular piece is for a new travel website. J. doesn't feel like explaining the web; this guy probably thinks a laptop is some new kind of banjo. Lucien set it up. J. hasn't worked for the web before but knew it was only a matter of time: new media is welfare for the middle class. A year ago the web didn't exist, and now J. has several hitherto unemployable acquaintances who were now picking up steady paychecks because of it. Fewer people are home in the afternoon eager to discuss what transpires on talk shows and cartoons and this means people are working. It was only a matter of time before those errant corporate dollars blew his way. He attracts that kind of weather.

J. checks the receipt nook in his wallet again, just to make sure. He makes a concerted effort to enjoy the scenery. It is hard: all trees look alike to him. The route slips between the places the government blasted through, the hills, and the scarred rock faces stare at each other from the sides of the road, grim, still grudgeful after all these years at their sunderance. Water trickles down the rock from unknown springs, high up springs, who knows what, this is nature, down the slopes, across the roots of intrepid trees, and wets the rock faces like perspiration on the brow of a boxer. The driver is taking J. deep in. Off the interstate. He is being taken in. Lucien set the gig up when J. called and expressed his serious doubts as to whether he could place a story about a fucking stamp. It was mostly a philosophical problem; they don't have to write about all the various events they attend, just enough to keep from looking like complete hacks. No one wants the game to be exposed, not the junketeers and not the p.r. folks who set the itineraries. Most of the time it is enough to pull out a notebook and scribble for appearance's sake, in between passes at the hors d'oeuvres table. After a couple of years, J. has learned to only write up the events where the number of expenses and the dollar-per-word bounty make coasting prohibitive. There are never any repercussions. Publicists continue to greet him warmly and hand out press material that remains unopened, he carries away promotional items by the bushel, he eats and drinks his fill. He remains on the List.

But this stamp problem. This stamp gig was so unusual, J. put it to Lucien as a kind of challenge: who in the world would possibly care about this event? What magazine employed copy editors who could bear to touch a comma of such a piece, what newspaper had a readership that consisted entirely of drooling and defenseless shut-ins? They'd been in rough straits before, Lucien and his journalist allies, but always came through in the end if they had to, placed the piece about Ronald McDonald's rap record (open-faced filet mignon burgers and chocolate margarita shakes at the press party), found the sympathetic editor who had column space for the plastic surgeon who specialized in Hollywood kindergartens (everyone who attended the press conference got a free estimate and a computer-generated hypothetical face to take home with them). But a postage stamp? It seemed ridiculous even by their degraded standards. In West Virginia yet. J. just wanted to know if the world had progressed to a point where such a thing was possible. He just wanted to know.

Lucien was calm and patient. He gave a little speech. He told J. to stick around his hotel room for a few minutes. A few minutes later the features editor of Time Warner's travel website rang and said he was thinking of running a piece on the Talcott celebration and would J. be interested. Like that.

Now the road dives between peaks, past towns persistent beyond the defeat of founding father ambition. The speckling of quiet houses and rusted trucks draws itself from the muck and develops a culture and evolves into strip malls, bright knots of gas stations and fast food outlets, before collapsing again into a barbarism of shacks and rusted trucks. The strip malls are reaching for perfection. Each time they enter into the outlands of a new strip mall, J. wonders if this time the franchisees and maverick entrepreneurs will get it right, if this time the ratios are correct and density, placement, brand will configure a new and final product. One beautiful single product with acreage and registers, with multiple fire exits and convenient business hours. But each creation is botched and maladjusted, it will not play with the other kids or has a morbid disposition, and subsides, inevitably, into the silence of black country road. And soon the strip malls disappear altogether and J. will see a sign for a town, and one or two lone houses jammed into hillside accelerate into a cluster of abodes and then thin out again. Presently he'll see the sign for the next town, all without ever passing what passes for a town in his definition. Not even a store beyond a gas station. He is confused.

Arnie says, "Nice and peaceful. Sure beats the city, huh?" Having assumed correctly that J. is not a son of the South.

"It certainly is green," J. says.

"First time in West Virginia?"

"Yeah."

"You're going to like it," Arnie assures. " 'The most northern of the southern, the most southern of the northern, the most western of the eastern, and the most eastern of the western.' That's what they say, and I can vouch for it. We've got everything here. Skiing in Beckley a good part of the year. If you get a chance over the weekend, you should check out the river. They have all sorts of white water rafting trips you can take."

"I'm not much of a water person," J. says. Which puts an end to the bumpkin patter for a while.

Content everlasting. The man at the website, sounded like a young guy, said they were looking for content. The website is set to launch in a few weeks. Eventually they want it to have a global aspect, but for the start they are focusing on gathering a lot of regional content. That way they pull in local advertisers, he explained. J. could hear computer keys tapping through the receiver. Time Warner is putting a lot of money into the launch, the man informed him. They want to make a big splash. He invited J. to the launch party, if J. was going to be in town. J. knew he was already invited; Time Warner is a mainstay of the List. All J. can think is *content*. It sounds so honest. Not stories, not articles, but content. Like it is a mineral. It is so honest of them.

Arnie and J. have been on small roads for over half an hour now, dancing along curved blacktop, past slide areas and deer crossings. The driver makes another attempt at conversation: "When I heard your name, I thought, Sutter, huh? Sounds like a Southern name."

"Maybe my ancestors were owned down here at some point."

"Maybe . . . ?" Arnie meets J.'s eyes in the rearview mirror and chuckles. "That's funny. You're funny." He starts to hum.

The light gives after a series of turns as the trees huddle together and snatch at the afternoon. There are no other cars on the road. Each time they clear one forbidding encroachment of hills, more livid peaks keep the car closed in. Arnie hums and taps his fingers on the steering wheel. This burp of paranoia: what if Caleb here is driving him up into the mountains, down to the creek, out to the lonesome spot where his family performs rituals. Boil him up in a pot, ritual sacrifice helps the crops grow. J. peers over the front seat waiting for the tree line to break. Taking the back roads indeed. After a few days the FBI will verify that he was on the flight to Yeager Airport, the woman in the window seat provides unenthusiastic affirmation, but after that no trail. Arnie's cousin the local constable. Maybe not even after a few days. No one knows where he is any more than he does. His editor will just think he flaked out on the assignment. Notorious tendency of freelancers to disappear near a deadline. Boil him up in a pot while they watch wrestling on TV. He figures even the most remote shack has a TV these days. The cable carrier in this region serves a special clientele, entire public access shows devoted to dark meat recipes.

As a joke, J. almost says, "So what do you do around here for fun?" but thinks better of it. I'm a real city boy, J. thinks, I'm a real jaded fuck. Eventually they clear the woods, passing first an unattended stand of native arts and crafts that seems not to have been open for some time, then a gas station and garage with a rogues gallery of cars and pickups in its lot. Arnie says they are getting close.

Content is king, they say. Rape and pillage time for the junketeer willing to put in the time to make the contacts. A whole new scale.

"This is Hinton," Arnie says. They had rounded a turn and now came across the biggest settlement in some time. Hinton is dropped down in the middle of a valley, a marble cupped by monstrous green hands. The car is separated from the town by the murky gray river that carved the valley; J. sees the low bridge that would have taken them into Hinton if they had turned left. A flat section of the town groups along the opposite bank, he spies a shopping center and above it the buildings inch up the mountain wall, thinning, a scattering of two- and three-story buildings that are probably the original town: old and distinguished structures. Arnie doesn't turn left. Arnie takes him right, away and parallel from the town, down the road that creeps along the river. A strip of small establishments perch on this side of the bank, a souvenir taxidermy shop, the Coast to Coast motel. Herb's Country Style promises chicken fried steak. Between the stores, J. can make out the other half of Hinton across the river, lurking among trees like a fugitive.

Arnie has stopped humming. "I usually only work Mondays and Tuesdays," he says, "but the festival is paying us almost double what we usually get. You staying at the Motor Lodge?"

"I'm not sure. If that's what they told you."

"Well, they said the Motor Lodge, so that's where I'm going to take you. If it turns out that's not where you're supposed to be, I'll wait around and take you to wherever you're supposed to be. How's that sound? We can go to Saskatchewan, I don't care." Arnie is flexible, apparently. "I heard Ben Vereen was coming. Is that true?"

"I'm not sure."

"I love Ben Vereen," Arnie says. "This is shaping up to be some big party.

Saying after a few years it could be bigger than the Nicholas County Spud and Splinter Festival. Good for the whole area." Up ahead J. sees the river jump out of a gigantic dam in exuberant streams, like hair through a comb, but they veer away from it; Arnie turns left across a black bridge that takes them over the rolling water. "Talcott's about ten miles on," Arnie continues. "That's where John Henry's from. But we're not going that far. Talcott's pretty small, so I guess that's why most of the stuff this weekend is being organized in Hinton. They're like sisters."

Past the bridge the road is unpopulated again. The road follows another branch of the river and J. looks down into tenebrous water. Trees march down right into the current and J. pictures a whole forest under the dark water, what existed before the dam raised the river. Maybe even a whole town sleeping under there. He wonders if the newspaper of the drowned town needs freelancers.

Arnie turns at a tall clapboard sign announcing the Talcott Motor Lodge. The sign has been recently repainted. He pulls up to the front door of the main building, a squat red structure with a tin roof. A statue of a railroad engineer tips its hat to all who pass.

"Here we are," Arnie says.

J. asks for a receipt.

After the killing is over, after the gunman has slid to the ground, after the gun smoke has dissipated into the invisible, the witnesses rouse themselves into this world again, find themselves waking in warm huddles reinforcing each other's humanity; they blink at their surroundings to squeeze violence from their eyes. Some gather their wits more quickly and run for help. A few possess a small measure of medical expertise and tend to the dying and shout reassuring words that are as much for the wounded as for themselves. There is a magnetism of families and friends, they are drawn together and inspect each other's bodies for damage. The witnesses thank God. The witnesses share what they have seen and fit their perspectives into one narrative through a system of sobbing barter. In these first few minutes a thousand different stories collide; this making of truth is violence too, out of which facts are formed.

Facts are Joan Acorn's trade this summer. She has recovered her purse and notepad but cannot find her pen. It is suddenly the most important thing in her life that she recover her pen. It's a Bic. She thinks she must have sent it flying when she heard the first shot and dropped to the prone position described by the personal security consultant her sorority retained to teach them about self-defense. Keep low, he said, and recited statistics about driveby shootings in the ghetto. As she looked up at him from the couch in the living room of her sorority house, Joan imagined him as the kind of man who instructed the ROTC guys in military lore. He was really butch. Joan found him sexy. He knew how to tell people things so they remained in their consciousness. The consultant enjoyed a vogue on her campus, he was a prophet of anticrime come to deliver them from the rape scare. When she heard the first shot Joan dropped between the folding chairs and sent her pen flying.

She sees her pen a few yards away, next to someone's lost sandal. A new wave of screaming starts; a new realization of what has happened thrashes around in traumatized skulls. Joan struggles to do what any journalist would do in this situation. The final event of John Henry Days was her first assignment, it turned out differently than expected, and she remembers instructions from last semester's Intro Journalism class. She crammed late-night in her pajamas with a friend, deciphering her lecture notes for the final and dropping microwave popcorn. Joan is single-minded. She navigates through the overturned chairs. Everything is so bright. People congregate in groups and pat each other's bodies. They dangle and sag. She makes her way to the sidewalk. Cars are hum still in the street, their doors open and mysterious and full of tales. It reminds her of a nuclear war movie.

She approaches an older couple dressed in identical green and red jogging suits. She identifies herself as a writer for the *Charleston Daily Mail* and asks them what they have seen. The witnesses point up to the bandstand. The witnesses point to the groups ministering to the dying. She canvasses the witnesses and tries to get the story. When Joan gets to the telephone outside the barbershop she tries to remember her parents' calling card number and has a little bit of difficulty.

Joan gets through to the editorial desk and informs a man about the killing spree. She sees a tan police car enter the square. Her use of the words killing spree is questioned by the man working the Sunday slot, who asks her to identify herself and slow down. Joan is the intern for the Life section of the *Charleston Daily Mail*. She had been very excited early in the spring that she might get the chance to write about fashion, a desire she expressed to her parents during their Sunday evening phone call. Her father got on the phone to her uncle. Her uncle, a successful lawyer who had many influential friends, got on the horn to the sales director of the *Charleston Daily Mail*, who made calls of his own. Then disaster struck. Around April Joan discovered that her three best friends were going to travel in Europe for the summer. Joan fumed; she wished they had told her earlier, they were supposed to be best friends. But she had already given her word committing to the internship and her parents told her that to back out would make her look irresponsible. In addition, they had paid for her trip to Europe the summer before and did not want to spoil her. A compromise in the form of a new car to facilitate her commute between home and office restored the family to its customary state of goodwill.

Joan tries to slow down on the phone. The slot man tells her to just slow down and tell him what happened exactly. For a second, the men standing over the journalist part and she can see his bloody chest and slack mouth. The sales director of the *Charleston Daily Mail* took her out to lunch the first day of her internship and described the history and traditions of the paper, pantomiming certain key moments with his hairy fingers. Joan's duties include opening mail, calling for art, and taking messages. There are occasional perks. One time the film editor said, anyone want a pass to a movie, and Joan took her best friend from childhood. In the movie they sat next to a beautiful news anchorman who had been on television for years and years. She made the best of things. Joan told her friends from high school, amid the silences that made apparent the divergent tacking of their lives, that she was going to write for the *Daily Mail*, but in fact she had little success convincing her boss of her specialness. The editor of the Life section does not seem fashionable or hip. He had been trapped by benefits and union security some years before. He is grizzled and has seen interns come and go, but Joan is an expert nagger. She is pert and brunette. In an impulse of inspired cruelty, he assigned her to write two hundred words on the stamp ceremony, to teach her about the dues all journalists must pay, no matter who their friends are. Joan was delighted and rose early Sunday morning and drove the fifty miles from Charleston to Talcott in her new car, which was equipped with a CD player.

The Sunday slot man reiterates his instructions to Joan. Just tell him slowly what happened. She perceives a stiffening in the postures of the men tending to one of the wounded and takes this as an indication of his worsening condition. She begins to cry. She cannot get the words to the slot man. She thinks, where, what, who, these are the essential questions a journalist must ask herself. And then Joan feels a warmth in her chest and she says in someone else's voice, "Talcott, West Virginia—A postal worker opened fire Sunday afternoon on a crowd of people gathered for the unveiling of a new postage stamp; critically wounding three people before being shot and killed."

**D**ave Brown's byline is a roach whose gradual infestation of the world's print media can only be sketchily documented. First sightings of the scourge can be traced to the late 1960s; numerous samples of the creature's spoor have been collected from the concert reviews section of *Crawdaddy*. The counterculture, it is hypothesized, proved an abundant food source for the emergent insect, which seemed to thrive on the scraps of the new pop culture, insinuating itself behind the baseboards of *Rolling Stone* and beneath the refrigerators of alternative weeklies. The organism traveled to new publishing empires by stowing away in the cargo holds of spectacle, a survival instinct that served it well in the following decade when a threefold increase in the number of print venues provided ample nesting opportunities. This moist, expanding media proved an exceptionally favorable environment for the byline and its appearances grew at an exponential rate. It has been observed crawling above a prison interview with Sirhan Sirhan in *Playboy* and lazily breeding in the *New York Times* during the heyday of singer-songwriters. Stubborn and tenacious, the byline was able to sustain itself through climatic changes in editorial style, its reproductive cycle seemingly unaffected by the insufferable aridity of the Reagan years. Today, no newsstand remains uninfested by Dave Brown's byline and its readily identifiable, unadorned, service-oriented prose.

On the afternoon of July 12, 1996, Dave Brown sits in the parking lot of the Talcott Motor Lodge in a beach chair, legs ajar, sunning his face with the optimistic silver of a tanning shield. He wears faded army cutoffs and bright red designer sneakers. His gray, untied shoelaces look as if they have been chewed. Dave nods at J. and gestures toward his thermos. "You want a drink?"

"What is it?"

"Gin and tonic."

J. shakes his head and drops his bags. He looks down at his key and searches for his room number on the rows of the motel behind him. The green motel building lounges low and fat; its two floors are stacked atop each other like two worms engaged in sexual congress. J. feels a few beads of sweat pop out from his underarms. "How long have you been here?" he asks, eyes tracing green ridges.

"I got in about an hour ago," Dave says, his head still tilted up to the sun. "Only flight I could get. I think we're the first ones here."

J. looks back at the hotel rooms. He asks Dave if he knows which of their fellow mercenaries will be attending the weekend's events.

"Beats me," Dave replies. "It's kind of a bum gig, and those are the ones where you never know who's going to show up. Frenchie I know, because I saw him at the *Esquire* thing last week and he said he was coming. Probably Tiny because he likes Southern food." He takes off his sunglasses and shakes his head. "I'm just here because I figured I'd kill some time before I head to L.A. for the TV press tour. Charleston seemed like a nice way station in between there and New York. Get some country air and that shit. I don't know what I was thinking."

J. shifts on his feet. His stomach complains again. "What's the buzz on the buffet?"

"I haven't heard anything yet. Local culture, hard to say. But then you gotta factor in the U.S. Post Office and you never know with government food. Sure you don't want a drink?"

"What time is it?"

"It's about four-thirty."

J. walks to the dry swimming pool, which looks like something he left soaking in his sink, a dirty pot caked with burnt leaves and grit. No lifeguard on duty. He drags over a beach chair, scraping flint, while Dave tips the thermos into a styrofoam cup and drops in some motel ice. J. takes a long sip and the buzzing in his head argues once more for his hunger. Dave Brown makes formidable gin and tonics. They sit and gossip for a few minutes about who they've seen at the last few events, discuss how the List always gets weird in the summer, thin and gawky, as the entertainment combine gears up for the fall. Everyone is in the Hamptons. L.A. keeps plugging along of course, in fact the last time J. saw Dave was at a summer blockbuster dog-and-pony show just before Memorial Day. Guns and car crashes keep everyone fed. The studio marketing people watched happily as hors d'oeuvre toothpicks were licked clean and abandoned on linen tablecloths. Travel pieces for fall publication sent the junketeers scrambling for malaria pills and sunblock. But then there are weird events like this one, odd meteors. J. feels a pain in his arm and slaps a mosquito into a bloody skid. Out in the country. This is a real die-hard gig if Dave, Tiny, and Frenchie are showing up. Which, J. observes, makes him a die-hard junketeer. Dave slathers some suntan lotion into his chest hair. Dave, the oldest one of them all, probably the first name on the List. No one knows for sure who conceived of the List, one or two prime suspects remain unconfirmed, but at a certain point the List required an inspiration, some muse of mooching, and no doubt it had to be Dave. The mastermind of the List sees Dave at a *Battle of the Network Stars* gala in the late seventies and is granted a vision. Dave with his oversized head screwed into a gnome's body, in his trademark president-for-life khaki jacket, with bulging pockets overflowing but never touched in public. He has pockets for his pockets. Survival gear: a compass with the open bar at due north, waterproof pens, jungle rot remedies and prescription-strength antacid. The mastermind of the List sees Dave, notes the inclination of the free drink in his hand and the next day his secretary is fathoms deep in his rolodex and recovering the names.

Dave digs into the motel ice bucket and freshens his drink. "So, J.," he begins, "word is you're going for the record." Mixing the ice cubes with his finger.

"Nah, I'm just on a jag."

"Really? How long have you been on this so-called jag, J.? Been pretty active."

"It's been about three months. Mid-April. I started with the Barbie thing." Mattel introduced its latest Barbie at an all-night party in FAO Schwarz. The new Barbie came with a Range Rover and vaginal cleft; J. and Monica the Publicist groped each other while miniature robot tanks circled their feet.

"I was there," Dave says, nodding. "A very elegant sushi spread."

"That's the one. Since then."

"Not bad. Nonstop? Moving around or just sticking around New York?" The implication being that it is fairly easy for one of their number to hit a press conference every day, score a doughnut or two, and split. If J.'s streak consists primarily of easy scores, his feat is unspectacular and quite possibly indicative of poor breeding.

"I've been pretty mobile," J. says. "I was in L.A. for two weeks for the blockbuster tour, but that's the most I was in one place and I've hit an event every day. I'm on a jag."

"Two weeks is a jag, three months is a binge." He winks, a sprightly flutter he had toiled on for days one dead summer in 1979. "Sure you're not going for the record?" he asks again. "Because if you've been junketeering that long nonstop, you've got a good start on the record."

"I don't want to be another Bobby Figgis," J. says. He is pretty dizzy from the gin and tonic; formerly a vile slick in his stomach, the drink has organized itself into an octopus-like creature that tugs and twists his insides.

"Nobody wants to be another Bobby Figgis. Just putting it out there. Let me tell you a story," Dave says. J. offers no resistance. "One time I was at this book party for Norman Mailer. I don't know which one, one of those goddamn things of his. I think I was going to review it for *Rolling Stone*. Or maybe I was just there, I can't remember—I reviewed one of his books for *Rolling Stone*, anyway. Or was it *People*? It's getting late and they've stopped bringing out the food so I'm stocking up on vittles. It was a nice spread. I had to reach over Capote, who was flailing his little rat paws in my way trying to block me. Are you with me?"

"You're in an hors d'oeuvre war with a drunken dwarf." It is a common enough occurrence in their line of business.

"We were two drunken dwarves trying to get in our God-given fill," Dave continues. "Bianca Jagger flirted with me. Coke was dirt cheap that year so you couldn't even get into the bathroom, even if you had to take a piss. You would have been home in your *Star Wars* pajamas. So George Plimpton comes up to me and says, 'Do you like Peking roast duck?' 'Do you like the Peking roast duck?' I look up at him. He's talking to me in that New England accent of his, like he was chipped off fucking Plymouth Rock. He says, 'Do you like the Peking roast duck?' and he goes off on this detailed story about the history of the dish and the special ovens they use and how in China they used to keep the royal ducks in this nice open area and feed them the best rice and grain. It gives the ducks a special flavor. It's like they're spicing them up before they're even dead. Only they—the ducks that is—think they're the king of the hill. The landed gentry of, what is it, the mallard family, the royalty who get the best food and have the best duck lifestyle. They sneer at the peasant ducks outside the gate. Plimpton's all spitting on me and grabbing for the duck on the table while he's telling me this story. But what they don't know, he says, he's stabbing a cracker in my eye, is that they're no better than the other ducks. They're all going to get eaten. It's just that some ducks get the better rice."

"That's a great story."

"Isn't it? Then he runs off to some other fab person in the room. And you know what the funny thing was? I'd never met him before. He called me by my name but he'd never met me before. It's a fucking mystery to this day. It's a fucking mystery."

"This is a parable of some sort."

"It's a tale told throughout the ages. You want a refill?"

J. excuses himself. He grabs his bags and discovers room 27 halfway down the second floor of the motel. He hears a car door slam. Another arrival. Sarcophagal air escapes from the room when he opens the door; he will swear to that. The room is a maroon slab. First thing, J. checks out the TV and finds it receives the standard array of channels. He smells wet cement. He sits down on the bedspread, a ribbed crimson sheath that looks like it has been used to drag for bait. Across the room, a faded print describes a railroad man squatting on the roof of a caboose, angry canyon walls receding behind him, his hand waving his cap in the air above his snarl of joy. Jesus Christ. J.'s stomach surges and he runs to the bathroom and vomits.

Benny waits for gravel to become hail. The sound means a guest needs a room. The highway coughs up people. It is a great and unknowable sea. Benny keeps them warm, if the heaters are working.

He walked the property that morning to make sure everything was ready. Josie was still asleep. His wife had earned an extra hour or two after all the work they'd done on the place the last few weeks. Benny ran his hands along the gutters and grabbed leaves, half-born insects. The ladder creaked beneath him and reminded him of his weight, or rather the increase in his weight. When Benny got nervous the food stuck to him. He didn't eat more, but the food stuck more. This nervousness then tipped into worry, because he didn't like to buy new clothes, and this in turn dispatched him to the public library, where he checked out books on the human metabolism. As he returned to the office, he stopped to obliterate with his shoe an anthill that had burst from the dirt, messy and teeming, overnight.

In room 14, Pamela Street thinks about her father.

Benny sits in the leather chair behind the registration desk. Out of habit he reaches over to the little stand but it is not there. He moved the TV into the back office, away from the front, because he wanted to make a good impression on his guests. He has nothing—not the afternoon movie, no soap— to occupy him now except his waiting. Benny feels something in his thinning hair and withdraws a twig that has snared a few precious strands. Removing them from the twig, he squints at the pearl knobs of the follicles. Three more down.

Benny and Josie had spent the better part of a month getting their humble inn up to muster. They repainted the rooms and defrosted the workhorse half-fridges, opened up a new case of sanitized glasses and deposited vials of miracle shampoo-conditioner on the shower ledges. It was a time of woe for mildew. He and Josie laid new carpet, they went down on their knees and into the silverfish. As Benny waits in the office, vacantly eyeing the sports scores, he hopes that all the reservations actually show; he borrowed money from the bank in Hinton to pay for all the improvements. If all the reservations arrive, it will be the first time he and Josie have reached full occupancy. The only time the No in the Vacancy sign had ever been illuminated was when Benny and Josie went to Acapulco for six days and seven nights for their wedding anniversary. To compensate for their venture's lack of history, Josie arbitrarily declares certain rooms Honeymoon Suites or haunted, but often forgets which is which, and sometimes she places a happy couple in a room with the ghost and is sick about it all night. Benny has had to restrain her physically from knocking on doors at 3 A.M. and telling guests to move two doors down.

Things have picked up in the last few years on account of the growing popularity of the dam and the lake. The Sandman and Coast to Coast gather most of the river traffic because they are closer to Hinton, but Benny and Josie catch their overflow. Strategically placed signs every quarter of a mile lure and tease. Local teens like to shoot buckshot at them. The Talcott Motor Lodge is a cozy budget motel off Route 3, but still proximate enough to the sights that tourists think that by staying there they are making some ingenious decision, distinguishing themselves from the other loudmouths of the tourist fray. The summer people swagger into the office damp and tired, sunburned and drained, tracking sand through the carpet. Always that detail: Benny imagines the grains jumping like fleas from the battlements of sneaker treads. The sand collects stubbornly between the bathroom tile, its sects flourish unpersecuted under carpet cover. The families are noise and the kids chase each other around the pool and slip and he can smell the litigation like coming rain. (He remembers then that he has forgotten to fill the pool, but it is too late to do anything about it, some of the guests have already arrived.) They demand amenities he and Josie cannot possibly provide. They are numerous and crack up the gravel in steady numbers, but he has never filled the place. Today, their place has advance reservations for every single room.

In room 29, Lawrence Flittings sits nude on the bed rubbing scented oils into his skin. It is a ritual he performs near the full moon that makes him feel more comfortable in his body.

In room 12, Alphonse Miggs brushes his finger along the bottom of the bathtub and contemplates the residue of abrasive cleanser powdering his fingertip.

Benny doesn't like the new posters. The Chamber of Commerce delivered the John Henry posters last week and he removed some of the pictures of the New River Gorge—a laughing family on a raft, the great Gorge Bridge striding across angry water—from the reception area as instructed. After staring at them over the last few days, his initial reaction has not changed. Benny finds the festival posters a little too garish. He is in the spirit of things; it is difficult to remain unmoved by the optimism of the town, and there's a good chance the events of the next few days will yield regular guests for his rooms in the long run. When Jack Cliff ran into him on the street and asked him if he was on board, Benny said, looking forward to it, Jack. But the posters seem so violent to him. The flashing sparks and sweat, John Henry's heaving black body. Josie loves them of course; they are typical of the town's railroad romance. Can't sit in a bar for ten minutes without some Joe going on about how their engineer grandfather did this or that. The wreck of old something or other. It isn't so glorious to Benny. The towns around here wouldn't exist if it hadn't been for the C&O, but a lot of people died laying track through the mountain. The cave-ins and dynamite. His neighbors, his wife, love all those violent stories. And for what. Look at it now. It's Amtrak, its CXS Transportation hauling crap from coast to coast. That's what he has to fight back saying ten times a day. It's just Amtrak.

In room 17, Dave Brown cleans out his thermos.

In room 27, J. Sutter sleeps and dreams of a blizzard of receipts, a million fluttering tallies that he captures on his tongue.

Benny looks at his rack of room keys, remembers screwing the hooks into the plasterboard. Each hook is a room and all the people who will stay there for a time. Lives converge on those hooks.

This weekend is going to be good for the town: that phrase is the going rate. Before his retirement, Josie's father had been a station man in Hinton for thirty years. They are railroad towns, Hinton and Talcott, and everybody who lives here has railroad in their bloodline. Not so Benny, whose family moved to Talcott when he was a teenager for reasons he still does not understand. He feels out of place when confronted with the railroad nostalgia of the two towns, that is to say nearly every waking moment. But as he waits for the next guest to arrive, he thinks perhaps he is learning to understand the mythology of his adopted home. He is learning what it is to wait for a train.

No one, it seems, wants to go to West Virginia. West Virginia contains many natural wonders. The New River Gorge is spectacular. A number of the bituminous coal concerns have informative tours and dioramas for the curious visitor. The historic stand at Harpers Ferry, to name another thing. And yet. Just last week at a bar on M Street in Washington, D.C., an inquisitive patron could have overheard this conversation between two postal employees:

POSTAL EMPLOYEE #1:

Pittsburgh I wouldn't mind. It's a big city. I have a college roommate in Pittsburgh.

POSTAL EMPLOYEE #2:

I don't know why they picked John Henry in the first place.

POSTAL EMPLOYEE #1:

You know. They got three white ones, you gotta mix it up these days. Nothing against John Henry. I just wish he was from somewhere else.

POSTAL EMPLOYEE #2:

Pecos Bill, Paul Bunyan—who's the other guy?

POSTAL EMPLOYEE #1:

Mighty Casey.

POSTAL EMPLOYEE #2:

(*sipping lager*)
"Casey at the Bat." I don't even know who Pecos Bill is.

POSTAL EMPLOYEE #1:

(*gritting his teeth*)
Nobody knows who the fuck Pecos Bill is. He wrestled a rattlesnake.

POSTAL EMPLOYEE #2:

You got Babe the Blue Ox in the Paul Bunyan one?

POSTAL EMPLOYEE #1:

That's exactly what I said. What's Paul Bunyan without Babe the Blue Ox? But we just did an animal series a few months ago.

POSTAL EMPLOYEE #2:
(*nodding ruefully*)
To take care of the animal lovers. We don't want to alienate that segment of stamp consumers. Not in Marvin Runyon's Post Office. Whose idea was this anyway for a Folk Hero series?

POSTAL EMPLOYEE #1:

Who do you think?

POSTAL EMPLOYEE #2:

Yeah.

POSTAL EMPLOYEE #1:
(*shaking his head*)
And he wants some target marketing people to go along. You know his big thing now. I don't know why it has to be me, but there you have it. I know the beds are going to kill me. I can feel that already. My back is fucking killing me already. It's enough to make me go—

POSTAL EMPLOYEE #2:
(*looking over his shoulder*)
Don't say it!

POSTAL EMPLOYEE #1:

I wasn't going to say that. I was going to say, go nuts. I actually talked to the son of a bitch mayor of the town. We got a registered letter from the Chamber of Commerce. They sent a registered letter to the Post Office like it's some kind of threat. The Post Office! They go, "Pittsburgh may be Steeltown U.S.A., but John Henry is Talcott's native son." So he gave in, canceled all the Pittsburgh plans that had already been planned out. Christ, this city is a fucking sewer in the summertime.

POSTAL EMPLOYEE #2:

It'll be good for you to get out of the city. Get some good country air.

**POSTAL EMPLOYEE #1:**

Why does everyone keep saying that? Country air, country air, everywhere I go. Watch me get a call from some guy in Minnesota saying we got to do the same thing there for Paul Bunyan. "An office of the United States Government can't show unfair treatment blah blah."

**POSTAL EMPLOYEE #2:**

I have some "relations" as they say, in West Virginia.

**POSTAL EMPLOYEE #1:**

(*rubbing a cigarette burn on the bar's surface*)
They're trying to use the John Henry thing to make the town into a tourist trap. The stamp gave them the idea apparently. All sorts of big fun.

**POSTAL EMPLOYEE #2:**

Tractor pull. Hayride.

**POSTAL EMPLOYEE #1:**

They got Ben Vereen coming.

**POSTAL EMPLOYEE #2:**

(*grinning*)
Pulling out all the stops. Look at it this way—you get to hang out with the stamp collectors.

**POSTAL EMPLOYEE #1:**

That's a pleasure.

**POSTAL EMPLOYEE #2:**

You can look forward to that.

**POSTAL EMPLOYEE #1:**

They always got those moist lips.

**POSTAL EMPLOYEE #2:**

They're always licking their lips because they got all those stamps but they can't lick 'em.

**POSTAL EMPLOYEE #1:**

Turns my stomach.

POSTAL EMPLOYEE #2:

They always try to be your best friend.

POSTAL EMPLOYEE #1:

Like I'm going to give them free stamps.

POSTAL EMPLOYEE #2:

Like we got stamps in our pockets that we're going to give them.
Maybe the Weirdo is going.

POSTAL EMPLOYEE #1:

If the Weirdo is there, fuck Runyon, I'm turning back.

POSTAL EMPLOYEE #2:

Shit yeah.
(*gesturing*)
Can we get another round?

Everything on him is free. His black Calvin Klein jeans hard won two years prior at a party celebrating the famous designer's spring line. Stacks and stacks of the jeans, up to the ceiling, but more pertinent than the company's publicity budget was the fear they might not have brought your size, or another journalist might beat you to your size, thus the resultant frenzy described the next day in Page Six of the *New York Post*. His T-shirt arrived in the mail one day with an advance copy of Public Enemy's latest release. Mickey Mouse heads festooned his socks, Goofy his boxer shorts. His shoes bounty from a Michael Jordan–Nike charity event, intended for the disadvantaged kids but everybody helped themselves so J. figured why not. They are a little tight, and pinch.

J. rummages through his canvas bag for some new clothes. They had been washed by Laundry in the hotel he'd stayed at the night before and charged to his hotel bill, which was in turn picked up by the record company that had invited him there. There is always an entity at the top who pays for things. While sifting through his bag, J. notices a log of tissue paper and opens it up. He remembers: at the end of the night he'd wrapped up a small ham sandwich from the food table to save for breakfast. One time he woke up with dozens of cocktail napkins in his pockets, all stuffed down in there. He pulled out the dingy bouquets from his trousers like a hobo magician. The sandwich still looks edible. J. picks off the dried brown edges from the ham, considers for a moment the wilted iceberg lettuce, and sticks the sandwich in his maw. He starts to feel better.

Strung out from the gin and tonic and the nap dream, which was antic and enervating and which he cannot recall, he wonders what time it is, how long he slept. The desk man at the motel gave him a press packet when he registered, checking his name off a list, but J. hasn't bothered to look at it so he doesn't know what time dinner is. It is still light out. Someone will come fetch him. Out of boredom he picks up the glossy folder of the press material. In a golden circle, John Henry pounds a railroad spike with a gigantic hammer. He has a big grin on his face. Behind him the other workers are bent over the track, small and human compared to the black titan in the foreground. Building the country mile by mile. This is the forging of a nation. This is some real hokey shit.

After the knock on his door, he hears Lawrence call his name. He reluctantly opens the door for the publicity man. Lawrence Flittings is tall and boyish, attired with his usual elegance in a light blue summer suit. Current New York style straight out of the lifestyle mags; a subscription card could fall from his navel at any moment. His blond hair is compact and slicked back with a particularly obedient mousse, considering the Southern humidity. He smiles at J., green eyes penetrating, and says, "I'm glad you could make it, J. Get here okay?"

Lawrence is a lieutenant at Lucien Joyce Associates, one of the most influential publicity firms in the country. Have their hands in everything from home electronics to beauty products to independent movies, an interdisciplinary and gangster army of hype. They'd publicize the debut twitch of a bean sprout, an unspectacular bud in a field of identical bean sprouts, if the money was right. Lawrence is Lucien's new right-hand man, replacing Chester, who is now in Development at Paramount. J. still runs into Chester at various events. Chester enthuses about his new job profusely and at length. The man has yet to connive one of his projects into the multiplexes; the scripts in question endure successive drafts, gain talent, lose talent, find new talent and sigh through more drafts. Chester draws up budgets, revises, revises again to accommodate the new people who have come aboard, and then the new people lose interest and the budgets are revised again. He is highly regarded and considered successful.

J. has yet to warm up to Lawrence. He still sees him as the new guy, a judgment that flatters J. somewhere because he has been around for so long. J. tells him he arrived without incident.

"How have you been? I haven't seen you since the Maverick Records event."

"The usual. Working a lot."

"I loved that piece about Whitney Houston. You're so clever."

"Thank you, Lawrence."

"I'm not the only one who thinks so, J.," Lawrence says, spinning the valve. The publicity man proceeds to name publicists and personages whose events J. has attended on his recent junketeering streak, the ones who have fed and housed J. over the last few months. J. thinks it is his way of saying, I know what you're up to. A smug little display of Lawrence's power, a momentary adumbration of the inner chambers. And another indicator that Lucien controls the List. As J. dangles in the door frame and listens to Lawrence's spiel, he makes a note to share this tidbit with One Eye, should One Eye show up this weekend.

J. nods and listens to Lawrence explain about the shuttle bus that will ferry them to the dinner venue in Pipestem, a resort town a few miles south. J. admits that he hasn't had a chance to look at the press material yet.

"Unfortunately," Lawrence frowns, almost sincerely, "I just talked to Ben Vereen's people and they told me he won't be able to attend tonight's dinner. He's taken ill, apparently. But the town people have lined up some local talent instead, so it should be splendid. It won't be the Puck Building, of course, but I think you and the boys will enjoy yourselves."

"I'm sure we will. I don't suppose Lucien is coming down here, is he?"

Lawrence smiles. "He's flying in tomorrow morning, actually. He's very anxious to see how this turns out. We've never done a whole town before. And we've worked with the government, but not the Post Office. We're all very excited. I'll tell him you asked about him." Lawrence pretends to glance at his watch. Duty done, time for the kiss-off. "I'll let you go, J., I'm sure you must be exhausted."

J. closes the door and is disappointed that there are only two locks. That bit about J. being exhausted—was that another dig at his junketeering streak? Streak, jag, binge. He crawls on top of the bed, swiping the publicity folder to the floor. He can expect Dave to make a few Bobby Figgis jokes at dinner. Junketeer jokes and junketeer chuckles all around the table. Public shame to reinforce their community's values. But behind the jokes there will be their very real discomfort with what he is doing. J. wishes he'd gotten the official lowdown from Lawrence on the exact nature of dinner.

He tries to remember why he started. He sees himself kissing Monica the Publicist at the Barbie event. They were on the second floor of FAO Schwarz in a display of radio-controlled toys. His hand moved down the back of her black publicity dress and he heard a whirring sound. The toys were active, autonomous rambunction, tanks mostly, with a few hot rods from the future thrown in the mix. The robots collided with each other and spun off. They ran into the bottom of shelves and got caught there, unable to understand why they could not progress. They let out whines of frustration. She bit into his tongue and he tasted his blood. The next evening he went to a TNT event for their latest Civil War movie, where he dined from a menu of authentic Confederate Army rations. It was kitschy. Everyone dug it and made ironic comments. The day after that he went to the Palladium to see the hot new band from England and the next thing he knew he was going for the record.

It has been six months since her father passed away, and she feels she may be ready to say good-bye to him. His remains are in storage.

Her father has been dead six months, but she isn't sure if she is able to make the final step and take care of the items in the storage facility.

Six months after his funeral, it is time to bury her father. The monthly storage fees are a bitch.

It is the first time Pamela Street has been out of the city in two years. She pulls the curtain string, looks out on the quiet grass and cement walkways in front of the Talcott Motor Lodge, looks past the blue slit of the empty swimming pool to the soup line of begging trees, and decides it is a welcome change from the air shaft that howls outside the window of her studio apartment. At this time of year the air shaft rattles with the exertions of air conditioners, reeks with the cooking exhaust of the Chinese takeout place on the first floor of the building. The smoke from below grits the yellow bricks of the air shaft black and brown, decrees the windows de facto antiwindows, portholes onto a sea of grease. She cracks the window of room 14. This is an honest to God breeze.

The funeral was the easy part. There was a mechanism of loss in place, the Yellow Pages were handy. The funeral salesmen brandished multiple-choice sheets, coffin make, viewing rooms by rank, appendixes referring affiliated firms that specialized in exotic disposal if you wanted to scatter the deceased's ashes into the sea near Ellis Island or out an airplane window circling over Coney Island. That was the easy part, the funeral salesmen were kind and efficient shepherds. But Mr. Street inconveniently died in the last week of the month, which left Pamela only a few days to take care of his things. His landlord, a ballbusting wretch of long standing, had been firm on this point, keen as he was on chopping the newly vacant apartment into two separate units. Pamela returned to the Yellow Pages to find a storage facility for her father's remains.

Pamela took trains and buses to the edges of New York City. There are rules about the placement of storage facilities, zoning laws. Many have enjoyed former lives as warehouses for industries that no longer exist or have relocated to more appropriate locations outside the city. The reconditioned warehouses now serve as repositories for things of no immediate purpose but infinite unquantifiable value. If you want to know what a person is about, all you have to do is look at what they put in storage. The superannuated but too expensive to throw away. Crates of illegal revolvers. Children who have moved away to start their own lives and have affixed their favors on new objects find their childhood possessions put in storage by parents who wait for their return. People move into new, smaller apartments and exile their too-much stuff into patient solitude until the day of their improved fortunes. People disappear into the world and leave clues in storage. *In storage* is optimism, everything temporary and defined, it promises a reversal of destiny and yet speaks in the dull syllables of finality, has the eloquence of a cemetery. Occasionally people remember an object during blank afternoons in their new kitchenettes, seek after it, realize that it is in storage and know it is gone forever. The possessions of the dead find their way into the gigantic and solemn storage facilities of New York City, interred there by family and attended by dust.

Pamela met the caretakers, fat cigar-smoking men who had no time for questions. They kept their eyes on the loading doors, greeted movers whom they had come to know during the course of their mutual interest in other people's things, scolded do-it-yourselfers who stared dumbfounded at the freight elevator doors. No one rushed her when she said she'd have to think about it and get back to them; they understood the traffic of their enterprise and knew there were others after her, just as there were others before her. Men in brown uniforms obligingly gave her tours of the spaces, asked her if she wanted nine-by-eleven or seven-by-five and directed her down dark corridors, switching on hanging bulbs at every turn. They brushed aside the lights' strings as if they were cobwebs. The men illuminated storage rooms that resembled the interiors of ancient ovens. Some rooms had doors that slid up and down, others had walls of metal grating that allowed her to see the other bins, the stuff of other people, bicycles of dead children, histories of upholstery, lamps from bolder decades, dartboards and family portraits. She couldn't judge spaces. They asked her if she was storing a studio or a one-bedroom or a two-bedroom, and she told them she was storing a museum.

After visiting a dozen storage places, Pamela decided on Dalmon, which is only two blocks from her house. Only two blocks away her neighborhood changes; Tenth Avenue broods near the river, where the city has different priorities. Dalmon has reasonable rates and even offered to move the material for her, at a small cost. It is very convenient. She met the movers the following Saturday at her father's apartment in Harlem. The movers were two young Dominican men who smiled a lot at her throughout the job, nice guys. She showed them the boxes that contained her father's John Henry museum and they urged dollies up the brownstone steps, coaxed carts through door frames, gouged walls. Pamela left the furniture, the plates, the rest of her father's things for the landlord to clean up, fuck him. The movers drove their van downtown and banished the boxes from her immediate responsibility.

No one wanted it. She made a few inquiries, called universities. Tuskeegee, Howard. She got lost in voice mail, mailed letters that did not receive responses.

She stalled out that spring. Pamela temped aimlessly, a migrant worker harvesting words per minute. The agency called her early in the morning if they had anything for her; otherwise she watched television in her pajamas and contemplated the bills from the storage facility, which distilled her hatred for John Henry into a convenient monthly statement.

Haunted by stuff. Hunched over ramen, in the same clothes she'd worn for days, she felt dazed. She was on the patch. She was off the patch. She was on the gum and smoking in between. She didn't go out that much, partly because she couldn't afford to, partly because going out did nothing for her mood. Her friends understood, her friends told her it was natural. It was part of the grieving process. Therapy diffuses: everyone knew the cant, the correct diagnosis. It was natural. It had nothing to do with her father, however, it had to do with John Henry, the original sheet music of ballads, railroad hammers, spikes and bits, playbills from the Broadway production, statues of the man and speculative paintings.

She thought about not paying the bills. When Dalmon finally unloaded the stuff (there must be auctions for such things, an entire culture based on the commerce of the dead or bankrupt, what did they do with what they bought), it would be like they were selling John Henry, not her father. This argument never got very far in her head. It was her father. She paid the bills on time and stopped eating out as much.

In May Pamela received a call from a representative of the town of Talcott, West Virginia. The months after her father's death marked the longest stretch in her life that she had not heard the name. The woman on the phone was very kind. The town was planning a festival to celebrate their town and

John Henry and wanted to know if they could buy her father's collection of material. She hated the name Talcott and refused, even though it was the obvious solution to her dilemma. The woman, Arlene, was persistent but Pamela did not budge. It wasn't a matter of money; they made a generous offer. She knew there were reasons, probably pertaining to the so-called grieving process, that she did not want to relinquish her burden.

In the end the matter was decided by the arrival of a handsome invitation from the Talcott Chamber of Commerce. Perhaps a few days out of the city would help her make up her mind.

J catches up with Dave Brown in the parking lot of the Talcott Motor Lodge. The night is clear and naked and swarming with so many anxious stars that it almost seems to him an invasion, a celestial troop movement auguring nothing good. In the cities it is safe because there are no stars, the light from a million apartment windows provides protection: they reduce the night into a vast purple mediocrity shielding against higher thought. J. nods at Dave, who is suited up in his bulging khaki jacket. Dave starts, "I think that in all my years of freelancing, I have never been to West Virginia. I've been all through Europe, South America. I saw Ali take out Frazier in the Thrilla in Manila—remind me to tell you about that sometime—I was one of the first people to interview Vaclav Havel—we talked about Lou Reed. The U.S.S.R., former U.S.S.R., Brazil, whatever. But I don't think I've ever been to West Virginia."

"Clear night," J. says.

"Clear now," Dave responds. "But that's weather for you."

"What's up, Dave? Hey, Bobby Figgis."

They turn to see Tiny and Frenchie, two fellow mercenaries in their covert war against the literate of America. Hail, hail. They encounter each other on the newsstands, they chafe against one another in the contributors' notes of glossy magazines, but primarily they meet like this, on the eve of war, hungry, sniffing comps and gratis, these things like smoke from a freebie battlefield on the other side of morning. At stake: the primal American right of free speech, the freedom, without fear of censor, to beguile, confuse and otherwise distract the people into plodding obeisance of pop. Their ideals: the holy inviolability of the receipt, two dollars a word, travel expenses. The junketeers are soldiers, and they hail each other. "What's up, Dave? Hey, Bobby Figgis."

"I hope you don't mind that I told Tiny about your streak," Dave says. "I ran into him at the ice machine earlier."

J. shrugs. He appraises his comrades. "Tiny, Frenchie. Good to see you."

The law of nicknames: contradictory or supremely apt, born of accidents and sticking for life or arbitrary and annoying. Tiny, of course, is not; he earned his nickname by not being so. At three hundred pounds, the man is hunger, gorging and grazing at the free spreads of life. If any person deserves to be on the List, it is Tiny, a creature who has evolved into the perfect mooching machine, leaving no glass undrained or napkin unstained by chicken skewer residue. He sucks up freebies in a banquet room like a baleen whale inhaling colonies of hapless plankton, swooping primeval and perfect, eyelids blinking slowly in the unlit fathoms of media. The dirigible prowls the food and travel magazine circuit; as a party trick he has been known to throw darts at a map of the world and name a princely dish native to that region, belching up its flavor on command, an archival gust from deep in his belly. Not to mention his thoroughly unwholesome fascination with curry.

Frenchie, for his part, retains an accent from his internment at a French boarding school during his adolescence. His parents were world-traveling sophisticates who unloaded their offspring with paid attendants half the year; the migrant's ways are in his blood. Tall and slender, proud owner of a shiny black mane, this lipless wonder has cultivated a satisfied Parisian air that serves him well while playing footsie with the editors of women's fashion magazines. For the world of international fashion is Frenchie's specialty, he knows where to buy rice cakes and had been linked in the gossip pages to that new Italian runway model before she discovered her bisexuality. She appeared to evaporate with every step and was perceived to be the marvelous avatar of a current brand of beauty. Frenchie took his expulsion from the empyrean badly; he had ascended from reporter-of to reported-upon, his name inflated in bold type among the gossip ledgers, and now he is back in the trenches. The other junketeers saw it coming; those they write about are not their kind, and mixing with them can only lead to heartbreak.

"No sign of the van?" Frenchie asks. He looks down at his suit and, distressed, returns the tips of his shirt collar to the outside of his jacket, where they sit like the wings of a shiny red bird.

"Should be here any minute," Dave says.

They are joined in the parking lot by a lithe young woman who is clearly not from around here; it is in her walk, a rapid skitter that places her from New York City. J. has found himself trying to slow down ever since he arrived at Yeager Airport, to get into the groove and pace of the state as a sign of openness to a different culture. The woman looks down the driveway and

lights a cigarette. Waiting, like them, but no reporter. J. and his fellow junketeers are in Talcott (or just outside it, he doesn't know) because they have
committed to a lifestyle: their lifestyle pays air freight and they board planes.
But why is she here? She wears faded jeans, a yellow blouse with a flower em-
broidered over her heart. She shifts in her boots, stamps out half a cigarette
and lights another while the junketeers shoot the shit and catch up.

"It's not here yet?" Lawrence fumes, emerging from the office with a cell
phone limp in his hand, no doubt making comparisons between the publicity
apparatus here and in New York and L.A. They don't know how to do things
here. "The van was supposed to be here ten minutes ago."

"Patience, Lawrence," Dave says.

Lawrence presses a few numbers into his phone, to beeps.

"We used to read the story of John Henry in kindergarten," Tiny says.
"The school board told the teachers they couldn't teach Little Black Sambo
anymore, so they switched over to this picture book of John Henry's competition. Positive imagery."

"You sound disappointed," J. says, glancing quickly at the woman for her
reaction.

"I was, a little. I don't mean to be un-p.c.," Tiny says. He is the kind of
man who says, "I don't mean to be un-p.c." a lot. "But I liked Little Black
Sambo. My mother used to read me Little Black Sambo when she tucked me
into bed at night. It's a cute story underneath."

"You were undisturbed by the eyeholes cut out of the pillow you lay your
little head on."

"They were different times, J."

"Did you hear I got a new job?"

"What?"

"It's at the department of no one gives a shit and you're my first client."

"Here it comes now," Frenchie says.

The battered blue van pulls up, New River Gorge Taxi stenciled on its
side. It looks like it has been tossed by tornadoes. Workhorse of the robust
fleet, J. says to himself. The driver, a ruddy-faced chap from the nabe, rolls
down the window and asks, "You all going to the Millhouse Inn?" His brown,
glinting hair is tucked precariously behind his tiny ears.

"All hacks in the back," Tiny says, already steering his body into the back
row. Frenchie climbs in next to him, makes a joke about there not being
enough room in the seat for him. J. is pressed between Dave and the young

woman. She's coming with them. Now he isn't the only black person. J. is grateful. If anything goes down in this cannibal region, he thinks, she will send word, and the story of J.'s martyrdom will live on in black fable.

"You're not coming?" Dave asks Lawrence, his hand on the door.

"I have my own car," he says.

"Big shot," Tiny mumbles as the van starts.

The chatter of the junketeers fills the van. They talk about who showed up at the party at the Fashion Café two weeks before and not one among them can remember what movie it promoted; about the night they attended the book party for the hot new memoir, something about a rough childhood, how they swooped down on the stack of review copies and the next day all ran into each other at the Strand bookstore, laughing at the coincidence, as they sold the review copies for cash. Tiny gloats over the money he gets for selling the cookbooks that arrive every day in his mailbox: *The Art of Southern Indian Cuisine, Tuscany Delight, The Master Crepe.* Tiny says, you can't eat recipes.

The woman's arm digs into J.'s side. She smiles an apology but does not speak. Maybe he'll talk to her at the dinner, so what brings you down here from the big city? How did I know? I could tell. J. closes his eyes to gather himself for the next few hours. Shut down for a bit before whatever god awful festivities are ahead of him. His stomach chews on itself loudly and he hopes that no one else hears it. Then he hears honking and the van lurches to the side. Peering through the windshield he sees the vehicle trying to run them off the road, the red pickup truck of his nightmares. So much depends upon a red pickup truck, filled with crackers. The pickup swerves in the lane parallel to them, dipping and zigging. The man in the passenger seat waves his pink fist out the window at them. Both drivers pounding their horns feverishly. "What the fuck is this! What the fuck is this!" Dave yells. They are being run off the road. Here it comes, J. thinks, this is how it goes down. The van capsized in a ditch. Open the door, I said open the damn door. What chew all doin' ridin' with nigruhs? We don't abide no consortin' with nigruhs in Summers County. Get out the car. Maybe one of his comrades puts up a little resistance against the taking of J. and the young lady. Then the ropes, the guns, the fire. The South will kill you.

"Slow down, slow down," Frenchie says. "It's all right."

"Are you fucking crazy?" the young woman shrieks. J. thinking, now she speaks.

"No, it's okay," Dave reassures, pointing out the window. "It's a friend of ours." And indeed, J. sees, the man in the passenger seat is none other than One Eye, come in from the cold.

"You know these men?" the driver asks.

"Sure, just pull over," Dave says. "It'll only take a second."

"You're the boss," the driver says, easing into the shoulder. The pickup pulls up in front of them and One Eye hops out, a scrambling, scarecrow figure with a short brown buzzcut. He is dressed like an idiot, with gray cloth trousers held up by red suspenders over a white striped shirt. A black eyepatch conceals his left eye.

One Eye removes his two black suitcases from the back of the pickup and offers a farewell to the man in the front seat before the red pickup takes off down the road. One Eye looks in the van and scrabbles into the passenger seat next to the driver, who shakes his head and frowns.

"What's up, fellows?" One Eye says. "I saw Tiny's fat fucking head in the window and knew it must be you."

"You had your one eye peeled," Tiny says.

"The great Cyclops," Frenchie adds.

"My plane was late and my ride had already left," One Eye explains. "So I hitched with Johnson there, figuring I'd catch up with you at the Millhouse."

"You're lucky Johnson had to run into town to buy some dry goods," Dave chuckles. Dave Brown—what could you do with Dave Brown? It is inert, the name just lays there, as resistible as his prose. His name does not lend itself to nickname shenanigans, playful permutations.

"He was a nice guy," One Eye says, cracking his knuckles. "More than I can say for you all. This is one sorry crew. No offense, ma'am, I'm not talking about you. Dave, of course, it wouldn't be a junket without Dave. Being down South must bring back memories of being on tour with the Allman Brothers, huh? Yes, we all miss Duane, it was a terrible loss. Tiny, of course, thought he could wrassle up some alligator fritters. Sorry to burst your bubble, Tiny, but we're a little north of weezie-ana. Frenchie, fuck you, I don't know about you, but J., poor J., I had such high hopes for you."

"He's our inspiration," Tiny pipes in.

"The great black hope," Frenchie says.

"Exactly. I had such high hopes. New York, New York. Wine, women and pop songs. And I find you here."

"He's going for the record," Dave offers.

"Tsk, tsk," One Eye shaking his head. "You can't see, but I'm making the station of the cross and praying for the soul of Bobby Figgis. Say it isn't so, J."

J., his name truncated to a single initial during childhood, does not need a nickname. "I'm on a jag," he says. He is a little embarrassed about how all their bullshitting appears to the woman next to him.

"Nonstop since April," Dave says, happy to be finally getting in his little digs before a proper audience. "Three-month bid."

"Three months in," One Eye says, taking stock, "Figgis was a wreck. You seem to be holding up."

"Jag."

"Hit an event every day," Frenchie counters. "He's going for the record."

"How's the book coming, Frenchie?" One Eye suddenly on J.'s side. If you wanted to shut Frenchie up, a quick rapier thrust to his ambition did the trick. Frenchie had spent his advance on clothes and lifestyle years before, without delivering word one of his manuscript, thus urging his comrades' initial envy to curdle into warming superiority, and then well-timed derision. If he wanted sympathy he should have never written those Talk of the Towns for the *New Yorker*, a sure friendship-killer in the freelance world. Frenchie does not say anything; One Eye's shiv dispatched him to the site of his more recent failure, to the bed he shared with his lost Italian model, her lost thighs.

One Eye had been blinded in a tragic ironic quotes accident a few years before. As he sat on a couch chatting with a publicist, a young freelancer stood above him, relating a droll tale of Manhattan mores as expressed in a new collection of short stories by that month's photogenic young writer. The bartender yelled out last call for the open bar, and One Eye jumped up on instinct, just as the freelancer punctuated his clever description by forming air quotations with the index and forefingers of his hands. The point in question was apparently very ironic, requiring a vigorous expression of the ironic quotes. The force of the irony, coupled with One Eye's eager and frantic upward movement, drove the freelancer's pincer fingers deep into the junketeer's eye socket.

J. reaches over and snaps One Eye's suspenders. "Where did you dig this up?"

"This is my Huck Finn outfit. I'm trying to gain trust, blend in."

"You look like an idiot."

"I know."

"Couldn't miss this one, eh? Where are you coming from?"

"Florida. I was visiting my parents."

"Okay time?"

"It's Florida."

"Figured you'd stop on down here for some more Southern hospitality."

"I'm on a secret mission," One Eye says. His good eye winks mysteriously. "A mission that could very well change the course of human events."

"It's hush-hush."

"I'll tell you about it later," One Eye murmurs. He turns back to face the road. He isn't kidding, J. thinks.

"I can't wait to see Ben Vereen," Tiny says.

"He canceled," J. informs him.

"What, creative differences?"

"No, he's sick," J. says, and the van continues its approach to the Millhouse Inn.

The List possessed a will and function. It sensed a need for itself, for an assemblage of likely suspects to get the word out. A group of men and women who could be called upon in times of need, individuals of good character and savvy, individuals who understood the pitch of the times. And the pitch of the *Times*. The public needed to know about the things that were being created by capable interests, a hunger existed among the public for the word, all that was needed was a reliable system to get the information to them. The List recognized the faces of itself: they turned out in bad weather, tired and hungry, night after night. Sometimes the ones who came got the word out; other times they took a few hours' reprieve from the chaos, a free meal and trinkets. The ultimate percentage was the thing that mattered, the unconquerable ratio of events covered to events not covered, that was the final concern.

The List pondered the faces of itself and reached out. The List kept abreast of the latest advances in information technology, contacting its charges by mail, later by fax, then email, whichever medium was most appropriate. The men and women on the List were astonished to find themselves contacted by email, having only just signed up for an email account a few days before and not having given their new email address to many people. They did not complain. It was convenient. If they wondered about the mechanism of the List, they kept their concern to themselves, or voiced it in low tones, during private moments. They feared expulsion. There had been a few cases of those who had abused the gift. One went mad. Another stopped filing and only showed up to eat from the banquet without giving in return. For the sin of not searching for outlets in which to deliver the word, this latter individual was deleted from the List and eventually became an editor. He looked at his colleagues from the outside, invited to only a fraction of the events he had been invited to before, and all remembered the look in his eyes.

The List was just. The List saw a discoloration on its person, watched as the discoloration described a face, and the face was added to the List. The faces the List plucked from its body were surprised. Some were new to the game, others old hands bitter for being overlooked for so long. Some appeared with much effort, others easy as pie. Some tried to figure out which event or article had been key, the one that blessed and graduated them, the one that had proved their worthiness. It was to no end. Shmoozers were passed over and the quiet diligent welcomed; the reverse was true just as often. It was inscrutable.

The List had been pushed from the earth by tectonic forces. The List possessed a specific gravity measurable by scientific instruments. The List contained weight and volume.

The List was aware of those in its charge. It knew if writers moved, switched from this newspaper to that magazine, if they died or retired, and updated itself accordingly. The men and women of the List were surprised at the promptness of the List's readjustment, but only the first time. After that first time they were surprised at nothing. Contact names were updated with military precision. The publicity firm rolls were never obsolete. If a bouncer at a club quit, or went to jail, or moved to a different club, his replacement was noted and identified to eliminate possible embarrassment. The quirks and pet names of maître d's at the popular restaurants were indexed. A harmony was achieved.

And the List rewarded the world. The percentage was maintained. Cover stories with witty headlines. Short and long reviews in the back of the book. Profiles of stars and magnates and web geniuses, insightful questions, silly questions, questions that begged still further questions, column inches adding up, fodder for the next iteration of the press packet. The public figure and the private citizen were rewarded. Those with dead careers walked among the living, resuscitated by a press release and attendant event at an appropriate venue. A financier who had done nothing real to speak of lately save collect interest threw a party to inform the public he was still alive. Around the Christmas shopping season a new gadget perched on a black pedestal, product of prodigious intellect, its virtues enumerated by those who had received it for free. The great ebb and flow of need, chronicled, subscribed to. A comeback. A meteoric rise. A next big thing, jostling for position in a year-end double issue. The reclusive author breaks her silence and grants interviews to justify her grandiose advance. The precocious upstart seen at the right parties. Behind the scenes at the award ceremony. The triumphant return. The inner life of. The secret world. The stories were told. There was a need. The List facilitated.

This inveigler of invites and slayer of crudités, this drink ticket fondler and slim tipper, open bar opportunist, master of vouchers, queue-jumping wrangler of receipts, goes by the name of J. Sutter, views the facade of the Millhouse Inn through reptilian eyes.

Is he supposed to take this place seriously? The walls of the rustic hotel and restaurant are obviously some factory concoction, J. sees that from yards away, the ridges and pocks identical from stone to stone. He can't figure out what style its designers tried to effect, colonial flourishes abut antebellum wood columns, modern double-pane windows nestle in artificially weathered frames of molting paint. Nice attempt by the toddler ivy along the walls, but hell, he discerns the wire firming it in place. But the water wheel is the biggest atrocity. The fountain jets force water over slats that do not move, the spray energetic and process of no natural movement, splashing into a cement pool lousy with plastic lily pads floating moronically, congregating near the drainage grate. Snug up against a hill, this establishment totally new, intended to service the legions of tourists who will flock here now for John Henry Days. They hope. A hipster kid with more hooks in his face than some ancient, uncatchable fish, strutting down Soho in seventies' bell-bottoms, has more period authenticity than this place. What is he doing here? He is going for the record, his works gurgling with slow, heavy fluids.

First things first when they hit the Social Room. Objective One: find a base of operations. Most of the tables had already been colonized by the other factions, but there is Frenchie tracking ahead, wading between chairs before the rest of them have finished taking stock of the room, on point, surveying, dithering a little between two tables to the far left of the podium before dropping his bag on one and motioning the other junketeers over. He nods to himself, second-guessing his choice, but no, this is it, this table is definitely it. As J. and the rest march to join him, they progress to Objective Two, libations, scanning the joint as they advance on their seats. Two bartenders barely out of their teens work their alchemy in a corner under ferns. John Henry Days employment largesse stealing labor from the fast food outlets, J. surmises. The junketeers take their seats and dispatch Tiny and Dave for drinks. A few citizens of Talcott and Hinton hover around the bar, but there is an opening on the left flank, a chink where Tiny or Dave might weasel in and dominate.

"I don't see a cash register," One Eye comments, sipping water.

"Me either," J. seconds.

These are some real white people, J. thinks, looking around. These people go into hair salons armed with pictures of stars on CBS television shows and demand. He is out of his element. He discovers the food table on the other side of the room. Looks like salad to start. His stomach grumbles again but he decides he can wait until the boys come back with the drinks. Bit of a line anyway. J. notices that the woman in the van has chosen a different table. Probably a good choice to keep her distance.

The drinks arrive, dock, find berth in waiting palms. Frenchie sniffs, asks, "This Gordon's or what?"

Tiny shakes his head. "No, tonight they're breaking out the good stuff. I asked the guy if he had any moonshine and he just looked at me. Was that un-p.c. of me?"

"Obviously you haven't heard of the great Talcott Moonshine War of Thirty-three," One Eye says over the rim of his glass. "You're stirring up old wounds."

J. has forgotten that afternoon's vomit incident but then he smells the gin. Bubbles break against his nose. He figures the ham sandwich he discovered in his suitcase has settled his stomach a bit. "Cheers," he says. Everybody's already drinking.

One Eye nods to the right, to an efficient-looking lady with a strong stride approaching their table, clipboard against her chest like armor. The handler. Can spot a handler a mile away, just as easily as she identified them. She introduces herself as Arlene. "I hope you had an easy trip out here," she says, smiling.

Nods all around. Tiny belches. J. thinks she is smiling at him more than the others. "I left some brochures with the press packets at the hotel," she says. "You should see what the county has to offer. Maybe you could include a little about the New River in your articles."

"Articles?" Tiny says under his breath.

"I saw them," Dave says, ever the appeaser when it came to the game. "Sounds like there's a lot of nice things in these parts."

*In these parts.* One Eye and J. look at each other: Dave is shameless.

"You should check it out if you get a chance," Arlene advises, retreating from the table. "Well, you enjoy yourselves tonight; tomorrow is a big day. I see you've already made yourselves at home. If you have any questions, or if you'd like to talk to the mayor or one of the event planners, feel free to grab me at any time." She departs, but not before smiling at J. again. Why was she smiling like that. Some kind of overcompensation for slavery or what? He leaves his seat to nab some salad, passing Lawrence on the way, who raises two fingers in greeting without breaking eye contact with the fellow he is talking to. The man is a pro.

It is a cafeteria salad, a Vegas all-you-can-eat salad, but J. doesn't mind. He has a good feeling about the main course. He swipes a brown wooden bowl and tries to ration himself, judging the length of the buffet versus the capacity of the bowl (always this necessary consideration of cubic space), he catches a glimpse of celery up ahead and makes a note to save precious room.

"Haven't these people ever heard of arugula?" Frenchie complains when he returns, looking a bit reticently at the fixings.

"Iceberg lettuce contains many important minerals," J. says.

The conversation in the room cuts out and at the podium Arlene asks for everyone's attention. She introduces Mayor Cliff and relinquishes the mike to a tall man with jagged gray hair and wolverine eyebrows. The skin of his face rough and sunken, eroded. Descended from railroad people, J. decides, he has timetable worry and collision fret in his genes. None of the other junketeers pay Cliff any mind; Dave is in the middle of an elaborate joke about a one-armed hooker.

The mayor says, "I'm glad you all came out here tonight to celebrate what our two towns have achieved in the past and what we will accomplish with this weekend." Feedback curses the air and a chubby teenager scrambles to minister to the p.a. system. When the screech ends, Cliff thanks him and continues. "We've all been working hard these last few weeks and months, and I know I'm not the only one who's glad that the day is finally here. My wife is very happy, I can tell you that. Charlotte—will you stand up? See that big grin on her face? That means no more 3 A.M. phone calls from Angel about her latest flower brainstorm. No more waking up to find Martin asleep on our doorstep with a report on the latest disaster." A good part of the room chuckles in recognition. J. sighs. "Now it's all paid off. So drink up, get some food and enjoy yourselves—you've earned it!"

Cliff takes a sip of water. "Some of you may have already heard that Ben Vereen will not be joining us tonight. I talked to his manager on the phone a few hours ago and he explained that while Mr. Vereen was very excited about coming down to Talcott, he was suffering from laryngitis and couldn't possibly perform." J. nibbles on a carrot and shakes his head. Laryngitis—probably resting after the vigorous and well-deserved ass-kicking he delivered upon his patently insane manager. "While this is a great blow—Mr. Vereen is an amazing performer loved the world over—we've arranged for some home-grown talent to appear after dinner. I won't reveal his identity right now, but I know that some of you have heard him before and know he will not disappoint." J. decides to tune him out. He doesn't need to listen to this homespun rubbish; he has all weekend to gather material, what little he needs. Will he have to do actual research? Who is he kidding. But he could always use a quote or two to round things out. Nine hundred to twelve hundred words—the website editor said they hadn't determined the average attention span of a web surfer, so they might trim his article if the next round of market research dictated. Twelve hundred words—he can excrete that modest sum in two hours no sweat, but a nice quote would spice it up. There is no need to listen tonight; he has two more days to badger some unsuspecting festival-goer into a colorful quote.

Cliff departed; in his stead ambles up some guy from the Post Office. Maybe ask that sister from the van her thoughts. She has something to say, J. figures. He sees her at the next table, listening to the Post Office guy, surrounded by the natives. Just as he is. J. looks around the room and confirms that they are the only black people in the joint. Honoring a black hero and them the only folks in the room. John Henry the American. He finishes off the last of the salad and looks over to see what is going on in the food area and he sees the red light.

He sees the red light and understands.

The red light at the head of a buffet table signifies one thing and one thing only: prime rib. J. has been waiting for this confirmation all day. In the airport he had glimpsed it in a vision and now it has come to pass. He sees himself cutting into the soft red meat, slicing first through the milky rind of fat, then gaining the meat and watching the blood extrude through dead pores at the loving, sedulous pressure of his cutting. J. sees the red light of the heating lamp at the far shore of the buffet table and immediately conjures mashed potatoes softening in essence of beef, the blood tinting the fluffy potato pink and refining it even purer, softer. This vision is the sublime distillation of all the buffets he's known, the one and true spirit summoned by caterly prayer. He waits for them to wheel out dinner, he waits to be fulfilled.

What makes him tick, this collector of stamps? He doesn't know himself. Alphonse Miggs sits in the Social Room of the Millhouse Inn, he sits on his hands at a table of eight, with seven folks he doesn't know. At the start of the evening his knuckles brushed against a lump in his jacket pocket. He withdrew a mothball and, supremely embarrassed, thrust it back where it came. He wasn't sure if anyone noticed his mark of shame. For the rest of the night he feels cursed with invisible pockets and all at the dinner can see his shame, the great pearl of naphthalene clinging to his person, smell the fumes of social incompetence emanating from it. Scoring their nostrils. The woman next to him, are her nostrils curling as she addresses him, is she sniffing him? She is about fifty years old, with a jubilant round face and well-pruned hedge of red hair. Noticing that he does not speak, noticing that he is one of two visitors from out of town at their table and not the black one, she introduces herself as the owner of the flower shop in Hinton. Her name is Angel and she smiles at Alphonse, exposing lips swabbed by red lipstick. Her accent elasticizes her words, jaw-jutting, sweet-sounding. She gestures at the glad ring of rainbow flowers around the podium, the looping green garlands dipping along the walls, and informs him that she spent hours devising pleasant arrangements for this weekend. Is she sniffing him? He nods at the vase in the center of the table, at the halfhearted burst of drooping tulips. He says they are very elegant. She thanks him and introduces him to her husband, a skinny man with a sun-cragged face who smiles a greeting at him before turning back to his conversation with the man next to him. She is in charge of all the floral arrangements, Angel explains, from tonight's dinner to Saturday's afternoon steeldriving exhibition and dinner, even the grand finale on Sunday, the stamp ceremony in town. As she recounts the preparations for each event her face seems to recapitulate the satellite emotions of each endeavor, the daisy hassle of Saturday's lunch, the gladiolus hell of the steeldriving match. It is the biggest job she has ever done, her distributor downright apoplectic at the size of her shipment, the shifting orders and delivery dates.

She has never commanded so many flowers before, it is a science, she could write a book about it, she jokes, but it all turned out fine in the end as anyone could plainly see and she got the name of her flower shop in the program. Which is good publicity. And where is Mr. Miggs from?

The drive from Silver Spring had been pleasant. It didn't matter where you lived, Alphonse believed, you go five minutes in any direction from your house and become a stranger in your own neighborhood. Windows, drapes, doorsteps, doors, each one harboring a stranger and not a neighbor, one of the great number that make up the rest of the world. All it takes is five minutes in any direction to find yourself in the nation. Drive six hours and what do you find?

In the Talcott Motor Lodge Alphonse had undressed, folding his driving clothes neatly and separately on the bedspread. Driving clothes, as if he were tooling around in a reconditioned Model T, white scarf trailing from his neck, but Alphonse Miggs has names and categories for his world, subsets and sub-subsets. The inventory eases navigation through the breakwater of his days. He then removed his black suit from the garment bag and hooked it on the bathroom door to let the steam soothe wrinkles. Stepping into the shower, he felt cleanser residue scrape his feet. He ran a fingernail along the surface of the tub, across the pattern of raised traction grooves arrayed in a flower pattern, and contemplated the white dust there. The packaged soap had no scent and did not foam. He used up the whole bar searching for lather.

He was the first to arrive. In general Alphonse prefers to be early; he sympathizes with movie mobsters who have run afoul of the organization and arrive at key meetings in public locations before the appointed time to test the vibe, but in this case he had merely misremembered the start of dinner. He was an hour early. Alphonse entered the Social Room and took a few awkward steps inside. No one paid him any mind. A blond woman steered her clipboard around the room, directing the staff by remote control, tapping her pen. Two bartenders with black bow ties arranged liquor bottles on their stand, swiveling the labels forward and crunching beer bottles into buckets of ice. Alphonse picked out a table that was neither too close to the podium nor too close to the wall. He wanted to fade, but he also wanted to see the proceedings. He sat in one chair, tried on the angle, and moved two chairs over. Baleful wail from the microphones. Everyone winced and stared at the teenager monkeying with the amp, the boy's hands skittered over knobs to tame the shriek. Silence then for a moment and the people returned to their tasks. Occasionally Alphonse caught the eye of one of them and they looked away quickly; it wasn't their job to figure out why he was sitting there so early. A teenage girl attacked his table, straightening the napkins and silverware, tickling the flowers into a pert attention. She skipped Alphonse's placement. He looked up at her and strained a smile from his face. She moved on to the next table. Alphonse turned his attention to the garden outside the French doors. Everything green and lush and orderly out there, darker greens coming to the fore, shadows brooding under leaves as a nearby mountain somewhere ate the sun.

A large man with a chef's hat rolled out serving tables through the kitchen door.

His philately newsletter announced the John Henry stamp that spring, reprinting word for word the USPS's release. A 113 million run in panes of twenty. Used to be commemorative stamps were something special, their limited runs hypothesizing scarcity down the line, bloating value. But there were so many now, issued so frequently that their significance dwindled. Alphonse Miggs collected railroad stamps.

He watched the people arrive. The preparations trickled to last-minute adjustments, an errand of tonic water, discipline of curtains and the other guests arrived. Five men in light summer-weight suits appeared at the door and the woman with the clipboard descended on them, introducing herself and gesticulating. The men looked city. Alphonse figured they were agents from the glorious USPS. They took measure of the room, looked down at the terra-cotta tile on the floor, the light blue trim of the moldings. The woman gestured at the tables, at the bar: sit anywhere you like, help yourself to the refreshments. The postal men chose a table up front. One man took his jacket off and draped it over the seatback, but seeing that his comrades did not join him, replaced his jacket on his shoulders. They proceeded to the bar one by one for seltzer water and a slice of lemon.

Natives of Talcott in exuberant summer clothes sallied forth, exchanging greetings for the second or third time that day. Alphonse watched the clipboard woman wave hello to them. They all knew each other. Perhaps he'd spoken to this woman on the phone, Arlene. The John Henry announcement drew him in and he called for more information, although he couldn't possibly think what more he could have needed; the press release had been quite thorough. The USPS under Runyon was very receptive to the public, maintained a line to answer questions, keep the dialogue open. The man who answered his call, after a not overlong and entirely decent wait on hold, informed him that if the gentleman was that interested in the Folk Heroes series, he might want to visit the town of Talcott, West Virginia, for their festival. He gave Alphonse a contact number and asked if he could help him with anything else. Civil servants get a bad rap, Alphonse thought. He called Arlene at the Visitors Center and she was delighted at his interest, the flowing signature scribbled on the business card enclosed with the information packet described a conscientious and caring nature. He made reservations.

Some later arrivals had no choice but to sit with the man. Guests staked claims for their parties, planting flags of purses and jackets, saving seats, savoring or ruing their place in the pecking order, made the best of things. Two couples sat down at Alphonse's table on the other side of the globe, as far from him as the rim would allow. One of the men nodded at Alphonse, and, not waiting for a response, looked into his lap as he slowly unfolded his napkin. Alphonse wondered if the table would fill up or if he'd remain out there on the ice cap. He made minute adjustments to the placement of his knife and fork. Contemplation of tines. Another local couple sat down between him and the other people, they greeted their friends, closing up the circle except for the seat to Alphonse's right. Alphonse sat on his hands.

An excited breeze teased the napes of all in the room: the salad table was open for business. The vanguard left their seats, heads darted toward, seats emptied in twos and threes. Alphonse hustled up to beat the queue. He garnered a fine spot in the top third and they heaved forward, reading and deciphering the feet before them. A shoulder dipped and this was taken for a sign. So tight together they must smell him. Were those beets he saw, that burgundy jelly ahead? Alphonse glimpsed a man at the podium looking over his papers. The man whispered into the microphone, hello, hello. The line bristled. They were going to miss the introduction, trapped by mixed greens on the other side of the room. The man walked away from the podium, merely testing sound, but the line hurried anyway. Iceberg lettuce, shavings of carrot, chickpeas, and a nice portion of beets.

When he returned to his table, the final empty seat had been filled by a young black woman, alone. He realized he hadn't seen a lot of black people so far, and since the others at the table did not acknowledge her, he assumed she was a visitor like him. She looked down at his bowl and walked to the salad bar. He had dolloped too much blue cheese dressing. Black people are African Americans now. Alphonse recalled again, he pondered the fact repeatedly, that the first commemorative stamp in the world had also been a railroad stamp, issued by Peru in 1871 to celebrate the twentieth anniversary of the South American railroad. (It is a sign.) And now John Henry, a railroad hero up there with Casey Jones, was getting his due in a commemorative stamp. Alphonse thought about the bustle of the room and the itinerary of the next few days. What he had come there to do. The woman on his left introduced herself as the owner of a flower shop. He listens and sits on his hands.

The table behind Alphonse is rambunctious and distracting. He turns around and sees five men, obviously not from Talcott: their revels are hermetic, and have nothing to do with what is going on in the room, the occasion. They drink heavily; one of their number, a gaudily dressed man with an eyepatch, returns from the bar pinching glasses together with professional poise, bearing refills for him and his friends before they have drained the drinks already in front of them. Angel tilts her head and clucks. The black woman on his right catches Alphonse's eyes and says they are a bunch of loud journalists from New York City. She says her name is Pamela.

Before they can speak further, the woman with the clipboard taps on the microphone for attention, her lacquered fingernails clawing at the air. Salad forks are set aside. She introduces herself as Arlene from the Visitors Center, and thanks everyone in the room for attending. Alphonse feels like an impostor, of course. He has been invited to this function, but most of the people in the room are locals, have worked directly on planning the weekend. His purpose swiftly comforts him. He is undercover. The mayor of Talcott replaces Arlene at the microphone and makes a few remarks. The other people at Alphonse's table laugh at an inside joke, a nugget of Talcott lore. Mayor Cliff is tall and gaunt. Thick gray curly hair writhes on his head, soft against the sharp ridges of his cheekbones. Alphonse isn't listening. Tonight is the warm-up, he thinks. Tomorrow the tourists and the rest of the town, the others beside the town luminaries getting fed in the Social Room. Tomorrow the celebration is open to the public, John Henry activities and John Henry barbecues, Sunday's trumpets-and-drums unveiling and the official release of the panes to the public on Monday. Bigger and bigger stages for the stamp. He will take his place and respond to his cue. Alphonse's local post office had recently outfitted the teller windows with bulletproof glass.

Alphonse sits up at the mention of the man from the Post Office, Parker Smith. He watches the man leave his comrades at the Post Office table (Alphonse's assessment had been correct) and shake hands with the mayor. Two perfect squares of gray perch in his black hair above his ears, almost the size of stamps, which amuses Alphonse slightly. Smith smiles and the emissary from the government addresses the people. "On behalf of Marvin Runyon, Postmaster General, and all of us at the United States Postal Service," he says, teeth twinkling, "I'd like to thank the good people of Talcott and Hinton for inviting us down for this wonderful occasion. I know you must be hungry and eager for the great food and musical entertainment the good people at the Chamber of Commerce have lined up for y'all, so I'll be brief. Did I say *y'all*? I'm sorry, I meant to say you all. Must be my Southern roots acting up. Haven't had so much Southern hospitality since I was a youngster visiting my grandparents in North Carolina."

Like a pro he waits for the chuckles to subside. People are so vain, Alphonse thinks. He watches Smith's face twitch into earnestness. "I was talking about this with some of my colleagues just a bit earlier—how you can't help but get caught up in the great history of this region. Talcott was instrumental in a great moment of our nation's growth—the forging of a national railroad, an effort unrivaled in human history. It was not without cost, as I'm sure you good people know only too well. How many of the folks who take Amtrak, or receive products shipped by CXS Transportation on the very railroad tracks just a few miles away, take the time to think about the good people of Talcott and Hinton whose grandparents and great-grandparents toiled under adverse conditions to bring this country together?" He takes faces in the crowd one by one with his eyes. "How often does one of those passengers on the train think about all the blood and sweat that made their journey possible? Part of what we at the Post Office hope to achieve by our issue of the Folk Heroes commemorative is to create awareness of the trials of men like John Henry, to invite Americans to walk in his shoes. That each time they use one of our Folk Heroes stamps, they think about the men who died to get us where we are today."

Is this man talking about a stamp or taking the beach at Normandy? Smith rallies for his final push: "But you all here today know much more about the sacrifices of railroad workers than I do," humble now, "it's your history. You don't need to hear me go on about it—your families have lived it. I just hope that this stamp, and the celebrations this weekend, can help tell the story of the sacrifices of men. John Henry was an Afro-American, born into slavery and freed by Mr. Lincoln's famous proclamation. But more importantly, he was an American. He helped build this nation into what it is today, and his great competition with the steam drill is a testament to the strength of the human spirit. The USPS is proud to honor such an American. Thank you."

A few minutes later, Alphonse finds himself in the food line next to

Pamela. They stand next to each other and do not speak and both know a little bit of token conversation is appropriate. They are seated at the same table and the night is already half over. But perhaps he is past the minuet of social graces. Alphonse decides to play his part, however—they can sift in vain through the clues later—and asks the woman what brought her to Talcott. Her face stiffens a bit and she says that her father collected John Henry memorabilia. That's interesting, Alphonse offers, because he is a collector as well, a collector of railroad stamps. Then her expression. He has seen the expression on her face before. It is the uncomprehending, loose shape faces adopt when he tells people he collects stamps. He informs her of the coincidence of the first commemorative being a railroad stamp, and here they are today. She looks puzzled and grabs a plate. The fumes of naphthalene swirl around him.

The old joke: what did the young lady say to her stamp-collecting suitor?

Philately will get you nowhere.

Pamela and Alphonse forage from the heated trays and do not speak again until the end of the night, after the commotion at the journalists' table has come to an end.

Applause, hands sliding toward slanted forks, as the Post Office man leaves the podium and Arlene announces that dinner will be ready presently. Not presently enough for J. He looks up at the thin, meek man with the polka-dot bow tie standing over their table. A press laminate hangs around his neck, abject and ridiculous. J. feels embarrassed for him; wearing a press laminate is so gauche. After waiting in vain for Frenchie to finish his story or for one of them to acknowledge his presence, the man finally clears his throat and says, "Arlene said you were some writers from New York City."

"That's right," Tiny says, "We thought we'd git ourselves down yonder for this shindig."

"My name is Broderick Honnicut," he declares, tapping the press laminate. "I'm a staff writer for the *Hinton Owl*. Thought I'd come over and say hello."

"Staff writer for the *Hinton Owl*," Frenchie considers, raising his eyebrows at his colleagues. "Well, well. I think I've seen your byline."

"You broke the story on the chicken rustling ring, I do believe," Tiny says.

"Chicken rustling . . . ?" Honnicut utters.

"The chicken-choking scandal," Tiny corrects himself.

"Turned out the cover-up went to the highest levels of government," Frenchie breaks in, taking the baton. "The town barber was implicated, according to a high-level source."

"The alderman got caught with his hand in the cookie jar," Tiny says.

No need to mess with this guy, J. thinks. He just came over to be friendly and he gets this. It is going to be a long night if the boys are this cantankerous early on. He twists in his seat to ponder the red light.

"Allegedly, Tiny," Dave admonishes, "always remember allegedly." He turns to Honnicut, smiling. J. knows he is about to set the guy up. "They're just joking with you. Say, tell me: What's the *Hinton Owl*'s motto?"

"I don't know what you mean," Honnicut says, growing flustered.

"You know what I'm talking about," Dave explains. "Every paper has a motto. The *New York Times* has 'All the News That's Fit to Print,' every great newspaper has to have a motto. Beneath your logo, there's a motto, right? What does it say?"

"It says," Honnicut stumbles, "it says, 'A Hoot and a Holler: The *Hinton Owl* Sees All.' "

Dave smiles. "That's catchy."

" 'A hoot and a snoot will keep you up all night,' " Frenchie says, and J. lights out for the food table. Because the red light is calling him. At the terminus of the buffet lies the sacred preserve of the Happy Hunting Grounds. Set above the cutting plate like a divine illumination, the red heating lamps warm the sweet meat. The red light is a beacon to the lost wayfarer, it is a tavern lamp after hours of wilderness black. J. experiences an involuntary physical response to the red light and begins to salivate. Sometimes he feels this in movie theaters, salivating at the glimpse of the red Exit sign. What a warm world it would be, he ponders, if we all slept under a red light at night.

When he returns, plate tottering, a sodden Babel of flavor, J. notes that Honnicut has departed. J. is grateful—he couldn't take much more of that. He looks around for One Eye, but can't see him anywhere, not even in the food line. No matter. J. has important business. The potatoes have declined his invitation, but J. still savors the pliable tang of overcooked heads of broccoli, carrots in star shapes, decobbed corn in pearly water. And the prime rib, the prime rib, aloft in its own juice, mottled with tiny globules of luscious melted fat. He showers the meat with salt, as if there could be anything greater in the universe than beef drenched heartily with salt. He possesses teeth sharpened by evolution for the gnashing of meat, a digestive system engineered for the disintegration of meat, and he means to utilize the gifts of nature to their fullest expression.

"This may be the New South, but they haven't caught up to everything, thank God," Tiny says. "This ain't no vegetarian menu."

"Amen to that," J. says.

"Ben Vereen was coming here?" Frenchie asks, incredulous. His plate is immured by empty glasses, mutilated limes groaning at their bottoms.

"It's a living," J. says. He gobbles prime rib and winces with pleasure, fighting telltale paroxysm. He needs the meat to pile on the liquor.

"How are they going to pay for all this?"

"Emptying the town coffers."

"No new basketball uniforms for the high school varsity team."

"Not the basketball uniforms!"

"Any of you actually writing this thing up?" Tiny asks, a yellow liquid glistening in his beard. He has filled twin plates with buffet mounds of horrific symmetry.

"I'm doing it for this travel site Time Warner is putting up on the web," J. informs him.

"Those guys are just throwing money away," Frenchie opined. "Fine with me."

"I got some outfit called *West Virginia Life* on the hook," Dave begins, "a monthly job they put out down here. But before I placed it I had been thinking about making it a New South piece. No one thinks about West Virginia. Throw in a few lines about the national parks and the white rafting stuff they got around here. It would have been a nice change of pace to do a trend thing after all these movie things I've been doing."

"Seems like a good peg," Frenchie says. "Though if I were writing it up, I could see focusing on the industrial age–information age angle. John Henry's man-against-machineness. That's still current, people can empathize with his struggle and get into it and all that shit."

"So you're going with Bob is Hip?" Tiny demands of Dave, his voice rising.

"Why not?"

"Are you sure it's not Bob's Alive!?" Tiny hisses.

It is an old argument. Freddie "the Bull" McGinty, before his unfortunate heart attack, had identified three elemental varieties of puff pieces, and over time the freelancer community had accepted his Anatomy of Puff. An early junketeer, the Bull (so named for his huge and cavernous nostrils) observed the nature of the List over time and posited that while all puff is tied by a golden cord to a subject, be it animal, vegetable or mineral, the pop expression of that subject can be reduced to three discrete schools of puff. For the sake of clarity, the Bull christened the archetypal subject Bob, and named the three essential manifestations of Bob as follows: Bob's Debut, Bob Returns, and Bob's Comeback. Each manifestation commanded its own distinct stock phrases and hyperbolic rhetoric.

Bob's Debut is obvious. Like lightning, Bob, the talented newcomer or long-struggling obscure artist, scorches the earth, his emergence charged by the profound electromagnetics of pre-Debut publicity and sometimes genuine merit. Such a glorious Debut deserves to be heralded in the glossy chambers of media. The out-of-nowhere record by the young lad from Leeds, the searching and surprisingly articulate second-person voice of the crab fisherman's roman à clef, the visionary directorial outing channeling the zeitgeist—all these works can be attributed to Bob, and Bob's Debut is a reliable story, the struggling talent is recognized, the indomitable vision championed. It makes good copy. This is the first manifestation of Bob.

Then comes Bob's Return. His sophomore record, aimless electronic noodling in some cuts, fame has gone to his head, but still listenable; the second novel, recapitulating some of the first's themes, somehow lacking, emboldened by success he tries to tackle too much; guaranteed by contract final-cut approval, the director esteems his instincts out of proportion, the special effects intrude and he can't trim it down to under two and a half hours. Bob's Return is well chronicled, he is a known quantity naturally pitched to editors, but not without hazards. He may have fallen out of favor among his initial champions and the long lead times of monthlies make cover stories a risky proposition. No editor wants to look at the cover of their magazine and see that they've showcased the profile of a celeb whose return had flopped miserably the week before. Editors guess, sniff the culture, and commit to Bob's Return, fingers crossed that the opening weekend box office will not be cursed, that the goddamned critics have not panned Bob's Return vehicle irredeemably to the mephitic baths of perdition. Weeklies and Sunday sections of major dailies have a leg up on the monthlies; if something magical happens, they can hitch a ride. This is the second manifestation of Bob.

Bob's Comeback is miraculous. It can occur two years after the doomed or mediocre Return, or twenty years. Many things could have happened in the intervening time to make Bob's Comeback printworthy: five crafty but overlooked novels consigned him to the twilight of midlist; three big-budget flops, two straight to video movies, one sitcom and a couple softcore thrillers fit only for the dingier cable outlets made a character actor of Bob; five very strange albums anointed Bob a critics' darling but a radio pariah. The long unchecked skid into obscurity. But then the comeback. Something shifts in pop. It helps if they have overcome a drug problem. Test screenings positive, publishing industry buzz a-flowing, advance radio airplay of the first single augurs good things. The publicity blows fire out of the cave, scaring the townsfolk, scaly thighs scraping in preparation for a rampage through the village. All the bad things the critics said are forgotten, the industry insiders rally around Bob, the author of the where-are-they-now? article is tendered his kill fee. Bob's Comeback makes covers. Equipped with a new look, a new agent, a new deal, Bob is back on top. Everybody loves an underdog, a redemption story. This is the third manifestation of Bob.

The Bull's musings were well received by his freelancing brethren. It brought order to their lives. Spat upon by editors, insulted by neophyte publicity minions, the junketeers embraced the woeful clarity of the trinity. By the time J. made the List, another variety had been identified and sanctioned by the junketeers. The trend piece. The phenomenon of the trend piece was brought to the table by a British music writer named Nigel Buttons, who had journeyed into the lounges and clubs of London, cozied up to DJs and promoters of tiny establishments situated at the bottoms of stairwells accessible only by alley, the garrets of demimonde, and decided that the three traditional categories could be expanded to include a new one: Bob Is Hip. By the addition of Bob Is Hip, Bob's other manifestations could be infused with new life by situating Bob in a scene or cultural eddy. Say Bob is a ukulele-playing gent who wears sunglasses on stage. If the evidence warrants, and even if it doesn't, Bob the ukulele-playing sunglasses-wearing gent can be insinuated within a burgeoning scene of ukulele-playing sunglasses-wearers—they have a culture and slang, they all sleep together, the romantic entanglements internecine. It is an exotic subculture that begs further exploration. Bob, blessed by a multirecord or multibook or multipicture deal, spotted by well-paid talent scouts with special acumen, takes an early lead on his cohorts and is now the glorious exponent of an underground movement. Depending on the circumstances, his Hip Debut promises a spectacular earthshaking realignment of pop; he finds his true voice in his Hip Return; the maundering and general getting-his-shit-together years of his decline are justified by the Hipness of his Comeback. The Bob Is Hip variation met with some initial protest until its endorsers suggested that creating novel catch phrases from "the new" or "post-" or devising witty neologisms for the nascent movement could ensure one's fame. A subculture is an amino acid soup out of which book deals crawl. More important, Bob Is Hip has broad applications. A manufacturer of blue jeans bruits its new tapered leg line. A junketeer attends and feasts at the event, but has no real peg to pitch the story. Armed with "The Neo Taper" and a broad manifesto, the blue jeans are a bona fide trend, no matter how short-lived, no matter how isolated. Presently, Bob Is Hip was a viable form of puff. Some junketeers jockeyed to grab credit for creating the quintessential Bob Is Hip piece, flailing their clippings in the air, neologisms underlined and backed up by concrete examples of their passage into con-

ventional usage, but there were many contenders and the issue was never settled. Bob's manifestations had become four.

Tiny started the argument in the Social Room because of a recent dis-
turbance among the junketeers. Since the days of Gutenberg, an ambient
hype wafted the world, throbbing and palpitating. From time to time, some
of that material cooled, forming bodies of dense publicity. Recently this phenomenon occurred more frequently. Everyone felt this change, it was tactile
and insistent. They found themselves in abstract rooms at events of no obvious purpose. Certainly there was a person/artifact/idea on display being promoted, but there was no peg, no impending release that it could be traced to.
Without a peg, the subjects in question were hard to sell to the editors of
newspapers and magazines. And yet the articles ran, the expenses were reimbursed, payroll cut the checks. The public liked them. Updates on well-
known public entities who were doing nothing at all, a computer marvel far
from implementation, musicians in coffee shops years from demos. The
undiscovered hired flacks before they needed them; the established but qui-
escent or loafing celeb retained publicity apparatus to remind the people of
their mere presence. Hence the new, hotly debated variety called Bob's Alive!
or Simply Bob. The golden cord had been severed and puff pieces roamed the
newsstands, unmoored to any release date. Simply Bob. Gossip columnists
had engaged in Simply Bob activities for years, some argued. A sighting at a
club or restaurant, walking the shar-pei on Fifth Avenue, cruising a downtown haberdashery: these engagements were memorialized by bold type in
the daily gossip columns. With junketeers munching and noshing at the tables of nonevent more frequently these days, and finding their reportage published, some sort of addition to the now-ossified varieties of Bob seemed
imminent.

J. doesn't have an opinion either way. While accustomed to thinking of
four varieties of Bob, his work will not change if Bob's Alive! is ratified and
passed by the body of junketeers. He will weather the rough seas of the
polemic. Puff is puff; it is puff. Observing the debate from the sidelines, he
will wait for the smoke to clear, and continue to perform his function as
he has for many years now. J. saws off a corner of prime rib and sticks it in his
mouth. One piece left. He decides to finish off the limp broccoli and save the
final bit of beef for the end.

Tiny rails against Bob's Alive! "I was against Bob Is Hip, too," he reminds
them with a snarl. "I never thought we should have gone that way. It's too dif-
fuse—this is a prime example."

"I remember your whining," Frenchie recalls.

"And now you want to go and bring in this Bob's Alive! thing. Is Talcott Alive?"

"I said New South," Dave corrects. "That's a trend piece. I can bring in improved race relations. It's Bob's Hip. Talcott is hip, they have a black hero. I can bring in Atlanta. I can bring in lots of stuff. Houston—Houston is hot now, it's attracting a lot of diversity."

"I'd go for Debut personally," Frenchie says.

"Debut?" Dave asks. "John Henry has been around for years, this town is a physical thing that has a history. I don't personally care to know what that history is, but it surely exists. I think trend is perfectly appropriate."

"See what I'm talking about?" Tiny thunders, spraying droplets of a substance from his beard like a dog shaking off rain. "You could make a case for Talcott as Debut, Comeback or Return or Hip. It's all jumbled up now. I'm accustomed to four varieties of puff and I like it like that. Four elements, four humors, four seasons, four varieties of puff. Otherwise why have categories at all? Why not make everything a category. A puff for every little thing."

"We already have that," One Eye interjects. "We call them magazines." One Eye has been quiet all night, and after his comment he looks back down at his food and prods corn. J. asks him if anything is wrong.

"Just thinking is all," One Eye says.

"Thinking about your secret mission?"

"What?"

"You said in the van. A mission that could change the course of human events."

One Eye's one eye narrows. He had forgotten he mentioned it. Dave, Tiny and Frenchie continue their argument. One Eye leans over to J. and whispers, "I'm taking my name off the List. Permanently."

"You renounce Satan and all his works? How do you intend to do that?"

"I have been plotting and planning, my friend, plotting and planning." His face illegible. "I've had this event circled in my filofax for some time now."

Before he can question One Eye further, J. sees Arlene go up to the podium. The musical entertainment. The red light beckons. Deciding he better get seconds on the prime rib before they close the food down, he throws his napkin on the seat and hustles. No hick is going to gyp him of his bounty. He removes himself and scurries over to the red light. One Eye looks disappointed, but J. figures he can pick up the conversation later. Arlene describes the singing prowess of one of the sons of Talcott, a boy who will go on to great things. This time J. doesn't take any vegetables. He asks for five proud slabs of prime rib. A young man departs one of the tables near the podium, a burly teenager with a soft balloon face. His baby fat has never gone away; it has chased the teenager's growth inch for inch, keeping in step, swelling proportionally. At the boy's table are an older man and woman—his mother and father, J. gathers. He hadn't noticed them before. That makes five black folks in the room. Who says integration can't work, he asks himself.

J. returns to the table, plate before him, the raja's rubies on a velvet bed. Dave and the others are watching the boy get himself together at the podium. He wears a black church suit and a brazen red tie clenched by a clumsy fat knot. His eyes and mouth, tiny things, disappear into his soft face like the buttons of a plush couch. The boy looks a little nervous, but then he starts to sing, and from the depths of him rouses a gorgeous baritone—it reels from the amplifiers like a flock of dazzling birds. The boy sings the "Ballad of John Henry." The boy sings,

> *John Henry was just a baby,*
> *When he fell on his mammy's knee;*
> *He picked up a hammer and a little piece of steel,*
> *Said, "This hammer will be the death of me, Lord, Lord,*
> *This hammer will be the death of me."*

> *John Henry was a very small boy*
> *Sitting on his father's knee,*
> *Said, "The Big Bend Tunnel on the C&O road*
> *Is gonna be the death of me, Lord, Lord,*
> *Is gonna be the death of me."*

> *John Henry went upon a mountain*
> *And came down on the side;*
> *The mountain was so tall, John Henry was so small,*
> *That he laid down his hammer and he cried, "Lord, Lord,"*
> *That he laid down his hammer and he cried.*

The rude talk that pestered the earlier speakers disperses. Lord, Lord: He hacks at primal truth and splinters off words and the men and women ache. Enraptured, all of them, openmouthed in beatitude and slack in delight at the nimble phrasings of the boy. Except for J. J. attacks the prime rib. He has not had his fill. He cuts off a piece ringed by a crust of blackened fat and sticks it in his mouth. It is a big piece, a hearty plug of meat, he doesn't know what time he'll eat tomorrow and he needs the meat. He rends tendrils of meat with his teeth, repositions them with his tongue, rends them further. He swallows quickly, another piece already impaled on his merciless tines, and the plug catches in his throat. He can't breathe.

The boy sings,

*John Henry told his captain,*
*"Captain go to town*
*And bring me back two twenty-pound hammers,*
*And I'll sure beat your steam drill down. Lord, Lord,*
*And I'll sure beat your steam drill down."*

*John Henry told his people,*
*"You know that I'm a man.*
*I can beat all the traps that have ever been made,*
*Or I'll die with my hammer in my hand, Lord, Lord,*
*Or I'll die with my hammer in my hand."*

*The steam drill set on the right-hand side,*
*John Henry was on the left.*
*He said, "I will beat that steam drill down*
*Or hammer my fool self to death, Lord, Lord,*
*Or hammer my fool self to death."*

It won't go down. He tries to swallow again but the plug will not oblige him. It is a stern and vengeful plug of meat. He tries to swallow again, panic trebling. Surely he isn't choking. It won't go down. He's going to die on a junket? This is some far-out shit, this is a fucking ironic way to go. Is he using ironic incorrectly? The copy editors are going to kill him. They are really cracking down on the misuse of the word ironic, it's like this global cabal of comma checkers and run-on sentences and fragments. Roaring in his ears. Why won't it go down? He finds it inconceivable that no one knows what is going on with him. They are looking at the boy and listening to his words. He has a problem asking for help. He does not want to look weak. And it might not be an emergency. Surely it will pass. The meat is just fucking with him. He could jump up, slam the table, knock over their free drinks, that would get their attention. But he's sitting there choking, quietly choking. Is this his pattern? That sounds like a diagnosis. And if he can self-diagnose, he can self-medicate. He has practice in that area. But you can't do that when your throat is stopped. Seduced by a red illumination. Bang, whimper, what the fuck.

The boy sings,

*John Henry dropped the ten-pound hammer,*
*And picked up the twenty-pound sledge;*
*Every time his hammer went down,*
*You could see that steel going through, Lord, Lord,*
*You could see that steel going through.*

*John Henry was just getting started,*
*Steam drill was half way down;*
*John Henry said, "You're ahead right now,*
*But I'll beat you on the last go-around, Lord, Lord,*
*I'll beat you on the last go-around."*

What's this guy singing? He's choking on the stubborn plug of meat. John Henry, John Henry. He works on the C&O Railroad. He pushes puff, he is going for the record. His muscles must be jumping out of his skin. It won't move, it sits like a bullet in his throat. No oxygen for me, thanks, I've had enough. Luke Cage the Marvel Comics superhero had bulletproof skin. At one point he had a sticker book where he kept stickers of Marvel Comics superheroes, they jumped out of the page, dynamic, Avengers Assemble and all that, muscles on full ripple, Luke Cage the jive-talking ex-con. This is what we get. Your whole life is supposed to flash before your eyes and this is what I get. Step into the light. Red light? What was up with that yellow shirt he wore anyway, some sleazy guy in a disco laying lines on the ladies, Luke Cage. He finds it incredible that in this crushing and collapsing time, he has the time to think these thoughts. But they say your life flashes before your eyes. I'm a sophisticated black man from New York City and I'm going to die down here. With cicadas, they got cicadas down here, don't they. I want roaches, real crumb-eating fucks from out of the drain.

The boy sings,

*John Henry told his shaker,*
*"Big boy, you better pray*
*For if I miss this six-foot steel,*
*To-morrow will be your burying day, Lord, Lord,*
*To-morrow will be your burying day."*

*The men that made that steam drill*
*Thought it was mighty fine;*
*John Henry drove his fourteen feet,*
*While the steam drill only made nine, Lord, Lord,*
*While the steam drill only made nine.*

*John Henry went home to his good little woman,*
*Said, "Polly Ann, fix my bed,*
*I want to lay down and get some rest,*
*I've an awful roaring in my head, Lord, Lord,*
*I've an awful roaring in my head."*

Isn't there something he is supposed to do? He feels like he is falling from a height. He can't think of it. He can excrete twelve hundred words in two hours and yet he can't think of any last words. How about an epitaph? He can't get farther than his name and the pertinent bookend dates. He slaps the table to get their attention. Their drinks jump. He sees a restaurant sign, yellow and deep blue, on the wall of a restaurant, on the walls of infinite restaurants. Who wants to be the guy in the picture turning blue? Black folks turn blue? Look for the telltale signs. Pictographs. Certainly public service announcements, like road signs and airport signs, need a simple language. Simple message, simple expression. Is that a journalistic axiom? He can't remember, and yet it sounds so official. Nobody notices his death. Sensation of falling. Who wants to be the blue guy in the choking picture on the wall of a cheap restaurant? Where is this place's sign? There must be laws about the placement of the signs, eating establishments must post them in convenient places. Federal law, but then maybe they vary from state to state. States' rights! States' rights, these people love their states' rights, signs on fountains, back of the bus, Rosa Parks. This place will fucking kill him. He should have known better. A black man has no business here, there's too much rough shit, too much history gone down here. The Northern flight, right: we wanted to get the fuck out. That's what they want, they want us dead. It's like the song says.

The boy sings,

*John Henry told his woman,*
*"Never wear black, wear blue."*
*She said, "John, don't never look back,*
*For, honey, I've been good to you, Lord, Lord,*
*For, honey, I've been good to you."*

*John Henry was a steeldriving man,*
*He drove in many a crew;*
*He has now gone back to the head of the line*
*To drive the heading on through, Lord, Lord,*
*To drive the heading on through.*

He stops falling. His body bursts and he is jerked up out of his seat. Involuntary Physical Response: the signs people keep on their lawns to repel burglars? He jumps out of his seat. My eyes must be popping out my head like some coon cartoon. His hands point to his throat. Can't these people see what's going on? The boy keeps singing. The pain is in his throat, around his throat and he would like them to make it stop. All these crackers looking up at me, looking up at the tree. Nobody doing nothing, just staring. They know how to watch a nigger die.

PART TWO

# MOTOR
# LODGE
# NOCTURNE

❖

The first blow shattered half the bones in the boy's hand and the second shattered the other half. There was no way he could stop his hammer from coming down the second time. He was swinging his next blow before his first struck the bit. That night in the grading camp someone said that they could hear the boy's scream all the way on top of the mountain and down in the shafts, louder than the sound of blasting. The boy's hand was all chewed up. The doctor would have to cut it off. The shale dust settled into the blood and melted into it like too-early snow. The other driver dropped his sledge and his shaker told one of the water carriers to run for help. They had stopped singing. This was time out of the Captain's timetable.

John Henry looked down at the boy. He had the build, but anyone could see he wasn't a shaker. Too much of the rabbit in him. The boss had told him the boy was a shaker on the west end and had been reassigned to fill in for L'il Bob. L'il Bob had been coughing fiercely the last few days and needed a day of fresh air to clear out his chest. He kept a bucket by his cot for what he spat up. No one mentioned miner's consumption, the black rot of the lungs caused by the foul air. Between the smoke from the lard and blackstrap candles, the rock dust and the blasting fumes it was a miracle they all weren't sick after a year in a tunnel. There was still time. L'il Bob didn't want to get caught coughing and lose his grip on the drill bit. It turned out the boy hadn't been a shaker on the west end; he'd carried water, and only for a week. What you needed were steady hands and speed, but what you needed most of all was faith. The sledge came down and drove the drill bit into the rock and the shaker had to twist the bit between blows to loosen the dust in the hole and keep the bit level for the next blow. Two quick shakes and a twist made the rock dust fly out of the hole. You had to have steady hands and speed, but you had to have faith. You had to know that the driver wasn't going to miss and smash your hands and ruin them. You had to hold it straight. John Henry and L'il Bob understood each other, which is why John Henry didn't like breaking in a new shaker. You had to hold it straight or you'd never hold anything in that hand again. The boy did fine for half the day, but then John Henry could see him get lazy or lose attention or maybe he just realized how crazy the job was. The candlelight was dim and useless. The candles in their hats sometimes snuffed out suddenly, the Lord blew them out, and the hammer fell mightily in darkness. The shaker's hands better be where they had to be when that happened. If the bit got dull, or the hole got too deep for a six-foot bit and they needed an eight-foot bit, the shaker had to replace it without letting the steeldriver miss a blow. The rhythm was all. L'il Bob did his work well. The boy did fine for a long time. But then he was slow, that one time, and the bit was not level. No question he would lose that hand.

He looked down at the boy. The boy sat on the ground, leaning against a powder can, looking at his hand and screaming to split his head open. The other driver, George, tended to him. He wrapped the rope around the boy's wrist to stop the blood. John Henry looked down at them. They were blackened by dust and oily with sweat, yellow and brown in the candlelight. This was time out of Captain Johnson's schedule. Every night Captain Johnson came with his tape to measure the day's heading. He started at the west end of the tunnel, took a measurement, and came around the mountain to the eastern cut and took a measurement. He could have sent one of the bosses but he did it personally. Captain Johnson had a schedule of convergence, of a moment when the final blast would break the mountain in two. Each morning the bosses changed the wooden shingles on the sign outside the cut. It was how far they had come. John Henry told the boy to quiet his screaming. He was not the first he had maimed.

He looked at his hands, the big dumb mules at the end of his arms. They did what they wanted. Palms like territories. It was stupid. Time it took the runner to get outside the tunnel, the time it took for help to arrive was lost time. John Henry bent over and lifted the boy from the ground and threw him over his shoulder, made a sack of him. He walked east, faster than going west ever was. They made ten feet a day with twelve-hour shifts. It was always faster getting out of the mountain than going in. He walked on the planks. The planks heaved up dust from beneath them with each step. He kicked a blasting cap out of his way and it skittered into a pile of dull bits the runners had left to the side. The hole they drilled that day was eight feet deep; probably the next morning the blasting crew would nestle the nitroglycerine inside it and blow it open to a few feet of heading. He told the boy to be still or else he'd drop him right there and the boy whimpered and was still. He asked the boy where he was from. The boy mentioned a town in Virginia, not far from the Reynolds plantation where John Henry had been born. Then the boy started screaming and John Henry let him. They were a quarter of a mile inside the mountain and John Henry could feel the mountain heave over him, breathing. He looked up and saw the one ugly crag that always taunted him from the ceiling of the tunnel whenever he passed. He remembered the day the blasting exposed the crag of rock and John Henry saw it for the first time, sneering at him, a spiteful beak of shale laughing at their little work, laughing at him. He worked under the crag for four days and each minute it cursed him. He was glad when they finally drove the heading past it and hoped that a charge would obliterate it. But when they reentered the tunnel after the smoke slowed and all the weakened stone from the roof of the tunnel had ceased falling, the crag was still there, angry and unforgiving, and John Henry damned it each time he walked by. The crag knew him.

The mouth of the tunnel was like an eye opening as they got closer to it. He tasted the change in the air. The ground shifted under his feet and all around him. Blasting in the west end. Some small pieces of shale tumbled from the roof of the tunnel but nothing big. Not this time. John Henry felt the back of his shirt wetting with the boy's blood. Yesterday a blast in the western cut shook out a large section of the arching in the east heading, and a stone from the cave-in crushed the skull of one of the drill runners, Paul. He'd never talked to Paul but John Henry knew he was from further south, Georgia. They buried him with the rest down the hill. No one knew if he had any family. He saw the light swimming in the gloom and as he stepped out of the tunnel he felt like Jonah stepping from Leviathan's belly. He knew the mountain was going to get him but the Lord had decided it would not be this day.

The blacksmiths at the mouth put down the bits they were sharpening to look at John Henry and the boy. They stood with some pick-and-shovel men and skinners and they all gawked at them. He saw the water carrier who had gone to get help standing with the boss. The carrier was out of breath and pointed at them. The boss frowned and told John Henry to put the boy in one of the mule carts. John Henry laid him down in the cart next to an empty crate of nitroglycerine and saw the boy's eyes. He had stopped screaming and yelping and he shivered all up and down his body, his eyes open to the sky. The boss said the doctor was in town and one of the men was going to have to take the boy there. John Henry walked away from the cart to a cistern. He dipped in a cup, two cups, and gulped the water down. He closed one nostril with a finger and blew forcefully, ejecting dust and snot, and repeated the process with the other nostril. The sun was almost down. He gulped at the air to take it into him.

The boss asked him what he was standing around for.

John Henry said he needed another shaker.

The boss spat into the ground and nodded. There was no shortage of niggers.

It was custom on nights like this, when they were far from home, to share stories of what they had seen on their journeys. For they understood things about each other that no outsider ever could. The stories passed the time through the night and sustained them.

And so it comes to pass that when the van returns them to the hearth of the Talcott Motor Lodge, Dave Brown, Tiny and Frenchie repair to a room to drink and tell each other stories. Frenchie had swiped two bottles of tonic water while the bartenders put away the liquor, Dave Brown shares his stock of gin and Tiny grants his room for their meeting. After the drinks have been passed around and each man has slaked his thirst, Dave Brown says that what happened to J. reminds him of something he had seen years before, when he was young. His comrades lean forward to listen to his story and Dave Brown begins his tale.

"They were the greatest rock and roll band in the world—do you understand what I mean when I say that? They were a thing that could never be again. Those days are over. Today the record companies have that kind of hysteria down to a science. It's a matter of mapping the demographics, man, but the thing about that time is, there wasn't a demographic. We were all the same thing. Mick was singing about stuff we all did. Fucking around with girls in the backseat, cruising up and down the streets looking for something we couldn't put our finger on but we knew it when we saw it. Satisfaction. We were all war babies. Mick and Keith knew what it was like to grow up in the fifties. It was the same over there as it was over here. They had the same parents. They were the war generation and we were the new generation."

"Flower power."

"You know me better than that. I'm saying it was different. It all seemed possible. That doesn't sound like me, but that's what it felt like and the Stones were a part of it. They made me want to write about music. Do you know what I mean? Talk to any rock writer of that time and they'll talk about the

Stones. You can argue for hours about the Apollonian and the Dionysian, but the dark wins every time so fuck the Beatles, just fuck 'em, perspective-wise. In the long view. I'd come back from college and sit in my room with my little record player with my hand on the needle and transcribe their lyrics. I filled a whole notebook with Stones lyrics and my annotations—which blues song Keith had taken what riff from, which words Mick was cribbing from who. Before they got their own voice. And I still consider that my first book. You can go to the Museum of Television and Radio in New York and look up their early appearances and see what I'm talking about. *Ready, Steady, Go* in sixty-four. The girls screaming, God, you can smell their panties. This fucking whiff. Can you imagine what it must have been like for parents to watch that on television with their children and realize that their fresh-faced daughters all wanted to fuck that mangy scarecrow guy on stage? Not kiss and nuzzle, but actually fuck Mick Jagger. Hell, I wanted to fuck Mick and I'm as straight at they come. You can still feel it in those old black-and-white museum pieces. I looked them up last year when I was researching this thing for *GQ*. I had some time to kill so I got out the tapes of *Ready, Steady, Go* and *T.A.M.I.* And it all held up. One of the museum interns came by and I thought it was my father going to tell me to turn it down.

"So those were the good old days. By the summer of sixty-nine all those screaming girls had stopped cutting their hair and let those Annette Funicello bobs go to hell. They burned their bobby socks and tramped around in dirty feet and had run away from home to join the fabulous furry freak carnival. Most of the Stones' TV appearances for the last few years had been on the news, not Ed Sullivan—they kept getting busted for various drug charges. Mostly a little pot, but that's what it was like back them. Getting busted for a little grass was big news. Brian Jones was a corpse at this point. He was always the ragged prophet of the group, standing off behind Mick with that airy look in his eyes and then he finally lost it. I feel it is one of my primal personal fucking tragedies that I never met the man. They found his body in a swimming pool and that was the first bad thing, I think. That should have told everybody that the gig was up.

"By that point I had started writing and was getting published. *Crawdaddy* gave me some regular work in the back of the book, and I got some San Francisco scene pieces into *Rolling Stone* so I thought I was a big shot. They were just little scene things but I thought I had hit the big time. So when the Stones came to America for their first tour in three years, I was front and center. They'd hired Mick Taylor, that dumb shit, to take Brian's place and got

B. B. King and Ike and Tina to open up for them. I caught them in Los Angeles at the start of the tour and even got into this party for them in the Hollywood Hills. This guy I knew had the same dealer as the guy throwing it and we just walked right in."

"Did you get to meet them?"

"Not until much later. I was a small fry, like I said. I met Mick later in New York during the Studio 54 days. But that was the older Mick. He was the elder statesman then, the settled-down and established rock star. Not Jumpin' Jack Flash. Not like then. The first time I ever saw them live was at the Forum on the kickoff of that sixty-nine tour. In L.A., I drove down for it. They were incredible, of course. They'd been out of circulation and their flock was waiting for them. The greatest rock and roll band in the world. They came out under red lights on the stage and immediately ripped into 'Jumpin' Jack Flash.' Mick came out with this Uncle Sam hat and a red, white and blue cape, dancing like the devil, slapping his hands together with that dance he always does, sticking his neck out like a chicken and bumping his groin against the air like he was fucking some invisible pussy. It's a gas gas gas. This was the Let It Bleed days, and Mick was doing his best satanic trip on the crowd and everybody loved it. 'Sympathy for the Devil'—on one level it went against the vibe the kids had been working, but still they all bought it. It was channeling the inverse of all that, it was the anti-matter but it worked. Keith still looked halfway human back then, he had this crazy black hair on his head that looked like two crows fucking. He had those long spider arms and held the guitar as far as he could from his body when he played, like he was holding this pot of steaming tar that was too hot for him. He ripped into the songs, just looking up at Mick now and again to see which way they'd take the crowd. Bill Wyman was on the left with his long woman's face, not doing much but doing his bit as usual and Charlie Watts just looking down at his kit, half his hawk face hidden by this sweep of brown hair, that was the look that was in, everybody had it. And Mick did his strut, hands waving the crowd up and urging them on. Sticking out those famous lips of his, he'd crack his body out like a hooker peddling blow jobs on Tenth Avenue. B. B. King and the Ikettes had stirred us all up all night and Mick took all that pent-up shit and released it. It was a wild night. I remember this guy standing next to me—he looked like a narc—and when the Stones came on he tapped me on the shoulder and passed me this skunky burnt-up joint. I was pretty high already and had seriously thought for the whole show that this guy, this schoolteacher next to me, was from the FBI. Just waiting to bust me. I was fucking obsessing on this guy all night. He didn't say anything or move the whole show, not even when the Ikettes were shaking their tits at us. So he passes me this joint and I look in his eyes and his pupils are the size of fucking quarters. He had eaten a few tabs of what, I don't know, that's what it looked like, and was desperately trying to keep his shit together. Then the Stones came on finally and snapped him out of it and he was back in reality, almost anyway. Who knows what he saw up there, but it snapped him out of it.

"The tour started from there and went all across the country, selling out everywhere. They made something like a million dollars over the course of it, and that's what got them into trouble. It was the time of free concerts and festivals and that's what the kids wanted. They demanded it. It was their right. Of course they wanted it all for free—they were Americans. Woodstock and Hyde Park and the Isle of Wight—that's what was going on. So the rock press got into the act. Ralph Gleason over at the *Chronicle* wrote a piece slamming the Stones for ripping off the kids and not giving anything back. Ralph thought they should give something back, basically accusing them of being sellouts. I always liked Ralph—he was one of the last moralists. So then *Rolling Stone* joined in the act and that pissed off the Stones to no end. Here was their comeback tour—they'd survived the drug busts and Brian's death, and now they were being reviled by their fans. Or the press, rather. At every press conference, it was like, 'so when are you going to do a free concert, when are you going to do something for the kids?' So what I'm saying is that already the concert had a bad vibe on it. It was born more out of p.r. than love for what the kids were trying to do."

"You've gone from 'we' to 'the kids.' "

"Have I? It was a long time ago. Maybe I'm just in journalist mode right now. I'm trying to be objective."

"And you sound like even more of a hippie than usual."

"I always talk like this."

"He's right—he always talks like this."

"But you went in for all that peace and love stuff, right? You always talk about it."

"I'm just trying to get some objectivity in my account, if that's okay with you, Tiny."

"I saw the Rolling Stones a few years ago on one of their farewell tours. One of their many farewell tours. I have a hard time reconciling. I'm trying, but I don't get it."

"You had to be there, Frenchie. It was a whole period that they were a part of. That's what I'm trying to get across."

"Don't get mad, I'm just saying. I'm more of a Hootie and the Blowfish man myself."

"All right, all right. So at the end of the tour, the Stones announce that they want to do their free concert thing and they want to hold it in San Francisco. Only the city fathers want this outrageous insurance bond for Golden Gate Park, the natural place to play, so they had to find someplace else. They retain Melvin Belli, this old school gangster lawyer–type to handle the arrangements. At this point Belli is handling the Manson defense down in L.A. Nice, right? He flies up to San Francisco and does some wrangling and massaging and secures the Altamont Speedway, this old stock car racing track out in the desert about forty miles outside of San Francisco. And it's on, December of 1969.

"We drove out there in Andy Farber's old Mustang early in the morning. I don't think you would've ever met Andy—he wrote the first really great mushroom piece—but he stopped writing in the early seventies and moved to Alabama to start a chicken farm. Andy and I were drinking this big jug of California red and smoking joints as we drove out there and it was a great morning. Sunny. We'd been up all night at the pad of this friend of his and we just kept going. And we headed out and every so often we pass a van or a car full of hippies and they honk and wave, and we wave back, it's all good fun. There's this great energy that we're all just going to hang out and listen to music and smoke some grass and maybe get laid and it's going to be a good time."

"Were you writing about it?"

"I hadn't intended to, but how couldn't I after what I saw? I found out *Rolling Stone* was putting together a package about it and I got to work. Unfortunately, I started getting sick the day after the concert, and that turned into pneumonia because I wouldn't stay in bed, and I couldn't get it done, which was a bummer. But I later included it in my book *Rock and Roll Memories*. I gave you a copy of it, remember?"

"I'm not sure I got that far."

"I see. Well, it's in there. It's the centerpiece of my chapter on the Death of the Sixties, which holds up as the final word on the subject, if you ask me. So we're passing people on the road, and the road out there was getting packed with kids and pretty soon we realized that all the cars pulled over to the side of the road weren't people stopping to get high—they're parking. We thought we were getting there early, but people had been camping out all night for this thing. There was no more parking up at the site and now you had to fucking park like miles away and trek up there. So Andy nosed into this little space and we started walking. It was a caravan. Thousands of pilgrims hoofing it up there. Little gangs of kids who had driven from all over the country, carrying baskets and coolers, passing wrinkled-up joints. Walking barefoot to the mount. You'd walk up one brown hill only to see two other slopes beyond it and all of them were crawling with people. Look back and you'd see even more people, the ones who got their shit together even later than you, and they were coming up behind. People banging tambourines and goofing. It was the convocation of the freak nation. No one knew.

"And of course it was a bigger mess once we actually got to the site. It was a quarter of a million people. All you could really see was heads in the distance for miles it looked like. Of course those people couldn't hear the amps, they just wanted to groove on the event. People sat down on the brown grass on their Indian mats and blankets, bunching up their sleeping bags as pillows. They'd dance a little hippie dance on one foot and then stop, everybody so fucked up. Girls were strutting around with their shirts off, tits flopping around with their crazy moves. Tits flopping all around—they didn't care. Long hair flowing. This was the ground zero of the counterculture at that moment in the world. They had caravaned from New York, hey let's go, man, and slept on the floor of vans or maybe they hitched all the way. They were yearning to be part of the free festival thing they'd heard about, this new happening. It was moving and horribly pathetic at the same time. You started to notice the bad freakouts little by little. One guy would be standing with his shirt off with his arms outstretched, staring off into the sun. And his mouth would start moving and he'd look confused and shocked, like he was realizing the worst thing in the world. Their friends would take them off to one of the Red Cross tents, which were totally overwhelmed. I later found out that Owlsey was there giving away free acid, and I don't know if that's what was causing it, but there was a lot of bad street acid making the rounds and that was doing serious damage. There were all these skinny malnourished dogs around, I remember that. They prowled around. The kids had found the dogs on the street and taken them in. Strays taking in strays. They couldn't take care of themselves and they'd take a dog in. It was a stimulating atmosphere with all the stuff going on; everyone wants to play with a dog, and the dogs were able to deal with the kids but you felt they were only one day away from total wildness. They sniffed around the trash and mud like they were sniffing what was coming and already adapted to it. Ready to go wild and ugly, like nature intended for them all along. It was messy enough. And then I started to see the Angels.

"The Angels had been providing security for the Dead for the last year or so. Jerry and the boys dug hanging out with them—they were these tough customers, dose-of-reality characters who put the up-against-the-wall in up-against-the-walls, motherfuckers. When the Stones finalized the San Francisco show, Rock Skully, the Dead's manager, set them up with the Hell's Angels. To keep things cool. Now, I've never bought into the Angels' mystique. I knew what they were before Altamont and I still know it. It was a stupid decision. The Stones bought the Oakland and San Francisco chapters of the Angels for five hundred dollars' worth of beer—Budweiser, their choice, I'm sure. I saw the first one after we sat down. Andy and I staked out some space next to a bunch of fifteen-year-olds and Andy immediately sacked out and I was lying back and taking in the scene. We were pretty far from the stage, and you could hear Santana faintly-playing, but I was in no rush to move up closer. Then I heard that hog sound, that backfiring farting sound of their motorcycles, and looked up and saw people trying to move out of the way. I saw the Angel coming toward me, with his long dark greasy hair and dingy club leather, astride this massive chopper. The motherfucker was driving his motorcycle through the crowd, just nosing it forward and revving it every few feet to scare the kids. He had this little square of black hair under his lip that was almost, but not quite, a Hitler mustache, but he had obviously cut it that way so that Hitler was the first thing you thought when you saw it. I couldn't see the Angel's eyes because of his mirrored sunglasses, but I could see that we were in his way and he wasn't making any motions to swerve away. I started trying to wake Andy, but he wasn't having it. We'd been up all night and he was totally out. His mouth open like a dead fish. So I started slapping him, trying to get him awake, but he still wasn't having it. I kept turning back to look at the Angel, who was still descending on us, slowly, like a shark, and then the Angel kind of did this slight nod thing and turned to the right. He smiled as he passed us and showed me his rickety brown teeth, what was left of them. From anyone else—on that day, in that scene, or anywhere else, for that matter—what he did would have been a simple kindness, but I looked into his teeth and knew he was trying to tell us that he could have run us over or not and it would have been the same thing.

"I left Andy there and started to walk around and the stories of the Angels started to trickle in. The Angels were getting violent. They attacked singly and in groups. Someone would accidentally brush against them and the Angels would whup them with a pool stick—they carried baseball bats and pool sticks that they filled with lead. These things connected with skulls. Or a kid might accidentally kick up some dust on one of their hogs and get beaten up. If an Angel started something, all of a sudden two or three other Angels would come swooping down and join in and help beat up whatever unfortunate soul had crossed their stupid white trash rules of propriety. They all had the same greasy look and feral eyes. They loved it—the dirt they wore on themselves was the natural progression from safe, middle-class hippie anarchy to total anarchy, anarchy in its natural state. When they laughed at one of the kids and picked on a flower child or couple and threw their Budweiser at the head of some kid in the middle of a freakout, they knew what they were doing. They were telling the kids that the Angels were the real deal. The kids were kids playing at something, and the Angels were that something all grown up."

"Now you've gone from 'we' to 'they' to 'the kids.' Weren't you the same age?"

"I was twenty-six at the time. I was a little too old to take it as seriously as, say, my younger brother did. I was just past the mark."

"So you didn't believe it all."

"I did or I wanted to—it's the same difference, isn't it?"

"All those people have straight jobs now, right? Run the country and what not?"

"That would be true."

"This is the elegy for the lost boomer."

"Like I said, I left Andy to his stupor and started walking the desert. The Altamont Speedway had agreed to hold the concert because the owners were basically bankrupt. It was in the middle of nowhere, just a mess of dead grass for miles in every direction, but now it had been taken over by the freaks. The towering amp scaffolds went up sixty feet in the air and the kids climbed up on them like black bugs. I saw one person climb halfway up and then lose his grip in a druggy haze, hang there for a minute, and then he fell down in the crowd where I lost him among the heads. I'd pass these abandoned stock cars here and there, rusted through and totally crashed up. Teenagers'd set up shop, spread out their Indian blanket on the backseat and ball. Some people didn't feel as modest and rolled around in sleeping bags, or out in the open, even. Well-heeled white chicks from Marin made the rounds asking for contributions to the Panther Defense Fund and giving speeches about the struggle. Like they were war widows. I was missing most of the action on stage, but I didn't care. I'd get there eventually. I was pretty fucked up, so I don't know why I'm casting so many aspersions on the kids, but I'd never seen so many people in such obvious trouble in one place before. The street acid was taking its toll. I got accosted by this head in a fringe leather jacket who peered at me through Peter Tork sunglasses. He grabbed on to me, dried grass in his hair, and kept jabbering at me until I finally had to knock him to the ground. He just looked up at me and smiled and said, 'You got it, man, you got it.' Everyone panting in communal, barefoot freakout. The sky had gone gray. The sun wasn't out anymore and the air was getting chilly. The p.a. warned people about bad acid, where to take lost children, and gave directions to the Red Cross tents. I saw a young woman with blood on her tie-dyed shirt and asked her if she needed any help. She said, 'It's beautiful, man. I just helped deliver a baby.' It's beautiful. She stumbled off and I just thought, what kind of woman who's about to give birth would come out into the desert for this? That's beautiful? People were getting seriously hurt. In the days after the concert, people kept mentioning that four people died and four babies were born, as if that was some kind of equation that balanced all the negativity out. But it didn't. Four babies born, two people run over by cars while they slept in sleeping bags, one guy passed out in an irrigation ditch and drowned in a puddle, and of course what happened during the Stones' set. It doesn't balance out.

"The Angels continued to crack heads open through each act. As the Jefferson Airplane started 'Revolution,' Marty Balin jumped off stage to break up a fight—the Angels had started picking on this black guy near the front of the stage and Marty jumped in to break it up. And the Angels turned their fangs on him and beat him unconscious. They beat the lead singer of the Jefferson Airplane unconscious. I was still far from the stage but I heard Paul Kantner—the guitarist—take the mike and start berating the Angels. So one of them grabbed a mike and told him to shut up. They were in control. I didn't like Marty personally—he had snubbed me at a party a few months before and though I retaliated by saying a few unkind things in print later on, I still held a grudge—but obviously the scene was now out of control. They'd beaten up a rock star, for Christ's sake. But the show went on. The Angels controlled the night.

"I woke up and it was dark. I had a little more stamina than Andy, but the last night's partying had finally caught up with me and I crawled into one of the junked cars and fell asleep. I vaguely remember doing that. I woke up and had all these seat springs digging into my back. I got out of the car and asked a kid if I'd missed the Stones and he told me that's what they were all waiting for. People had ripped down the speedway fencing to make bonfires, so that lit things up a bit, I could see people dancing naked in the orange glow. You know, burn, baby, burn. Shit. And the film crew's lights helped. The Maysles brothers were filming the concert—Mick was jealous that the Woodstock movie was coming out in a few weeks and he wasn't in it, so he got the Maysles to film his own free concert. People were singing Stones songs like that would summon them out of their trailer and then an Angel would glide by and drown them out with his motorcycle. But then one time the hog sound didn't cut out. It got louder and the sea of people parted and this wedge of Angels came driving up through the people like an arrow. And between their motorcycles came the Stones, protected from the crowd by their bad-ass bodyguards. The screaming got massively loud. I got myself into the wake of the Harleys and pushed myself forward to the stage. I felt the thousands at my back, hungering behind me. As the Angels helped the Stones up onstage, I saw that it was full of people. Angels, hangers-on, anyone who could still stand and control their body was up there. It was ridiculous, man. I weaseled my way to the right, and got a pretty good view. At one point one of the cameramen zoomed in on me, but I never made it into the movie.

"The big banks of lights showered the stage with a hellish red light from above. There was barely enough room onstage for the band with all those fucking Angels, but the Stones took their places. I saw this German shepherd, one of the Angels' dogs, hoof around the mikes, eyes as greedy and hungry as those of its masters. Behind me, the miles of people pushed forward. It was the moment they had all been waiting for. Deliverance time. It was night and the greatest rock and roll band in the world was going to take them to their reward. And then it broke—Keith started to drag his claws across the strings and Mick twirled his black and orange cape and they started into 'Carol.' The crowd surged forward all of a sudden—we were as close together as we could have been and they wanted more. More people wanted in. It all came down to this, I thought. A few yards away, this hepcat in a Nehru jacket—Nehru jacket, shit—tumbled into one of the Angel's hogs because the crowd pushed him and of course first one then two Angels started beating him. I was pushed forward by the shift in the crowd so I lost sight of it—the last I saw of him was a volley of pool sticks coming down on his head like lightning. The Stones must've known it was too violent in the crowd to play, I know for a fact they knew what was going on, but they kept playing. Thing is, it wasn't even that great a set. Totally uninspired. All the energy they'd had in L.A. had totally dissipated by the end of the tour. They were doing the show, they were doing what they did best, but they couldn't hide the fact that it had been a long couple of months. Maybe they didn't take a stronger stand against the Angels because they just wanted it to be over. They just wanted to play their final set and get the fuck out of America. They'd been bullied by what the press and what the public expected, the pop had shifted and forced them into this. Or maybe they were scared of the Angels, of what they had wrought, and if that was the case then they should never have gone into 'Sympathy for the Devil.' It was just stupid. Mick in his Satan mode asked the crowd to please allow him to introduce himself, lit up all red against the black desert night, and the Angels took their places. The Angels brought their wrath upon the hippies, raising their baseball bats and pool sticks upon the heads of the kids. The kids all clambered and rushed up to get up to the front of the stage, they ran up to the Gates and the Angels swung down on them. Mick tried to stop it and the Stones quit the song. Mick said, cool it, cut it out. As if he were still in control. The Angels dragged away some people and things calmed down a bit. Mick joked, "Something funny always happens when we start that song," as if he thought that you could say the words of the spell and then act surprised when you smelled brimstone.

"I was exhausted. Andy and I had been going on for too many hours before we even got there for us to enjoy the concert, no matter how it went down in the end. But to put up with this, with my body dehydrated and my head throbbing with a red wine hangover? Shit, man. It was fucking unreal. And it only got worse.

"I'd seen him before when the Stones appeared with the Angels and everybody started moving forward. Tall, skinny black cat in a lime green suit and black shirt—he stuck out. He'd waded past me and was two or three people in front of me, closer to the stage. Now there were two or three Angels right in front of that part of the stage and I'd been watching them suck back Budweiser and push people who got too close. They'd been laughing and pointing at suckers in the crowd and were definitely guys to watch out for. I had gone up as close as I wanted to get and was happy where I was; I got into that space at a concert where you've staked out a spot, your legs are braced to prevent being moved, and I was glad that there was a human buffer between me and the Angels. I saw the Angels getting more and more anxious as the Stones started up. That was the most horrible thing. I saw what was going to happen. I saw them start to fixate on the black dude and choose him. I don't know how I knew it, but I knew they had chosen him before it came to actual violence. The black dude was bobbing his head and dancing and I saw the look in the Angels' eyes and knew.

"Up onstage, the Stones started into 'Under My Thumb.' After what happened with 'Sympathy,' I think they convinced themselves that they were going to get through this song without a hassle. So they kept playing all through what happened and later claimed that they didn't know that anything had gone on. It was like a Vietnam GI saying he didn't know there were children in the hut he just torched.

"What happened was an Angel touched his hair. One of the Angels came up to the black dude and laughed and grabbed a big chunk of his Afro. His dirty paw went for it once and the dude moved his head away, and then the Angel sneered and the fucker went for it again, this time getting his hand deep into the guy's Afro. The guy jerked his head away and swung at the Angel with his right, not putting the Angel down but knocking him back a few steps. The two other Angels came up to join their buddy in his fun—it was quick—and the black guy went down, just kind of dipped and when he came back up I could see the gun in his hand, a little nickel-plated revolver he'd pulled out of his pocket or something. He kind of bounced up from the ground and had a gun in his hand. And then I saw the knife. The guy was looking at the Angels who were hassling him but didn't see the Angel at his back who swooped out of the crowd—this greasy creep came up behind him, grabbed his arm to steady his kill and sunk the knife into his back. The Angel followed through with his thrust, pushing the black dude forward and suddenly the wolves just ate him up, they dragged him away. The girls were screaming. I rushed forward to follow them and a space had cleared where they had him on the ground, half a dozen Angels standing over him. Blood already gushing out from his clothes. He said—these were his last words—'I wasn't going to shoot you,' and one of the Angels lifted a garbage can high over his head and brought it down into his face. Then the other Angels joined in and kicked his head and body with their motorcycle boots, laying into the black guy like they were going to wipe him out totally, like they were going to make him and his fucking extinct then and there. And we stood in a ring watching. There was this kid next to me, a teenager with curly red hair and this silly suede bandito hat on his head, who started to move forward and I held his arm and told him, 'You can't do anything.' The Angels would have killed him and me too if we'd dared do anything. We understood that there was nothing we could do and stood there watching this horrible event. The Angels possessed the night.

"It was horrible and we watched it. All the negativity of the day, of all that year, came down to this violence that we witnessed. And those thousands at my back who weren't right there and didn't see it could feel it. The Angels did what the people demanded, even if they didn't know they demanded it. They were going with the flow. They kicked and stomped him until he was just a puddle and when he wasn't moving anymore they stopped. He was flat on his back in the dirt, his elbows dug into the ground propping up his hands like weeds and I could see into his skull. I could see the stuff of his brain. A young guy moved forward to help him and the Angel with the knife told him to back off. He was going to die, it's too late, the Angel said, and there wasn't anything you can do about it. We stood there like that for a minute, the Angel defending his kill, and then the Angels took off. Two guys came up and took the man's body to the Red Cross tent. His girlfriend, a blond from Berkeley, followed them, sobbing hysterically. She was wearing a crocheted dress. You don't see crocheted dresses anymore. And onstage the Stones played 'Under My Thumb,' a song about getting over on your girlfriend, to hundreds of thousands while the Angels performed their sacrifice."

"Sacrifice to what?"

"To the culture. The kids had brought a new thing into the world, but they hadn't paid for it yet. It had to be paid for."

"Why did he have a gun?"

"For protection, I guess. And he needed it. He died in the Red Cross tent. He'd lost too much blood and there was no way they were going to get him to a hospital in time anyway. The Rolling Stones flew away in the helicopter and left us in the desert. And we found our way back to our cars and went home."

"So this guy is like the Crispus Attucks of the seventies."

"That's a new spin."

"Alas, who cries for the lost counterculture?"

"Who indeed."

"What was his name?"

"His name? I can't remember."

"What about Andy?"

"I didn't see him until the next day. I caught a ride with some Haight-Ashbury kids."

"And what about the Angels?"

"The Angels split."

S ometimes it happens. Nothing he can put his finger on, an effect maybe like the reverse of dynamite: noise and fire, white light, these elements flying not apart but together into a compact thing. Him, an afternoon. Putting the ruin back together to what it was. Looking over the past few hours, what does he see: an extra ribbon of bacon at breakfast, half an hour less sleep, a portion of seconds considering the dead robin next to the birch tree at the side of the road he walked here. Nothing really and yet he feels different. The peculiarities of this morning collect, they persist, stand at odd attention on his self like iron shavings on a magnet, drawn by invisible forces. Charged, attracting this day and life to him he sits on a stump and writes his song.

A drying puddle bristling with gnats; twigs like lizard legs, all knees; a cobweb on his brow. A breeze.

He's on the top of the hill. He has to let out the tune he's been humming under his mind for the last few days now. Try a line and let it hang in the air. The last word of the next line comes first, it shines, obvious, newly there, and the rest of the line creeps up on it. That's half a verse right there. Like picking a pocket. Sometimes he thinks rhyming is cheating. First man to rhyme building a whole new world should take his place with the man who invented brick. He's practically stealing the song today; it's not his but he's got his fingers on it and that's half the battle.

Where's that chord from. Some man like him hundreds of years ago sitting on a rock, arthritis not so bad today, a wind came out of nowhere and knocked the clouds away, then this chord on his fingers, been in his fingertips all night: plucks the chord on his mandolin, something else, whatever instrument the man favors. Zebra sinew stretched tight across a torso of wood that makes sound. Sounds good. So good he thinks he invented it, he's the first person in history to do this thing.

Feeling like today he's just nothing but himself. Nothing but a man.

He can only go so far before he has to go back to the beginning. Memorize it, chase after that lost word in the verse he just thought up, got it, sing it again and again. Verse, verse, verse, taking the story of the man farther and getting it down this afternoon before he forgets it.

Add the love of a good woman. A hero needs a woman. Name her Polly Ann, after her.

He holds out his hat in taverns after he sings, the coins waterfall, silver down. He'll try this song out tonight. Somewhere he stopped feeling east. He's been following the rails, seeing what he can get out of this town before the next calls him on. The rails lead west. But now the air has changed and he has to face it: he's more west than east now, he's in the Western territory. He doesn't think he wants to go that much farther. Some fellow told him once that there's a whole country of songs out there, the guy passing him the jug after they traded tunes. That may be true. But there's something today about this song, about how easy it is, that maybe there's just this song. Taps his foot along to keep the beat.

Weight of suspenders on his shoulders, where his shadow falls away from him and the leaf half in the shade. Nothing really and yet.

Maybe it's the *Lord, Lord* that makes it work today. Sitting there in the verse, an anchor. Forget Big Bend. *Lord, Lord* is the real mountain in this song, thrown up from his bedrock and looming. It reminds him of something he knows about himself. And if he took the time, maybe he could take each of his words today and link it back to something that happened to him. His father or mother, something that happened one day. Some of the words he wouldn't know where they came from. Might take years, might take his deathbed. To figure it all out. Or maybe it's the whole thing together that makes it all important.

Then. Everything that collected on him has fallen away. What happened anyway? It's like that. Exhausted half the feeling, used up half the magic and didn't know he was closer to the end than he was to the beginning. Too busy to mourn. And now the day is no longer charged and all he has is his creation. Twigs just twigs, puddles just puddles. Spent.

Song done? Not yet. He knows that. Like a dollar bill it changes hands. Others will hear it and add a verse, goose the rhythm, slow it down to fit their mood, temperament, to fit the resonance set up in them by the arrangement of plates on the kitchen table that morning. Same thing he did: scuffed shoes, an old guitar, easy in crescentic afternoon like a layabout in a hammock, got all day for a song. He wasn't there at Big Bend. This is his own John Henry, who he figures is a man like himself, just trying to get along. And if the man who taught him the song has his own John Henry, let him. The next man will have his. Someone else will change his verses and today's John Henry will be gone, or secret in altered lines like memory.

He'll try it out tonight. Next week someone who half-remembers it will sing it again. Maybe even at the same moment he's singing his version in some other town along the rails, their *Lord, Lord*s hitting at the same time like two steeldrivers working the tunnel side by side.

Benny said he didn't want to go anyway, so the missing invitation didn't disturb him and he dismissed Josie's soundings about the so-called snub with a robotic downward wave of his hand, always the same gesture, she'd seen it a hundred times. Too preoccupied to deal with any matter these last few weeks unless it pertained to "the preparations," unless it was keeping vigil for the UPS truck ferrying the new cartons of toilet paper or negotiating with Bob and Frank's Hotel-Motel Supply on the issue of the replacement key chains, which had arrived as botched blue plastic diamonds with the words "Titcut Motor Lodge" etched into their faces. This last matter, with its attendant pockets of voice mail vacuum, ran up their phone bill to unheralded scale. Bob and Frank's Hotel-Motel Supply mailed them the original purchase order for the key chains with Benny's invalid scratches marked in yellow highlighter. It was inarguable: it did indeed look as if he'd written Titcut, and the supply company was apparently reluctant to redo their order free of charge. Benny doesn't possess the same facility in dealing with people as Josie, and so it fell naturally and tacitly to her to harangue, nag and needle the succession of representatives from the supply company, Bob, Frank, Frank, Jr., whoever was unfortunate enough to answer the phone, about the Key Chain Affair. Benny demanded daily updates. With so many details commanding his attention, the ephemera of the preparations coursing in swift orbits, he did not have the time or inclination to endlessly debate the matter of the missing invitation, which in his mind had already been settled. He settled it himself. He talked to Mayor Cliff about it, and had been assured that the missing invitation was a mistake and no more than that; the politician even made a joking reference to the Fred Letter Office, as the Post Office had been called years before, owing to the former postmaster's legendary scattered faculties. Mr. and Mrs. Scott were invited to the opening night banquet at the Millhouse Inn, he assured Benny; Benny and Josie had pitched in to make this weekend special and were expected. But when Josie discovered that Charlotte Cliff had helped out with mailing the invitations, she knew exactly why theirs did not make it to the battered red mailbox that stood in spinster vigil at the foot of the parking lot. Of course she could not tell her husband why; all she could do was raise the matter repeatedly and obsessively, lob it into the air of their living room and watch it fall dead to the ground, as if she were a child sentenced to desultory indoor play on a rainy afternoon. She knew exactly. And she did not want to go.

Which suited Benny fine. The start of John Henry Days went off without a problem, the guests arrived, the rooms filled, no bother except for the matter of the dirty swimming pool, oh and the lounge chairs the New York journalists had left in the parking lot, which Benny had to move back so that they would not get pulverized by an inattentive driver. Friday night: he wanted nothing more than to take his customary stool at Bucky's and drink with his mates. He did not want to see his fellow citizens put on airs, pat themselves on the back and generally try to pretend that a plateful of lukewarm grub at the Millhouse was some high society event.

Benny drives out to Hinton and Josie stirs a packet of macaroni and cheese. No doubt the food at the Millhouse is a step up the culinary ladder from her meal, but she is happy with her macaroni and cheese and settles into her bed with a copy of a Judith Krantz romance one of the guests had left in her room. The book opens naturally to the naughty bits, neatly foreshadowing the heroine's assignations. Josie knows how far she has to wade through boring bits, she sees the floozy pages ahead. She reads and sometimes looks at the bell above her bed, to the signal linked to the grubby yellow button outside the office. Once a pleasant pearl color, the button is now shellacked by pilgrims' greasy deposits; from the front doors of all-night gas stations, coffeepots, circulated cash and gripped steering wheels, this substance makes its way to the motel office buzzer. But tonight the NO VACANCY sign keeps them away, and all of the guests are at the Millhouse. No one rings. She always jumps when the bell rings. She falls asleep to the theme from *The Tonight Show*.

Benny's snoring wakes her hours later and she remembers the ghost.

Josie feels it is her daily circuit through the rooms that gives her insight into the ghost. She senses its comings and goings; they share a bond as lifelong (and afterlife) residents of the region. She is a daughter of Hinton and bound to the place by history and family, the ghost attached to the mountain by its mountain death. No wonder Benny cannot sense the specter; her husband is a longtime resident, but he is not *of* the town. He cannot see the sense of her argument that under a mountain full of ghosts, their outpost, situated between the towns of Hinton and Talcott, is a natural place a ghost will wander to and make a home. What did her husband think he was doing by choosing this tract of land? It is a solemn recess between the places people had chosen to live. How about next to the Three Rivers Bridge? she asked. Too close to the Coast to Coast, he said. How about closer to Talcott, just a little closer, not here in the damned belly button of Big Bend. Too far from the New River traffic, he said. And now they have a ghost.

The guest register is complete. Benny Scott is a thorough and fastidious bookkeeper. It took him a long time to pick the registers out of the supply catalog and he is happy with his choice, the black leatherette binding and generous spacing of lines somehow jibing with an unarticulated idea of the essential nature of his motel. Their motel, rather. It would be entirely possible then, if a bit time-consuming, to make a concordance between Josie's archive of haunted rooms and the immediately previous occupants of said haunted rooms. Which people had slept there the night before the ghost visited the room. Families of four, say, or isolated men on excursions into the land, young couples making their way out of the national park. It would be a simple matter to interview Josie and match up the dates and rooms with Benny's crabbed notations in the guest register. Such a foray into the woman's mentality would reveal that, unknown to Josie, her tracking of the itinerant ghost through the Talcott Motor Lodge corresponds to evidence she finds on her morning rounds: material wrapped up in tissue paper at the bottom of the bathroom trash can; a certain scent that greets her when she opens up the doors after checkout time; the tea-leaves sheets. A subconscious equation. The movement of the invisible ghost, as perhaps is only appropriate, is inferred by Josie through the unseen.

The first thing Josie thought when Benny, beaming, that sweet-foolish grin on his face, told her that they were all booked for the weekend of July 12, the weekend of John Henry Days, was that there was no avoiding the ghost. The haunted room would be filled. Benny has come to take Josie's ghost stories as a joke, what other choice has he, even when holding her arms to keep her from marching out of the apartment to warn a guest in the dark A.M., to tell them to beware, to look out for dancing shimmers, to move to the next room over or sleep with the light on and say a prayer. He has no choice but to make a joke out of it. Yes, she conceded once, the haunted room changes, it is inconsistent, but that isn't her fault; the ghost likes to mix it up. The rooms of the motel are essentially the same; if Benny were in the ghost's position, she tried to explain, tied to Big Bend by spectral contract, tied to the motel on the base of the mountain by convenience and ghostly whim, wouldn't he want to change rooms from time to time, trade the daguerreo-type of the Hinton Station in room 13 for the bright cheer of Chessie, the C&O's feline mascot, smiling from the side of a railroad car on the wall of room 26? (This a thinly veiled reference to the fact that Benny does not get sick of anything, and resists with a certain glum aplomb any of his wife's ef-forts to redecorate their apartment.) Seems kind of picky for a ghost, Benny said. Perhaps he's a member of Triple A, he said, maybe one of their approved hotels might be more his style. Josie threw up her hands. If the ghost moved from room to room, it wasn't her fault. If Benny wanted to switch chores and make the beds and wash the bedding out back in the cantankerous washing machines, he'd get well acquainted with the comings and goings of the ghost himself. Mr. Comedian had nothing to say to that. With the motel's high va-cancy rate, it is easy to accommodate Josie's edicts about where a guest can sleep and where he can't. But if they are all booked up there could be no such finagling. Someone was going to have an unexpected roommate.

None of the guests had ever complained of the ghost when accidentally given the keys to its latest roost. They were lucky, Josie reasons, for the en-tity's mercy: the ghost sleeps peacefully next to them, occasionally stealing the covers and leaving merely an imperceptible depression on the pillow, or perhaps the ghost hikes to the next room over, eschewing the hassle of man-ifestation and its attendant miscreancy. But tonight. She had feigned exhaus-tion that morning to avoid seeing the face of the unlucky soul who would sleep in the haunted room. She'd spent Thursday on a search and destroy mission against the smell of mildew and dampness, dropping lethal payloads of aerosol roses on the first floor, on the second floor, complained of agonized trigger finger at the end of the day and Benny let her sleep late. She avoided the front office all afternoon, and Benny took her trepidation for pouting over the missing invitation. She let him. He took her fear for a joke. He doesn't know the ghost like she does.

The first ghost any child of the region hears of is John Henry. Each time a train leaves the Talcott station and rushes into Big Bend Tunnel, the engi-neer blows the whistle for old John Henry, poor John Henry. His was the tri-umph of the human spirit, her father told her, and if you dare enter the tunnel you will hear his hammer singing in the darkness. This is the deathlessness of the human spirit, her father told her, fingers in her blond pigtails, which were moist from her chewing. Big Bend is alive with the ghosts of men. The mountain eats the sun and delivers the towns to the ghost world every day.

Her father was the Hinton station man and knew these things; his father was an engineer and had told him these things when he was as young as she was. Her mother told him not to scare her and he smiled. If she's old enough to stay up later than she's supposed to, he said, she's old enough to hear the tales of Big Bend. Men died in the tunnel, he said. His father had helped remove the bodies from the cave-in of 1883, the bodies of men he knew, and where did she think that souls went when they died violent deaths. They linger on angry. And did she hear the whistle blow just now, her father asked and she nodded. That's the engineer blowing the whistle to ask Big Bend to save his life, to let the train through its big heart of rock.

She has avoided the situation but can no longer. She gets out of bed, no need to worry about waking Benny from his gin sleep. Josie had fallen asleep in her faded pink robe; she puts on her slippers and leaves the apartment to read the guest register. Surely the guests are back from the Millhouse by now. She reads the name of the guest in room 27 and goes to warn J. Sutter of the vengeance of the ghost. She tightens her robe against the night with trembling hands and walks up the stairs. Benny will be angry with her, but he needn't know. She pads up the stairs. Josie knocks three times on the door. She can see the shred of light at the closed curtains so she knows that the man is awake. She waits and knocks again. She thinks about getting the key and letting herself in to leave a note but decides against it. Benny would really be mad at that. She waits five more minutes for an answer and finally returns to her bed.

Benny is still snoring. Saturday mornings, after Friday nights at Bucky's, find Benny cranky until the coffee kicks in. He'll tell her about who he saw at the bar, Rob, Nelson, Arm. She'll tell him about going to room 27 and he'll make a joke about it. And maybe she'll tell him a joke Arm told her once, one she is certain Arm has never told his friend. When Armand Cliff and Josie dated in high school (which Charlotte Cliff had never forgiven her for and which neither she nor Arm had ever informed Benny about, it was before he had come to Talcott), he took her into Big Bend Tunnel, just inside the entrance. They stood in puddles and kissed. She got suddenly scared at the dead space, heard the hammer swinging in the darkness, this insistent pounding, and she asked Arm, what about John Henry. Arm said, you want John Henry? and put her hand on his crotch. Which Josie still thinks is a funny joke after all these years, but she doesn't think Benny will appreciate it.

Bobby Figgis began his career as a stock watcher for *The Wall Street Journal*. He possessed an MBA from Harvard and decided to become a journalist to cover the games and strategy of his fellow alumni. He had always had ambitions and now that he had jumped through the hoops his parents had held for him, he was going to pursue them. He wrote small articles about fluctuations in the market that were praised by his superiors.

Bobby Figgis met an editor at *New York* magazine and dazzled her with his teeth. She proposed that he write an article about the new class of young urban professionals. It seemed like an obvious fit. Bobby knew the players from his school days. He rang his old acquaintances. He instructed the photographer as to which Upper East Side apartments to shoot. His article made the cover of the magazine and at another party he met more people who asked him to write for them. For a while he had a thing with the editor at *New York* magazine, but she broke it off. She considered him her find, and resented the attentions of those she perceived to be her competitors.

Bobby Figgis quit his job at *The Wall Street Journal* and went freelance to cover the world of the new Wall Street warriors. He was in key with his time. He had a stock set of adjectives and knew the bouncers at several trendy downtown nightclubs. He knew them by name. One day he found himself on the List. It surprised him because he had heard stories about the List but did not believe he had paid his dues yet. He still had this thing about paying his dues, one of many abstract ideals instilled by his parents, and he found it hard to shake.

Soon Bobby Figgis had entree to the best parties in the city. Publishing parties and movie parties and big-time fashion parties where he worried, not without cause, about dandruff. He expanded his specialty. He married a stockbroker he had dated in business school. It hadn't worked out before but now they just clicked. She looked good on his arm, she had lost weight, and she liked to charge into the office each morning to tell her coworkers of the party she had attended the night before. She wasn't bragging, she was sharing the details of her life as anyone would. She had to be at work at six in the morning because of the foreign markets and soon she could no longer attend as many functions. He started fucking around.

One day Bobby Figgis bet another member of the List that he could do an event every day for a year. Bobby had become quite a bullshitter at this point and his fellow junketeer said why don't we put some money on it. They shook hands. The next day Bobby remembered the bet and pledged not to drink any more during the week, only on weekends from then on but he forgot his pledge once he got something to eat, around two in the afternoon. He ate and attended a party thrown by the Elite Model Agency that night and nailed the first day of his bet.

Bobby Figgis made it through the first week fine. A week of nightly junketeering was no big feat. Publicity cycles ebbed and flowed, all junketeers found themselves pulling a full week from time to time. It was part of the job. After two weeks he grew tired, however. It was the same food night after night, it seemed to him. His colleague reminded him of his bet and he continued, cursing the afternoon light when it woke him.

A thought emerged in the minds of the junketeers, almost simultaneously, as Bobby Figgis entered the third month of his bet. That there might be some kind of record involved. The younger junketeers consulted the older junketeers and it turned out that Bobby Figgis had entered into new terrain. He had set a record for the longest bout of junketeering anyone could remember. Bobby Figgis had entered into new terrain.

They asked him if he had taken a day off and he replied that he had not. They asked him if he wrote about all the products or human beings or concepts the events were intended to promote and he replied that he filed the usual amount. It became official. Rules were drawn up for future challenges to the record. Junketeers began to wager on the wager. Everyone wondered how far he could go. His wife had stopped speaking to him some time before. She punished herself for her husband's obsession by driving herself at work. Bobby Figgis stuck to the wager and departed every afternoon or evening to an event or events described on the List, which arrived by fax every noon.

Bobby Figgis lost weight and did not seem his old self. This occurred in the sixth month of the bet. He interviewed this week's starlet in her suite at the Sherry Netherland Hotel and sometimes answered his questions for her. He attended computer conventions at the Jacob Javits Center and asked the bright young geniuses of Silicon Valley if their data compression devices could store things other than data. His jokes, always stiff, became obtuse and seemed to refer to a new brand of humor. A noticeable lack of affect. His fellow junketeers waited for him to throw in the towel. He had nothing to prove anymore. The man he had bet informed him that the contract was void. He could stop his odyssey short of the agreed-upon year with honor. He did not stop.

In the ninth month Bobby Figgis attended a video game convention. He was flown out to Arizona by a kids' gaming magazine that lasted only one issue. He walked down the rows of the convention hall to a symphony of electronic beeps, whistles and gunfire. Middle-aged men aimed electronic machine guns at screens, decimating street criminals in a game endorsed by the U.S. Department of Justice. Sword blades directed by joysticks hacked at dark-skinned creatures. The monsters exploded in vivid pixelated death and were replaced by identical monsters. There was no end to the monsters. They came from within the machines. Bobby's skin felt on fire. The middle-aged men loosened their ties and took aim. Bobby stopped before a strange machine. A young techie put down his sandwich and urged Bobby into a black body suit equipped with sensors. Bobby put on gloves and stuck his head into a heavy black helmet. He stepped into the gyroscope and said he was ready. The techie pressed a button and the gyroscope began to move. The screen inside the helmet blazed brilliantly into his eyes, describing a high resolution dream that did not seem to end.

Bobby Figgis returned to New York the next day. He did not file the story on the video game convention. He stopped filing any stories. He showed up at events but had dropped all pretense. Bobby Figgis had established a record of nonstop junketeering that no one dared match. He smelled bad. Some of the regular suppliers to the List barred him from their events. Everyone felt a little awkward about this. His picture was taped up at movie premieres with a prohibition against his entry. Stories continued to circulate. His wife was long gone. Soon he attended only the subterranean events that are the fear of all junketeers, events without names, held in places without addresses. He disappeared. He was never seen again. The keeper of the List deleted his name after a time. He had been devoured by pop.

Yes, her father would have loved it and probably would have stormed the microphone to make a speech. And perhaps they would have let him speak. First the mayor, then the man from the Post Office, and then her father takes the podium to deliver a few remarks. She's heard each sentence before, ten years before or fifteen years, he stitches the stiff threads of ancient and favorite rants into one bitter shroud for John Henry the man and his times. He runs over the allotted time and people shift in their seats, strangling the necks of napkin birds in their laps. Mr. Street has not even approached his point, whatever that may be. One or two repeated sentences, the blurred edges of phrases make the people wonder if he is drunk and they listen more closely following this lapse—is he drunk or crazy. Obviously he feels for John Henry keenly but there is a pace to the night, when they will drink and when they will eat and who will speak and that boy at the end who will sing. The mayor wonders if they need this man's collection of artifacts as much as he thought they did. Maybe they can hire someone to make things out of plaster and call them replicas of the genuine article. The tourists will have already paid their entrance fee and tourists never feel completely ripped off at tourist places, no matter how much they have been misled. The tourists are glad to be out of the house, and the real is so hard to come by these days, they understand and expect these deceptions. Maybe if the kitchen staff brings out the food, the guests will slowly get up to get something to eat, and Mr. Street will get the message.

Pamela sits in a plastic chair outside her motel room, legs crossed, right hand cupping her left elbow, expelling colonies of smoke from her mouth at regular intervals. The smoke lights out into the dark lands and swirls away by forces into diasporic scattering. She looks down into the foiled maw of her pack and counts the cigarettes, placing her nervousness and resulting hunger for smokes on one hand, and the dwindling number of smokes and her imprisonment at the hotel on the other hand. She is stuck at the hotel until morning, which would be fine if she were sleeping. But she can't sleep, even though she turned the picture of John Henry walking down railroad tracks to face the wall. Rather than making her feel at home—her parents' house had been crammed with mawkish pictures like that—the motel picture bullied her into ruinous confessions. She dragged a chair from the empty pool and sits outside her door, smoking, sometimes watching the crackling blue death of insects in the coils of the bug trap, sometimes watching her cigarette tip wither to ash. Sometimes the face of the choking man at dinner creeps up, his thrashing body and bulging eyes, and she shivers.

Talcott. She had heard the name thousands of times over the years, her father shaping the name as paradise or proving ground or just another town on a map depending on his mood. How far is she from the town itself? She still hasn't seen it. The Motor Lodge is on the outskirts and the Millhouse Inn is part of the town of Pipestem. The black laborers on the C&O weren't allowed in town, she remembers that factoid from her father's sermons, they lived in shanties near the work camps and were allowed into town only for one hour on Friday afternoons to buy supplies. She wondered if any of their shanty town remained, and if it was part of the weekend's festivities. Take a walk through John Henry Town! Here's the man's very own lean-to, notice the spaces between planks allowing nice cross-ventilation in the summertime, and the tar-paper roof protecting a full 35 percent of the abode from the rain and snow. No, it isn't here. If it were, her father would have put it on a flatbed and driven it up to their apartment as part of his collection. Probably would have slept in it too, poured some scotch into a clay jar and sat inside there at night, tapping his foot to some old work song and sipping from the jug of 'shine. Where they lived after they walked away from the plantations, pieces of paper signed by a magistrate in their hands, to trade tobacco and cotton for the currency of the industrial South. Coal and steel. And layin' the line.

*Layin' the line*, out of her father's mouth, became this all-purpose non sequitur that testified to balance in the world, whether the matter be existential or quotidian. Stub a toe? Layin' the line. Passing grades in chemistry? Layin' the line. Summer heartbreak, a backed-up toilet, walking pneumonia, winning three bucks in Lotto. Layin' the line, girl. You were layin' the line whatever you did, trudging through dust until you returned to it.

It began, like most obsessions, as a harmless interest. She was six, her family returning from Delaware from a visit with her grandparents when her mother noticed an antique store by the side of the highway. They stopped. It was a good point to stretch their legs. While Pamela provoked to no avail the scarred old tomcat perched on a barrel, its green eyes squinting timeless feline reproach, and her mother peered through a glass counter at what can only be described as the heirlooms of the damned, her father discovered something in the recesses of the musty store, past a neighborhood of decapitated street signs named for trees native to North America. It was a ceramic figure about three feet tall, its base a short expanse of railroad track supporting a hunched black man with a hammer poised to slam a railroad spike that jutted from the track precociously. Her father prowled around the object like a wrestler. Sections of it were chipped away, a bit from the man's cranium, a crescent of his cheek, exposing the crude white matter beneath. Her father called Pamela and her mother over to that corner of the roadside antique store, where lawn jockeys of variegated expression and purpose gathered, arms tired. The figure of John Henry layin' the line was surrounded on all sides by small men in red outfits hefting the strange burden of gold rings. The hammer's impending but stalled convergence with the spike had a spooky presence to it and Pamela felt a chill: it was a fragment of something larger fallen from above, eternal forces glimpsed for a second. She asked her father what it was. He told her it was John Henry, and John Henry sat in the backseat with her all the way back to Harlem, swaddled in her favorite red blanket, her blanket.

She exhales smoke into the night air, aiming for a denomination of gnats a few yards away. So it is sibling rivalry, she thinks. John Henry took her blanket. It started with that. At first she and her mother made fun of the little creature. Her father placed it in the doorway next to the umbrella stand so that it was the first thing you saw when you unlocked the three locks, that tumbling line of security, pushed in the slow door and entered their apartment. Sometimes they'd talk in his voice, a deep "How do you do?" and chuckle at their stupid joke. The hardware store thrived, it was on a corner with a lot of traffic and had a domain. Mr. Street hung his shingle at the right time, at the right place, and he joked with the handymen who did odd jobs in the neighborhood, he swept down on homeowners and renters as they dozed along the aisles looking for something to unstop the drain or punish the truant hinge, understanding exactly when their postures intimated defeat before the long and stocked shelves of Street Hardware. A man of his age and success could use a hobby. Model airplanes, collecting stamps, or John Henry: he had earned the solace of taking his mind off things. And as the pictures of Mrs. Street's family came down to make room for framed, faded sheet music and photographs of the Big Bend Tunnel and woodcuts of a hero, she thought, the man has earned it.

She hears laughter from down the row of rooms. It is one in the morning. Pamela breaks the rules of cigarette rationing she set a few minutes before and lights another Newport while still exhaling the smoke from its predecessor. Then how do you trace the course of an addiction. It is a child. It feeds off nurture and care, it learns how to crawl and learns cunning and suddenly it is its own being, willful and scheming every second at survival.

The hobby grew. The traces of its development were savored and polished by Mr. Street, he talked to the artifacts when no one was around, or he thought no one was around, or he thought everyone was asleep and he had John Henry to himself. Chronicles of mechanical production. Yellowed and tattered handwritten drafts of ballads, nibbled and yellowed published versions of the ballads for drawing room amateurs, early sound recordings—one hundred twenty versions of the song and counting. Ink scratched into paper at midnight by hopeful songsmiths under lantern flicker; Yellen & Company Music printed sheet music, a tavern favorite in some localities; the recordings, expression of those written notes, piled up in their sleeves in alphabetical order, subcategorized by region. Fat 78s preserving the croaks of bluesmen who chronicled the showdown at C&O's Big Bend Tunnel, dainty 45s from sixties English bands that garnished the fable with paisley chords and frenetic sitar of the psychedelic sound, eight-track tapes of Johnny Cash on pills singing of John Henry, C-60 bootleg cassettes of Johnny Cash on pills singing of John Henry. Recording equipment necessary for the 3 A.M. playback of said recordings.

Mr. Street made weekend pilgrimages to antiquities shows and fairs, he wrote to terse P.O. boxes in the back of obscure magazines unavailable on any newsstand. Certainly not in their neighborhood. He assembled John Henry. A playbill from the Broadway show and the original score. The very trousers and shirt Paul Robeson wore during the show's troubled and truncated run. Did Mr. Street decline the temptation to wear the clothes from time to time? Pamela cannot find any way he could have. Hammers. Ten-pound and twenty-pound sledges in pairs. He rubbed brown oil into their handles with one of her old T-shirts, loving the wood as it was said John Henry did, to keep the wood limber, to allow it to absorb the shock of each blow. A grizzled old geezer from Charleston showed up at their apartment one Sunday night and opened a suitcase containing five of what he claimed were actual drill bits used by the Big Bend Tunnel crew, long rusted javelins with mashed plug ends. Her father bought them all, the new school clothes could wait, and hung them over the mantel, five fingers of a railroad hand.

At one point he proclaimed, over a pot of string beans entwined with bloated flats of bacon, his artifacts the largest collection of John Henry in the world. None stepped forward to dispute his claim. Some houses smelled of dogs or cats. The Street household smelled of her father's rotting mania and the sour reek of Pamela's and her mother's snuffed lives. He tried to acquire one of Palmer Hayden's famous paintings of John Henry, a piece of the Harlem Renaissance. The owners wouldn't budge. Like he had the money. He settled for a poster and in the dining room John Henry sprawled dead on his back, surrounded by the witnesses of his feat, arms spread wide like Christ's and his hammer in his hand, he died with his hammer in his hand. One time her father disappeared for two weeks to hunt down an old Adirondack hermit he'd heard of, to tape record from the man's drooling lips a variant of the John Henry ballad, which had been told to him by his grandfather, supposedly a Big Bend worker who had toiled with John Henry. Her father had cleaned out the receipts from the hardware store for the trip, leaving Pamela and her mother with no money and the Street women ate tuna fish and macaroni and cheese for two weeks. The tape turned out to be unintelligible, the old hermit muttered dementia but if you listened hard enough, and her father did with all his life, you could hear the big man's name.

The air is cool. This is the country. She hears steps down the cement walkway. Pamela sees it is the writer, the one who choked at dinner. He walks slowly and timorously, as if on a listing deck. He looks up from the ground and sees her, lifts a hand. "Still up?" he asks.

"How are you feeling?" She blows out smoke through her nostrils.

"Better," he mumbles. He raises the soda can. "This should help," he says. He doesn't sound as if he believes it.

"That was pretty scary."

His eyes dip down again. "Well, the guy saw what was going on and knew what to do." They give their names to each other and he apologizes for his colleagues' behavior in the van. He tells her they get a little excited sometimes.

"No problem," she says. "I lived next to a fraternity house in college." He smiles at this and she offers him a cigarette.

"My throat," he says, shaking his head. He asks her what brought her down here.

"My father collected John Henry material," she says. "It was his hobby. They want to buy it for a museum they're planning." She is entirely truthful.

"Must be a big collection," the writer says.

"It is," she answers and she lights another cigarette. One of the rooms down the line opens and the man with the eye patch pokes his head out. He yells out the man's name and waves his arm in circles.

"Maybe I'll see you tomorrow," he says.

"Probably."

Tomorrow she has an appointment to meet Mayor Cliff to hear his personal appeal. She has already decided not to give it to them.

S oon it will be time for the night rider to take his journey. His head is full of steam. He can feel the pressure in his head build to shift pistons, he can see by the few remaining drops in the brown bottle of Quint's Elixir that his boiler is well fed. Soon the car will begin to move.

He had the workers haul the parlor car from the yards to his home, they pulled the car down the gentle slope to the southern edge of his estate, where at night the sagging spray of weeping willows might look like speeding countryside. At midnight he lounges on the plush cushions of the parlor car, a vintage model from the Wagner Palace-Car Company, well appointed, elegant, generous in comfort for the distance traveler. Each time he enters the car he is delighted anew by the deep pile carpeting, the exquisite plush upholstery of the armchairs and couches, the lovely drag of the silk curtains and the beveled French mirrors. He watches the lantern light crackle in the chandelier and swim across black walnut paneling and marquetry fit for the first-class cabins of riverboat and steamships. No spittoons: the insalubrious brown wash that covers too many train floors these days will not be tolerated in his sanctum. He prefers the craftsmanship of Wagner to Pullman, but of course Pullman thought it out more completely, he understood the need of luxury and amenity and his current dominance in the field is undisputed. This is the fruit of competition and he will not have it any other way. Still the Wagners had a class all their own, even if he did, finally, have to hire away one of Pullman's porters to care for his private car. The porter comes in every morning after his night rides and dusts and arranges, removing the empty bottles of laudanum, dark tincture of opium, from the waste bin and wiping clean occasional vomit from the water basin in the washroom. The parlor car ferries one passenger, and he gets the best service.

There is a splashing in the pond. His wife recently ordered the pond restocked with carp, and they are perhaps splashing in the water, sensing his anticipation, the impending departure. He pulls out his timepiece, for if he is not mistaken, his head is aswim and it is time for his parlor car to move.

All aboard! The engineer makes his magic and the parlor car begins to crawl across the grounds. On the grass the ones who remain behind wave at the locomotive—they wave their hats and kerchiefs at the departing train, great thunderous waves of steam rolling up around them. The whistle cleaves the air.

They call it the Great Connection, this route through the anger of the Allegheny mountains that opens up the tidewaters of the Atlantic to the currents of Mississippi. He thinks, these are the times of connection, of routes between people for things. He feeds the magnificent and hungry connection, the child of industry, and watches it grow. The transcontinental is complete, the oceans are joined: done. He was not there at the joining, he had other business to attend to, but he knows the details of the race for the one-hundredth meridian, the convergence at Promontory Point, where the pig-tailed Chinamen of the Union Pacific collided with the Irish paddies of the Central Pacific and the final, ceremonial gold spikes were driven home by the silver-plated sledgehammer and the nation was joined. The telegraph operator sent back one word, "Done." And so it was. And his work is that work in miniature, connecting Virginia Central to Cincinnati, he wants Huntington by seventy-three and he will have it. His boys will have to move earth, but he will have it.

The car is fast, fast as galloping hallucination. It has found the tracks of the C&O's western heading, or where the tracks will be when they push the heading through. The people who have never been in a train before this day tilt their bodies to the windows and take in the Virginia countryside, seeing speed itself, collecting description to share with the people at home when they have completed their journey on the iron horse. He likes variety. Tonight he sees twin girls in blue petticoats, a cotton speculator with pince-nez, mail-order brides clutching their worlds in black-watch carpetbags. (Those he conjures depend on his mood, which is in turn predicated on the density of that night's mixture, the number of drops he has placed in the glass of water. Crescent of lemon hooked onto the rim of the glass, from his very own lemon trees. He's not good at faces: the eyes are missing, and the lips and teeth.) He approaches a dignified gentleman who studies the land outside the window in silent measure. He likes to talk to his passengers on his night ride. And where are you traveling, sir? Going to Cincinnati to visit family. Splendid, splendid. And how are you enjoying your ride? Yes, quite pleasant. First time traveling by rail? You've been on the Erie. Did you enjoy it? Oh, the Susquehanna is a beautiful sight, and a remarkable piece of engineering. I've heard something about that, the delays, but with recent disputes between Vanderbilt and the Erie gang, it's no wonder there's been a decline in service. Did you hear that they have to relay their entire track? It's all six-foot gauge they have up there, and that's the problem. It's not compatible. Our entire track is standard gauge, it conforms to the American standard. It will stand the test of time. That's very kind, sir, that's a very nice thing to say. It is smooth, isn't it? The right-of-way was planned meticulously by our survey-ors before we laid an inch of rail. Notice that there aren't those jarring turns that you experience on the Erie and some of the smaller lines. We planned it out.

Here comes the news butcher. What do you have? *Harper's, Munsey's*, the latest issue of *Punch*. Nothing for me, thank you, although this gentleman might require something. Not hiding any erotic literature under those mag-azines, I hope? I'm just joking, carry on. You're a good boy. The Union News Company hires only the best and brightest young men for their services. Many of them stay with the railroad, sir, I've seen it happen. They get the railroad fever and become ticket masters and engineers and even conductors. I've seen it happen time and time again. (His wife has never seen him like this, his emotional rigidity playing no small role in her late neurasthenia. Exam-ples of their eccentric and fragmenting relationship are—but not limited to—wordless dinners where the only sounds are the shuffling of servants and his dried lips sucking soup; violent conjugal relations that correlate to Sunday morning sermons about the weaknesses of the flesh; and his strict orders that he is not to be disturbed in his parlor car and her fear, so strong, that prevents her from even glancing at it. In his car he can be one of the people, garrulous and solicitous to his opium-bred specter guests. Quite a potent draft, Quint's Elixir, available at the pharmacy until recently.) Your wife remains uncon-vinced? Traveling by coach and will meet you in Cincinnati, I see. Well, you'll beat her there by days. I understand perfectly. My very own mother refuses to step foot on one of my trains, despite my protests. She thinks it's the work of the devil. Of course you have to consider when she was born. I might have been frightened, too, by those early locomotives, with their flying soot and noisome engines. But we're modern men, you and I, we understand the fu-ture, don't we?

I've been to Atlanta many times. The lines to Atlanta are much improved and I can assure you of a comfortable ride. Do you have business there? (And he fights the temptation to mention the war. He can't remember this ghost's particulars, how he made him, so it is best not to raise the topic. He could tell him that he knows why the Confederates lost the war. Simple mathematics. Between Philadelphia's Baldwin and Paterson's triad of Rogers, Danforth and New Jersey Iron Works, the Union could count on a new locomotive every day and miles of rail, while the Confederates had to convert the Tredegar Iron Works to produce ordnance. He visited Baldwin just last week; they know their duty. The Rebels ripped up their precious track to make armor plating for their ships and shell casings, while the Northern lines extended their mileage and kept the supply lines open and Lincoln's war chest paid them to ferry troops and freight. Handsomely reimbursed for patriotic duty. It was simple mathematics, to him it is obvious, but he does not know his guest well enough to share his knowledge, he does not want to open a wound.) Textiles. Well, I hope that one day you will have occasion to use the C&O in your business. Our express service is nonpareil, I can assure you. Our deliveries are always on time. (He uses his line's express service himself, to receive parcels from Quint's Medicinal Supply. It's his connection, one might say.) And isn't that the most marvelous thing? We are bringing all of our isolated towns into the fabric of the nation. Much has been said about the importance of the transcontinental—yes it is quite an achievement—but I think the greater boon is to the points in-between, the smaller towns and depots we are passing as we speak. I have an English friend who used to derive much amusement from what he called our nation's predilection for laying track through lands that had not been settled yet. He called it making a railroad line from the town of Nowhere-Special to Nowhere-in-Particular. He made sport of it. But look at us now. The people come. Like this town here, Talcott, the one outside the window there. Ten years ago this was wilderness. Now look at it. It is a depot, and the next day it is a community. And they need things. The grain states can send their goods to Philadelphia, and a woman in Kansas can order a new dress from New England. Did you know they refer to our line as the Great Connection? We've opened the Atlantic to the Midwest. Think of that. The rails are still, and always will be, the car of the people, as they say, but think of these new opportunities. The future of the railroad is to tend to the needs of the people, and not just their travel needs, mark my words. This is the spur of capital at work, my friend. But you are a man of business and I'm sure you understand. The cow towns of Sante Fe will want your fine goods, sir. And we will help bring them to them.

It's best to close the window now. We are approaching the Big Bend Tunnel and the air is not the best. The fumes accumulate, you understand. It took us almost three years to blast through it. We could have gone around, but that would have added precious time to the journey, and time is everything. Arduous work, of course, but with the new steam drills, the work of excavation is much more rapid and efficient. God made the mountains and man made the steam drill. True mechanical marvels, sir. If you ever have the occasion to see one of these machines, you will not be disappointed. But we should close the windows now, I can see it up ahead.

Junketeer lore holds that when One Eye lost his eye, he gained sight into other spectra. Blinded by the irony of the times, he could peer into realms denied the average man, where cause and effect have no sway, logic no authority, where the only laws are the dim edicts of the supernatural. Alas, One Eye demonstrates no useful feats of prognostication. He declines to say sooth. He cannot foresee the weekend box office tally or channel the *Publishers Weekly* best-seller list. When chance places him before a sitcom, it is not within his power to perceive which actor will tumble into boozy tailspin and tell all, or determine who is fated to hawk baubles in a brightly colored infomercial, who will follow James Dean around Dead Man's Curve. He does none of these things and does not pretend to. But when it comes to one-eyed men with eye patches, you project, J. thinks. You want magic these days. Conjure women and oracular witches stirring lizards in cauldrons don't just fall off trees, so you take them where you can get them.

"I didn't mean to break up your interlude," One Eye says, tilting his head toward Pamela.

"Just talking," J. answers. "I had to get a soda for my throat."

"How is it?"

"Raw." His throat shivers with a tremulous pain. After—after the commotion, after the application of Mr. Heimlich's Maneuver, the subsequent launch of the pernicious plug of beef from esophageal berth and the tracking of its salival contrail across the Social Room—a man introduced himself as a doctor. The local general practitioner, another railroad son, this one equipped with wire-rim spectacles and pockmarked crimson cheeks. J. forgets his name, but why not Dr. Willoughby? Dr. Willoughby was kind and knew the town's secret scars, thumbs hooked codgerly into his green suspenders. Suitable enough. Doc Willoughby told him he might want to check in with the hospital. After serious choking incidents, he said, the trauma to the throat tissues can sometimes induce them to swell up hours later, impeding the breathing passage. A post-choking choking. Better to be safe than sorry, he said. J. declined of course.

"Why didn't you say something sooner to let us know what was happening?" One Eye asks, at once angry and apologetic.

"I was trying. You didn't see."

"I didn't know you were choking. You looked so peaceful at first, I thought you were sneaking a fart, to tell you the truth."

"Someone saw, thank God."

"He's a stamp collector?"

"He collects railroad stamps."

"Christ."

"You're telling me." J. looks down at his soda and wipes away a wash of condensation. I'm glad the stamp collector was there, he tells himself.

One Eye stiffens, and the expression he had in the van and the Millhouse returns to his face. "It was a sign, J."

"A sign I should chew thoroughly before swallowing." J. isn't sure he is ready for a conversation right now. He wants to crawl into his musty sheets and stare at the water stains on his ceiling until they align themselves into pools of sleep he might dip in.

"You can look at it that way if you want."

"There something you want to talk about, One Eye? I should get some sleep."

One Eye motions him into his room. J. glances back down the walkway to where Pamela had been sitting, but she's disappeared. He sits down in the lime green vinyl seat by the desk and places his hands on his knees. "Not hanging out with Dave and the guys?" Custom calls for a night cap or three in someone's room on gigs like this, bullshitting against the darkness. J. has a legitimate excuse, a near-death experience being a perfectly legit excuse, but what is One Eye doing hanging out solo in his room. He isn't usually the sullen one.

One Eye deflects a spray of papers from his bed and sits down. "What I told you earlier about the List," he says, his one eye blank and deep in the mesmer routine he likes to use from time to time. For effect. This time he's cranked it up a notch to piercing. "I wasn't joking."

"You plan to take yourself off it," scoffing, "might as well appeal to the pope for special dispensation."

"I'm serious. I know who controls it. It's Lucien."

"What makes you so sure?"

"I've been thinking about it for months. At first I thought it was a consortium. We talked about that, remember?" One Eye brings up his investigation from time to time, over plastic plates in vintage ballrooms and on couches along the walls of blood-red downtown lounges. He shares his suspicions about the architects of the List: are they a consortium of publicity firms or solitary and mean-spirited visionaries? J. thinks it is a game. Something to pass the time during the many dull moments at events. When One Eye abandoned the idea of a consortium on the grounds that the List possessed an aesthetic purity and a malicious logic that could never be achieved by committee, J. nodded his head and nibbled chicken saté off a skewer. Might as well be discussing puffs of smoke above the grassy knoll. And when One Eye decided that the likely suspects were Lucien Joyce Associates and Patricia Klein Public Relations, J. agreed and continued to nuzzle the bottom of his beer. It is talk to kill time. No one really cares. Do people wonder how televisions, VCRs and computers work, or do they care merely that they work, that they are good, that good folk in lab coats have fashioned devices to round our misshapen hours. The List keeps them working and that is the important thing. J. says he remembers their many conversations on the topic.

"It's not PKR," One Eye says, leaning forward in a posture that might have been described as earnest if one did not know him.

"You finally decided on Lucien." Half of half a yawn executed just then.

"Patricia Klein didn't feel right," One Eye continues, trying to ignore J.'s slack expression. "They're too specialized. They have big-name clients, but they're not diversified enough. And I doubt Patricia has the cunning, to tell you the truth, for this kind of system. I had pretty much decided it was Lucien when I talked to Chester." One Eye almost shaking; he needs to tell someone: this is big stuff. "I cornered Chester at an animal rights benefit in Beverly Hills. I figured it was time to interrogate him. It wasn't a List event, I didn't see any junketeers or the usual flacks around and Chester had been out two years. This was last month. He was circling the room, pressing the flesh, and I cornered him. He was glad to see me."

"Good old Chester," J. nods. "He knew how to liven up things."

"He's not dead."

"You don't see him at events. Same thing."

"Yeah. It was like old times. To tell you the truth, I'm not sure Chester is happy out there in Hollywood. They have a different style and Chester is a little too . . ."

"New York."

"Right, for them. Anyhow, I got him drunk and got it out of him. The lowdown. It took three martinis and a lot of the old One Eye stare, but I got it out of him eventually."

"So spill it." J. checks the time on the bedside digital clock. More common than Gideons in hotel rooms nowadays.

"It's Lucien," One Eye says. "It's been him all along. He knew the game before he even started his own agency, from when he was a party promoter in the disco days. He knew the game from the street. He knew all the players from when he was just a wannabe dropping invites on tables in clubs. He had a perspective. Chester says he let him in on the List after he'd been with LJA a few years. Calls him into his office with this big production about earning trust and shows him the List. Then it became Chester's job to do the routine maintenance, you know, addresses and contact numbers. Lucien still chose the names, but Chester kept it running smoothly."

"Until he quit. Was he fired or did he quit?"

"He quit. He wanted to go to Hollywood. Go Hollywood. And Lucien didn't take too well to that. He's very protective of his boys and doesn't like to see them leave the nest and get out from under his thumb. A few months ago for no reason—according to Chester—Lucien cut him off the List. He still liked to go to L.A. events for old times' sake. They haven't spoken since."

"Mommy didn't like it that he was running around with loose Hollywood starlets. So Chester talked."

"Chester talked and here we are today."

J. thinks about his throat. Is it swelling up? One Eye's revelation is interesting in the abstract, but J. doesn't have it in him to dwell on it. He is too enervated and wrung. "You could always not go," J. says. "No one's forcing you to these things."

One Eye clucks his teeth. "You're going for the record and telling me this." J. doesn't say anything. "It's not about willpower. It's beyond willpower. Deleting my name has a symbolic power that will sustain my decision."

"They'll just put you back on. They'll notice and put you back on."

"I'll start with this one thing."

J. stands to go. This can wait until the morning, after he suffocates on his own throat. In the raw minutes following the stamp collector's rescue, Tiny retrieved the plug of beef and asked him, "You going to eat this?" Maybe he should have kept it as a souvenir. Get it bronzed. Don't soldiers save as souvenirs the bullets and shrapnel cut from their flesh? Soldiers' kids play with them. "And how do you intend to accomplish this Houdini bit?" J. asks.

"First, we break into Lawrence's room."

"What?"

"To see if he has the List. We'll hit his copy, and then we'll hit Lucien's."

"I'll be in jail and you'll get off scot-free," J. says, backing away. "White people can get away with that, not black people. Not down here. We get caught, if they don't string me up, I'll get railroaded for sassing the judge or something. You're laughing but I'm not joking. I'll be laying asphalt with the work gang."

"This isn't Mississippi in the fifties, J.," One Eye says, cocking his head.

"It's always Mississippi in the fifties," J. answers. "Go ahead."

"I've checked it all out. Lawrence is leaving at noon to pick up Lucien in Charleston. Lay out the master's slippers and pipe. Forty-five minutes there, forty-five minutes back, that's more than enough time to get into his copy of the List. Lucien doesn't trust anyone except his assistant, so they bring it wherever they go on their hard drives. Email and fax it from their laptops."

"There's no other copy in Lucien's super-secret safe deposit box?"

"Chester says Lucien keeps a backup in his office, but he writes over it from his laptop copy. Any changes we make will be put on the backup copy on Monday."

J. shakes his head. He likes the man, but Chester isn't the easiest person to trust, not with that penciled-in mustache of his. But then, J. remembers, Chester shaved off or erased the wisp because it didn't fly in Los Angeles. So maybe that was something. "How do we get into his room?"

"I like that, J. That means you're working it out in that gifted brain of yours. You're coming around."

"You haven't answered me."

"When you needed that receipt to cover that party you threw in your room at Game Expo Ninety-five, who did you come to?"

"You." One Eye had purchased receipt-forging gear at a restaurant supply store and helped out his amigos when circumstances demanded some expense sheet finagling, for a 10 percent fee.

"When you needed a copy of Nexis software and a password for some last-minute research, who did you call?" Given to One Eye by an intern he deflowered in a janitor's closet at the *Washington Post* a few summers back.

"I get the point."

"Think about it. Wouldn't it be great to fuck Lucien up? It's his baby. You know he gets off on it. Making the monkeys dance. Pulling the strings."

"From hell's heart, I stab at ya, baby."

"Maybe."

"You want to spend more time with your little girl," J. opines. "Watch her grow. You've been away too long."

"I don't have a little girl."

"I know, but it's something you could say to explain this business."

"This is no life for a grown-up."

J. gulps, thinking once again of the doctor's warning. He finds himself gulping forcefully since his beef misadventure to test the swelling or not swelling of his throat tissues, dispatching inverse trial balloons to test the weather of pain down there. The can of ginger ale, quaffed at selected intervals, will help in his experiment. It didn't get better or worse in the hours after the choking; his throat just plain hurts. He sipped water out of plastic motel glasses as thin as physics allowed, water that hinted at sulfur. Who knows what swamp the pipes were connected to? Dismal Swamp. He decided to switch up to ginger ale. "You'd like me to believe there are high stakes involved. But it's just a game. What made you come to this," J. asks, "after all this time?"

"I already lost one eye. One eye—what's next? I'll open a press release, get a paper cut that gets infected and I'll die because antibiotics don't work anymore. I'll get botulism from some spoiled peas at a buffet. Or I could choke to death on pigs-in-a-blanket, eh? Plus I want to show them I can do it."

"Proving what?"

"At the very least it'll be a fun prank. A spy mission. What do you say?" One Eye's one eye winks.

"Let me think about it."

"That's a halfway yes. I knew you had the spark, J. Ever since I saw you snag that bottle of Stoli and put it under your coat at that Random House fete."

"Good night, One Eye."

"So you're in?"

"I'll have to talk to you in the morning, One Eye. Let me get my shit together and I'll talk to you in the morning."

Alphonse Miggs lies on his bed half-naked, contemplating the fissures of a mothball. His striped boxer shorts almost reach his knees, the tops of his socks almost reach his knees, out of his T-shirt extrude soft fishbelly arms. He hasn't removed his shoes yet. Lying on the bed with his shoes on is something he would never do at home, not even on the pullout sofa in the basement where he sleeps these days, and is a luxury. He is in room 12 of the Talcott Motor Lodge, in a museum of previous guests' scratches and gouges, grateful to have a place to call his own.

The mothball's surface is too pocked and imperfect to roll away.

Rarely in his recent memory has he been as happy as when he unpacked his clothes. In any drawer he pleased. He had saved this task (extra-special treat) for after the banquet. In the top drawer Alphonse delicately placed his underwear and socks, in the second his shirts, and in the last his pants. One, two, three. Every item of clothing level in his palm as if he were handling packages of moody nitroglycerine. In the ledge above the sink he placed his travel kit just so. Eleanor was not there to stop or move his placements and each time his hand departed one of his possessions he felt a blush of freedom. A bona fide sensation.

Putting clothes in any old drawer feels like a political act because recently in the Miggses' household, 1244 Violet Lane, there has unfolded a cold war over spaces. It happens in every household of course, someone picks out a favorite chair or side of the couch; over time someone comes to a choice, or all at once—on the first day the new chair arrives in the house and is claimed. In Alphonse's home the usual pattern of domestic boundary erection has attained the aspect of warfare, with the attendant gamesmanship of posturing, deployment, arcane strategy. Not to mention hurt feelings on both sides.

Alphonse and Eleanor married for all the usual reasons: fear of death, fear of being alone, the compulsion to repeat the mistakes and debacles of their parents' marriage. It was a small ceremony; Eleanor's six-year-old niece caught the bouquet, leading to jokes at the expense of Eleanor's unmarried older sister, whom everybody pretended was not a lesbian. On the honeymoon cruise they made brief love several times, with the lights on for the first time ever, as there was no one who could see them except whatever beings lived in the darkness outside the porthole. Eventually they bought a home.

The prefabricated house at 1244 Violet Lane came equipped in its natural state with nooks and cubbies. These were areas in rooms that would offend the eye if not occupied by a thing or object. That corner in the living room. That somehow frightening blank spot in the foyer. The mantel, with its unbroken plane that spoke of manifest destiny. These were areas that needed to be filled or else something else might roost there that was unwanted, a negative feeling or perception. A great flood of refugees from knickknackland set up lean-tos where appropriate, dispossessed tchotchkes earned citizenship. Artificial flowers insinuated into the small nook between the bay windows in the dining room and doilies accepted their missions with a grim certitude that belied their frilly edges. Alphonse's second-place trophy from his senior year achievement in the hundred-yard dash posed in the foyer on a three-legged table whose radius forbid objects larger than single-flower vases or small pictures, perfect for the submajestic dimensions of the die-cast second-place trophy. Whether the architects of the house placed these nooks out of a farsighted sense of need or mere perversity is beyond telling, but Alphonse and Eleanor passed the test with flying colors and swiftly the house looked lived in. Together they chose where things went.

A routine of married life settled in. For the first couple of years Alphonse spent an inordinate amount of time looking at his hands. Lifelines and their mysteries crisscrossed and terminated in his palms. His cuticles obtained nicks and imperfections that healed over time and he observed the process. Alphonse tried to read something there, a clue or two. He took this preoccupation as a symptom of incompleteness, despite what surface appearances told him. He had a good job, for example; middle management was only a better tie away. Around him the house was in great shape, as they outgrew the wisdom of the home decorating magazines. Sometimes they entertained other married couples of their acquaintance for dinner to discuss the issues of the day. But still. Then one afternoon, in his doctor's office as he waited for his annual physical, Alphonse discovered an article about hobbies. It caught his eye. The article elaborated about a psychological need common to most folks, a hole that needs filling. Stamp collecting, the article suggested, was a wholesome interest amenable to the beginner but equally rewarding for the seasoned collector. He showed the article to Eleanor, who nodded, and he sent away for a starter kit from one of the philately companies recommended in the article.

The basement proved perfect for this new interest. The basement was great for storage and one day would make a fine barracks for the washer and dryer, but in the early period of their marriage served only as the home of the fuse box, oft-worshiped during hurricane season. Then the stamps arrived. He scraped a table down the stairs, untangled an extension cord to power the lamp and created a space for himself not far from the water heater. Above him spiders wove secretions into traps amid a maze of bent copper tubing. The basement became a place that was completely his, different from the communal nooks and cabinets and drawers upstairs, the spaces that testified to their shared effort to make a home together. They agreed where to put the vase, the porcelain unicorn, together they ratified the placement of the wedding picture, but the basement was his. An inequity blossomed. It was a full third of the house's cubic space and he had claimed it. It was a place to masturbate and think about the world and mount his stamps, glory over his collection of railroad stamps.

Stamps like to be touched in a certain way. Soak them until they are wet to separate them from envelopes, and when they are wet enough they have to be handled just so. With tongs. It is his hobby. And so it went on for years. She never went down there. And then Eleanor retaliated. It took years but it happened.

With Eleanor lately there has been this flurry of clubs. It is almost as if he looked up one day and she'd gone through the Yellow Pages or ripped off every contact number from every flyer in every laundromat in town. Or maybe one club leads to another club, a pyramid scheme of interest and hobby. She makes one friend and the friend is a clue to another friend in another club. "It's just something to pass the time," she says when he asks her to explain the newest prop in her repertoire, the next alien thing she has brought into the house, bylaws or instructional literature. When she says this she is returning his stamp excuse to him and it is not lost on either party.

She is on the steering committee of two maybe three charities now. The book club. Every month there's another discounted hardcover from the local big chain. He's never heard of the books before he takes them into his hands and reads the dust covers. They seem to be about women overcoming, or women suffering, and then there is a little note of triumph at the end. Eleanor affects a note of irritation whenever he asks a simple question about the books. Sometimes he'll be reading a philately magazine and will look up to see Eleanor squinting at him over the hardcover edge as if he lives in its pages. It seems the only time she cooks nowadays is to test out the storage capabilities of her latest acquisition from her plastics club. In this club the membership requirements are that you like to get together to trade plastic food storage devices. He opens the door after a long, a too long, day at work, to a smell fit for the kitchen of a really fancy restaurant, one they might visit on a special occasion, if they still celebrated their anniversary for example. But there will be nothing on the dining room table except the honed gleam of the wood polish. In the kitchen the grand repast is already interred in her plastic containers, in flat lozenges, in sleek cylinders, in deep rectangles with rounded corners. Half a liter, liter and two liter and in between. The tops are available in many different colors, everything stacks inside everything else conveniently. The plastic is opaque and he can barely make out the contents. He'll tilt one and watch a brown liquid collect in the bottom corner. Eleanor will be in the living room with a book while he inspects container after container. The things in the plastic containers are not leftovers in the strict sense for they have been prepared specifically for storage. She throws them out the next day in preparation for the next configuration of containers. Sometimes he'll happen into the kitchen during the cleaning ritual. Certain orange globules of grease resist the capabilities of the soft side of the sponge and force her to turn it over to the abrasive side. Then the plastic becomes clean.

The storage devices necessitated her membership in a recipe club so she could have novel foodstuffs with which to fill her containers, which in turn required the purchase of cookbooks. Exotic recipes from foreign lands necessitated the purchase of rare herbs, ingredients that would never be used again yet required still more storage. His cereal was exiled to a not as convenient cabinet, displaced by carmine dust (for color) and lime green relishes (for tangy aftertaste). He went downstairs one day and noticed his World War II spy novels, all twenty years' worth, in boxes on the floor of the basement; their homelands upstairs had been invaded by cookbooks. His racing trophy was on the floor next to them; it had been displaced by a group photograph of the steering committee of the Clothes for Orphans fund-raising dinner. He has no idea where things he might need are stored these days. Scissors, duct tape, the menus of establishments that deliver food, they have been replaced by Eleanor's diverse materials and cannot be found. How could he not see it as revenge for the basement?

Perhaps they had had a decent conversation lately but about what he doesn't know.

Perhaps he'd feel better if she had bruises on the inside of her thighs or worked late at the office or constantly returned to him thin excuses, but instead it's these clubs. As a gesture—no, it was more than that it was an attempt at de-escalation—he said she could use his computer down in the basement, but Eleanor was adamant about getting her own. Instead she took him up on his other offer, made a decade and a half before, to use the guest room as her office, and in there she made a clubhouse for her clubs. Her new computer makes invitations and bulletins and flyers a snap. The new word processing programs make everyone into a desktop publisher. Slowly she mastered fonts. They had not used the pullout sofa in the guest room for years; she moved a desk in its place, and one of her club friends helped her move the sofa downstairs one afternoon. Now Alphonse sleeps there nights. They had long before grown bored with each other's bodies and laid off the sex thing. Some nights he comes out only for food.

The drawers in room 12 are uncontested and his.

He can hear periodic laughter from one of the rooms down the row. Probably those journalists. They have their fun and he has his. For about an hour now he has been staring at the mothball. The small moon on the bedside table. From a few feet away it looks smooth but the more he looks at it the more the imperfections become apparent. His eyes dip between granules and go as far into the thing as they can, then clamber on to the next ridge. He has decided to make the thing into his lucky charm. Certainly there is a reason he chose that suit as his last suit, and a reason the mothball decided to come along.

This night he saved a man's life. He was the first to recognize the symptoms of choking, drilled into him by years of staring at the walls of restaurants as he ate by himself, with his paper already read and still half a plate of his greasy meal left on the plate. At such moments there is little to read except choking prevention signs and the wretched faces of his fellow diners. Alphonse was the first to notice that the black man was choking. Two years earlier he saved the life of a woman at The Chew Shack when she indulged too enthusiastically in a plate of all-you-can-eat shrimp. He knew what to do. But he found himself staring at the black man. It seemed as if every feature of the man's face, as it was manipulated and contorted by suffocation, became discrete and separate from the rest. His bowed left eyebrow one object, his twitching right nostril part of something else. Each of these things could be collected and put in a separate mount on its own page in one of his stamp volumes. A special edition series. In its special place on a basement shelf. It was only when he realized his indifference to whether the man lived or died that Alphonse jumped up to help. The man didn't say thanks, but given the excitement, Alphonse didn't blame him.

He props himself on his elbows, peering down the soft, foreign slope of his body, fixating on his knees and the slack skin congealed into those ugly lumps. Then he finally removes his shoes. The heels of his blue-toed socks are stiff with blood. He bought new shoes for the occasion and they break him in as much as he breaks them in. His heels are raw and torn and tarred with dried blood. He hasn't felt the pain because all he's felt since he arrived in Talcott is this feeling of inevitability.

J lies on his bed in room 27 of the Talcott Motor Lodge, weary and hurting, the whitecaps of the untamed mattress cresting and dropping below his body, and he tries to get his shit together. He has a few more minutes to go before he tests his throat again. So far so good. Did he almost die? And with a piece due, even. He figures he'll write the piece in the airport on Sunday and email it to the editor at the website. A bloodless edit will follow, emails lob back and forth, and one day an electronic burp with his byline will float up into the web morass, a little bubble of content he will never see. Fart in a bathtub. The new innovation of the internet, its expansion of the already deep abstraction of his job, appeals to him. He files and a check arrives. He mails in receipts paperclipped to an expense form and a reimbursement arrives. It's always tricky with a startup. They might hold his expense form up to the light and question every line or be totally scattered and push his paper through without a glance. J. always leans to the side of discretion and doesn't pad too much on his first assignment for a venue; best to earn trust and abuse it later.

He gets assignments. He is a successful freelancer.

His thoughts touch on his proposal, he prowls his tideline and nudges that dried jellyfish thing with his toe. A book agent called him up last year, after a big article of his ran in one of the music magazines, a gonzoish account of a weekend spent in Compton with a troupe of notorious gangsta rappers. No journalist wanted to talk to them after an incident where they sent a writer to the hospital for nibbling without permission at some of the band's chicken in their dressing room. The magazine called J. up and he said sure, he'd spend a weekend with them if someone was picking up the tab. Knowing that there was always someone picking up the tab. The weekend was uneventful—the rappers had a new album coming out, and older and more practical, and understanding the brief half-life of a pop act, they needed their friends in the media—but gussied up with teen slang, a little reefer scent dabbed here and there and a nice set piece where a hanger-on gave J. a tour of his gun collection, the piece pimprolled with street cred. It made the editors hard and went over big with the well-bred suburban white boys who made up the magazine's readership and bought the group's records, J.'s authentic details providing material for their performances before the bathroom mirror, and a book agent who had staked out hip turf called him to ask if he had any book ideas. J. thought for a moment and mentioned one or two things that he'd been mulling over, and the agent said, that's all well and good, but how about something about rap music? J. circled around the idea. He admitted that he had wanted to write a social history of hip-hop at one point, when he was younger. The agent offered some words of encouragement, pray elucidate. They spoke for a few more minutes and J. agreed to put some of it down on paper. The music of his teenage years. Interview Kool Herc, visit the old Bronx basketball courts where the DJ pioneer threw his jams in the late seventies, armed with his famous monster sound system, his cobbled-together and gaffer's-taped sound system; J.'d lean on the chain-link fence and wonder what it would have been like to be at ground zero. The majesty of a playground or ball court seen through a chain-link fence, a world cut by diamond wire. The start of something. This had been his idea when he was younger. The agent called a few months later to check his progress and asked, what about gangsta culture, he wanted something more of what J. had put in that article he had seen. The violent subculture of men who lived like outlaws. J. said he'd write a proposal; maybe he could work it out. He made notes, or notes to himself to make notes. He was gestating, he told himself. He gestated for months before he understood that he is too old now. Both he and the music are too jaded. They grew up together and are too old to pretend that there is anything but publicity.

He lies on his free sheets on his free bed and thinks, no money down. Three months into his junketeering streak he tells himself he feels fine. Except for what happened earlier that evening, J. has tuned himself perfectly to the rhythm of events, found parity between what had been his life before and what his life is going for the record. They struggle and win brief inches, but neither side wins him. He neither wants to go home and take a few days off nor submit himself mindlessly to the flux of events. Is this what Bobby Figgis thought at this point? That he was in control, before pop consumed him. One Eye intimating that he wanted out, and to have J. help him tunnel under the wall. Now One Eye pretends he cares. Maybe he is sincere. He's not supposed to give a fuck; that's why he was put on the List in the first place. The intent of the List is to have a reliable group of people on call who don't give a fuck, who want things for free. The List wants key Americans. And the junketeers are quintessential Americans, J. thinks. They want and want now and someone else is picking up the check. Such model and exemplary citizens that people listen to what they have to say. They follow our lead.

J. takes another sip of ginger ale and waits. He still breathes. Is he so bored that he'll actually be reduced to reading press material to fall asleep? Maybe he is already over the line and doesn't even know it. There's John Henry on the glossy cover of the press packet. The first time he heard of him was in the fifth grade, in a cartoon. Mrs. Goodwin's boys and girls squirmed in anticipation whenever she wheeled in the projector at the start of class, notes of optimistic juvenile code were smuggled up and down the rows, tiny necks extended to read the white tape along the side of the tin canisters, because when that boxy gray cart with the metal frog perched atop it rolled into the room everyone knew they were going to waste a nice chunk of hour. Mrs. Goodwin was a young woman. She would have been around the same age J. was now. Which meant that no matter how old and wise she looked back then, she knew nothing at all. Late that spring her stomach began to swell and in the last class of the year, New York summer banging on the windows, she told the boys and girls that she wouldn't be back next year because of the baby. They all felt betrayed. She smiled and told them to remember that she also taught seventh grade and would return, they would be reunited in junior high to pick up the latest installment of *Warriner's Grammar*. She never came back, but by then her former charges had graduated to novel distractions and no longer felt so attached to teachers, no matter how motherly.

The day the projector rolled into town Mrs. Goodwin told them they were going to see a film about a great American hero who helped build America. (Looking back, J. questions the purview of the class. Mrs. Goodwin taught English, but was this story English or History or Social Studies. What is the exact line of demarcation between History and Social Studies, for that matter.) Mrs. Goodwin—whose kind manner conscripted each of the students, one by one over the course of the year, into calling her Mommy, drawing grateful laughter from the other kids who were happy that it was not their day for that embarrassing error—instructed Madeline Moses to pull down the yellow blinds, those old broad and curved slats that instructed their own elementaries of grime. Alex Minkow turned out the lights and Andrew Schneider volunteered to work the projector, choosing at that very moment his lot in life. Young Andrew's hand flickered over the stiff apparatus, the crotchety projector initially resistant to his fiddling, and the cartoon began.

J. remembers the bold colors and blocky limbs of the people first. Now J. links them to Malevich in his peasant period, sees the elemental forms of cones and squares lodged in their arms, legs and faces, social systems inexorable in the skin, but back then the people just looked strong. People of the Earth. Plankton legions of dust swirled in the swath of projector light. What else does he remember. That it was the first time he saw a black mother and father in a cartoon. John Henry's parents held him the day he was born and John Henry was born big, forty pounds and gifted with speech straight out the womb. He demanded food, two pigs, a generation of chickens, acres of collard greens, yams by the bushel, and a pot of gravy to wash it all down. He ate the food in great inhalations (J. wondering from the summit of the Talcott Motor Lodge, who is that little boy down there in the classroom who shares his name, and where did they get that food. He was born a slave. His parents were slaves. Where did they get all that food?), he ate it all up and belched and informed his parents that he was going to die at the Big Bend Tunnel on the C&O Railroad. Casual, like that. Such talk from a kid one-day old. The child J. took it all in stride. They were taught about Greek gods, and prophesying witches popped up everywhere you looked, scurrying around the Doric columns like rats. Curses, omens, the odd swan rapist: they were as common as eviction notices, overdue bills, utilities shut off for lack of payment. The gods said how-do-you-do all the time, why not in the glowing shack of this cartoon, depicted by the animators as a warm haven bathed in gold light, where a young black boy was born with a hammer in his hand. (J. almost forgets that part, the most important part of his birth, right? "John Henry was born with a hammer in his hand." Warning to pregnant women to watch out for excessive amounts of iron in their diets. Perhaps Mrs. Goodwin wondered at this part just what was kicking in her stomach.) John Henry's mother, a fleshy woman with chocolate skin and pinchable face, told her bouncing baby boy to get some rest: born that day and already talking about dying. There it was. Womb-wet and already saddled with the knowledge of his destiny and doomed to fulfill it. (Talk about baggage.)

The cartoon furnished the children with a montage of the doomed man's adolescent feats. Big as a man at the age of six, he outran horses, chucked boulders, played hopscotch across chasms. (A hormonal imbalance causing spectacular and unnatural growth, J. notes as he rubs his throat, and a hyperactivity calling for a prescription of Ritalin.) But he always loved his hammer. He smashed rocks, knocked over trees, pounded tidal waves from silent lakes with a blow from his mighty hammer. (Criminal mischief, mucking up the environment, our nation's greatest resource.) And of course the medium of animation well suited for these shenanigans. The children cheered him, reminded of that afternoon's later appointment with Tom and Jerry and other luminaries of Looney Tunes and Hanna-Barbera. Primary color mayhem. John Henry tore shit up, summoning havoc in a manner familiar to the sons and daughters of television.

And then came the day for John Henry to go out into the world. He said good-bye to his parents and followed the mountains into the distance, imposing sledge resting on one shoulder like a loyal falcon, his belongings wrapped up snug on the end of a stick across the other shoulder. (And where did that trope enter the world: the hobo's possessions wrapped up in a red cloth and knotted on the end of a stick. Footloose into the American adventure.) He walked into the sun. Free. No mention of slavery. This was a cartoon for kids. They were assigned one-page essays on the life of Martin Luther King, Jr., year in and year out, instructed sternly not to plagiarize from encyclopedias and the standard texts. Learning to paraphrase. No one wanted to be the kid, usually Marnie Pomerantz, who was asked if her parents had helped her with her homework. Points off for not mentioning the March on Washington. When the teacher mentioned slavery, swiftly, usually only in terms of Mr. Lincoln's proclamation, as if the peculiar institution only came to be in its ending, invariably two or three white kids turned around to look at J., putty faces full of something, curiosity or compassion he didn't know, they always looked away when he met their eyes and he grew warm. (Or did he stare straight ahead fixated on the stapler on the teacher's desk and merely see them fuzzy in his peripheral vision. Which version flatters the boy he wants himself to be.) But no mention of slavery in the cartoon. Were they supposed to take his walk from home in search of his fate as the slave's walk from the plantation? No, the children were supposed to find their own experience in John Henry's retreating back and his parents' tears: Mom closing the door after tucking them in, their first day of school, the view from the old school bus ferrying them to camp. These American particulars, because John Henry was an American. J. lay on his bed in the Talcott Motor Lodge. He walked from a slave economy into an industrial economy, the twentieth century loomed and man-killing machines, steam-spitting machines. There was a black kid in every grade. The one in Mrs. Goodwin's fifth grade class was named J. Of the children who looked at him at the mention of slavery, none were Jason or Patrick, whose parents had raised them well and were glad they brought black friends into their homes to play, they talked about it in their beds at night while they watched Johnny Carson before proceeding to the more pressing matter of the building going co-op.

The projector clicked off frames, twenty-four per second, creating motion on the white screen that pulled down from a metal rectangle screwed above the blackboard. The bulb raged through the frames, Commodore Andrew Schneider waiting for impending mishap with his hand on the rudder. John Henry found work on the railroad, the Chesapeake & Ohio, driving from Washington, D.C., to Cincinnati, the very same C&O named by the steeldriving man on his nativity. He was glad to get the job. The Captain welcomed him aboard and extended a hand. (In a more monochrome world this freed slave worked for pennies, wandering from job to job in search of circumstances promised in the good Mr. Lincoln's proclamation. The railroads hired the niggers for pennies; you could tell a nigger what to do like you couldn't tell an Irishman, no matter how down and out the immigrant was.) In four-color glory, John Henry worked two-handed, crashing down one hammer on a spike while the other swung up in ecstatic arc, sparks erupting in blasts and gusts of orange and red; he made fire, he left the other workers in the dust as he moved west, ever west, with two unerring compass hammers in his hands. John Henry was always smiling. Even though the sparks burst up and dominated the frame, his smile shone through. (Testifying to an overlooked part of his myth: formidable teeth that overcame the primitive dental technology of his day.) In the cartoon the other railroad workers were white men who set down their sledges in wondrous admiration as John Henry outpaced them, outraced them, fulfilled their nation's destiny with what he had in his arms.

Adam Horning had a nosebleed and tore off a piece of college rule loose leaf and stuck it up there. He could have gone to the bathroom and loitered there a while according to his custom, but today they had an exciting cartoon. John Henry mashed the spikes into the ground, driving a mythology into the ground, as if carving it letter by letter into the earth would make the dreams of men live. All admired his strength and fortitude and if the great man entertained dark thoughts after his fate—the image of which had radiated in his head since that first light beyond his mother's legs, he took his death into him with his first breath—who could tell. He smiled and swung. And all the children in the room, in their private school uniforms, immediately distrusted the man from the mechanical company in his white suit, cosmopolitan venality writ in the seams of his fancy-dan clothes, so distant from the rough cloth of John Henry and his merry band. This big-city charlatan came down South with Yankee lies, and said his machine could drive steel faster than any man alive. What did J. and his classmates think of this used car salesman bragging about his machine. The animators clearly had a fun time with it. The machine was silly and big as a barn, part hot rod, part vacuum cleaner, all discombobulated monstrosity familiar to them from the blueprints of Wile E. Coyote. A junkyard machine whose purpose, for all its bulk, was finally expressed in a meek little square that moved up and down when the huckster turned on the device. This little square block was to beat John Henry's hammer? Clouds of steam exited pipes, the metal creature shook furiously, all to a ridiculous chorus of toots and whistles. It was the foolish dream of a mad scientist, and yet the railroad workers were in awe. In fear. Except for our man John Henry, who saw in this comic and elaborate concoction the seamless assembly of his fate. John Henry spat into his hands and said he could lick any machine made of man and could drive more steel than that hunk of junk any day of the week. (Hubris, sin of the Greeks. One of them, anyway.) He wasn't going to be replaced by big-city devilment.

The contest was arranged on a sunny afternoon. The referee stepped up with a stopwatch, chest cut by black and white stripes, an anachronistic joke not lost on the inmates of Mrs. Goodwin's fifth grade class. John Henry stood with his big smile, hammer at the ready, and the salesman clambered up the machine and took roost in the tractor seat on top. The salesman pulled a lever and the small dustclotted speakers of the projector filled the classroom with the sound of hooting and chugging and put-put-putting. The steam machine rushed ahead of John Henry, the tiny metal block pushing the ready spikes down into the earth at a healthy clip. John Henry swung his hammer home but he couldn't catch up. His smile was gone and sweat streamed into a mouth tight with strain. The onlookers worried after their local hero while the Yankee on top of the machine sneered and twisted his mustache. (And these rosy-cheeked folks are the ancestors of his hosts—the ones who had watched him choke at dinner—the hardworking founders of Talcott watched John Henry lose.) The machine pulled farther ahead and it seemed all was lost. The children ensnared in the clutches of suspense, rapt at their desks; not one spitball splattered a neck, doodles went undoodled. The institutional clock above the classroom door, the first lover to these children and the best one, faithful to each despite a thousand furtive assignations an hour, ticked neglected. And then they saw John Henry smile. John Henry's smile returned and his hammer pummeled the earth; little black action waves of force emanated from the ground and soon the sound of the pounding drowned out the corny whistling of the machine. This earthshaking man. The makers of the cartoon kept close on the hammer. (Cheap and easy to repeat a couple of animation cels over and over again.) The sound, the beating heart of man, grew louder and louder. Wasn't no machine going to beat this man down. The referee's face filled the screen, which was pulled down over the blackboard to obscure a sentence diagram in chalk, he looked down at his stopwatch and blew his whistle, cheeks billowing out. John Henry pounded down the last spike, looked back at the groaning folly so far behind him, the failing machine, and fell to the ground. The witnesses jumped up and down and the salesman threw his big-city chapeau to the ground and said, Darn! Foiled again. The music of victory (standard victory music familiar to J. even then, before its untold repetitions in films and television shows over the next two decades, the young learned their responses early and thoroughly) swelled in symphonic crackling mono and then died—John Henry wasn't moving. He was flat on his back in the dirt. A doctor rushed up to him, stethoscope around his neck. John Henry raised his head: did I beat it? The doctor said yes, and took the hero's wrist between his hands. (This cartoon doctor deigned to touch nigger flesh, of all nineteenth-century Southern doctors this man served all of God's children with equal care, such is the magic of Talcott.) Old doc shook his head. John Henry was dead. He died with a hammer in his hand, just as he said he would on the day he was born. He beat the machine and died doing it.

The screen returned to whiteness and the tail of the reel slapped around and around until Andrew Schneider turned off the machine. After the cartoon finished, J. was sure Mrs. Goodwin had led a discussion about the lessons of John Henry's story and its ambiguous ending, but he doesn't remember it now. Mrs. Goodwin, why did he die at the end? Mrs. Goodwin, if he beat the steam engine, why did he have to die? Did he win or lose?

PART THREE

# ON THE
# EFFECTS OF
# COUNTRY
# AIR

❖

The assistant paymaster delivered word of the contest with the week's wages. He walked the camp. He talked to the men. He looked down at his ledger and looked into the eyes of each man and gave him his pay. The assistant paymaster counted out coins slowly as if the men did not understand the meaning of wages. As if the men did not know how to count money and did not know what they had earned for their labor. It was payday and all the men knew he was coming. They had learned not to rush up to him and crowd him like begging dogs. He paid each man as he got to his name on the list, which did not follow any order but his own. The list was not determined by name or salary or seniority on the site. It was determined by the mind of the assistant paymaster and over time the men had learned their places in the order. John Henry was toward the back of the list and he waited in his shanty for the assistant paymaster with a dull and rigid patience. As the strongest driver he was paid the most. Most of the men did not resent his salary because they knew they could not beat him and that was a natural fact. Some did resent him. The assistant paymaster gave John Henry his wages for the week and told him that Captain Johnson wanted a contest tomorrow.

The company could not stop talk about the deaths. The men had been told not to talk about life on the mountain and had seen with their own eyes men banished from the site for complaining about the conditions, the injuries and the hours and the deaths. But neither Captain Johnson nor his bosses could keep the men from talking about the mountain at night. Camp life could not be tamed by daylight threat. Night was a release from the mountain in the shadow of the mountain, beneath the outline of the thing against dark blue night. They drank and wagered and told stories, and when they drank their tongues loosed and they dwelled on the violence. Jokes curdled quickly at night and lately the men dwelled on the cave-in at the western cut. It was like a trick, the mountain. The shale resisted hammers, steel and blasting but it gave to rain and wind. Water from Heaven melted the rock of the mountain and the rainwater was red on the ground. After rain, their boots were caked with red grit from the puddles. The first day after last week's rain, the roof at the mouth of the western cut gave way, crashing through the timber arching, and killed five graders who stood there to get out of the sun. It was a trick. In the shade of the cut the mountain came down on them like a hammer and killed them. A cry went up. The other men mucked out the rock and pulled out the bodies. They knew the men were dead but hurried anyway. When the doctor arrived he looked at the twisted bodies and talked to Captain Johnson. They talked and Captain Johnson gestured to one of the bosses. The men buried the dead men in the fill of the western cut and no warning from the company was going to stop the talk in the camp.

John Henry held his pay and stepped out into the sun. The cheer of payday animated the men in the camp. The men who drank their wages swiftly and had gone a day or two without whiskey drank. Debts were repaid. Some men with families calculated how much money to send home. John Henry fingered coins in his hand and considered the cunning of Captain Johnson. A contest raised the spirits of the men, even if they all knew who would win. One day John Henry would be beaten. Men bet on the challenger and men bet on John Henry. The excitement, John Henry knew, would put the cave-in out of the minds of the men. Until the next accident. The contest would cure the discontent throughout the camp.

L'il Bob scampered over and wondered to his partner, who will challenge you? John Henry didn't know. When the word came a few hours later that it was O'Shea he was not surprised. He lifted his eyebrows slightly and no more. He knew the Irishman did not like getting paid less than a nigger. Captain Johnson kept O'Shea in the western cut for that very reason. He didn't want to know what would happen if the Irishman had to work next to John Henry every day. The black man's hammer on steel might sound like coins to him, the sound of coins falling out of his pocket. He might decide to use his hammer for something else besides eating into the mountain. Take a swing. O'Shea had arms like stovepipes. Yet it was probably Captain Johnson's idea that the two men compete in the steel driving contest. The winner got fifty dollars; probably O'Shea would get a bonus if he beat the black. The white men would bet on O'Shea and the black men would bet on John Henry. The contest between the races would distract them from the mountain's vengeance all the more. If the black man won it would make the men feel good about themselves and they would forget about the mountain for a time. If the white man won it would remind them of their place in this world and the hate would drive the work. The work progressed in either event. Captain Johnson had a timetable.

That night L'il Bob said that Irishman was foolish, and John Henry shrugged. The Irish workers were a step up from the blacks, but not that much. Low competed against lower. L'il Bob on payday was a happy man. He thought up lines he could sing for tomorrow's contest and told them to his partner. He sang, Shake the drill and turn it 'round, I'll beat that white man down. John Henry cocked his head. L'il Bob said, Shake the drill and turn it 'round, I'll beat that Irishman down. How's that? It's better, John Henry said. O'Shea and his tribe wouldn't like it, but the bosses wouldn't get angry and take it out on them for days. L'il Bob told jokes he thought up as he held the drill bit for John Henry. John Henry would look at the man in the darkness of the tunnel and see a slit of a smile on his lips. It was a joke he would hear later. L'il Bob on payday told his jokes over card games. He made his coworkers lose track of their cards and he took their money at the end of the hand: full house. The blacksmith named Ford asked L'il Bob if his boy were going to beat the Irishman tomorrow or should he put his money on the underdog. Ford looked at John Henry while he said this to see his reaction. The steeldriver said nothing and L'il Bob said, have you lost your sense? Must be crazy—sure playing cards like you're crazy or maybe you just like giving your money away. Ford grunted and anted.

John Henry turned to bed early that night. He had never been beaten by another man's hammer but pride is a sin. He took his rest. The payday carousing tried to keep him awake but he willed himself to sleep and dreamed of the contest as a fistfight between the white man and the black man over the fill of the western cut. The dead watched the contest from beneath the rock. He saw through their eyes staring up at himself as he crushed the face of the white man. He did not need his hammer for that.

S unglasses: where are they? Sunglasses prevent arrest for reckless eye-balling.

Here they are.

So armed, thus fortified, J. traverses the hazy border between parking lot gravel and the half-tamed dirt of country road shoulder, a disputed area this, every rain betrays the ceasefire in a violent push, every car wheel in and out of the Talcott Motor Lodge shifts the balance of power, foreign aid. The frontier a gritty smudge two steps wide, two steps and he is out on the road, before noon, with a mountain to his left and a river on the right. He feels not so bad this morning, not hungover and half-mast, things seem in order, synapses fire apace, the information gets through, and the freebie sunglasses dull the rapier sunlight jabbing through the leaves. Safe in sunglasses, and his throat doesn't hurt at all.

He looks through the haggard trees to the opposite bank of the river, where railroad tracks skirt the base of still another green mountain like an iron hem. Rounds a turn in the road and in this deviation feels the motel, his room, his stuff, drift off behind him. Just him in the woods, traveling down one of the three disobedient channels that vex the mountains: the road, the river and the tracks. The road he walks on has the worst of it, he thinks. Stuck between two troublesome neighbors and too broke to move. The road tiptoes in asphalt slippers around a mountain that is always throwing trash into its paved yard from high peaks, dirt and leaves and TV dinner containers, while the river on the other side keeps trying to sneak the boundary over, eating shore here and there, taking liberties with the survey line every spring under the guise of sprucing up the yard. Don't mind me, chum, just pruning these hedges. He follows the easy bump of a distant ridge with his UV-protected eyes and feels sweat roll. The day is hot and cloudless. This isn't J.'s neighborhood at all. Disputes all around him, but none of them his affair, and he likes it that way.

Just passing through, thanks. He lives in unlikely times, ambles through the valley of an unlikely Saturday morning. On the underside of his planet, or deep beneath it. Talcott, West Virginia: the world you walk on every day not knowing it's down there. He feels good, the dirt crushed under his sneakers is a sure and accountable sound, certainly not sidewalk or hotel tile or ballroom carpet, able syncopation against the fluid strumming of the river beside him. Occasionally a bird sitting in, a horn player stepping inside this day's establishment to see what's shaking. He takes a deep breath and walks west. One of his comrades—Dave Brown or Frenchie—knocked on his door early that morning, shouting something about the taxi that would ferry them to breakfast. J. yelled him away and slept—five minutes or an hour, it didn't matter and he didn't know; he clutched the sheets to his neck as if they were flimsy lapels in a sudden and seeking rain, he got up when he was good and ready. On his own itinerary. He dressed in freebie clothes, he took his time and opened the door of his room when he felt ready. Forsaking a free meal, even, such is the magic of this morning.

He thinks it's funny that he is walking west, into town for supplies. I'll take a bag of flour and two yards of cloth for the missus, thanks, Clem, pay for the goods with company scrip. The railroad had a monopoly grip on all the citizens of Talcott and Hinton, it owned the town store and overcharged more than a Brooklyn bodega. Isn't that the way it worked back then, he'd seen something along those lines on a PBS documentary. Before unions and pamphlet-waving reds. Abortive insurrection beat down by imported Pinkerton talent who arrived on the seven o'clock locomotive in menacing slo-mo at dusk, red light swimming in the folds of their long leather coats, suspicious bulges where holsters usually hang. The troublemakers find their shacks burned down and everyone learns from the lesson, keeps quiet, and the grocer stacks toy currency. Syrup for the colicky babe. Nerve tonic for the addled lady of the house. To assuage the monthlies. The grocer gives the goods away for free, fake money with the C&O logo makes everything look like a freebie. J. decides he will pay for his own breakfast when he gets into town.

An orange butterfly stumbles from the trees on the riverbank, startling J. and activating his metropolitan crazy pigeon reflex: one hand rises to shield his head from birdshit, the other straightens to karate chop. But it is just a butterfly, a silver ball upset by invisible bumpers and flippers, and it ricochets away. This is the country, it is safe. He feels good, trying to remind himself, good, and it is best to suppress his natural inclinations and go with the flow. Immortal even. Seems to J. that if you have a near-death experience, you are invincible for a time. Unless you're in the trenches, the chances of almost dying twice in the space of a few days are remote. Astronomical. Cars will bounce off him, drive-by gunfire perforate his body's outline in the wall behind him. He made it through the night, he is golden. Bring on the burning barn with the family of kittens inside; J. is ready.

He finally drifted off at 4 A.M., between gulps, and slept dreamlessly. He rose from bed without his customary stiffness (that odd ratcheting-up of himself that always reminded him of a rollercoaster car clicking up to its first big fall of the day) and disorientation about where he was, what hotel and mission. His mood almost derailed when he ventured down to the front office to find out about a lift into town and the woman at the front desk looked at him as if she'd seen a ghost. (A spook.) She pulled her bathrobe to her chicken neck and asked him if he was staying in room 27. He answered in the affirmative, answered her tentative question as to how he had slept with an over-enthusiastic simile that called up the familiar image of blissful nurslings in their cribs. She seemed relieved, then concerned anew at this response, and at the collapse of her thin eyebrows J. quickly rerouted the conversation to the matter of transport. Turned out the New River Gorge Taxi wasn't scheduled for another pickup until later that morning; J. had missed the breakfast run. He asked her how far it was to town.

There's a car behind him, the first car since he started walking, and he fights the vision his paranoia prepares for him: the truck jags right just as it reaches him, sends his body flying into the river and his body washes up weeks later on some littoral strip downriver, wherever this river ends up once it splashes past these mountains. No one around to witness this anonymous violence and no one to identify his body, the fish have eaten his identification (pollution has given them a taste for crisp plastic and magnetic strips). But then he remembers his invincibility, and this morning's distaste for his customary scenarios. Exhale your city self into this cool country air, this place can absorb all of you and more. It isn't a truck, he sees as it rounds the turn, but a Chevy Nova of a perky green shade, with hubcaps of spinning rust. The driver, a middle-aged brunette who sucks a cigarette and squints through smoke as they pass; in the passenger seat a little girl with a round moon face stares at J., turning in her seat to watch him recede as they speed on to town. And perhaps her oddly sharp gaze disturbs him for a moment, but then they are gone, he is alone again in the paralyzed landscape. See, nothing to worry about here.

Walk down the road until you get to the bridge, take a left, the woman at the front desk told him, it's about two and a half miles. He calculated that to be a forty-five minute walk, and here it is, not so bad at all even though it is something that wouldn't normally occur to him. A receiptless span of time. What else had the stamp collector ejected from his gut last night. To make him feel like this. He makes a list of pertinent phenomena. The choking thing had sobered him up immediately, leeching booze from him as desperately as his blood wrenched oxygen from blue depleted blood. He'd forsaken the drinking session in Tiny's room, and the ginger ale rehydrated him after a couple days of serious junketeering and its attendant effects. Although he hadn't slept that long, he'd slept on his own schedule and not publicity's. The facilities at the Motor Lodge, the lack of them, had forced him to leave his room for food. And finally, he is getting some air. Serious routine-breaking in the last twelve hours on all fronts. Maybe it is more than that. Thinking back, he hasn't felt this clear in months. (Such is the bad posture of his nights, slouching always into dipso inclinations.) Grateful body. Have to give the stamp collector a proper thanks at some point.

J. comes to a spot where the shoulder widens and he spies an opening in the trees and gossiping brush that slides down to the river. People park here and go fishing, he figures, old grandpa teaching little Jimmy about bait and life. Or teenagers smoking joints and throwing beer cans into the river and making out: he sees some sun-bleached cigarette butts and what appear to be a large pair of jockey shorts at the edge of the parking area. A lark: the trail down to the river is steep and he makes his way down to the bank slowly, prodding upslope dirt to its premature retirement on the bank, trading steady poplar branch for steadying hemlock trunk until he makes it the thirty slanted yards to the semicircle stretch of mud.

Except for the railroad tracks across the river he can't see any sign of civilization. And the silver loop of an old can's pull-top in the sand, but nothing else. Out of the sunlight and in the shade of the trees crouched around the bank, J. feels his body cool and he slips into an even deeper silence, even though the brown river is louder than the empty road. Time out of the world. A little downstream the water blows over a sill of rocks that sends white curtains twisting and twirling. For an instant J. sees himself clinging to one of those rocks, but he can't figure out if that momentary image is a scene of final hard-won safety or just a reprieve before the battle for the shore. He has half a mind to sit but decides instead to make an oath, some stentorian declaration of himself and purposes. Isn't that what you do in places like this, among nature, out of the hurly-burly, no one to hear but those who won't tattle: make an oath. Hurl one. Same thing as laying a road or nailing railroad tracks into frigid dirt, that's making an oath too, saying *I am*. And if it was good enough for his hosts this weekend, it is good enough for him, he figures. He is an American, fuck it, he has his Social Security card in his pocket at that very moment.

He can't think of anything. He gives it a full five minutes and decides to take a piss instead.

He takes one last look and clambers up the dirt. He approaches town and whistles without recognition the tune he heard at dinner the night before.

It does not take Guy Johnson long to realize that he is the bug. From beneath the creature's russet carapace erupt segmented legs bristling with tiny spurs. Soft antennae droop from its head in a dejected parabola half as long as its body. The bug probably discovered the lemon sour with its antennae, but that is conjecture for entomology is not Guy's field. At the university entomology is housed on the other side of campus from the humanities and he never has occasion to visit there. Guy has been watching the bug for a while now. Reconstructing likely narratives is Guy's enterprise these days, and it extends even to his rest break, as he sits on the hard mattress staring at the floor. The bug sniffed around the room until it arrived at its present location a few feet from Guy's bed, straddling a gritty slit between two floorboards; its movements before he first noticed it are unknowable. Nibbling and sniffing at the candy he dropped a few minutes before, the bug discovers what he discovered, that the enticing discovery is in actuality a trick, and the tongue will curdle on it. Yet it feasts.

He wonders if the proper word is mandible, not tongue. If one jumps to conclusions, one will corrupt the research. One wrong step and one is investigating an entirely incorrect avenue. He unlaces his shoe, fingers clenched around it in a traditional insect-squashing manner and he places it slowly, not without a touch of sadism, above the inquisitive creature. He stays his hand, watching. He waits for the insect to tire or grow sickened of its find. The lemon sour is too big, there is no way in God's green earth that the insect can devour it all. But it does not tire. It nibbles, making progress imperceptible to the eye, and Guy replaces the shoe on his foot. He realizes he is the bug. They do what they must.

When he departed this morning, his papers were spread across the room according to the manner in which he had organized his vast materials, which is to say not organized at all but entirely submissive to the disorder of this project. Transcribed versions of the ballad crouched beneath correspondence received from his informants, notes tossed off in an elusive moment of inspiration secreted themselves in a sheaf of entirely unrelated sections. Amber scraps bickered in piles, contradicting each other in a crumbling din; one half of an interview skulked in one pile while the other half brooded in a pile across the room. He rode herd over crafty fugitives. If he were to die tomorrow, no one would be equipped to make sense of his investigation. He did not have a choice but to let his research roam as it pleased. If all his accumulations were organized properly in well-marked folders, in coherent groups, he would be lying, declaring that he had bested this dragon. He has not. He cannot make sense of any of it. He can savor one or two triumphs, of course. Guy has disentangled the John Henry tale from the John Hardy tale and traced their commingling in certain ballad variants. He has eliminated the false leads generated by regional versions, disentangled the Alabama State Southern and Norfolk & Western from the Chesapeake & Ohio. All those routes in a gnarl. Still he has refused to organize his material to reflect this. He is transfixed and paralyzed by the confusion, and when he returned from this morning's interviews and saw that in addition to making his bed and sweeping the floor Mrs. Thompson had erected one looming and impenetrable stack from his strewn papers, his initial flush of anger eased into gratitude. She had reminded him that he had still not found his way into the mountain.

It had started as such a modest proposition: to trace the origin and transmission of one of the ballads he and Howard had collected for *The Negro and His Songs* and *Negro Workaday Songs*. He had done his best to preserve Negro songs for posterity; now he would concentrate on a single one, "The Ballad of John Henry," explore the regional variants, separate the Irish and Scottish influences from the Negro derivations, and excavate deeper still, determine if the great steeldriver truly lived. If he had known the journey he was about to embark upon! It had brought him here to the very mouth of the Nile in the first true heat of summer. As the end of the academic calendar closed, a trip up here had seemed the perfect balm. It would be work, doubtless, but the prospect of remaining in North Carolina without interruption disheartened him. He had completed the advance work. The dispatches he posted to all corners of the country—from the largest metropolitan newspapers to the smallest county gazette—in appeal for any knowledge of John Henry, no matter how small or half-remembered, had resulted in hundreds of responses. Pick-and-shovel men from Mississippi replied with personal favorites, retired engineers from defunct lines related what they still retained of the old worksong, descendants of railroad men, former hoboes and dockhands, the eloquent and the illiterate alike offered up precious clues. (He looks balefully at the tower on the floor and shakes his head.) This is the method of gathering folklore, accumulating, sifting, tracking with ineffectual magnifying glass the footprints of ghosts. But he had not reckoned on the variety and plenitude of the accounts. No, he had not foreseen the true extent of this adventure at all.

One man against the mountain of contradictory evidence! He has been here three days. Three days, and Guy thinks he can see a little into John Henry's dilemma: the farther he drives, the deeper the darkness he creates around himself. "The Ballad of John Henry" has picked up freight from every work camp, wharf and saloon in this land; its route is wherever men work and live, and now its cars brim with what the men have hoisted aboard, their passions and dreams. Whole crates full of names, the names of women they have loved and the towns in which they toiled. He sorted through that mess and what he found was Big Bend Tunnel in Talcott, West Virginia. Now that he is here, he is left with the human respondents, and they are a disappointing bunch. Each interview he conducts dodges, feints like a boxer. Whether he is following up on correspondence or randomly canvassing longtime residents and old-timers, he cannot get two stories to coincide. One informant maintains the contest never happened, another maintains her long-dead grandfather took her on his knee and related the story as a true adventure. One insists the Chesapeake & Ohio never used a steam drill in these parts, and the next claims to have helped the Burleigh salesman set up the drill for the contest but cannot remember his own name. Some have heard the ballad so many times that they manufacture their own spectatorship, stealing lines from the song and offering these in their eyewitness accounts.

Each time Guy peers into their milky eyes, observes their slow and exhausted movements as they greet him at the door, he is reminded anew of his problem. He has come too late. One by one the first-person accounts collapse under his interrogations into second-person accounts, or worse, complete falsehood. The contest (if indeed there was a contest, he corrects himself) took place over fifty years ago in 1871 or 1872. But some brain-fogged Hinton and Talcott men place the drilling contest in the 1880s, the 1890s, long after the completion of Big Bend, countering historical record and immediately casting shadow on all they say. Even more maddening, they often repudiate their written testimony altogether, remembering events differently once Guy appears on their doorstep. In one letter, a man claimed to have seen the event with his own eyes; when Guy addressed him in person, the informant admitted to have toiled on the western cut, not the eastern, and merely heard the tale repeated from another. Guy opens his satchel and presents as rebuttal their replies to his newspaper advertisements and all they can do is shrug, or shake their heads in confusion, admitting to a faulty memory at times. He adds this morning's interviews to Mrs. Thompson's pile. What's another spade of dirt thrown up on a mountain?

Soon the boy will knock on the door of his room to fetch him. He would be lost without Herbert to guide him. His adventures upon his arrival assured him of that. The train ride from Chapel Hill had been routine enough, if beset by numerous delays, but once he retrieved his bags and stood on the blanched, worn planks of the Hinton Station platform, his trials began in earnest. The station manager, a stocky white man with a thick mustache and acute gaze, took one look at Guy and irritation twisted his countenance; when asked where one might find the McCreery Hotel, the man gestured vaguely over his shoulder and returned to his timetables. Guy's overtures to other white men at the station met with similar failure. Finally, what he should have done once he got off the passenger car became clear, and he approached one of the Negro men who sat across the street from the station in the rickety chairs arranged in front of Riff's Mercantile. The man introduced himself as Al and assured Guy that the easiest thing to do, given the circumstances, would be to take him to McCreery's himself. Guy should have wondered then what the "circumstances" were; actually, he should have already been aware. He voiced his concern that he was interrupting the man from his discussion, and the men chuckled.

He was the boy from the city. As Al helped him with his bags and led him down Third Avenue to the hotel, he asked Guy what kind of business he had in town. "I'm looking into the legend of John Henry," he responded, thinking in a moment of self-importance that this might impress the man, for his little work would help spread the names of Hinton and Talcott and their importance to an American legend. Al looked at him with a queer expression. He muttered, "Funny line of work," bid the bags jump in his palms, and they did not speak again until they arrived at the establishment, when Guy offered to pay him for his trouble.

Al shook his head. "Sure you want to stay here?" the man asked. "They other places you might want—"

Guy cut him off, thanked him and was promptly refused a room by the proprietor of McCreery's, who informed him that he was not in the habit of giving rooms to niggers. Al was still waiting outside, intently tilting a match into his corncob pipe as if this were the first time he had attempted this maneuver. He took one of Guy's bags and led him to Mrs. Thompson's house. She let rooms, he said. Guy lugged in his wake. Of course McCreery's had assumed he was white from the university letterhead upon which he had sent his request for a reservation. His earnestness to get to Hinton, coupled with the numerous dispatches he had posted under the whiteface of scholarly research, had caused him to forget the grip of Jim Crow, ever clenched around his people. Unlikely, yes, but there he was with sweat on his neck and dumb embarrassment on his face.

He rises from the bed, brushes aside the dusty brown curtain and watches Mrs. Thompson pin the wash to the line. He sees the shirt he left on his bed this morning; he had not asked her to clean it, but there it billowed. Guy has already enjoyed too much of her kindness. She opened up her house to him without a moment's thought. Her price was more than fair, indeed he would save a considerable amount of money on room and board by accepting the hospitality of Mrs. Thompson. When he wasn't pondering John Henry, his energies shifted to worry over his budget. It had been hard enough convincing the department of the worth of his research, and he is concerned the sum they eventually disbursed to him might not be sufficient. He maintains meticulous account of his expenditures, ever mindful of leaving an opening one of his more malicious colleagues might exploit. A Negro in the world of academia must be twice the scholar, and twice the tactician, of his white colleagues.

Mrs. Thompson was a rawboned woman with a quick stride and keen intensity; Guy imagined her hurrying from task to task around her house with ruthless efficiency. She rarely had the occasion to take in a boarder, she explained as she showed him up the stairs, past sepia photographs of her clan, but when she did she always enjoyed the company. Guy was to stay in her son's room, she told him; her boy had moved to Chicago, where he had a good job on the killing floor of a slaughterhouse, and had recently taken a wife. The room was bare, save for the bed and the dresser; the Thompson boy had taken all he possessed when he moved North. Once Guy was settled, he joined her in the parlor and, after employing the usual methods of setting an informant at ease, asked her about John Henry.

"That's an old story," she said simply, face betraying nothing.

He had established previously that her father had worked for the Chesapeake & Ohio a few years after the completion of the tunnel, and inquired if he had ever shared any information about the tale.

"Can't live around here without hearing about ol' John Henry," she granted, but offered no more.

He was not advancing the heading, as it were. He pressed her, attempting to talk around the subject before broaching it anew. She told him about her husband, who had died in a railroad accident some years before, told him about how hot it got around here in the summer time, and how often the ice salesman came around, but when he tried to bring up John Henry, all she would offer was, "Can't live around here without hearing all those old stories," and returned to him that obscure expression. She left to prepare dinner, which turned out to be fried fish and biscuits, a delicious meal that consoled the professor after his long trip. Over this repast they talked about life in the town, and the relationship between Hinton and Talcott, which slept on the other side of the mountain, but he never did get anything out of her that related to his investigation.

His first interview the next morning resulted in similar exasperation. One of the many responses he received from his advertisement in the *Hinton Independent* had tantalized Guy with its possibility. "Dear sir," it began, "I am writing on behalf of my father, who as a young boy carried water for the C&O on the Big Bend job and witnessed with his own eyes the struggle of 'Big' John Henry and the steam drill, to which you are inquiring. As my father is in poor health, and of weakened constitution, he urged me to write you to inform you of his knowledge, which he is willing to share with you in exchange for a small fee to help defray the bills from the doctor, as well as his medicine. He has always related to me his stories of those Big Bend days . . ." From there the informant wandered into a secondhand account replete with the customary details of the legend, but he redeemed himself by his residence in Hinton, as well as his direct relation to a person who had toiled on the construction, a person who, most important, was still among the living. Once Mrs. Thompson advised him that the man lived in town, a short walk away, Guy decided to make it his first stop. In retrospect, he misinterpreted the expression on her face as he departed.

It was, to say the least, a disappointing encounter, relieved only by its brevity. "You wrote me?" Mr. McLaugherty asked through the screen door. Between his heavily freckled cheeks, his nostrils widened as if confronted by a ghastly stench.

"About John Henry, yes," Guy offered. "This is the letter you sent."

"Let me see that." After extending a callused hand through the door, he reviewed the contents of the letter, looking up at Guy every few lines. Finally he said, "I don't know where you got that, but I don't have nothing to say about that letter, boy." He shut firm the inside door, hazarding one last appraisal of Professor Johnson before he turned away: "I see it's been a long time since I been to North Carolina." It later struck Guy that in addition to Mr. McLaugherty's obvious prejudice in matters of race, appealing for money from a Negro might not have been the most pleasant prospect for the man. What bothered him the most was that when Chappell arrived, he would have access to McLaugherty and those like him.

On his return to Mrs. Thompson's there was a young Negro boy waiting for him in the parlor. "Sir, my name is Herbert Standard," he said with an extended hand. "Mrs. Thompson told me you needed someone to take you around." Mrs. Thompson nodded from the kitchen doorway, drying her hands on a thin kitchen towel, and could not help but smile.

Herbert was a youth of twelve years, a student at the local colored school, Lincoln. Guy quickly gleaned that the young man possessed a quick mind and exceptional manners, not to mention a patient disposition, this latter quality being the most appropriate for their enterprise, given Guy's apparent inability to ingratiate himself to the local populace. It was soon revealed, in addition, that the boy was well regarded in the community, among whites and Negroes alike, in Hinton as well as Talcott, and with him as pilot, Guy was able to advance his heading.

Guy looks at his watch. He has another ten minutes before they climb into the Standards' wagon and start out to Talcott for the next scheduled interviews. He has two more days before he must return. There is still much to do; while he tells himself he should take pride in what he has accomplished so far, the customary feelings of well-being attendant to satisfaction evade him. In the journals, Cox's John Hardy hypothesis is receiving no small measure of interest at the moment, but what Guy has collected from his informants discounts the theory that the outlaw Hardy and steeldriving Henry were the same person. Guy's larger sample of variants reveals that while the John Hardy songs possess numerous lines common to the most popular John Henry songs, the Hardy songs have more similarities to Irish and Scottish ballads than to Negro workaday songs. From all the evidence, the Hardy songs are confined to the Appalachia area, and sung by whites, whereas the Henry songs have been disseminated all over by itinerant Negro workers, who carried the song from construction camp to construction camp; the song traveled the rails with the men who laid the rails, from state to state, accruing texture from all who came to hear and sing it. This is not to mention the problem of dates. Hardy was hanged in 1894 for his crimes; John Henry's fateful race, however, is said to have occurred in 1871. Cox may have uncovered informants who maintain that the man who beat the steam drill and the villain hanged in Welch in 1894 were one and the same, but that would make Henry one improbably long-lived steeldriver. Most of Guy's interviews—and he has collected far more informants than Cox—place John Henry in his thirties when he came to Big Bend; it is, at the very least, unlikely that after forty years of steeldriving the same man was able to make the kind of mischief attributed to Hardy. (One can always count on white folks to get a bit confused when it comes to describing the age of colored people.) When Guy's book is published, it will contain, if nothing else, this contribution to the study of these songs: John Hardy is a white song and John Henry a colored song. At least that one thing! But he still feels a bit of envy for Cox, for John Hardy was, without a doubt, a real, breathing person. His colorful life, his gambling exploits, sundry criminal activities and the murder that got him hanged are a matter of public record, verifiable from newspaper accounts. Ex-Governor McCorkle, who signed the death warrant, is still alive and available. In the strange case of John Henry, however, all Guy can rely on is what people can wring from the years, hard-fought drips and drabs.

*When the book is published.* Guy is not the first to come here to study folk songs—two have been here before—but he is the first to devote an entire study to John Henry and his legend. Until Chappell arrives, he thinks, amending his statement. Guy won the race to get here first, but Chappell possesses the better credentials. When Guy first proposed this trip to his department, he was sure that their initial reprovals were the fault of Chappell, who has talked of his own John Henry study for years, but has yet to come down here himself. "There has already been work in the area of darky songs," Professor Asbell told him, waving his spectacles as if shooing away a mouse. "Do you truly believe these ditties to be an appropriate avenue of scholarly research? Especially for a young professor trying to establish a reputation?" It took months of cajoling and nagging; ultimately Guy had to produce all the correspondence he received from his advertisements before he garnered what little support he has now.

Who else is there to preserve the body of Negro folklore against the march of time? White folks? He remembers hearing Milton Reed's address at the New York conference. Guy thanks God that Reed is not planning a full-length study of John Henry; the man is apparently satisfied with his paper on the "ribald" versions of the ballad. Reed takes the tale of John Henry to be the God's truth—it coincides with his romanticization of the Negro, his ascription to the colored people qualities Reed cannot find in his own. When

Reed delivered his paper in New York, Guy cringed as Reed gloried over the more vulgar versions of the ballad—the ones containing verses attributing a voracious carnal appetite to the steeldriver and describing extravagant sexual conquests—and he did not like the look in Reed's eyes. He resembled a carnival barker gleefully describing the nether parts of the Hottentot Venus, with his frothy thin lips and wild eyes. Reed's research started from the veracity of the John Henry legend and proceeded from there; in the songs he found confirmation of his ideas about the bestial aspects of the Negro. For Guy, the question of whether the John Henry legend rests on a factual basis is, after all, not of much significance. No matter which way it is answered the fact is that the legend itself is a reality, a living functioning thing in the folk life of the Negro.

Then why, he asks himself as he watches Mrs. Thompson tend to her wash, does he continue to hope that each new informant will give him the affirmative, irrefutable proof?

He made much progress with Herbert's aid. Herbert introduces Guy and his business, and it seems that having one of their own community vouch for this bespectacled colored stranger, who claims to be a college professor, makes the reluctant loose their lips, and the already-inclined to speak more volubly. Their work is cut out for them; Hinton is a town of five thousand, Talcott another two hundred. Most of them, naturally, claim to have firsthand knowledge of the event, and although the present and former C&O workers he has contacted lead them to others, the task remains monumental. If only he had arrived here sooner! Decades before. The few people he can find who lived here at the time of the construction of the tunnel and are still with us offer their fanciful and extravagant stories; the years have pulled a veil across their memories. On occasion his mind tries to convince him that he is not even in the right place, but he defeats these nefarious schemes of his intellect. He is in the right place—after all the false leads of the myriad variants naming the Cruzee Tunnel or the Alabama State Southern railroad or whatever locale was simply the closest to where the respondent resided—Big Bend is the tunnel named in three fourths of the ballads. Or 70 percent, more precisely. Yesterday Herbert took him out to the place itself, to the place where John Henry met his Waterloo. He could not help but feel a bit of disappointment. He had imagined after all this time a monstrous cavern, a gate into the pits of hell. As he stood there, looking up at the gray arching of the mouth, he might have been on the threshold of any railway tunnel in any part of this land. It was unremarkable in its surface effects, and yet it had generated out of its rich soil such an abundant crop of lore. Among the Negro workers John Henry has become a byword, a synonym for superstrength and superendurance. He is their standard of comparison, they talk him and sing him as they work and loaf. But here, he whispered to himself, I can see merely a mountain, and nothing more. I can study the legend but I cannot conceive of the man.

Here is the neat problem of weighing of evidence and the discovery of truth, the challenge he has set for himself. He understands the rules of this particular competition. When someone like Mr. Curry, an old-time Hinton resident who worked as a mechanical engineer on the site almost from start to finish, claims on paper that there was no steam drill used, but reverses himself as they sit on his porch drinking tea, Guy understands that this setback is to be expected. When one considers the abnormalities and errors to which the human memory is subject, especially when it is dealing with something far in the past and tinged with the dramatic, such occurrences are to be expected, indeed counted upon. But his heart sinks nonetheless. Herbert's own grandfather is such a case. Guy met the colored gentleman at his home four miles east of Talcott. His cottage overlooked the Greenbrier River, and Guy thought the man truly blessed to live in such a bucolic locale, in the very embrace of nature. "John Henry," Mr. Standard began before trailing off, "John Henry?" He seemed to address the river itself, and not his visitor. He was such a slight man that his physical body seemed to disappear beneath his clothes; his bones were like tent poles sturdying his shirt and trousers. "Which John Henry do you want to know about?" Mr. Standard murmured. "I known so many John Henrys."

"The one who worked on the Big Bend Tunnel," Guy offered. He waited patiently, with his pen flat against his notebook.

Whereupon Mr. Standard expounded upon how small Talcott was when he moved there fifty years before, about the day the Hinton roundhouse burned down, and what kind of fish ran in the Greenbrier at this time of year. When Guy finally met success in returning the subject to the steeldriver, Herbert's grandfather said, "I don't know any John Henry. Who's that?"

On the trip back to town, Herbert apologized for his grandfather, explaining that just a few years ago he used to tell him John Henry stories all the time, but now he has trouble remembering anything at all. If only Guy had made it up here years before. Even a year might have made the difference. In terms of oral testimony, at any rate. Documents remain elusive, yesterday and today. In that tower of paper by the door, there is no evidence that a steam drill was used here. Some positive evidence, yes, from second-person accounts, but no paper trail. Captain Johnson, the contractor for the site, died years ago and left no journals or work papers of his job on Big Bend. The Chesapeake & Ohio files for this job were lost in a fire—convenient enough for the railroad company, given their deplorable safety record. It is an undisputed fact that the C&O used a steam drill on the nearby Lewis Tunnel in 1871. It is an undisputed fact that despite the unreliable nature of the machine, it was certainly cost effective—about 5.5 cents an inch versus the 11.2 cents an inch for human labor. Of the forty steam drills sold by the Burleigh Rock Drill Company, three are unaccounted for; if one takes into account that the drilling contest was arranged when a Burleigh salesman came to demonstrate its effectiveness, and that John Henry's success resulted in a failed sale, it makes sense that there would be no paper record. And given the machine's tendency to failure—as some versions of the ballads sneer, "Your hole's done choke and your drill's done broke"—it is possible that a man could have beat the machine. Again, he catches himself. The veracity of the man's existence has no bearing on his mission here.

Herbert knocks on the door and Guy answers that he'll be downstairs soon. He truly is a clever boy; Guy wishes there were more opportunities for him in this town. He searches the floor for the insect, but it has disappeared, abandoning the lemon sour. Too much to digest. Herbert and Guy are to return to Talcott this afternoon. Mr. Arnett, a retired conductor on the C&O, told Guy yesterday that his great-uncle was a foreman on the Big Bend job and saw the race with—what else—"his own eyes." He gave Herbert directions; the man is a bit of hermit, from his relative's description. "All these people talk about the day of the race around these parts, but they never seen it with their own eyes. If anybody seen it," Mr. Arnett insisted, "it's my uncle." Guy is exhausted, his morale depleted, but what other course is there for him? This is my profession, he reminds himself. He puts on his coat, grabs his satchel and his hand starts for the doorknob. But he has forgotten something. He opens his billfold and removes the paper. Each morning when he leaves his house, to prepare himself for his daily battle with university intrigue, he reads what he has written there. Since he arrived in Hinton, he consults it whenever he is about to begin another foray into the field. He reads, *we make our own machines and devise our own contests in which to engage them.*

He shuts the door behind him, thinking, perhaps this will be the one.

E'ven when he doesn't want to Bobby hears the song. Since the day he was born. Always and especially today.

He's about to leave the house with his shirttail hanging out when his mother stops him and reminds. He can't go out the house looking like that, not today.

When he's not at his father's garage handing his father his tools and putting them back on the peg when his father is done using them, sometimes Bobby goes out back to the little pond and watches the frogs leap.

Sometimes he goes to the library and looks at the snake book. He knows right where it is on the shelf. He can get a ride home usually because everybody knows him, it's not too bad.

But today he's not doing either of those things. The frogs don't come out when it's hot like this until the shade gets over the water and it's the big fair today so the library is closed, like when Miss Fletcher is sick and the sign says closed. Today he's going out to the tree.

And sometimes he goes into the tunnel and listens to the hammers, but he's not doing that right now. Maybe later, even though he's wearing his new sneakers and the tunnel is full of puddles and he'll ruin them. There was a bit of a fuss because when he came home last night, he was so tired he just lay on his bed and fell asleep like that in his good clothes. Then when his mother came to dress him this morning she said don't do that again.

But there were nice people last night at the big dinner and after he sang the song he got an extra piece of cake. That man liked the song so much he jumped up and fell over so Bobby kept singing because the man liked it so much. If you understand sometimes you can act funny like that. John Henry makes you do funny stuff like that sometimes. It was for the John Henry Days that everybody was waiting for and today is the day.

He finds the trail easily, it's where it always is. You can't see it if you don't know where it is, it starts right there between those two trees. Two feet in, the pine trees huddle like two big men. Bobby squeezes between them and he's in the forest. The trail winds and avoids trees. You can move branches but not trees.

He's bigger than he was when he first started coming here. Stabbing sticks once at eye level now hit his chest; sticks that once got stuck in his hair now try to get into his belly button. Born big, his father says, and he just got bigger. When he hit thirteen he stopped growing because he was already as big as a man. That's how his father explains it to him when Bobby sometimes borrows a T-shirt that is too small for him. He likes it when he goes to work with his father and they sit together in the truck both wearing his father's shirts.

There are slim pine cones and big fat pine cones. There's no grass, in other places but not here. Every Sunday Bobby has to clean the driveway and he has to sweep away the pine needles. But he doesn't have to do that in the woods and more and more of the brown pine needles come down and make it so he can't even see the ground. It's all brown pine needles and pine cones that slowly lose their nut color and get gray as they go back to nature. He doesn't have to pick those up either.

When he notices that his shoelaces are untied, flopping off his sneakers, he stops to tie them and that takes five minutes. Usually if he looks at the floor of the forest and concentrates, he can make ants and bugs come out. First one black one maybe and then maybe two black ones then there's a whole lot of bugs around him. Today he's kneeling for so long working on his shoelaces that they come out without him even thinking about them and con-centrating. There a red one with a black butt, like its mother was a black one and its father a red one and they race-mixed. They're going to be in trouble if they find out.

Then there is the other thing that happens when he is still. He hears the music better. His mother said she used to sing the song to him when he was in her belly and he remembers it. That's why. But he thinks it is because it is around all of them, coming through your fingertips if you lean your hand on a tree or touch dirt. You can feel it then especially. His father shakes his head when Bobby tries to tell him this thought.

He was happy that they were happy to hear him sing John Henry last night. They always like it when he sings it, it's the only song he knows. He first heard a recording of it when he was little, on the radio; he started singing it right along with the voice on the radio and his mother said, listen to that!

She said he had true musical ability. He had heard it before, all along, every day, but for the first time he heard the words. But when they tried to make him sing other songs he just sang the John Henry words to the music. It would be the Star Spangled Banner or Swing Low Sweet Chariot and he'd sing the John Henry words. They didn't get mad or anything but they stopped trying to make him sing other songs. He only likes to sing John Henry. His mother said to his father, you never know about the things that occur to the boy.

This morning his father said they should pay him if they want him to sing. Bobby works with his father in his father's garage handing him tools and getting stuff for him and gets his pay in allowance. He stopped going to school when he was thirteen. He was bigger than the other kids and his mother said God has other plans for him. Since then he goes with his father to work and everybody knows him. He's not allowed to touch the cash register after that time when he did and his father had to drive all the way out to Mr. Beecher's house to get the change back. His mother said to his father that night, what do you expect, things occur to the boy sometimes. Today is the festival so his father will go only if he gets a beep that someone needs a tow for their car.

He's almost where there's a small clearing and it's white bark trees that are naked until high up and then they have little branches with little leaves. He passes the old tree that fell over years before and now is all green with moss. One time he stepped on it just to see what would happen and the old wood started pouring out like sand. Now there is moss in the hole he made because that was a long time ago. He told his father about it at dinner and his father said it was going back to nature. Everything goes back to nature, he said. The light from the clearing starts coming into the trail and the dark green leaves get light green. When he gets into the little clearing he walks over to the tree that has the mark he made in the bark. When the other people come they won't even notice the mark because it looks like a scratch. He knows other people come there because sometimes he trips on a rock and there are letters on it. The other people put initials on the rocks, but he doesn't. He was being sneaky when he made the mark. He was being sneaky when he borrowed the hammer.

He borrowed it from the Visitors Center when Miss Carmine was not around. He thought maybe she was in the bathroom. When he walked into the Visitors Center it was empty for the first time since he had decided to borrow the hammer so he walked up to the wall where it was hung with nails with a little sign under it and took it. He tried to put it under his shirt but it was too big so he ran. He ran up Temple and then down Third Street and then he started walking. He put it under his jacket and the handle stuck out but nobody looked at him funny when he walked by them. He felt like a bug with the frogs looking at him.

When he goes to the pond the frogs get scared and jump across the water making circles or go underwater. If he stands still they start to come back like magic. He'll look into the water close to the edge and see a frog sticking its eyes and mouth about the water. It looks like leaves but it is a frog. They are the same color up there but the legs of the frog are brown and look like twigs. That way no one can see them. Then there will be a bunch of frogs there with just their heads above the water, all of them trying to act like they're leaves. He'll see a flying bug like maybe a dragonfly start getting close to them and Bobby will say, watch out, you're going to get it. If the flying bug gets too close the frogs jump at it and try to put it in their mouth. They have been watching out for bugs to eat. They do that all day. Sometimes they go underwater but a lot of the time they wait for flying bugs. That's why he felt like a bug when he carried the hammer. He could be a flying bug people were on the lookout for.

It wasn't heavy. He wasn't John Henry but he carried the hammer without trouble. He walked in the woods. When he got it to the clearing he moved the brown pine needles apart with his sneakers and then he dug with his hands until the hole was big enough. Then he put the hammer in it and put dirt and pine needles on top of it. When his mother said what have you been doing, he said, nothing. If someone had said to him, did you take the hammer, he would have said yes. But no one did.

He moves the dirt off the hammer. It is a hammer like John Henry had. Since it has been in the ground the wood of the handle has gotten wet and it is damp and cool when he touches it. The wood of the handle was already split in the middle when he borrowed it. In the woods the handle will get old and crumbly like the other trees and branches that fall. Maybe it will get termites. The head of the hammer has little dents and many scratches on it. Maybe it will rust in the woods like the metal in the cars in the back of his father's garage. If the hammer is out here it can get old and older and go back into the ground. It can be part of the forest and the mountain again. It will take a long time but already if he sticks his fingernail into the wood he can scratch it because it is soft. He covers up the hammer. He starts back down the trail. The John Henry Days is today and everybody is going to be there. His mother said there will be a lot of fun stuff to do.

If you ask him why he took the hammer, he would say, because it wants to go back to nature. And his mother would tell you, you never know what occurs to the boy.

Every day in that place reduced his notions. Reduced the first day by the serried fluorescent rods in the ceiling panels; diminished by the pallid green light on the neutral prefab sections of the cubicles; made entirely small by the rectitude of the scratchproof desks, which were not alive with the artifacts of fabled counterculture, like maybe vermilion-tinted bongs encrusted with resinous murk, or rainbow posters detailing the famous gigs of the psychedelic dead, not even an errant roach, a little something to lubricate the old brainstem under deadline. Downright corporate, J. thought when he first walked into the offices of the *Downtown News*, the oldest and largest alternative weekly in the U.S. of A., consulted each week by J. as the supreme hipster tipsheet. No bumper stickers preaching common sense about big issues like whales or unionized grapes—they were forbidden, he learned later—nowhere was there tacked up a funny cartoon with a clever pun about Uncle Sam. Notions reduced apace as he discovered the intelligence behind the height and placement of the flimsy cubicle walls, which fostered the illusion of privacy but at all angles abetted intrusion, random observation by those at the top of the masthead. That first day when his boss, Metro editor Winslow Kramer, left for lunch, J. hazarded a call to Freddie, to find out which one of the bars that tolerated, indeed relied upon, underage drinkers, they would meet at later. And if any girls were coming. Turned out, Freddie remembered, that Monday at The Blue and Gold was Greta's night, and she was a capricious old bat who might let you buy one beer, get comfortable, and then card the whole table on the second round, kicking them out after everyone, it seemed, had left their driver's licenses at home. They were about to decide on another amenable establishment when he felt the man's eyes upon him. He was a short white guy with slick black hair, dressed in neatly pressed khakis and a light blue oxford pinned down by red suspenders. The man looked into J. and of course knew he was sneaking a personal phone call when there were a million stories in the naked city waiting to be told. He walked on, nodding slightly to himself, and of course making a note to berate

Winslow Kramer about the necessity of sedulous and go-get-'em interns. J. hurried off the phone and thought, it's just like Big Brother. They were living in the year of the book and if you looked around you could see it was all true.

Was the prim buttoned-down man the publisher? J. wondered. The liquor magnate Reinhart Becker, who had purchased the ailing *News* out of financial boredom, fiscal inertia, in order to expand his empire into the realm of the printed word. According to the paper's vigilant media columnist, who regularly railed at the man in the name of free speech and an independent press, Becker wanted to sit on his acquisition for a few years and sell it at a nice profit when the market was right. Or was the man who made the rounds of the cubicles the new editor in chief, Jimmy Banks? Jimmy Banks, who had been one of the early editors of the *News* during its famous fifties era, gone on to various big-name dailies in all the big markets, even soldiered through a stint at *Time* magazine, before coming home to his first love, you never truly leave your first love, the *Downtown News*. J., staggering through a dizzy bout of rookie paranoia, walked over to the candy machines for a Snickers. In the first scenario the circumspect air of the man marked him as a farmer patrolling the hen house, counting the eggs he'll take to market soon. In the second scenario his weary, distracted calm said that he'd seen it all before, interns will slack off, it's part of the business, and it doesn't really matter as long as they put the paper to bed on time. In either case, J. still felt like he fucked up, and he returned to collecting phone numbers for the factchecker of the exposé of the parking meter scandal.

"It's not what I thought it would be like," J. told Winslow Kramer on Tuesday, and Kramer told him that's what everybody said: They think everybody's smoking Humbolt joints in the bathroom. He explained that these were the new offices. The *News* had recently moved into this space after thirty years on Fourteenth Street and things were different. Becker Distilleries owned the property and had forced the paper into the building because they had trouble finding tenants, despite the recent blossoming of the economy. Now they were finally collecting rent on the place.

"He's a real bastard," Kramer said, "but he leaves us alone." J. remembered the boycott two years earlier, called by the staff on the eve of the sale. At the tail inches of the columns and reviews, the writers urged the readers not to buy the paper the following week if the sale went through, to show Management that they didn't want to read a paper published by a liquor manufacturer who engineered ad campaigns to urge underage drinking and put up big billboards in minority neighborhoods, just bad vibes any way you looked at it, who knew what kind of changes this supporter of various conservative groups might impose on this vanguard of the left. The sale went through, and newsstand sales dropped the next week, but nothing major, comparable to certain heatstroke weeks in the summer when the folks still in town were too weak to read, or when January blizzards kept the citizens indoors and uninformed about city hall's sundry machinations.

J. had noticed no change in the paper over the last few years. He was a diligent reader of the *News*; he rushed out to buy the paper every Wednesday, turning first to the music reviews in the early days of his education, then to the movie reviews, and then after a time finding himself with a flashlight in the subterrain of the front of the book, discovering in bits and pieces the covert scheme of democracy and how it kept the people in check, in ignorance, in obeisance, etc. This was stuff he didn't find in the papers his parents read: puppet governments below the equator, kickbacks to the mayor's pals, lead paint potato chips for the kids in the projects. Stuff in the drinking water, a chemical whose name J. always forgot, the *News* reporter had discovered secret documents. Journalists were getting assassinated in Central America and the intellectuals of Pan-Africanism died in plane "accidents." His parents were in on it, J. had come to realize, by their deep middle-class sin. They were complacent and a fascist government needed people to be complacent, to turn a blind eye. So he read.

He listened. He was on the inside now. Word around the office, murmured along the labyrinthine cubicles, held that Reagan was sure to be reelected next week; the paper had done all they could for Mondale, but it was a lost cause, the country overflowed with simpletons who refused to see. But that wasn't going to stop J.; he was turning eighteen on the very day of the election, and he was going to vote for the first time. J. had read with deep anger the statistics of voter turnout among young adults and minorities in an article published by the organization he was now a part of, he clucked at the sorry numbers, recognizing that apathy was a major tool of the oppressors down in Washington, he said amen to the condemnatory tone of the article, he shook his head solemnly when the writer pointed out that the numbers were caused, surely and sadly, by the effects of disenfranchisement, institutional racism, the sheer failure of the country's education system. Amen.

The writer's name was Andy Halloran and J. hoped to meet him in the coming months. There was no telling who he might be. No one in the office looked like what he thought they would. Winslow Kramer, for example, did not wear the black leather jacket and dirty jeans in which J. had attired him after reading the man's music reviews for years. J. had clipped the article Kramer wrote about a crazy night in CBGBs with the Ramones, when Dee Dee was too fucked up to play, passed out in the middle of a song, and Kramer climbed on up, grabbed the man's bass from the tacky stage, and filled in for the rest of the set. The *News* had the best music section of any mag he'd read, and Kramer had a byline J. always searched for on the contents page. Or used to. He hadn't written for a while. When Kramer called to tell him he got the internship, he was surprised that the rocker was covering the Metro desk, the post J. had requested, where the real battles lay. More surprised when Kramer asked him not to wear aftershave or cologne; since his overdose a year and a half before he was sensitive to chemicals, he explained, the bouquet of modern life left him faint and panting and grasping for his inhaler. In person that first day, Kramer sported the bowl haircut of a penitent, and wore new dark blue jeans and a faded green T-shirt without a slogan or a band's name. Brown freckles dotted his sunken cheeks, a swarm of bugs eating their way out from within. On the desk there was a picture of Kramer and a bleary Patti Smith, taken in some downtown alley, but nothing else to link the man with J.'s notions.

The first day J. said, "I liked that piece you did about the Gang of Four show a while back. I thought you really got it. The atmosphere."

Kramer looked at J. distantly, a bit fearfully. "Thank you," he whispered.

"I was there, at Danceteria that night." The age limit was eighteen, but J. and Freddie followed in the wake of some beautiful older girls in platinum Warhol wigs and got through the front door. They weaseled up to the front of the stage, in the front of the jaded crowd, and rescued the song list taped to the microphone stand when the band finished playing. J. and Freddie fought over who deserved the night's distilled essence more, who was the bigger fan, but J. walked home with it.

Kramer said, "Yeah?" and took some papers to the Xerox room.

Still, the place was pretty fucking cool. There was a little chair next to Kramer's desk, and they sat close together in the tiny cubicle. Kramer talked in low, mellow tones, and had an appointment outside the office every afternoon, with the acupuncturist, with his analyst, with Narcotics Anonymous, which left J. alone with the daily papers to mine for promising stories, or to find holes in the mainstream version of events that they might excavate. He answered the phones and told writers and sources that Kramer had stepped out but would be back soon. People stopped by the cubicle to look for

Kramer and J. wondered, was that Lynn Fields, was that Ron K. C. Speath, was that skinny guy Billy Pagels, who had written the excellent piece about Grandmaster Flash and the Furious Five. J. was a lucky man, so he believed, and so his friends seconded, telling him as much from their college dormitories between keg parties. The *Downtown News* was the only paper that covered rap music in any way, reviewed Whodini and Run DMC singles. James Baldwin had editorialized in these pages, Lorraine Hansberry had essayed a few words about the direction of black theater. J.'s parents were glad he was doing something beyond working at that electronics store; they wanted him to become a lawyer and didn't like the fact that he had deferred from college for a year. They thought he would never go and get a degree, follow the plan, that he'd lay around their house and watch television until he was thirty, never get beyond working the record counter at Crazy Eddie's. The internship showed them that he wasn't just fucking around, even though he did go out every night with friends; sometimes forgot his keys and woke his parents up at two in the morning with Budweiser on his breath. Or he hoped it would show them.

He put on a song and dance for them Tuesday night at dinner. "Have you heard about Eleanor Bumpurs?" he challenged his parents, in between mouthfuls of Lake Tung-Ting Shrimp, which had been delivered to their door just minutes earlier from their local favorite. Free fortune cookies and an orange.

"Of course," his father said, "it was in the *Times* today."

"It's another example of a larger pattern of police attacks against the black community," J. said.

"I thought she was mentally ill," J.'s mother said, tearing the corner of a plastic packet of soy sauce.

J. had discovered the article when Kramer disappeared early in the morning to go to the allergist. Eleanor Bumpurs was a sixty-nine-year-old Afro-American woman who had been killed by the Emergency Services Unit as they tried to evict her from her city-owned apartment. The piece was a few pages into the Metro section of the *Times*, a small and terse square of type. Six cops had gone in, warned in advance that the woman had mental problems. According to the police, after they broke down the door, the three-hundred-pound Mrs. Bumpurs came at them with a knife, and the men who had received certificates from a program that taught them how to deal with the mentally ill killed her. Officer Sullivan shot her twice with a shotgun.

"Yeah, she was sick, but the cops knew that when they went in," J.

pointed out. "They were *Emergency Services*, that's their job to handle this stuff."

"That's terrible," J.'s mother said, as a ball of gray meat rolled out of dumpling sheath. "Can you pass the salt, Andrew?" J.'s mother said, gesturing toward her husband.

"Eighty-nine dollars a month. That was her rent. Is that worth a human life? There's a pattern here," J. insisted. He clipped the article and showed it to Kramer when he returned, sniffing, pharmacy bag in his claw, from the allergist. Kramer called Noah Blumenthal, his point man on such matters, and by the end of the day, after negotiations in the editor in chief's office (somewhere down the hall out there), the piece was out of the Metro section and into the feature well. J. felt he had discovered the outrage for the paper, he had contributed his first thing to the *Downtown News*. At dinner, he reiterated some of the dialogue from Kramer's and Blumenthal's conversations, to demonstrate to his parents the justice of his deferred education. "The cops are taking their cues from Koch and Reagan that black people don't matter," J. informed his parents. "Can you imagine what it will be like if Reagan gets reelected next week? It's going to be a field day on black people."

"Too bad that Mondale's such a wimp," J.'s father said.

"That's going to be the message we send to the cops: That it's okay. Eleanor Bumpurs killed in her own home! Michael Stewart choked to death by subway cops—anyone could be next," J. protested, attacking the broccoli on his plate, saving the shrimp for last, his strategy with this particular dish.

"That's why we always say save money for cabs home. It's not safe on the subways at night," J.'s father said.

"Right. But still—this is a police state we're living in!" Cab fare cut into his bar money. He always took the subway home. Simple economics.

On Friday, Kramer looked pale and didn't say much all morning. Less than usual. He spent a long time in the bathroom and when he came back he said that he had to visit the doctor immediately. (J. later recalled he had used an antifungal aerosol spray that morning.) There was a headline meeting at noon, so J. would have to go in his place. Jimmy Banks had seen the Bumpurs piece, but there might be some unforeseen questions, and if that happened J. was to give whatever information he could. Kramer rubbed his throat. "These meetings are pretty simple," he wheezed. "You'll probably not have to do anything, don't worry about it. Just sit there."

J. was going to enter the inner sanctum of the paper. On Thursday he had walked to the editor in chief's office to deliver a reimbursement form for one of Kramer's writers but the door was closed, and the secretary said she'd take the form, it was all right. J. had read the Noah Blumenthal piece; as in all the man's work, righteous anger reverberated between the quotes and facts, as if meticulous research and the journalistic method were all that kept the man from becoming a homicidal vigilante. With disregard for department policies, with seemingly premeditated intent. Blumenthal in person, when he came in to drop off some factchecking material, was quite and nervous. Kramer told J. later that he lived with his mother in Queens and had only recently conquered a phobia about the subway. J. read the piece again before the headline meeting to make sure he could answer any question that might come up, perhaps regarding the one or two missing quotes Blumenthal was supposed to insert on Monday, or the missing sentence that started the third paragraph, which Kramer and Blumenthal were still arguing about. Who knew what they might ask. He wanted to be prepared.

This was the kind of work he wanted to do, J. thought, squinting at the printout and underlining with his finger dot matrix outrage. These were real stories. He had been raised in a cocoon, programmed for achievement, but there was a whole city out there that was unruly and didn't give a shit about plans. And he wanted to take his place in it. He wanted to know where reporters got their statistics about rates of crime, and how they requested secret files the government and big business didn't want the public to know. The clandestine order that made things go. Blumenthal had read Emergency Services' protocols on the use of deadly physical force and had interviewed Eleanor Bumpurs's case counselor. The reporter had looked up Officer Sullivan's record of nineteen years on the police force and had seen a pattern there. He found things that converged in one place and time from different parts of the city, like people on a subway car, and violence was the result. J. felt a part of the Bumpurs piece, he had turned Kramer on to it, and though it was a small step it was his first, and that's how you learn to walk, he thought.

A few minutes before noon, Freddie called J. from his dorm room at NYU to give him the lowdown on the night. Sophie's was the ticket: they'd spend the night on Avenue A, and Julia was going to bring some of her friends maybe, they were still negotiating, and then J. looked at the clock and saw he was late for the meeting.

He ran between the cubicles, left and right, skidded down the blue tile floor. The door to the editor in chief's office was closed. He was too late. Kramer was going to kill him. The secretary looked up at him, and raised her eyebrows to say, yes? "I'm supposed to be in the meeting," J. said.

"So go right in," she said, and pawed the in-box.

He turned the handle slowly.

It turned out that the white guy with suspenders was Jimmy Banks, the editor in chief, and he sat behind a desk of black metal with his hands clasped together. Behind him on the wall, framed covers of the *Downtown News*'s first few issues hung in parallel authority, to remind the people in the room of tradition in solid black and white ink beyond reproach, reiterating quaint outrages of a simpler city. There were ten others in the room, those whom J. had seen designated by bylines and their editorial maneuverings over the years, but he did not know whose face belonged to which riveting personal essay, which exposé, which descent into the downtown after-hours abyss in search of the first piece about the new raging drug. They slouched indolently in chairs, drooped on the floor, in the stiff gray cushions of the couch along the back wall, drinking coffee and diet soda, notebooks agape. They looked at J. but did not say anything. He sat along the back wall, on the floor, next to a thin woman with black fingernails, black dress and oily, glinting dyed black hair. He did not intend to speak unless addressed. He listened to the old hands of the *Downtown News* to see how it worked.

"Bumpurs—I'm trying to riff on that."

"Cops and Bumpurs. Do the Bump. Bump me in the morning and didn't just walk away."

"Bump, jump, lump, stump . . ."

"The cops knock on the door and—"

"Knockin' on Heaven's Door."

"Maybe we should focus on the cops."

"Knock knock. Who's there? Cop. Cop who? Cop come to kill ya."

"How about Shooting Range in High Bridge? You know, because they have those rooms in the basement of the precinct for target practice."

"Did anyone besides the cops see that she had a knife, or just them? Because that's something. That's an angle."

"High Bridge Target Range. Target Practice."

"Bumpurs, Bumpurs, Bumpurs . . ."

"Permanent Eviction."

"Her family says there's no way she could have attacked them because she had a heart condition. And arthritis."

"Shotgun, High Bridge: The Blankety Blank of Blankety Blank."

"Are NYC Cops the City's Secret Police?"

"Go Nazi—secret police, Gestapo, something along those lines."

"Are NYC Cops the City's Gestapo?"

"Gestapo on 174th Street."

"This isn't a Sidney Lumet film."

"Hump, mump, dump, pump . . . I'm thinking."

"Jackboots on 174th Street."

"Franklin, you're barred from the rest of the meeting. The rest of you focus on the race thing. I think that's it."

"It's not a very riffable name."

"What's wrong with Permanent Eviction?"

"Race and Rent. Of Race and Rent."

"The Devil and Officer Sullivan."

"The Case of Officer Sullivan."

"Are You Next?"

"How about a Tale of Two Cities? You see, High Bridge is one city, and Chelsea is the other, then we can bring the Raymond case and compare the different responses to—"

"I thought we killed that piece. I thought we agreed to kill that piece."

"But now we have a peg again. It's fresh again. Uptown, Downtown, the two different standards—"

"Forget it. Blumenthal doesn't mention it. Where's the cop from?"

"Italian, from somewhere in Queens. Forest Hills."

"The Italian Stallion Meets the Great Black Something."

"Isn't Sullivan an Irish name?"

"Bumpurs Bumpurs Bumpurs . . ."

"Focus on the victim."

"Deadly Physical Force."

"Anyone see *Cheers* last night?"

"Have Gun, Will Evict."

"Ah ha."

"Law of the Landlord."

"New Lease on Life."

"What the hell does that mean?"

"I don't know."

"Settling Arrears."

"Arrears of Death."

"Why is this so much fucking trouble? Maybe we should skip it for now and come back to it."

"Past Due. In for Arrears. Are NYC Cops the New Debt Collectors?"

"Will you get off the fucking interrogatory hed? Save it for the subhed, Christ."

"No one saw *Cheers* last night?"

"Thinking, I'm thinking."

"High Noon in High Bridge. Showdown on 174th Street. Was Eleanor Bumpurs Gunned Down in Cold Blood?"

"The Executioner's Song."

"In Cold Blood."

"We used that last week. And you—you're back on the goddamned interrogatory hed again."

"Black and Blue! She's black, they're blue!

"We get it."

"Bumpurs Bumpurs Bumpurs."

"The Fire This Time, go for the Baldwin thing. They threw garbage at the cops the next day, right, from the rooftops—The Fire This Time."

"But it wasn't flaming garbage."

"I heard it was molotov cocktails."

"It was a bag of trash."

"Whatever. I still think The Fire This Time works."

"Maybe they'll riot."

"A Shooting on 174th Street."

"A Killing on 174th Street."

"Maybe we should get someone to write a sidebar over the weekend. To get the black angle."

"Who?"

"I don't know, what about our boy Malefi?"

"He hasn't been returning my phone calls lately."

"Why not?"

"Too busy?"

"What, busy changing his name again? What about the guy who wrote the graffiti piece two weeks ago. We put it on the cover. Is he . . ."

"You mean is he . . ."

"Yeah, is he black, Afro-American, what do you think I mean?"

"No. He's a professor at NYU."

Jimmy Banks looked over at J. J. had his arms drawn around his knees in a cannonball position. "You," Banks pointed. "What's your name?"

"J. Sutter," he answered. "I'm the intern, I'm Winslow Kramer's intern."

He embraced his legs tighter. "He asked me to come in case you needed to know anything. About the piece."

"Intern," Banks said, nodding and looking down at his desk. "It's probably too late for a sidebar anyway." He nodded some more and then abandoned his thought. "Everybody put your thinking caps on or else it's Bloodbath on 174th Street."

"I still like Of Race and Rent."

"Maybe we should just go with Bloodbath on 174th Street."

"Anyone else? Okay, Bloodbath on 174th Street it is."

"Bumpurs Bumpurs Bumpurs."

The individual who wishes to purchase a gun in the state of Maryland must endure a seven-day waiting period, and for some this may be the most difficult part of the application process. The ten-dollar application fee, which is forwarded to the Superintendent of the Maryland State Police, should be no hassle; excavation in the living room couch may cover the deficit if the applicant is a few coppers short. Scribbling in the lines and scratching the X's across the boxes regarding name, address, occupation, place and date of birth, height, weight, race, eye and hair color and signature will be a small hurdle, but most of this information has probably been memorized over time, and the gun dealer may be able to provide aid without breaking any laws. The section regarding a history of crimes of violence (the usual: abduction; arson; burglary in the first, second and third degree; escape; kidnapping; manslaughter, excepting involuntary manslaughter; mayhem; murder; rape; robbery; robbery with a deadly weapon; carjacking or armed carjacking; sexual offense in the first degree; and sodomy; or an attempt to commit any of the aforesaid offenses; or assault with intent to commit any other offense punishable by imprisonment for more than a year) may knock out a few. Checking the wrong box next to questions regarding one's status as a habitual drunkard; addict or a habitual user of narcotics, barbiturates or amphetamines; and spending more than thirty consecutive days in any medical institution for treatment of a mental disorder or disorders (unless there is attached to the application a physician's certificate, issued within thirty days prior to the date of application, certifying that the applicant is capable of possessing a pistol or revolver without undue danger to himself or herself, or to others), may cause the individual to be turned down, unless fate intervenes and the application is reviewed by the State Police around quitting time or just before an office party celebrating the retirement of a valued member of the department, someone perhaps named Sal. The individual must be twenty-one or older, no excuses, and fugitives from justice will be denied permits for obvious reasons. This is all laid out in Article 27, Subsection 442 of Maryland's gun legislation. The application does not include Rorschach tests, questions about whether the glass is half-full or half-empty, or the proclivity to hold mock trials, while dressed in one's underpants, in which the worthiness of the human race is weighed by a jury of the individual's stuffed animal collection. There are a lot of questions that are not asked in the gun dealerships of the state of Maryland, but for some the hardest part of the application may be the seven-day waiting period. It may be hell for some.

Once the individual has the new gun in possession, he/she may maintain it for use in his/her residence or business. The new gun owner may feel an urge to walk around town packing heat, but this is a real no-no. The individual can't just walk around with a gun in his or her pocket; there are laws against that. It may be transported to a gun shop for repairs, from place of legal purchase, to a formal or informal target shoot, sport shooting event, for hunting and trapping, to dog obedience training class or show, or organized military activity, and the weapon must be unloaded and placed in an enclosed case or holster, with the ammunition maintained in a separate, closed container. But walking around with a gun? That's reserved for officers of the peace, and employees of security or detective firms, and requires a permit. The application for a carry permit is a bit tougher, at times a head-scratcher.

West Virginia is a popular gun-running state, on a per-capita basis, in the top five, based on how many guns bought in the state are traced to out-of-state crimes per one hundred thousand population in the originating state. Eventually people who want to buy guns in West Virginia for export get to know the shortcuts and just jet over the state line, slap down the cash and cross back over the state line. The number of out-of-state guns used in crimes within the borders of West Virginia is comparably small. And yet it does happen from time to time. At the most unlikeliest of times, at the hands of the most unlikeliest of people, it happens.

Learned people keep track of the numbers, draw up studies, make arguments. In this landmass of numbers, riven by valleys of rarity and tormented by summits of likelihood, there are landmarks. An out-of-state gun used at a public event in a lethal fashion, unclassifiable as a crime of passion or monetary gain, by an individual who does not fit the standard profile of a perpetrator of a violent crime. Such events skew. They draw more media attention than the routine gas station robbery or umpteenth depredation against the dignity of the humble convenience store. The public is inured against such mundane crimes. They yawn. But in the case of the spectacular crime, soul-searching may be initiated, becalmed dinner conversations snap sail at the mention, suspicious appraisal of one's neighbors occurs up and down the rows of the planned community. Such a case will be a landmark in a stream of statistics and stand apart for a time. A blip on the graph. But once the names have been removed, the particularities expunged in the name of scientific method, such a case may indeed skew, but be consumed into the mean nonetheless. Statistics will swallow the aberration, if the aberration can endure the seven-day waiting period.

The place mats of Herb's Country Style aspire to the perspectives of mountain divinities, bought in bulk and fixing a century of scrabbling human achievement in its just form on the diaphanous paper. The map is rough drawn, poorly reproduced, wholly sketch. Squiggly indecisive lines worm among straight, rivers contend against manmade roads and routes. Pamela can easily pick out the friends of this establishment. Their names are bold on the map, two buildings down from Herb's the Coast to Coast Offers Free Continental Breakfast In-Room Coffee 25" Remote TV Pool; Magnificent Bluestone Dam Tours Available a little south of here, past where two rivers diverge. The edificial advertisements of local big-guns row along the bottom of the paper, landmarks on the avenue, granite enticements distinctly detailed. Appealing to the practical and fit and promising all sorts of adventures in the New River Gorge National Park, Lowell Hardware in the Historic District Carries All Your Camping Needs (And Some You Don't Know About), while the McKeever Lodge in Pipestem whispers luxury into the ears of the less rugged, announcing All Sorts of Special Themes and Menus, such as Seafood, Italian and Western, to be digested in the 25 Fully Equipped, Deluxe Cottages. The final advertisement perches on the right corner, olde-style letters urging her to visit John Henry Monument and Big Bend Tunnels. A Summers County Favorite.

In the upper left adjacent to a brown coffee cup eclipse a harpoon called N jabs away from her. She doesn't see her motel. Route 3 trudges east and off the map into mottled formica terrain. She moved her plate because she didn't want to look at it. She cleaned her plate except for two hashbrown kernels at the edge of a pool of ketchup. Pamela can't eat them because they remind her of the fight outside her apartment building the week before and look like knocked-out teeth. No point trying to figure out the cause of it: two crack-heads fighting over God knows what, and once the puncher saw the damage he'd inflicted on the punchee, he helped his friend to his feet to hoof it out of there before the cops arrived. When she left her apartment to come to Talcott, the dried blood was still visible on the pavement.

Herb's Country Style is situated in a locale more peaceful than her neighborhood—no ambulance wails, no crack vials or needles glinting, no homeless living or dead to step over—but despite those leagues the universal coffeeshop protocols are still enforced, even out here in international waters. The waitress keeps her java refills coming as they settle into tacit exchanges of cupfuls and murmured gratitude, and when J. sits down in Pamela's booth the waitress follows standard operating procedure. She asks, "Separate checks?"

Pamela becomes one of the locals when J. opens the door; the chime dispatches all heads to the entrance to check the identity of the latest arrival, and Pamela joins in enthusiastically, avoiding herself in this game. J. looks more energetic than he did last night outside the motel, his step no longer uneasy. He's regained the swagger he and his comrades had the previous evening. The locals take gauge of him to see where they can place him, if they know him, then they return back to their food, nodding or squinting to their companions in shared appraisal. Pamela feels a tinge of envy: it must be nice to know where everything lays. He isn't from around here, not in that shirt and not with those sunglasses. In that skin. She considers inviting him to sit with her, deciding before the thought is finished she doesn't feel like talking. She needs to prepare herself for her discussion with Mayor Cliff. She fishes another cigarette out of her pack for cover activity but then J. is at her table asking if he can join her. "Help yourself," her mouth moves.

He slides into the red vinyl across from her and she glances out of the glass. Pamela has not been into the town proper yet; so far she's seen the same view since she's arrived. It seems that every place she's seen so is precarious. The back of Herb's looks out on the river, but here in the front her view is the familiar sight of mountain creeping on the road, a slope of green and gray that pushes up out of vision. Kind of like skyscrapers, she thinks; the sky is up there somewhere.

"I missed the taxi," J. says, his hand darting for the plastic menu behind the napkin dispenser.

"Your friends just left," she answers. She shared the van with them over here and they entered the place together. All the faces turned to them and looked away again. Ritual of the chime. Pamela diverged from the journalists and sat alone in a booth by the window. She asked the waitress if they sold cigarettes and was referred to the gas station next door. When she returned with packs to spare, her food was already on the table, like that. Her bill, too, upside down and waiting. "Feeling better today?" Pamela asks. He looks better.

"Oh I'm up and at 'em."

Perhaps his sunglasses hide dark circles, but his voice isn't as low and raspy as his friends' were this morning in the van. He's the only one of them who doesn't look hungover. "This kid," Pamela starts, "when I was in third grade, this kid in my class choked on a hot dog. The teacher came over and gave him the Heimlich and a little piece of hot dog shot out of his mouth. It looked like a cigar."

"Was his name Frank?"

She tries to remember. Is this another one of those it's a small world moments? "I forget his name." She doesn't get it until an hour later.

The waitress fills her cup and takes J.'s order. Pamela lights a cigarette, sees she has one going and tamps out the surplus. She catches J. watching this and thinks, he should be the last one to judge, after his and his friends' antics. Compulsive drinkers, compulsive smokers. Everyone on hair-trigger behavior. He asks her if it is her first time in West Virginia.

"My father used to come here a lot to find stuff for his collection, but he never brought us down." Now she may be bringing it all back to where it came from. Two hours to kill before her meeting with the mayor. The mayor seemed pretty mellow, judging from his speech last night. "What about you?" she asks.

"First time," he answers. "This isn't my usual beat. I'm down here doing a travel piece for a new website."

"On the internet."

"We prefer the term Information Superhighway. What do you do?" he says, and they could be back in New York.

"I'm a temp."

"How do you like it?"

"Have you ever temped?"

"No."

"You wouldn't ask that if you had. Typing and filing, usually. They call you up and you head out."

"Just like me."

"The agency doesn't send me to places like this. They have a strict policy."

"You should have them look into it. This place could use a good proofreader," tapping the menu, "unless 'Pried Fish' is some Southern delicacy I'm unaware of."

She asks him how long he's been a journalist and thinks, gay? The way he talks reminds her of Royce. Whenever she and Royce went out he'd look around the room and pick out the waffling straight boys. The curious or closeted. Or so he claimed with some authority. Not that there wasn't proof of his abilities; she'd forgiven him for what happened when she introduced him to the new fellow she'd started seeing. Forgiven him and him: it was her luck. J.'s not that bad-looking. That Hawaiian shirt is pretty loud, makes him stick out more than he does already. Black people around here are pretty country from what she's seen so far. What room is he staying in? Not on her floor: upstairs somewhere. Leaving tomorrow. Haven't been laid in— He does live in New York though. She shakes her head. That kind of thinking leads nowhere. Also a drinking problem, probably. Blond girls or he's gay. Maybe introduce him to Royce when they get back to New York so he can do his trick.

(It takes her about four seconds to concoct this narrative.)

THE WAITRESS DROPS J.'s plate on his place mat with one hand and refills Pamela's coffee with the other. Her greasy spoon movements are honed, delicate, and were it not for the refutations of every single object in his field of vision he could be at the ballet, observing a master. The place mat features a crudely drawn map of Hinton. He studied it when he sat down, glad to be out of the heat and glad to be done with his exercise. A giant star marked Herb's location; the restaurant tottered on the bank of the New River. North a bit (this thing drawn to scale?) a bridge crossed the river and ended up at the foot of the town. Six, seven, eight blocks long and five "avenues" wide. He is far from home. Then south of the main part of town is a little strip of streets on the bank of the river. Not as many historic locations marked there, must be the newer part of town; when he got close to Herb's and could see across the river he spotted a large supermarket over there. Then there are all these corny ads at the bottom, tourist traps. He can't see his motel on the map. He isn't tired exactly but wouldn't mind a ride back. Sees the ad for the John Henry Monument and asks, "You going to the steeldriving thing this afternoon?"

"Think so."

"It's going to be a re-creation of the John Henry race, right?" Gloomy Gus only opens her mouth to stick a cigarette in it. "Two guys banging nails into the ground to see who can go faster?"

Pamela executes with practiced ease an expression of sublime boredom. She exhales smoke through her nose and says, "Actually John Henry didn't lay track. That's what everybody pictures, but that wasn't his actual job. He worked in the tunnel. One guy would hold a drill bit horizontal like this and the steeldriver would hammer it into the rock to make a hole. Then they'd put dynamite in the hole when it was deep enough and blow it up to advance the tunnel. Then they'd start over again."

"I thought John Henry was made up but these people really take him seriously." Sticking a piece of bacon into his mouth.

"That is the question. Big Bend Tunnel is the place named in most of the ballads, and that's over in Talcott. The songs identify the C&O Railroad and they're the ones who put the line in. So it fits that it comes from a true story."

"But that doesn't mean it actually happened—the race itself. He has, what, a heart attack once he beats the drill? Or he's struck down from above."

"Want to rain on the parade, don't you?" she says, starting to grin. "There are two books about it. My father had the first editions, he would . . . Two folklorists—Louis Chappell and Guy Johnson—came down in the twenties or thirties to interview people around here and find out if he really lived or not. They found some people who said he did and some who said he didn't," nodding to the locals in other booths of the restaurant, the representative natives. "Some of the people who worked on the tunnel said they'd witnessed the contest and some said no way it ever happened. Their granddad had told them John Henry worked in Big Bend, or he didn't. Most of the people were dead by the time they got down here, so a lot of it was secondhand anyway."

"So what was the upshot?"

"One of the writers, the white man, Chappell, believed that the contest happened, and the other guy, Guy Johnson—who was black—thought there wasn't enough proof. They interviewed the same people, a year or two apart and got different stories from them. Talcott and Hinton obviously think he existed. My father did."

The white guy believes but the black guy doesn't. He knocks some morsels around on his plate. The eggs aren't that bad but you'd think she'd put out her cigarette while he's eating. Just courtesy. Or maybe she's telling him she didn't want him to sit there. "He was an academic?" J. asks. Was that tense right? She's using the past tense for her father.

"John Henry was just his hobby," she says. "He owned a hardware store. But he started this hobby of collecting whatever he could find about it. Just whatever he could dig up. Memorabilia."

"And what's your take on it? Think he existed?"

"Are you working now? Are you interviewing me?"

"If you want to look at it that way."

"You're not writing any of this down."

"I have a good memory. If you want I can pretend to write it down. Do you have a pen?"

The door chimes. They turn to look at a ponytailed man roll his wheelchair through the front with practiced fluidity. Pamela says, "I'm not a good person to interview. I just came here to get rid of my father's stuff."

"How much did he have—how big is his collection?"

"Boxes and boxes."

"You're not the sentimental sort."

"It's not doing me any good. It's taking up space and I'm paying for it."

Masterstroke here is to change the subject. He's been watching her tear off the scalloped edges of the place mat and fold them into little balls. Doing that when she's not puffing away. Pretty good-looking though, regardless. He'll change the subject here. "Can a man actually beat a steam drill?"

"Am I your main source for this piece?"

"This is all terribly helpful background. You're an expert."

She squints. "The first mechanical drills weren't that well put together. The bits wore out quickly, they kept breaking down. And in rock like this— all these mountains are soft shale—they'd get stuck in all the dust."

"A geologist and a historian."

"You have no idea," she says. The left corner of her mouth tilts ambiguously but declines to commit to an interpretable expression. Certainly seems to have some issues, J. thinks. "The drills were so unreliable," Pamela continues, "that a really strong steeldriver probably could beat one of them under the right conditions—comparing the speeds of great steeldrivers and the speed of the first drills. If the contest wasn't too long. It was a timed contest. It's within the realm of physical possibility."

"The power of positive thinking."

"It's all speculation. But no proof he didn't do it."

"Or that he did."

"Not sure if you want to say that too loud around here, if you know what I mean."

J. looks over her shoulder seeking rabblerousers and rednecks, someone to make him feel ill at ease, discovers mere men in plaid shirts sawing at chicken fried. When he returns to her face, Pamela is smiling; she says, "I don't think you have to worry about anything. Those two professors—Chappell and Johnson—tried to find the employment records for the C&O in this region but they were told they'd been burned in a fire. A lot of men died here and the railroad didn't want the bad publicity. It was a company town so the newspapers didn't keep a record of the accidents—they might have been lost in a fire or burned up on purpose—there were a lot of reasons why they wouldn't have kept records. And if they did keep track of their black workers, well, John and Henry were the most common names for freed slaves, so if there was a record of him, it wouldn't mean that he was *the* John Henry."

"John Henry is Bob Smith."

"John Doe."

She had released her hair from the bun she had last night and the light through the windows livens the ends of the strands to a glowing copper. Her father had a John Henry fixation. Some sixties guy catching that nationalist fever, getting radicalized by Frantz Fanon, save up for a dashiki, revolutionary consciousness. Latches on to the steeldriver as an ideal of black masculinity in a castrating country. Issues, daddy issues. The last event for John Henry Days is tomorrow afternoon, so that leaves a day and a half to make any possible move. Knock on the door of her room: I saw the light on. (Hide that smirk, she's sitting right across from you.) But she also lives in New York, so maybe he could just lay the groundwork over the next day. He has a legit excuse, he's working on a story. And then what in New York. Is she just depressed over her father's death—no telling how long ago he died—or depressed in general. Every waking day, a history of it, John Henry. Definitely issues of some sort, inevitably they bleed over into the bedroom. She's good-looking and all that but he didn't have time for another New York City nutjob. Is he even her type? He doesn't have time for a relationship anyway, beyond his and Monica's arrangement. I'm no prize, I'm going for the record.

(It takes him about five seconds to concoct this narrative.)

She's a thin broth but let's say there's a story here, J. says to himself. She has a strange manner and is currently surrounded by rolled-up bits of paper and is disappearing behind a blue haze but let's say there's a story here. He starts thinking up follow-up questions he can ask her later.

There is a peaceful listlessness in the way the towncar glides through these valleys that makes Lucien think this is the way things were meant to be all along. That in the shrinking dregs of the Ice Age glaciers retreated and scraped through mountains in order to facilitate these modern highways; the final and supreme use of accumulated eons of pulverized stone is gravel for highway shoulders; the succession of rivers they pass merely affirms their progress like milestones, and the water cycle is just a little something on the side. He has come to believe that the intent of geological dynamism is modern convenience. Everything, in fact, all these ancient mechanisms. Somehow four fingers becomes the most practical arrangement, the opposable thumb and that whole mess, and on this day the driver steers the luxury automobile across tempered asphalt with accomplished digits. Is there a liquid that makes the air conditioner work, the way there is Freon in refrigerators? This substance biding its time through humdrum epochs for its ultimate deployment against Southern humidity, the prevention of perspiration stains on Lucien's suit. The inexorable tending towardness of all things.

Heady thoughts of a p.r. flack on a Saturday morning.

Lawrence Flittings, his right-hand man, dependable lieutenant, sits to his left and answers Lucien's questions with care. Lucien gazes at the passing hills and inquires about the preparations without listening to Lawrence's rehearsed answers. He knows Lawrence has taken care of every grubby detail but understands that the man needs to prove his efficiency, and hence this game. Lawrence is as close as Lucien has ever come to having an efficient gay assistant without having a bona fide efficient gay assistant. Lucien asks, How is the hotel, how was the dinner last night, which junketeers have made the trip?

What Lucien really wants to know is if Lawrence can name those trees. Crawling along the mountainside, all the way up to the cracked peaks, the trees march unperturbed by the incline, stand up straight despite the insinuations of gravity. They must have strong roots, all intertwined underground.

They work together to keep from rolling down the slope, to provide for Lucien's delectation a calming introduction to the natural beauty of West Virginia. The hotel is small but comfortable, Lawrence says, the dinner last night was enjoyed by all, the usual suspects from the media pool are in attendance, and now Lucien lobs a poser: Do you know the names of those trees, Lawrence?

There is nothing in his laptop or in his post-it festooned clipboard to aid him. Lawrence says swiftly, "I don't know," and Lucien nods, looking out the window all the while. If the driver can help them out with a little native lore, he does not say. Lucien has to keep Lawrence on his toes. He looks into the future: Next time they have an out-of-town event, Lawrence will research all the local flora and fauna, just in case. But Lucien will not ask the next time. Lawrence will wait for the question but it will not come, then he'll try to slip his new knowledge into the conversation somehow. Listen to that red-breasted robin, Lucien, it's their mating season and that is their mating call.

These trees do not dissemble. They are true to their natures, like Lucien. Lawrence his first day on the job probably imagined he was coming to work for a Mike Ovitz, or a fashioner of summer blockbusters. A postmodern Barnum in a slimming Italian suit. All who meet Lucien expect such, such is his reputation, misearned. Certainly he surprised Lawrence immediately, in those first few days (he must have) with his humility and soft, careful speech. Oh, he thunders now and again, but only at those who understand thunder and will listen to nothing else. Certainly he surprised Lawrence with his sincerity over time. (Ticking off here his favorite attributes.) Lucien is not, as many believe him to be, fake. Such a label implies premeditation, that the inner man does not match the outer man and fakery is involved. But he is no counterfeiter. From time to time, after the lights have been turned out and the surly emanations of the streetlights fill his bedroom or in odd moments at well-attended events when he is in between greetings and small talk and alone in a crowd before he has decided on his next strategic interaction, Lucien will find himself lost in his landscape. How he stumbled there is not important, which sign he misinterpreted that led him into this introspective cul-de-sac, what is important is that he is face to face with his character and must account for what he has become, and in those moments he will not flinch. He can describe the man he sees with merciless acuity, recognize the hunched and shriveled creature before him and there, it happens, he extends his arms without reluctance or disgust to embrace his true self. And there is no disagreement between Lucien at that moment of sudden confrontation and Lucien at this very moment, on the job, timecard perforated, en route to his latest assignment. No false front, he does not dissemble, he is exactly as he appears to be.

The miles retreat. Lawrence says it's not that much farther, and Lucien thinks, all these trees are for me. To delight his eye. He wonders if the natural drift of his thoughts makes him a narcissist, but then reassures himself that he is only substituting the concept of Lucien for the larger family of man. For simplicity's sake. He's thinking about all humanity, not just himself. That business about the jungle shaping four fingers and a thumb and thus their smooth ride this morning: all three of them, Lucien, Lawrence and the driver, enjoy the monkey's good fortune. And everyone on the road ahead and behind him, on all the roads leading to and shunting off this highway. Lucien's I is a democratic beast, many-headed, fork-tongued. Neolithic toolmakers shaped arrowheads, these skills developed over time and now the chrome doorhandle of this vehicle is shaped just so. The magnitude of chrome doorhandles disproves his narcissism once and for all. There are millions and millions of chrome doorhandles in use around the globe, turned by peasant and king alike, facilitated by perfected manufacturing process, millions, allowing swift and easy egress from vehicles, nooked betwixt palm and metacarpals. He is not alone in receipt of the neolithic toolmakers' gifts. Heck, people are opening doors everywhere.

The miles retreat and Lawrence says again, it is not much farther. Soon they will be in Talcott. Lucien has a patchwork idea of the town stitched by pop culture. He has borrowed elements of that idea on more than one occasion, to underscore the home-style virtues of a new home-style lemonade or to reconfigure a dull-witted celebrity's platitudes into a front-porch wisdom that journalists will pick up on and in turn deliver to the people. To present things just so. Folks pick up on these flourishes very quickly. When he first started in this business and was coming to understand his facility for making people believe things and was much taken with the language of his therapist, Lucien thought he was tapping into the collective unconscious. But now he thinks it's simply the atmosphere. That air is an admixture of nitrogen, oxygen, trace gases, and one of these trace gases is American cliché and we breathe it in with our first breath. Peering past miles they have yet to travel, Lucien pictures Talcott and sees the tall spire of the town church, a crowd of parishioners glad-handing with the pastor on Sunday morning, a blond child in a bright striped shirt waving a sparkler on July Fourth and a glass pitcher of lemonade pimpled by condensation. We know that the lemonade is home-made because there are seeds swirling in the bottom of the pitcher and that detail is what makes it true. Talcott is an American small town and contains virtues.

Lucien thinks, maybe the trick about doing a town is making the thing into the idea. He has never done a town before.

Thinks back. He treated Mayor Cliff as he would any other client. He did not talk down to the man just because he was from another neck of the woods and knew nothing about being seated at the best table. No one client is dumber than another; they are all merely clients. Mayor Cliff had just de-parted the matinee of a popular Broadway show and had sunset plans for the observation deck of the Empire State Building. He had rolled the Playbill into a grubby tube and from time to time during the discussion it unfurled and he rolled it anew. The mayor explained that the wife had never been to the Big Apple and this trip was a perfect opportunity to mix business with pleasure. The wife was out shopping, he said as he unzipped his purple track jacket to reveal a joke T-shirt. The joke was lost on Lucien. Something about woodchucks. Lucien did not allow this miscommunication, this symbol of their cultural difference, to alter his prepared remarks although perhaps he was a little sad that Mrs. Cliff had not come along as well, so that afterward the couple could discuss his words, and an hour or two hours from then, Lu-cien would feel his ears burn.

Lucien said to the mayor, "This is my office and that is my guest chair. We have a process we have to do now and I want you to be comfortable. This is what I do in the getting to know the client stage, you have questions and want to be reassured. Your time is valuable so I'll be honest with you: I sell light bulbs. Yes. It generally takes time for the appropriateness of this anal-ogy to settle in so I will ask you, do you know how fragile light bulbs are? It's always the filament that breaks before the glass. You've knocked over lamps, I've knocked over lamps, knocking over lamps is the side racket of every American. They're very fragile. It's the filament. Fil-a-ment. Sounds like a word you'd use to describe a god. 'A thousand lovely filaments falling down her divine shoulders.' Fragile and yet they light up the whole world. These tiny crimps of metal. Hit the switch and a million electrons jump off the fil-ament into darkness and light up the room. These are tiny electrons that are full of energy.

"My point takes a bit to get around to. I go, and what are we? We are energy too. This is Einstein talking here, not me. Just then. Now I'm back. Look at my hand. Yours will do just as well of course, but look at my hand. The knuckles here say that's where the bones meet, so I have bones. The tendons stretch here and so I have muscles beneath my skin. If I pinch my fingertip like this it goes white because I cut off the blood flow. I have capillaries and veins and inside them blood. You understand my point. There are smaller and smaller systems, down to blood cells and the specialized tiny bits inside them and we can go smaller still into atoms. Blood cells and tiny atoms that you and I need to live and that's energy. Split the atom and that's energy. Energy to destroy a city or light it up or power a sun. These are natural processes. The windows of my office are tinted to cut out the UV—too much of that will give you cancer, but the point is that the sun is a giant light bulb. I'm reinforcing my opening gambit. It is a series of atomic explosions, a billion splitting atoms. The light of the sun takes a day or two to reach us, there is universal constant involved, but there it is. The sun is a big ball of splitting atoms that allows life on earth and in my hand I have atoms, I have a sun. We all have suns in our hands, inner light, every object, and all they need are a little something to initiate the reaction. That's why I say I'm in the light bulb business. I'm just trying to let a little something out.

"I handle celebrities. I handle shiny new cars from Europe. These cars have a power in their names, these European imports, because to American ears they sound exotic and so they want them straight out the gate and this makes my job a little easier. They are already leaking light before I ever get my hands on them. Look into my eyes. Then some things come to me dull and I have to get to work. Otherwise they remain dim. The duller something is the duller you feel and that's where the elbow grease comes in. I have handled paperweights and toasters and politicians. Organized events for them that are like setting up mirrors to reflect their inner radiance to best effect. No, I can't name any of my political clients, I have signed nondisclosure agreements and such things are the holy word, but rest assured you have seen the light glinting off the teeth of my political clients and have pulled the lever for them, chum. A company that produces lawn sprinklers once approached me, and now I feel the satisfaction of a job well done when I drive through upstate suburbs to visit friends or clients and see rainbows caught in the spray of sprinklers I have helped out. This is missionary work. I've helped TV pilots get along. Some are still in syndication as we speak. I have never done a hubcap, but I hope with all my heart that one day I will. I've had my eye on a few and now it's a matter of contacting the manufacturers. Pro bono. It sounds ridiculous but love is often ridiculous to those on the outside. Take the elevator down to the street and wait five minutes for a ridiculous couple to walk by, what are they wearing, something ridiculous, mismatched socks, you might have a little chuckle but you will envy with all your heart the inarguable adoration in their smiles. I am coming around to my point: I have never done a town before, sir, and I would love to. To give the world your light.

"What I want to do is establish the brand superiority of Talcott for all things Talcott-related. The name of your town, Talcott, Tallll-cott, it rolls off the tongue and that's half the battle. The sound of things is half my job. Egon. 'A coffee table is not a coffee table unless it is an Egon coffee table.' How many times have you heard this phrase? Sounds so good and right you might think it's Solomon that said it, it's something from the Bible and handed down. I didn't make it up, wish I had, but this is not an advertising agency I run here, those offices and cubicles you passed out there are not the offices and cubicles of an advertising agency, but I helped to get out the truth of Egon coffee tables to the people and now you know this simple truth about coffee tables as well as you know your wife's maiden name. Her maiden name is what she was before. Now she is something else. Do you ever think about that? I'm talking about the lines that divide you from one stage to another. The natural image is the cocoon. Light bulbs, cocoons, I'm coming back to light bulbs, don't fret. What I'm really talking about is the exact moment between the cocoon and the butterfly, the moment of change, the exact instant when the potential is released into light because that is what we are discussing at the moment. This is where we are now with your town. Would you like some water?

"A coffee table is not a coffee table . . . I didn't make that up. I'm not that clever. But I did my humble effort to urge Egon coffee tables into deserving living rooms across the country. They are stark and scratchproof and fit easily into any preexisting design motif or lack thereof, they do not stick out, are unobtrusive, but they have their own subtle radiance. They shine in their own right. I don't know you. I can't describe your life, but I know the world. The world is full of undiscovered treasures waiting to reveal their true light. Are you a kind man? Are you a forgiving man? I don't know, I've just met you, sir. I have picked up on a few things. You cross your legs and uncross your legs and you have that thing you do with your chin. I have learned that you are an attentive listener, but if I said I knew you I would be lying so I'm not going to insult you by saying that I do. But I know the world, and it is full of light.

Here and there, it leaks out, and this is where I come in. Lumens and lumens. Talcott is full of light. It is a silent star. It is a superheated solar furnace that is dark and waiting to become light. You have plans and ideas. I will give them to the world. All I ever do is release radiance. This is light bulbs, sir, and this is why I say I am in the light bulb business. This is light bulbs."

It's like living in a bum's tin cup; one thing rattles and they all rattle together. Right now he hears everything except the words he strains to remember, all his neighbors' livid faces horde around him, but he cannot make out the shrouded face he seeks back there in the snow when he shivered with a broken face. Stick a baboon in front of a piano and that's what this building sounds like at all hours. Before Mickey it was the Mailers arguing, and their cheap things falling on firetrap floors as he knocked her around. The fight lasted an hour and he didn't get a single word down all the while. Tomorrow what blood she cannot remove from her housedress will be seen on the wash line outside, pinned to those looping linen grins across the facade of every tenement, one every story, dangling ropes bearing dun-tending sheets, underwear, pajamas. Love and hate and gossip hung out there. Fistfights and puberty. If the damned yelping doesn't tell you, all you have to do is look for baby clothes on the wash lines to see who just delivered. The familiar clothes of the dead disappear suddenly. The Mailers' fight finally stops and then it's Mickey, because it is Saturday night, crashing wide the front door and making his rot-gut stumble up the stairwell, finally thrown out of the last basement dive of the night and mistaking every door for his. He lives on the top floor, so floor after floor of mistakes. When he tries his keys in their locks, one by one they say, move along, Mickey, and he fumbles along to the next apartment. Jake thinks "Move along, Mickey" might make a good saloon song; he'll try after he gets the John Henry ballad out of him and on paper. When Mickey finally gets inside his place, it's a gang of drunks yelping down Essex, then a baby, or a gang of babies, or those wretches who live in the basement. If all other distractions cease, there are always the rheumy bitches in the basement, who cough up things from their lungs at remarkable volume, things that must be chairs or wardrobes from the sound of it. He has never seen them, only heard the heavy basement door scrape behind their scurrying, so he is left to imagine what they look like from their harrowing coughing fits. Ruth says they're gypsies. Everything's cramped. In the heaving tenement, in their two rooms, Jake looks down at his music-paper, hands stoppers at his ears, pressing hard until all he hears is his own heart bass-drum in his skull. But he can't remember the words. A song is just words on paper until it is sung, that's what they say at the office, but he can't even get that far. Every minute he spends struggling against the disharmony of his world is money out of pocket; in his line Saturday is the biggest night. The dance halls and beer joints and vaudeville houses are overflowing at this hour, this is the time he waits for all week. After a year of Saturday nights his blood naturally jumps at this hour, and he thinks of all the people spilling in and out of establishments, fumbling through gaudy signs for the key into this evening. But Mr. Yellen is off to the Philadelphia office on Monday morning and if Jake doesn't get the manuscript to him before his departure, he has to wait another week. That won't do. Uptown at Cunningham's Rosie Clifford is beginning the first set of her week-long engagement, and he should be there plugging. Buying beer for Handsome Boy Morton and his band, seeding the gallery with chorus slips. Instead Slim is probably there in his place, plugging the latest song from Ames Bros., probably a drinking song, knowing them, another attempt at the next "Down Where the Wurzburger Flows." They can try as much as they want but Ames Bros. hasn't had the stuff since Dolzier and Finch moved over to Patriot, and everybody knows it. Songs like that don't just happen, million-sellers. Yes, Jake should be there tonight, plugging for old man Yellen, going song for song with his rivals, but he's here, with still-born sheet-music on his lap and lyrics that have picked up stakes, nowhere to be found. Now it sounds like somebody's getting killed out there. The coppers playing dice when they should be out protecting the citizens. It would be quieter at the office on Twenty-eighth, but some of the real contract men, as opposed to aspiring tune-smiths like Jake, might be there, filling up the warren of little rooms with cigar smoke, and they'll crack wise with him. What are you doing at that piano, song-plugger? Particularly if they're playing whist and tipping elbows. He'll take a lot of ribbing. He's just an errand boy to them, even after a year. They are the artists and he might as well be one of the Negroes who drop off the boxes of sheet music at the novelty stores. As if their scribbled songs sell themselves. As if with dozens of music publishers hustling every day and night at the same joints, trying to get the attention of the same talent, trying to get the ear of the public, their songs just sell themselves. Most of them are hacks anyway, rhyming *sandwiches* with *languages* and *Doherty* with *majority*, the dumbest stuff, trying to copy whatever song made it big last week. If this week it's tot songs, those hacks are thinking about Little Sally and her red balloon, temperance songs this week if that's what the papers are talking about, beer-drinking songs the next week. Stealing whole-sale the melody of the latest saloon favorite, trading Molly for Dolly, but they'll stuff newspaper into their pianos to stifle the sound because they think their fellow songsters in the next rooms are going to steal from them. A gang of thieves. One step above rag-pickers, the way they root around looking for some scrap to sell. They have the gall to look down on him. Least with this John Henry song, if he can remember it, he's trying to do something unex-pected, bring back a ballad after all this hopped-up ragtime stuff everybody's doing today. The two-step is big so they got to make up songs to two-step to. It's a merry-go-round. He looks at the upright in the corner. Maybe if he could play around on its yellowed keys, the night he heard the John Henry song would come back. But he can't touch it if Victoria is in the house, he's learned that. His baby sleeps through every aggravation the street and tene-ment assails her with, but let Jake play one note on the upright and open go her eyes and wide goes her mouth and out comes the wailing. Even if he sticks newspaper on the strings to muffle like they do at the office and plays as softly as possible, she's crying. Cacophony upon cacophony in this ram-shackle, and his baby girl can't bear a note of actual music. It could be a million-seller, it could be what everyone in every saloon needs if only they heard it once, and his baby will scream like a banshee. Smart thing to do would be to sell the damned thing anyway. Big Danny ain't coming back. Back when the police closed down McGinty's, on account Man McGinty wasn't giving the syndicate their proper take of the back room stuss game, Big Danny broke into the saloon the next day in broad daylight and rolled the rickety upright straight out the front door. For wages earned and owed—Big Danny had been knocking the keys for four months and only got paid for two. He stayed on for the free liquor, but it gets to a point. Once he got the piano out on the sidewalk, he had nowhere to put it, because the house rules at the flop he called home said that every one of his possessions was to be stolen the minute he left the premises, and he was tired of combing the shelves of the corner pawn to buy back his pilfered stuff. So he called up from the street, Jake looked down into the Essex hustle, and a few hours later Jake was explaining to Ruth why this beaten-up piano was taking up precious space in their tiny two rooms. Victoria wasn't born yet, but once she arrived they'd need all the space they could get, and that hunk of junk was out of tune and out of place. Smart thing to do would be to sell it. He saw Big Danny one more time after he brought the piano over. Looked like he'd been dragged out of the Hudson. Big Danny said, I've placed songs with every top-notcher at Tony Pastor's and now look at me. Jake gave him some bills. McGinty might have been tight with the cash, but no one else was going to hire Big Danny, no legit place, not with those opium eyes of his. Word was Big Danny had disappeared into a Pell Street hop den, disappeared down with the Orientals, and that was months ago. Best to sell it and buy things for Victoria, pay off the doctor. Makes him feel awful bad to think about Big Danny like that, Big Danny's the one who broke him in after Old Man Yellen recruited him. "You got the lungs," Yellen told Jake the day he picked him out of the choir, "you got working papers?" He had working papers, he had a valise full of neckties. Jake's first job had been selling neckties for a friend of his father, but after Yellen came that day, he hadn't set foot in his father's friend's necktie shop since, or his father's synagogue now that he thinks about it. Getting a chance to sing was the only reason he went there anyway at that point. Guy walks in says he can get paid to sing, what does he need to go back to synagogue for? Singing for free. Jake was entering into a long-standing Tin Pan Alley tradition, he later discovered. All the publishers come down and canvass the Lower East Side synagogues in search of strong pipes to steal from the choirs. You need a new plugger, you come downtown. Jake noticed Yellen's suit right off, it wasn't none of that cheap Orchard Street stuff; see a guy in a nice suit like that and no way he was going to go for one of Jake's cheap neckties, it was a skill he had learned from doors shut in his face. The guy had made something of himself. Of course one of those doors not shut in his face revealed Ruth (who said her father was not home but of course he saw her father plenty once Jake started courting her) so he has to thank the job for that at least. "Can you read music?" Yellen asked him when they stepped outside. Yes, he could read music, was he a blind man? It was also the last time he wore his threadbare Sabbath suit, too; first thing he got paid, one of the contract composers tipped him to a tailor on Thirty-fourth Street where all the guys went. Sure Jake could read music. He got the job and that night was his introduction to New York City at night. Big Danny his guide inside. They met up in front of the Alhambra, at eight o'clock as Yellen instructed. Jake was early, watched the couples swagger arm in arm through the beautiful doors to be devoured by globed light. The night was young and the couples made their way up to Fourteenth Street seeking any available mischief, a promising joint, the men in tilted brown derbies and tight checked suits, the women in pinching corsets that unclenched into long dresses, faces painted to coquettish blush beneath hats plucked completely except for one long feather. He had never been inside the famous Alhambra, or any of the other places on that bustling row. A gorilla tapped his shoulder and introduced himself—Big Danny. Big Danny said he'd been playing a game of spot the rube, and look it, he'd won. He was still big then, could have been mistaken for a strong-arm man, and talk about lungs. He was a boomer, no fooling, and when he started in on the plug, he got the song heard above all the saloon racket. Could be a full orchestra playing a march and you'd still hear Danny. Big Danny, Jake's guide for the night, showed him the ropes and only talked down to him occasionally, when he asked a stupid question or spent one moment too many wide-eyed at one of the chorus girls. (They kicked so high.) Big Danny said, Staff notes into bank notes, that's the word, and we're the men who get the songs out there. You got to know what kind of place you're working. If it's a dance hall, and you got couples trying to have a good time, you plug the rag, something that will get them all two-stepping. If you know the bandleader and your firm has a reputation, maybe all you got to do is buy him a drink and he'll play the song next thing. Maybe you got to buy drinks for the whole band, so remember what everybody drinks, do they got a taste for beer or do they got a taste for whiskey. Dance hall, it's a rag so it's an instrumental and you don't have to pay stooges to sing the chorus, just clap your hands in time to get them dancing. But a saloon, once you get the song in the hands of the bandleader or the singer, you got to get the chorus slips out there into people's hands, lay some coin on a beer-bummer so they'll join the refrain. Once again you got to remember if they want money or drinks. Some of these rummies'll do it for a shot. Once the band gets to the refrain, that's when you start booming. You start singing loud. Louder than the singer if you have to but you got to get the crowd on your side. The people you gave the slips to, they're joining in, too. What do you think the rest of the crowd's going to do? Join in and remember. Could be the first time the song's been played in public, just got back from the printer's that morning, but they see you and a bunch of stooges singing it and they think it's already a hit. Everybody knows the song but them. You have to believe that too—that the song is a hit. It might be "Lost Little Child" with a couple of words changed, or maybe one of the boys slowed it down, or maybe it's the tenth coon song you tried to plug that day. But you gotta believe it's a hit or else they're never gonna believe it. That's what's going to get them into the music stores and five-and-dimes looking to buy the sheet music. This is the way we do it now. Got million-sellers all the time now, and this is how they start, with us, boy. We plug 'em, we get 'em in the hands of the right people to play 'em, and people buy 'em. He blew out a tart cloud of cigar smoke. Jake was dizzy, felt he'd been on the dance floor ten numbers in a row. He figured if he could sell neckties he could sell songs. Big Danny nodded to the bouncer and they went inside. Jacob watched and played stooge. At the Alhambra, Big Danny waited for the tearjerker to end (it was the summer's hit, "No Flowers for Amelia," with the melody reworked and an extra chorus, another Whitman Bros. hackjob) and approached the bandleader with professional copies of Yellen's latest drinking song, and ten minutes later Big Danny was singing the refrain, with Jacob backing him up from the other side of the room, winking, reading words from the chorus slip. At Cunningham's half an hour later, Big Danny took the headliner in a bear hug between her sets—she looked like a limp daisy grabbed by a gorilla (they went way back together he said later)—and she sang the song first thing when she got back onstage, a rags-to-riches yarn with an easy chorus that the crowd would have picked up on even if Big Danny and Jake hadn't been booming it out. But they were booming and Jake couldn't stop laughing. It was a new kind of singing; he felt like a newspaper boy hawking a gory headline, or one of those chest cases holding sandwich boards for the latest remedy that he couldn't afford. At the Arabian Nights Jake got swept up in the final chorus and bumped into a Bowery boy and got a face full of stale beer and peanut shells. Lucky that's all he got. They got thrown out of Leary's, the first but not that last time Jake would be tossed out like a slop bucket by management for no good reason. At Bob Preston's Variety, Big Danny bought the entire band beer, and they cheated him, tucking the professional copies (stark, no frills, without the fetching cover art that attracted the civilians, back sides bereft of the usual cheap advertisements for nerve tonic and rocking horses) underneath the music of their scheduled set and never got around to Yellen's song. Big Danny bunched the chorus slips into balls and threw them around the room as the people danced to competitors' songs. It happens. They're at the mercy of the musicians. Place after place, from saloon to burlesque house and back again, bribing and cajoling, failing or not, they moved the music in the modern way, the little guys in the new industry. The next morning Jacob had become Jake, pruned his surname too, to a simple Rose. His parents didn't cotton to that, no sir, but this is America, this is the twentieth century. A guy's got to get ahead. His father still gives him grief about it, but Jake gives grief back when he catches his father crouching over his kid, speaking that dead language to Victoria even though he's told the man he doesn't want him speaking that around her. Old man's hovering over his baby girl like an old world ghost. This is the twentieth century and there's his gloomy father trying to import a Lithuanian village into Jake's two tiny rooms. Victoria's a classy name, a royal name, and royalty doesn't need any peasant stuff dragging her back. His father makes a vague old world grunt whenever Jake says this is the twentieth century, and the sound isn't musical at all. To heck with it all, Jake hasn't the time. Barely enough time for the sun, some days. He started sleeping past noon once the rhythm came in. He learned the flow of the New York City evening, which joints hit their peak at what time, distinguished the drinking joints from the dancing joints, memorized the bouncers' names and the tactics of competing pluggers. He made the rounds, wore down shoes that his cousin resoled for free if Jake told him stories about bawdy houses and what went on inside them. He got the songs out there in a good percentage. He'd pick up the new batch from the office on Twenty-eighth Street every night and hear the contract men in their cubicles attempting alchemy on their battered pianos and thought to himself, they shouldn't call it Tin Pan Alley because all their racket sounds like tin pans clanging together, but because more often than not what they conjure up is just tin and not the gold of a bona fide hit. It didn't take him long to figure out that if you became a contract man, a composer or a lyricist, you got a decent salary plus royalties. Knock out a few popular songs and you're set up on Easy Street. He looks at those drunks at the office banging away at their plagiarized ditties and thinks, half these guys started out pluggers like him and they got nothing on him. But he's the littlest cog in the machine. The women work in the daytime, demonstrating numbers in music shops and department stores, and the men work at night, plugging the dance halls. The songwriters knock them out, then above them the hit-makers spend their royalties. And above them the publisher got the best of it. The walls of Yellen's office are crammed with framed copies of hits and above the names of the songwriters is his name, bigger than everything. Big Danny, before he got on the hop, before he got fired, said the minute he figures out the system it changes, a guy can hardly keep up. Some places got music machines, player pianos that play songs that are already set, and there's no use for a plugger when they got a machine to do it. No need for a musician that breathes and bleeds when you got a machine to do it. Some places now got kinetoscopes showing motion pictures of what the lyrics say, so you don't have to imagine what a song's about, it's up there on the wall in a picture. First it was slide shows and now it's kinetoscopes. From where we are, out there hoofing it from place to place, we can't see the whole thing. You ask Yellen about the distribution and he'll tell you about how this new printer can cut up thousands of copies a day, and how long it takes for the train to get it from here to Chicago and Philadelphia, and how much he makes off the ads on the back, and how when Harper's prints a song, how many of their readers will buy it the next week. We're just two guys, Jake. They got more than twenty music publishers on the Alley alone, and that's not including the big guys like Von Tilzer moving uptown. We're just two pluggers and they got a whole system over us. Jake said, this is the twentieth century. Big Danny said, no fooling. Now outside some man is beating his horse. How is a man supposed to get ahead with all this noise. He doesn't know how Ruth and Victoria can sleep through this night after night. They slept through him being beaten, it was only two blocks away. He rubs his bent nose and drags a finger across the groove in his cheek. With his bashed-up face he looks like any Bowery brawler. No longer the choirboy. This is what the street has done to him. What gang they were from there was no way of telling, but they beat him good, came out from beneath one of the El struts and knocked him down with a brick. It was the first heavy snow of winter and he cut his plugging short because no one was out, but short meant it was still late. With his face pushed down into the piled snow he could still smell the horse manure beneath it. They cut his pockets straight out of his trousers and grabbed his meager bills. Sent that night's songs soaring on a gust. But maybe his wife and child didn't hear him because the snow swallowed all his screams. They left him in the snow, with a different face, a different nose and exploded cheeks that now testify to violence before uninterested juries of passersby, and only the people who knew him before say his kid looks just like him. This city is a crime. He pulled himself from the snow and leaned against the El, on one of the odd bluffs the wind made because it didn't know what to make of elevated trains, he rested on halfhearted dunes and cutoff cliffs of snow. The mayor gets himself elected on a reform platform and still the gangs own the streets and the coppers turn a blind eye. Stephen Foster got paid ten dollars for "Oh! Susanna" and made millions for his publisher and died broke of drink at a Bowery flophouse just over there. He tried to lift himself up. You can fall into the city and no one will ever find you. When the snow melts they will find his body and a bunch of frozen drunks no one missed. He scraped frozen blood from his eyes and peered into the snow. He felt like he was at the bottom of an hourglass, it was coming down so hard. The man came up the street singing. Jake never saw his face. He had to have seen Jake, or at least the dark wings of blood around him. But he didn't stop. No one cares about their fellow man. He walked by singing that John Henry song, coming up the street right in between the tracks above. It was only when Jake finally marshaled himself out of the blizzard and Ruth had cleaned his face and he was falling into bed like it was a chute that he was able to think, that was a pretty good song. To a guy like him, you hear a melody like that and think it will be a tough plug. It doesn't have the syncopated push of a rag, the rollicking swagger of a saloon song. It does not describe the orphan girl's escape from the sinful life when the millionaire falls in love with her and then they take tea with Carnegie. But it has a power. The song of the horse getting beat reminds him of him getting beat, and some of the lyrics start coming back. He's got to get them down on paper before they go away again, even if they were pounded into him that night. He touches his scar, and remembers how he hauled himself up from out of the snow. *John Henry went home to his good little woman, Said, Polly Ann, fix my bed, I want to lay down and get some rest, I've an awful roaring in my head, Lord, Lord, I've an awful roaring in my head.* Ruth's tiny hands wrung the rag into the basin and turned the clean water pink. What the man was doing out in that kind of weather, who knows. Why he was singing that particular song, who knows. Walking into the wind, beneath the elevated, maybe it was the tracks that made him think of the song. Jake looked it up and no one had published a version of the ballad. Asked one of the contract men about it, the guy said, yeah I know that old song, what do you care about that slow stuff for? Jake thought with everybody chasing after the latest fashion, a ballad was going to sneak through. Yellen has coon songs coming out of his ears, and there is no way Jake is going to be the millionth guy to rhyme *mother* with *love her*, no matter how misty-eyed it makes the room. Him and Ruth and the kid moved into these two rooms and it was better than living with the airshaft blowing God knows what sickness into Victoria's lungs. With all the garbage they throw down there it's no wonder the gypsies in the basement are sick, but that isn't going to happen to his little girl. Now they have a front room and their bedroom looks out on the street and when it gets warmer they can sit on the fire escape. They got air now, but it costs money. This John Henry isn't going to be a million-seller, but it'll show the old man he has initiative. A fellow's got to start somewhere. This is the twentieth century and you got to make your own luck.

Sneaky Petes, both of them, aware of being in plain sight, sans excuses, without a hall pass, up the stairs from One Eye's room, on tiptoe past the mastications of the ice machine and in front of room 29 of the Talcott Motor Lodge.

                                    J.

This is stupid.

                              ONE EYE
*(squinting with socket and eye alike, over a loop of keys)*
You're fucking up my movie.

                                    J.

We didn't synchronize our watches.

                              ONE EYE
*(two keys down in failure and on to the next)*
I got enough time for both of us. Time it takes them to get back and
forth from Charleston we still have plenty of time. Man!

                                    J.

*(looking over his shoulder)*
I thought you said you could open it.

                              ONE EYE
*(with John Henry-like hubris)*
I can open any lock made of man. With what I got here. Just be glad
they don't have those electric card things here yet.

                                    J.

Who'd you write the piece for?

ONE EYE

*Locksmith Today.* I met the editor at a conference. We were—fuck—
digging at this lobster salad they had laid out. He said he'd throw
some work my way, then a month later he calls me and says the oldest practicing locksmith in the world is retiring and they want an
interview. The IRS was on me for some delinquencies, I don't even
know how I got back on the grid in the first place, how they tracked
me down I still don't know, so I needed the money. Went out to
Jersey and talked to the guy. Man!

J.

*(in halfhearted sarcasm halfheartedly delivered)*
Have all day apparently.

ONE EYE

I'm getting it. He was liquidating his shop, we were drinking and he
gives me a set of his master keys. Said he had a one-eyed friend in
the army, back in dubya dubya two.

J.

The big one. Wait—there's a car coming.

ONE EYE

Who is it?

J.

*(recognizing the logo of a leading package-delivery service)*
Just Federal Express. Strangely, I don't know, I've changed my mind
about this mission for some reason.

ONE EYE

*(pushing against the palace gate in the manner of Hercules)*
Here it is.

J.

*(stepping into the den of Ali Baba)*
Close it.

ONE EYE

*(remarking, not for the last time, on the repetitive nature of existence and
the disquieting universality of modern human experience)*
I think this room is exactly identical to mine.

J.

*(a grammarian)*
That's redundant. If it's identical it's exactly.

ONE EYE

*(very like a sailor)*
Will you just shut the f—

J.

*(with a practical air)*
I don't see it. What if he took it with him?

ONE EYE

*(not too proud)*
Didn't think of that. How do you like that?

J.

*(pensively, index finger tapping chin)*
Knowing Lawrence, you're in a cheap motel in the middle of
nowhere, and you have this computer, so—

ONE EYE

*(recalling adolescent pornography-concealment procedures)*
It's under the bed.

J.

*(ditto)*
It's probably under the bed.

ONE EYE

*(brandishing)*
Okay.

J.

Don't look at me, I'm a Mac guy.

ONE EYE

*(even as human endeavor is simplified by the advances of technology, some
dilemmas yet await the intrepid inventor)*
That's not the problem. Gotta wait.

J.

*(still capable of colorful imagery despite the rigors of prodigious journalistic output)*
See how long it takes to boot up? They got like hamsters running around in there to power the thing.

ONE EYE

*(lobbyist for the free enterprise system)*
Spare me. All you artistic types and your precious Macintoshes. You gotta face reality. Even I can see that and I only got—

J.

Yeah, yeah, you only got one eye. We're still waiting though.

ONE EYE

*(with the casual aplomb of a jack of all trades)*
Okay. Just gotta find the file. C drive . . .

J.

*(examining)*
What's all these jars?

ONE EYE

What's all this—Hey, looks like Lawrence is working on a book.

J.

*(in a flash of horror over years wasted, all that lost time)*
Yeah?

ONE EYE

I think it's a memoir. Here: "I was a sickly child . . ."

J.

*(as if lost in wonder among the capacious aisles of a glamorous new pharmacy)*
Got tons of hair gel here.

ONE EYE

*(drawn once again to the disquieting universality of modern human experience)*
"Oftentimes I would go to the window and watch some of the

neighborhood boys engaged in the activities typical to that stage of childhood. Oh! How I would long to join in their games."

J.

He's got some serious NASA-type black ops hair gel here.

ONE EYE

*(contemplating class differences)*
Here's something about an erotic attachment to his governess.

J.

Will you just find the file?

ONE EYE

No, yeah. You be the lookout.
*(charitably)*
Still, it's not that bad if you like that sort of thing. Hmm. Okay here are his work files. Organized little fucker.

J.

Well.

ONE EYE

I'm sure it's in here. Just have to find the file name . . .

J.

*(looking between curtain and frame)*
Try Bottom Feeders, Moochers . . .

ONE EYE

Looking through this stuff . . .

J.

*(as Linnaeus might)*
Barnacles, Pilot Fish, Leeches . . .

ONE EYE

Try this . . .

J.

*(what is there about looking outward through a window that engenders in susceptible natures the contemplation of inward mysteries)*

Layabouts . . . You know I felt so good this morning when I woke up this morning. It was revelation. Almost. Just woke up—

ONE EYE
*(with help from the trade winds, discovering the route to the Indies)*
This is it! We're all here, look at it. All of us—Hey, me and Dave have the same middle name—

J.
*(a skeptic)*
Let me see.

ONE EYE
*(for the benefit of the audience)*
Watch the window, man. Says it was last updated yesterday. Man, they got everybody in here. I didn't know Abe was one of us, I mean yeah he's always around but I thought he was just tagging along. He's totally undercover. This is crazy. What kind of diabolical . . .

J.
*(alas)*
Shit! It's them!

ONE EYE
*(allaying)*
What are they doing? Are they coming up here or are they checking Lucien in?

J.
*(unallayed)*
They're . . . Man, they're splitting up. Lawrence is coming up here. Can't get out now, you damn idiot.

ONE EYE
*(forgoing an exclamation of Eureka)*
We'll hide.

J.
Lock the door!

ONE EYE
*(with an ontological aside)*
Was the door locked when we came in?

J.
I don't know. You're the one that opened it.

ONE EYE
*(and yet a return to the womb impossible at this juncture)*
Put everything back the way it was.

J.
*(with a keen eye for symmetry)*
I think that was little more to the left.

ONE EYE
You do it then, I wasn't even the one that touched it.

J.
Go out the bathroom window.

ONE EYE
*(on the nature of a paint-gummed window crank)*
It's one of those things that only open like two inches.

J.
'sus Christ. I'm not gonna hide in there, you crazy?

ONE EYE
*(stepping into the tub)*
Pull the curtain back, pull it back.

J.
Shh! Move over, I can't— What if—

ONE EYE
Probably takes like five showers a day . . .

J.
Shut up, he's at the door.
*(sotto voce, to himself, glum tones)*
And I felt so good when I got up this morning.

E xcerpts from *Hamm's Stamp Gossip*, "The Year in Review."

Lick 'em if you got 'em, folks! It's that time of year again when **Good Old Hamm the Stamp Man** looks back on the last twelve months, takes out the tongs and says, was 1996 Fine or Very Fine? Well, the experts all agree—1996 was darn Near Mint! I don't know about you, my philatelic friends, but I'm still trying to catch my breath over the totally fab new record set when the **Sweden Three Skilling color error** went up for auction. Can anyone say 2.2 million dollars? That's the kind of moolah that says, this ain't no **self-adhesive duck stamp** you're talking about here. It was the proverbial "shot heard around the world" of stamp collecting! Certainly the high mark (or should I say watermark?) in a year when many rare stamps traded hands at record prices. Hey, anyone out there have 2.2 million they can lend me? I'm good for it!

Frolicking Philately! Did the **USPS** go crazy this year or what? What's **Marvin Runyon** smoking over there—old **cut squares**? Just kidding, Marv! But he sure has kept us all busy—this year the post office issued 89 **commemorative stamps**, 22 **definitives**, 13 **special stamps** and 1 **Priority Mail** issue. How's a guy supposed to keep up with that? The most popular issue turned out to be (drum roll, please!) the **James Dean** commemorative. This will be no surprise to the lovely ladies of stampdom, who have been cooing over this particular issue since the day it was first announced (you know who you are!). Just another example of the genius behind the Postal Service's new "open" selection process. Guess James Dean is a "Rebel with a Cause"—to celebrate!

And what about **Stampgate**? The world of collectors is still reeling over the so-called **"Nixon Error,"** in which 160 stamps of the

**Richard Nixon** issue were discovered with the red intaglio printing of the former President's name upside down. Oops! When the stamps in question were later revealed to be just printer's waste, Tricky Dick had to admit, "I am not a genuine error." I'm still a **McGovern** man myself.

But it wasn't all fun and games. There has been some speculation that the sad events of July 14 in the town of Hinton, West Virginia, at the unveiling of the **John Henry** stamp, may affect the price of the issue. Everyone knows a stamp with "a story" tends to bring out the worst traits in the philatelic community, but you've heard me go on about "the ghouls" before, so I'll spare the sermon. In the end, only time will tell if the morbid history of **General Issue 3083–3086** inflates the value of the John Henry stamp by itself, or the entire **Folk Heroes** set.

Adventure as she steps on the bridge. Sneaking out of the potluck dinner of the left bank, those tenacious houses a spyglass away from the main settlement, the grub and gasoline and trinket salesmen who drum their fingers waiting for tourists, that varied fare. Across the riveted threshold of the bridge is the banquet of civilization, she can see it, the town of Hinton, laid out before her. The bridge is a couple a hundred yards of concrete fast over impelled water. She looks over the guardrail and below. Looks around for witnesses, spits, sees her water dwindle and disappear before it joins that other water. She is stationary over things running away.

Quaint is always the word. Up a ways she sees the American spiral of a barbershop pole. The first building to greet her as she crosses the street is the First Baptist Church and she sees the sign: Temple Street. None of the buildings are over five or six stories—why push your luck when you've already chosen godforsaken land. There are a few level blocks of stores and other establishments before the town eases up the mountain and becomes residences until incline disallows. She doesn't see any cigarette butts on the sidewalk or gutters, notes this, fingers her pack. The streets are busy. The few traffic lights earn their keep, herd. Toddlers extend chubby fingers to parental assurance and at intersections the young are kept from cars. Dawdlers point into shops and all shops are open and she can sense that this activity is unusual. The town bristles with the promise of John Henry Days.

She looks at her map as others do, just another tourist, unfolding and squinting, fixing what she sees in the sunlight into what the Chamber of Commerce says. It turns out she is right in front of where she has been told to go.

The sign says closed but the doors of the bank swing wide on stiff hinges. Where's the bulletproof glass? It looks like an outlaw's easy score, a still life of trust. Only wooden slats keep the patrons from the tellers, wide enough to stick a hand through. She can't help it. Pamela is no thief but the vigilance and paranoia bred into her from generations of city dwelling often produce this inverse appreciation of opportunities; years of keeping her purse close by, her bags locked between her feet on the subway, have opened her eyes to the unattended.

"You must be Miss Street," a voice declares. Padding up the marble comes a thin old white lady in a John Henry T-shirt and khaki shorts, sunglasses dangling on her bosom. "I'm Janet," she says, extending a browned arm. "Jack will be out in a jiff. We're just going crazy around here today."

Janet leads her to one of the desks at the back of the bank, and Pamela sits in the customer's seat like she has to beg them not to foreclose. Janet departs behind teller windows and says hurriedly, in tailgating syllables, "We're just going crazy around here today, I'm like a chicken with its head cut off."

Pamela doesn't see an ashtray.

She wonders if she is early. She checks her watch against the slim black hands of the clock on the wall, finds they are in concordance. If you can't trust the clock of a bank.

The plaque says President. The door opens inward, releasing the dull letters to the sunlight inside the office until they blaze and burn off. "I'll be down there soon," goes the mayor's voice as he comes into view, in light blue pants and short-sleeved oxford shirt, striped blue tie, holding the door open for his visitor, a chubby man dressed in a pinching railroad engineer's overalls, "just some things to take care of." Cliff smiles at Pamela and says, "You're here."

The man in the overalls, obviously not a real engineer even in Pamela's citified eyes, lifts his cap to her as he passes, summoning a fan of brown hair from the back of his scalp.

Cliff makes a quick call after he directs Pamela to a brown leather chair, "just a sec." Lyndon B. Johnson's hangdog visage pulls her eyes to a wall of pictures in Cliff's office. Next to Lyndon is a photograph containing evanescent grays that fade into white mist as they near the frame. The caption tells her it is the C&O passenger station, Hinton, ca. 1900; six men in dark coats loiter and pose beneath the canopy of the plank building. Cliff says, "Tell them we're not going to pay for it if it doesn't get here by three." Pamela's eyes drop to a picture of an old locomotive, a C&O track gang, the C&O cafeteria. "What do you mean only two gross?" Mayor Cliff and his wife probably, his son probably, on a white porch, Cliff holding up a certificate she can't read. His son in a football uniform, arm flexed Charles Atlas style. Mayor Cliff and his wife, and his son in a wheelchair, the porch now equipped with a ramp. "Thanks for coming down," Cliff says to Pamela.

"This is a nice town. It's nice to get out of the city."

"I was up in New York City just recently. Heckuva time, me and the wife. Greatest city in the world. But there's no way I could live there, if you pardon me."

Pamela nods.

"Well then, I take it you had a nice time at dinner last night? Sorry I didn't get to say hi in person, but I was just on the run the entire time. Would've liked to have held it here of course, but we just don't have the uh appropriate venue at the moment. Arlene took care of you all right?"

"About my father's collection—"

"I'm sure you'll see this afternoon what a great addition it will make to our community. There's the monument, of course, overlooking the tunnel for about twenty-five years, they put it up for the centennial, the Ruritan have had a little stand up there, but for what we're thinking about the museum, your father's collection would be a real plus. I read that inventory you faxed Arlene, it's pretty impressive, what he acquired over the years. Had his own museum up there in New York?"

"He ran it out of his apartment. Had a little sign up and people were supposed to just walk in off the street."

The phone rings. Cliff looks at it, looks at Pamela, lets it ring, drips hands onto his thighs. "Sure. We'd give it a great home down here. I could show you the plans we had drawn up, but we sent them back to—this architect we hired hadn't seen our proposed site, got the shape of the lot all wrong, but he's working on it. Maybe I'll have a copy sent over to the motel anyway so you can see. It's the old A.M.E. church, it burned down a couple years ago and the plot has just been sitting there. It's town land now and it's not too far from here. Talcott's just too small, unincorporated, that's why we're stepping in here, Hinton is." The ring is the ring of eighties office phones, and sounds ancient to Pamela, almost prehistoric. The row of buttons along the bottom of the phone are translucent squares and fill and blink with yellow light when a call comes in. The ringing stops. "No way they have the resources over there," Cliff continues, "and we have Route 20 right there and the traffic from the national park. Figure it's just like turning on a light bulb. Flick that switch and we'll have all sorts of visitors coming through here. Arlene talked to you about the money?"

"I think the money is great. It's very generous."

"But you, what's the saying, you can't put a price on memories, right?"

Janet pops her head in. "Sorry, Jack, that was Bob, he says he'll see you there."

Cliff frowns at the interruption. "Of course I'll see him there, if I wanted to take the call I would have picked up . . ." He smiles quickly at Pamela and remembers something from his to-do list, asks, "Hey, Janet, is this okay?" He glances down at his clothes, pulling at seams.

"It's fine, look great," Janet says, ducking out.

Cliff nods to himself. The motion passed, the ratification of his ensemble spurs his heart. He says, "Sorry. So . . . It'll all have a nice home here, you can be sure of that. We have a lot of stuff already, this is after all the true home of John Henry and we have a lot of stuff passed down through the generations. We're all railroad people here and the father passes it to the son. It belongs here. You should have seen what we said to the Post Office when they wanted to bring out the stamp in Pittsburgh. We wrote them, boy, this is John Henry's home. And when we heard about your father's collection and how we were thinking of making this an annual thing every July, we looked at that inventory you sent and we just knew. It was like a light bulb going on in our heads. Light bulbs. Haven't had any other offers on it, have you?"

"You're the first to take an interest in it, that's why I came down here. I'm just paying the storage space on it now, to tell you the truth."

"So you closed up the museum when your father passed on?"

"Couldn't, just don't have the time to run it."

"I understand perfectly, you're a young lady, have your life to live in New York. Pardon me—hotline, got to take this . . . Hello, honey. No just put whatever doesn't fit in the fridge and we can take it out later . . . did you call Arm and see if he needed a ride over?"

Pamela's attention drifts to the wall of photographs again, to its constellation of affection. Her eyes dart between the faces of the father and the son. The nose and ears passed down between generations. What else is passed down. Resemblance is only the start of it. Most of it happens under the skin. There are other things, you squander them, use up what is good not knowing it is good before it is all used up. Then what are you left with? Nose and ears.

Convenient interruption to this line of thought, Cliff moves over and sits on the edge of his desk, closer to Pamela and now partition between her and the photographs. He says, "Sorry about that. Where . . . yes, your father. That's why we're so glad you came down. We're trying to do the same thing. Teach the people about John Henry, educate the people about the history of the region and the history of Hinton and Talcott. When you see what we have organized today, you're gonna have a kick. We have two men from town going to have a steeldriving race, all sorts of music and things, we hired this band from Charleston, I haven't heard them but they sure come highly recommended, play a lot of music from the region from what I understand."

Is she staring perhaps a bit too blankly? Cliff purses his lips and shifts his tone. "But we don't want to rush you," he says, smiling. "You just have a good time this weekend and enjoy yourself with all that's going on. Didn't expect you to hand it over right now, did we? That's why we brought you down here, so you can see for yourself what we're doing down here. Think of it as us carrying on your father's good work, what he was trying to do with his own museum before he passed on. No universities or anything contact you about his collection?"

"It's not exactly like people are clamoring me."

"Heh. It's kind of specialized."

"What are you going to charge?"

"I thought Arlene already discussed the figure," Cliff murmurs, rearing back with a where did I put my glasses expression. "We've gone over the number quite a bit, I think—"

"Not pay, I mean charge." Something new to her in her voice. What did she care? Here she is asking. "For the museum. What kind of admission are you going to charge people to see John Henry."

He relaxes. "Oh that. It's kind of early, but if you're worried about that, don't worry about that, it won't be cheap I mean it won't be expensive. Most of the people come through here, it's families on vacation, families with kids and that kind of thing. Most of the admission would go to upkeep. The physical plant, the, preserve the physical condition of the exhibits themselves. Want to put a first-rate burglar alarm in there, too. Don't know if Arlene told you had a break-in at the Visitors Center and someone made off with one of the sledges we had on display. Probably just some kids having fun and I can understand that, I have a son of my own and he was a bit of a hell-raiser but it was the property of a private citizen who let us put it out there for the visitors to see, so we're very concerned about the security issue. So one thing we're going to put our fees to is protecting the displays, make sure nothing happens to the items your father went to such great lengths . . . Is that a real huge concern, the fee? I mean is that a deal-breaker?"

"No, I—just wondering. My father didn't charge. I think he just wanted the company, to tell you the truth. But the sign he put up, you almost had to be already looking for it to see it." Her head darts toward the photographs on the wall. "Is that your son right there?"

"That's Armand." The collapse of his eyebrows and emergence of fault lines in his brow mark an emotion swiftly put into check before his smile asserts itself broadly, victorious over turbulence. "Quite a football player before the accident. You should have seen him play."

"They're here!" Janet aslant in the door, doorknob absorbing her weight.

"About time. Why don't you bring a box in here, take a look at them." He returns to Pamela. "There's going to be a taxi to take you to the grounds, right?"

"Yes."

The box is ungainly but Janet does not struggle despite her shallow physicality. A box of feathers. Cliff takes the box to his desk and slits the top with an engraved letter opener. They dig around in the packing peanuts, the bank president and his assistant, treasure hunters over cardboard flaps. "Oh, they're beautiful," Janet sighs.

"Pretty smart if you ask my opinion." He tosses a cellophane package into Pamela's lap. "What do you think?"

It is a hammer, a green hammer formed from mealy green foam. She bends it through the package and it obediently oozes back into its original shape. She looks up at the duo and nods.

"Keep it," Cliff says, pleased. "We're gonna be tossing them out, to the kids. It's a keepsake."

Out on the sidewalk and out in the sunlight, Pamela bites the cellophane and removes the hammer. She doesn't see a garbage can and tucks the plastic into her back pocket. She grips the handle in her hand and it collapses on its pores. Thinks, ten-pound sledge, twenty-pound sledge. She takes it between her hands and compresses it into a ball, releases it and watches it wiggle like larvae. Two little white kids speed past her to catch up with their parents. In the minutes she has been inside the number of people on this slim street has doubled. She thinks back to the map in Herb's Family Style and in her head unfurls a weird image of ant specks skittering along a tiny grid designated Hinton. People move past her in every direction. She is stationary in the rushing people. She is jostled and wonders where she is supposed to be right now.

The town is lousy with John Henry Days.

J. and Monica the Publicist were fucking biweekly, or not. Sometimes biweekly they fell asleep in a soaked tangle on Monica the Publicist's bed, in their event clothes, shoes hooked on sheets. They had an arrangement. More than one morning they discovered house keys dangling in the front door, out there all night, daring someone to rob or kill them while they dozed in boozy prostration. Whoever was annoyed most by the morning sunlight on their faces got out of bed to pull the blinds. After a time the alarm clock by the bed waked them with traffic reports of highways they never traveled on. Monica the Publicist had to be at work at nine and did not allow J. to stay in her apartment. Nor did he wish to. She took a shower and dressed for work while J. tried to wring as much sleep as he could from the morning, waking for a few seconds as Monica opened a drawer in search for the correct underwear or turned on a faucet, and then falling back to sleep again. When Monica finished her preparations for another day of publicity, she slapped J., he slipped into his shoes and they left the apartment. At the newsstand in the subway Monica bought a medium coffee and J. bought the dailies. There they separated with a terse kiss. The train Monica took to work was the same one that provided J. with the most direct route home, but they wanted to be free of each other as soon as possible, so J. caught a train on the platform below that forced him to transfer two times before he arrived at his station. It was easier, this tacit arrangement.

The next time they saw one another after these biweekly sessions, a night or a week later at an event, when it was made apparent once again that they were part of something larger, cog and flywheel, they did not speak to each other. Monica made her rounds, talking to the key players in attendance that night, her boss, the client, the journalists, avoiding J., who talked to his fellow junketeers and drank heartily and filled his stomach, disdaining Monica. It took time to build, their need. The second time they saw each other at an event, one of them would say hello; they took turns so neither felt the other had the upper hand. The second time after their biweekly session, they talked for whole minutes to catch up on what had happened in their lives since they were last in bed. J. made a deadline, or broke a deadline, had a run-in with the copy department, got a big assignment. Monica planned an event that came off well, failed to engineer some nice press, got a big client. They were glad to see each other, and often linked eyes from opposite sides of the room, communicating much in those glances. But it was the second time. They went home separately. The third time after their biweekly session, when two weeks had gone by, when they had reset, they spent as much time together as possible, holding hands, this was warmth, they danced if it was appropriate at that particular event. They made jokes about the other people in the room, kissed if no one was looking, it felt daring, they got reacquainted with the smell of their bodies. It was nice to see each other again. At the end of the night they went uptown, invariably uptown to Monica the Publicist's apartment on the Upper West Side, and fell into her bed.

It was not a love nest; she lived there. She lived in a new building of dark glass and steel, in a one-bedroom apartment with beige walls and beige carpeting. She never had anything inside the refrigerator except wilted vegetables and takeout Chinese containers full of moldering things. She owned a water purifier that bulged like a malignancy on the kitchen sink faucet. The blinds had come with the apartment; the cleaning lady kept them gleaming and white. Monica still had the glasses she bought when she got her first apartment a few years before, and they comforted her, artifacts of soothing continuity. J. used them to drink water sometimes, in the middle of the night to ward off hangover. A year after their pattern had insinuated its simple rules, he noticed the pictures on the table next to the bed. She identified the members of her family for him. Periodically he would notice them for the first time and ask her about them. She'd tell him that she already told him who they were months ago, and he'd say he remembered even though he didn't. Occasionally, suddenly upset anew by something her boss had said that morning or irritated by the inflection in J.'s voice, she exiled him to the couch, and sometimes he sulked there for his own obscure reasons. He lay down on the segmented couch, sheetless and prey to the circulated air.

After the first few times J. entered Monica the Publicist's apartment building, the doorman began to say hi to him. Hey, my man, he said, winking, white gloves quick to tug the burnished handles of the doors. He had witnessed J.'s arrival and probably had a few theories; he had seen the other men Monica brought home, he saw her on the many nights she came home alone and he probably had a few theories. Then he was replaced by a man who knew nothing of J.'s arrival to the complex, and this new doorman said nothing. There was a gym on the second floor, and a sign-up sheet for the jacuzzi on the third.

Of course they despised each other. Other lovers appeared, were wined and dined, escorted them to events, retreated back into the city. These brief romances with the scavengers and anglers of the city intersected with but did not perturb J. and Monica the Publicist's arrangement. It was not a hush thing, it was not a keep quiet thing, but neither mentioned their biweekly partner to their new lovers; there was no need, two nights a month was not a particularly large section of time, suspect only after months and months, and the relationships never lasted long enough to force them to the juncture of revelation. Nor were these would-be rescuers from the arrangement worth discussing during the biweekly assignations. There was the stockbroker who desperately wanted to meet celebrities and left Monica standing, vodka gimlet in her hand, as he tried to woo the Nigerian lingerie model by the bathroom door; there was the time J. showed up with the calculating new conscript in the factchecking department who was transformed horribly after a cosmopolitan and had to be cut loose, bad news, colleagues made jokes for weeks. Sometimes, at an event, J. or Monica would see these new arrivals, and they resisted the urge to interrupt the deep conversation by the canapés (did his face ever seem that alive when she talked to him, did her face ever seem that illuminated from within when he told her a story, no not at all, they had an arrangement), resisted the impulse to swoop down with drink tickets and spirit away the engaged biweekly partner with a lascivious come-on. There was no need. The events came and went, and so did the new people.

Once in a while one of them said I love you, to flat sonant agreement from the other pillow, and it always took them a while to fall asleep when that happened.

Passion at first when it appeared as if their relationship might one day accord with conventional ideals. J. saw Monica first, as she handed out press packets by the coat-check room one night. He thought she was pretty. Monica met him a few events later, when she came over to massage a junketeer who was conversing with him. She introduced herself, as was her custom at events, because she never knew where a stranger might fall in the scheme of things. They ended up kissing a few events later, a friendly good night peck on the cheek that quickened sweetly. As they would never do again once the arrangement asserted itself, they did the normal things, saw movies and ate at restaurants. Monica put the dinners on her corporate credit card because J.

was a writer and expensible. He bought her flowers. Their comrades in the business, on both sides of the events game, thought they made a nice couple. They were a good-looking couple, and besides how are you going to meet anyone real in this business. The cab rides back to Monica the Publicist's home often embarrassed the drivers in those first months, but J. tipped well, and there were worse things that could happen in a cab.

One of them wanted to end it, and the other did not put up a fight. Neither could recall exactly who brought it up; they each had their own motives. Apart from their individual reasons, there was one common to many citizens in the metropolis: They believed there was something more in this city waiting to be discovered, something just for them. They parted as friends. J. had never left any item in the dark building and that simplified matters. It had curdled, things like that curdled and there was nothing that could be done about it except move on. The city was big. Two weeks later they were back in Monica's bed, and two weeks after that, too.

Of course they loved each other. The ceiling above the bed twinkled with a universe of events, they picked out and named the familiar constellations to make sense of their lot in life. Whole mythologies up there, sundry pantheons. There blazed the Doughnut, right there, the loose ring of stars named after a certain kind of event held in formerly hip establishments groaning through the final days of their decline, where the salsa was tepid and deracinated, the greens inevitably soggy and depressed. There, a quadrant below, was the Greenstein Belt, named after the Park Avenue plastic surgeon whose clients booked large banquet halls in the fancier hotels to hawk eponymous perfume, where the sick lighting livened the scars of designer surgery into ugly relief. There, spinning there, was Ursus, whose distant, serried stars signified publishing events where the literary heavyweights who had done their best work in the fifties smoked cigars, got into fights over who would be remembered sixty years from now and puzzled over feminist attacks on their hirsute corpus. They came quickly, in silence always, and disengaged and chatted about their private constellations, arid boredom drying their secretions swiftly, they picked out stars until one realized that the other had not said anything for some time, and they were alone.

Biweekly and biweekly through years. They had squabbles like any couple. One spring Monica adopted a distracted air, nibbled petulantly at crackers, arrived late and departed early at events. She waited for J. to comment on the change in her behavior, for she felt it was obvious that inside her something was shifting and so she exaggerated the symptoms to get his attention, and when he did not remark upon it she told him one night in her bed that she wanted to leave the publicity racket. She had a friend who had a farm and had been invited to spend a few months there, to clear her mind, rearrange her priorities, whatever, it was a healthy and nurturing environment with fresh air and farm animals. J. chuckled and said he'd like to see that. He slept on the couch the rest of that night, found his advances disdained two weeks later, and did not accompany Monica to her apartment. Their arrangement resumed two weeks after that, but various precedents had been set. Half a year later, when J. lamented what he perceived to be a certain hollowness within him and confessed to revisiting the old book proposal, Monica scoffed and said that would be the day. He rebuffed her two weeks later, they resumed two weeks after that and then they were even.

Certainly in a city of contracts and bargains, of pacts and compromises, theirs was not the most decrepit. It made sense. Certainly the city had produced unions more unholy than theirs, brokered alliances more profane and withering. They endured, they held each other, plummeting through fads and flavors of the month, through a universe of events and beyond, in fevered biweekly embrace, deep into cold pop.

In a different world perhaps. If he were a soldier instead of a mercenary, and she a healer instead of a handler. Circumstances had thrown them together, life under pop had forced them to find solace wherever they could. He was a soldier in the French village, he brought her chocolates and stockings, real treasures in these times of scarcity. She was a nurse tending the wounds of our boys, she taught him that it is enough to make it alive to the end of the day, that it was okay for a man to cry. Always the sound of the shelling to remind them of what the world had come to. After the Armistice, they'd go their separate ways, return to their former lives. But this war was peculiar. It would not end, it discovered new markets every day, the fighting spilled over into new demographics each day, none could remain neutral in this conflict, and no side could ever win. So it continued, and the soldier and the nurse comforted each other. In a different world perhaps.

Look, there's Paul Robeson on Broadway, in his dressing room backstage at the 44th Street Theatre, winter of 1940. He is John Henry. For one more performance, anyway, because they've closed the show. Everybody hates it. Word is it's a real stinker. And word is getting around. They had a short run in Philly a couple of weeks ago, and the critics hated it. Normal people, too. They reworked it, stuck chewing gum in the breaches, cast off here in New York last week, but they're still waist-deep in bilge, good intentions bobbing around them along with other buoyant sundries. So the money guys are strapping on life jackets aboard the good ship *John Henry*. Every man for himself!

Blame, point the finger: The scrivener responsible is one Roark Bradford, who adapted the musical from his 1931 novel. A best-seller, that. Standing there deliberating in the bookstore, one look at the author bio and they knew they were in good hands. "Roark Bradford is amply qualified to write about the Negro," it read. "He had a Negro for a nurse and Negroes for playmates when he was growing up. He has seen them at work in the fields, in the levee camps, and on the river. He knows them in their homes, in church, at their picnics and their funerals." Very impressive credentials indeed. Especially that bit about the picnics. He might as well have a Ph.D. in Negroes. His mastery of the Negro idiom is quite startling. The reader is invited along as big bad John Henry swaggers through a series of picaresque adventures, such as picking cotton ("Hold yo' fingers a little bent and let yo' hands pass by de bolls. Efn they's nigger blood in yo' fingers de cotton will stick an follow."), loading cotton on to a steamship ("You's a cotton-rollin' man on the *Big Jim White*, so wrassle dat cotton down. Hit's cotton and you's a nigger. So wrassle hit down, son!"), and rousting hogs ("Line up, you bullies, and make yo' shoulders bare! 'Cause when I h'ists dese hogs outn de pen, you gonter think hit's rainin' hogs on yo' weary back."). The pages, they turn themselves.

Romance as well as action between the thick blue covers. Transplanted to the colorful world of Louisiana river life, John Henry's big test here is his relationship with Julie Ann. It is love at first sight and they have much in common. "I's six feet tall, too," she purrs, "and I got blue gums and gray eyes." Hearty recommendations all. If only Julie Ann could keep her hands off that nigger Sam, that good for nothin' specimen of N'awlins lowlife. They hang around the wharf, snort coke, sip whiskey. At the end of the chronicle, John Henry, upset by Julie Ann's latest dalliance with Sam, stalks the dock and discovers that his captain has retained the services of a steam winch that loads "cotton like ten niggers." It is ambiguous whether it is John Henry's romantic woes or the steam winch's affront to his prowess that causes him to call for a race with the machine, such is de 'nigmatic 'fect of Bradford's prose. At any rate, he croaks in the middle. Julie Ann rushes to finish the race herself, she croaks, and the star-crossed lovers are united in death. The book flew off the shelves. Of course it would make a lovely musical.

Paul Robeson sits in his dressing room. Soon he'll walk onstage. Out there the audience doublechecks seat numbers and squints at the programs. The next day boxes and boxes of unused programs will fill the alley behind the theater. In these moments before the performance he holds all the words tight. The people out there, the tilted heads arrayed from orchestra to balcony, are not his first audience. Twenty years in the business, he's had some experience. In a debating contest in high school he stood before his teachers and recited some Toussaint-L'Ouverture. As Napoleon dispatched thirty thousand troops to Haiti to squash insurrection, L'Ouverture told his people, "My children, France comes to make us slaves. God gave us liberty; France has no right to take it away. Burn the cities, destroy the harvests, tear up the roads with cannon, poison the wells, show the white man the hell he comes to make!" The Haitians kicked the French's butts; Paul Robeson came in third place in the debating contest. He said he didn't understand the meaning of the words, what it was to say those words to white people, he just thought it was a good speech. This was before he came to make his own speeches. Around this period he also played Othello for the first time, his comet role, returning and returning to him throughout his days. The performance was a fundraiser for a class trip to Washington, D.C. He was a hit. It didn't matter that he couldn't join the field trip because the hotel didn't allow black people to touch their sheets. Later on when he had some juice he'd cancel shows in segregated theaters, but this was before.

What are bad notices, critics' snipes, when you've been pulverized and punished bodily. At Rutgers he played football. The man was big, what can you say? At his first practice they jumped him, piled on him, broke bones. He got up. These were his own teammates. Next practice one of them drove cleats through his hand. He kept playing. They laid off him once the season started and it was the opposing team's turn to bloody him, when they weren't forfeiting, preferring to lose rather than share the field with the black man. He knocked them around. He scored. He won games for them but what exactly is his expression out there on the grass, it's hard to make out, let alone interpret. What is he thinking.

They thought he was going to be the next Booker T. Washington. Smart colored fellow like him. He dropped his law career to perform. Made his mark working with Eugene O'Neill, in *All God's Chillun Got Wings* and *The Emperor Jones*. In *God's Chillun* the races mix. A white actress touches his hand in one scene and they thought there might be rioting. There was no rioting. That would come later. Good reviews mostly, although there were naysayers; some white critics thought the play was an insult to the white race, some black critics thought it was an insult to the black race. Around this time segments of the black press started to get on his back for playing the "shiftless moron" and the "lazy, good-natured, lolling darkey." Not the last time they'd make this point. His singing career got into full swing around this time, too; performing bills mixing black spirituals with secular songs, he hit upon a new formula. In *Show Boat* he sang "Ol' Man River," drawing deep OOOs from deep black wells. Sang around this country and then in other countries. Visited Africa, Europe. Sold out the Albert Hall in Merry Olde. Stayed away as much as he could from the U.S. of A. for ten years.

It was when he traveled that he began to change.

Outside his dressing room, the bustle of preparations, location of props.

In Moscow he dined with the Prime Minister. Eisenstein had invited him over; turned out he was into Touissant, too, and wanted to make a film about the man. Small world. They probably discussed this by a samovar. He dug the Soviets and they dug him. One night at the theater, a little Russian kid ran up to Paul Robeson, encircled his tiny arms around the big man's legs and implored him to stay, saying he'll be happy if he stays in the bosom of Mother Russia. Little moppet. Pretty moving. He moved on. Hung out with the Loyalists during the Spanish Civil War. The soldiers adored him. It wasn't every day an international celebrity toured the front lines. He made the rounds, waved out the window of the Buick. Occasionally shells passed over his head. There was something changing in the world and in him, too. He said, "I belong to an oppressed race, discriminated against, one that could not live if fascism triumphed in the world." All those people dying over there were dying here, in him. He said, "I have found that where forces have been the same, whether people weave, build, pick cotton, or dig in the mines, they understand the common language of work, suffering and protest." The Negro sharecropper, the Welsh miner, the Slavic farmer. He said, "Folk music is as much a creation of a mass of people as a language. One person throws in a phrase. Then another—and when, as a singer, I walk from among the people, onto the platform, to sing back to the people the songs they have created, I can feel a great unity." We are our songs. He said, "I am sick of playing Stepin Fetchit comics and savages with leopard skin and spear."

He came back to America a new man.

Tonight he's John Henry. Already in costume. Dark blue dungarees held up by a broad brown leather belt. Sleeveless T-shirt, brown cowboy hat. The dialogue is terrible, the characters racist, the situation appalling, but in John Henry, a man of the land, Paul Robeson sees the folk. The masses. He wants to represent the experiences of the common man. Out of this folktale, even if diverted down ruined streams, flows the truth of men and women. They sacrifice and give. It didn't turn out the way he wanted it to. Some guy in the press said even Robeson "could not carry on his back 800 pounds of bad play." Ouch. But he is trying. He'll be back on Broadway and knock 'em dead in "Othello."

Someone knocks on his door, hey it's five minutes to curtain, Mr. Robeson.

This is a turning point. No thunderbolts from the sky or neuron-zapping epiphany, nothing flashy, but there was something going on inside him. Where was America when the blood of the Loyalists spilled in rivers? Where was America when the blood of the lynched spilled in rivers? He performed at rallies for the Communist Party, benefits for socialist causes. No card-carrying member, but still. Brushes are made for tarring. Down in D.C. Hoover opened a file. He was always opening files. Open a file on a box of cherries for being too red. The file got fat, that's what FBI files do. Still performing, making movies, making the scene on Broadway again in "Othello" but Paul Robeson's making speeches, too. Defending the Soviet Union, watch out. In Paris '49, he said, "It is unthinkable that American Negroes would go to war on behalf of those who have oppressed us for generations against a country which in one generation has raised our people to the full dignity of mankind." Actually, he didn't say that, but the Associated Press attributed the remarks to him and there you have it. Who is this Negro to speak this way? Here we are trying to get this Cold War thing off the ground, and there's this guy talking our heads off about human dignity. Called before the House Un-American Activities Committee, he did not denounce himself. The paper of record said, "We want him to keep singing and being Paul Robeson." They cannot recognize this man.

Boy, it's cold outside. Pitiless New York winters get inside the bones. Inside the dressing room the steam heat clangs.

A few months later they rioted in Peekskill. New Jersey, that is. An anti–Paul Robeson riot. This lefty arts group asks him to do a benefit and all heck breaks loose. Not in our town. Goon squads roved, red-blooded Americans of multiple epithets and a single hue. Dirty Commie, Dirty Nigger, Dirty Jew. The mob smashed the stage to kindling, which came in handy when an individual or individuals later burned a cross. They sent Robeson fans, assorted fellow travelers to the hospital. The cops stood by with their arms crossed: Do you hear anything? Nope. You? Nope.

After that, it just ain't the same. Concert tours cancelled. Theater owners hated pinkos or feared repercussions. Sympathetic venues couldn't book him because of threats. You get a phone call in the middle of the night, you have a family, what choice do you have. He couldn't make a living. He became the first American banned from television when an appearance on Eleanor Roosevelt's NBC show was called off. If his country had gone mad, maybe overseas would be better. They loved him overseas. But get this—the State Department pulled his passport. It would be "detrimental to the interests of the United States Government" for him to go abroad and speak on black rights. He's "one of the most dangerous men in the world." If he signed a paper saying he wouldn't make any speeches, everything would be copacetic. But he wouldn't do it.

Stuck here. Exiled to his own country, he started to fall apart. Got more and more broke. A man with a voice like that, and he can't even open his mouth. He began to talk about the pentatonic scale. He had a theory about the pentatonic scale. The ubiquity and universality of the pentatonic scale in folk music around the globe proved the brotherhood of man. By studying the pentatonic scale we can peer into human truths. The commonality of the folk. Pentatonic scale this, pentatonic scale that. Trip on the rug and it was the pentatonic scale. Beset by mental as well as physical problems, he slid. After a couple of years, things loosened up but the years of confinement had taken their toll. When the withdrawal of his passport was finally declared illegal in '58, he settled in England, where successive breakdowns finished his career. Suicide attempts, electroshock treatments, overmedication. He was a plate of scrambled eggs. As the civil rights movement reached fruition, as he sat across the ocean, far from the front lines, and few remembered his name. When he returned to New York in '64, the newspapers gloried over his reduced capabilities. Look at Goliath, hobbled now. DISILLUSIONED NATIVE SON, went one headline. A reader wrote a letter back. It said, "That's John Henry himself you're insulting."

Maybe he should have been a baker. His great-great-grandfather was born into slavery, purchased his freedom and became a baker. He baked bread for the Revolutionary Army, and the story goes that George Washington himself thanked him personally for his patriotic contribution. So maybe he should have been a baker.

Hey, Mr. Robeson. Hey, Mr. Robeson, goes a voice outside the dressing room door. It's time. The people are waiting.

He is John Henry tonight.

*I*t's me. *Calling to see if you're back in town. Give me a call. I'm at work.*
*This is Gene in factchecking calling about your piece. Just have one or two queries, if you could call me back today that would be great.*

*Hey, J., this is Marshall, calling on Friday around three-thirty. Hey, man, hate to bug you again about that contract, you have to send that in before you can get paid, so . . . send it in! Have a nice weekend.*

*This is your Aunt Jennifer calling about your father's birthday. I'll be home all night.*

*Gene in fact-checking again. Guess you didn't have time to get back to me yesterday. Legal has a few queries about your piece, that last section where you say "it's so easy even a dimwit can do it." Do you have a source on that, that dimwit thing? Is that in their press material or did you just, where did you get that from is what I'm asking. Thanks.*

HE ERASES EVERYTHING. The answering machine company had prominently advertised the salient feature of its new product—Keep Track of Your Messages from a Remote Location—and he can't, by his sights, get more remote than he is now. He presses a button and is free. This is modern technology. One time he forgot his ATM number and he became less than human, see-through, he waved his hands in the faces of other people but they could not see or hear him. This was how he felt. He wandered the streets for a few hours without currency or an identity until his ATM number returned to his recall as suddenly as it had disappeared. It had been something of an existential dilemma and troubling but it hadn't happened since.

*This is Herb in Accounts Payable at Saturn Publishing. I'm still waiting on that Social Security number, sir, we can't pay you unless we get a Social Security number for you. I assume you have one.*

Checking his messages reminds him of the record so he starts thinking about how he'll fill the requirements next week. There's that paperweight thing on Tuesday so that's taken care of. He can probably skip lunch that day, probably breakfast too because Sharp always puts out a nice spread for their products, and if this new paperweight is half as good as the buzz maintains, they'll really go all out . . . He catches himself salivating at the idea and blames One Eye. One Eye's crackpot mission to get himself off the List had undone all the good work J. had put in this morning. He had shaken off his conditioning for a few hours and it had required much effort, renunciation, reserve-tapping struggle. Real hair-shirt stuff, this morning. Then, like that, corralled into that dumbass business and he stood in the bathtub waiting for Lawrence to leave. They were lucky they didn't get caught. He slid back into custom too easily.

*Hello, J., it's Elaine. The piece looks great. There were just one or two things I changed so I'm going to fax you the new version and tell me what you think. We're closing the issue in half an hour, so if you can get back to me before then, great.*

He walks over to the bathroom and urinates. Feels so at home in this place he forgets to tend to his fly. He has half an hour until the taxi comes back for another run to the festival site. Pamela will be there. He opens up the press packet so that he'll be able carry on a conversation.

*This is Margaret at Legend returning your call. About that check, I'm going to have to check with someone in processing to check out what happened to your check. My assistant says she remembers seeing the check request form so it should have gone in and the check should have gone out, so I don't know what happened.*

He reads, "The C&O railroad provided a great opportunity for the slaves freed by Mr. Lincoln's Proclamation. The C&O paid the passage to West Virginia for any freed black willing to work and provided the first salary some of those men had ever seen. The laborers came from all over, from as far north as New Jersey and as far south as the Florida panhandle. When work on the Big Bend Tunnel finished many stayed with the railroad for the rest of their lives. They were proud to join the C&O family."

*It's me again. I don't know if you're mad or what or I don't even know. When you get this message call me.*

He stops. But what if he doesn't go to the paperweight event on Tuesday or skips whatever event (he'll have to look it up) is going on Monday? It isn't as if he bet anyone any money that he could do it. Go for the record. It is a competition between him and himself. Or him and the List. Depended on how you looked at it. He had bet himself he could do it. Hadn't he? Looking back it seems to him that he just started doing it and it made a certain kind of sense so he kept going. It wasn't even particularly hard, going for it. If he deposits that check that should have arrived by now it will take five days for it to clear. The company is based in New York, is in fact one of the biggest magazine concerns in New York, but their bank is in Idaho and it takes five days for their checks to clear. (How quickly his cars jump the tracks, are derailed.)

*J., long time no see, it's Jane Almond from Hotshot Media calling you again about that event at Haze on Tuesday, it's for that new paperweight Sharp is launching. I'm going to put you on the list plus-one, but you should get there early because I know a lot of people are coming. Love ya!*

He checks the digital clock, faithful ally through an infinity of hotel rooms, and reads on. "While it was hazardous work, the C&O utilized all the best safety procedures of the day to provide the healthiest working conditions for its men."

*J., it's Mark. Someone on the business side put a red flag on some of your reimbursements for the L.A. trip. Got it right here on my desk, see you put down lunch one column, but then the receipt you put in there lists three margaritas. You know if it was up to me, but they're really cracking down on that sort of thing here since we got bought, so.*

He skips ahead. "Those who say that John Henry is a mere legend will risk the ire of local residents. Many of the older residents recall being told the story of the great competition by grandparents or uncles who were employees on the C&O and witnessed the race with their own eyes." Lucky he didn't get beat up in that diner this morning.

*J.—good news. This is Victor. We're finally going to run that luxury doorknob piece it looks like. Turns out we have some space in the section because one of our writers went AWOL. I know it's been a while but do you have any factchecking material you can send me on that? I hope this is still the right number.*

"The foreman and the drill salesman ran to get the results of the race. By the time the referee fired his shot signaling the end of the competition, John Henry had drilled a total of fourteen feet. The poor steam drill, however, had only drilled nine feet. John Henry had triumphed over the nefarious machine!"

*Hey, J.—hey, that rhymes. Umm it's Evelyn and I'm going to send out that kill fee today, but I don't think I said it was for the whole thing. If you look at the contract, it's a twenty-five percent kill fee for things now ever since we got that new editor in chief. Sorry about that. Gimme a call.*

He realizes that he hadn't thought of the record for whole hours, not until he got back into his room. Seeing the room, being back in the room reminded him that he was only a temporary guest here. He is one in a series of people who are given the key and this is only one in an uninterrupted series of assignments. Best to keep thinking of it as such, not expect too much from whatever kinds of encounters he has with Pamela, and plan for next week's streak of junketeering.

*This is Gene in factchecking again. Just . . . give me a call when you get in.*

"Some say that the great steeldriver was laid to rest with his beloved hammer in the fill near the eastern portal of the tunnel. There are others who insist that John Henry sleeps on top of Big Bend mountain, where a log church once stood. But if you ask the old-timers of the area, they'll tell you that the bones of the legendary hero lie in the old Negro cemetery that still stands in the northern slope."

*Hey, it's Jane from Hotshot. I can't remember if I called you back about that paperweight thing, but it's still on for Tuesday and you're plus-one. Love ya!*

He sees himself holding cotton candy at the festival and telling Pamela, "You know, there's no doubt that the great John Henry lies on the northern slope. At the old Negro cemetery, you know the one," dispensing this like some metropolitan cocktail party tidbit. He'll probably get some ribbing from the others if he's hanging there talking to Pamela with his nose all open. One Eye will say something. Best to avoid his friend for now. Immediately following their escapade, when they were safe in the parking lot, once they were out of the bathtub, his monocular comrade tried to enlist him in the next mission: to break into Lucien's room and hit the master. He smelled the asphalt bake as One Eye cried, "It's Lucien that bastard! I knew it was him. We go in there, we'll just take our names off, click click, that'll show 'em."

"It's one thing if you want to know who runs the List. Fine," J. said. "It's an elegant idea in its way, a machine to keep the media-saturated society up and running. Deserves a patent, or at least a franchise agreement so that other cities can get in on the action. Now you know who thought it up. Here's a lollipop. But it's one, stupid to try that trick again and think you won't get caught and two, if you don't want to go to events just don't go. No one is forcing you. There's no gun at your back. Lucien walks in and pals or no pals he'll probably call the cops to teach you a lesson." Thinking, these white boys think they can do anything mighty-whitey style. Like there are no consequences.

"I'm talking symbolism here. Symbolism is important. Many important events in human history have happened because of symbolism. You got your Boston Tea Party, dump the shit in the harbor, love that dirty water, you got all kinds of shit, giving blankets full of smallpox to the Indians. Our country is built on symbolism. Look, answer me a question. Why are you going for the record?"

"How are smallpox blankets symbolic?"

"Of contempt, contempt. We come in peace and we try to kill 'em off with courtesy. 'Oh, snuggle up in these innocent-looking blankets, Chief, no one's going to suspect these lovely quilted jobbies.' Why don't you just answer the question?"

"To see if I can. To prove I can."

"Prove what to who?"

"It's a circular argument, but yeah, to prove I can to myself."

"It's a symbol of something to yourself even if you don't know what it is. So who are you to deny me my own private symbolism, not matter how silly it may seem to you when you're doing the same thing? You're like the symbolism referee trying to throw me out the game."

"Delete yourself. But leave me out of it."

"You have your machine to beat and I have mine."

They left it at that.

*J., got a quick copy query for you. Do you want it dimwit with a hyphen like dim hyphen wit or do you want it one word dimwit? I've been going back and forth with the copy department about this and we're stumped. Give me a ring when you get this.*

Perhaps going for the record had been inevitable ever since he found himself on the List. Those years before. Like this competition had been waiting for him the whole time and he hadn't known it.

*This is a message for J. Sutter. This is Mr. Ardin in Accounts Payable. I received your message of the sixth about your check for the May issue and I'm not sure who you talked to in the office before, but they were incorrect about the procedure. If you were paid the incorrect amount for an article, you have to ask us to send you a Form 199, send that back to us, care of me, along with the check, and we will cut a check for the correct amount. It should take about sixty to ninety days to process.*

He still has a few minutes and decides to wait outside for his ride. There's a lot more traffic on the road, all of it heading west and that's where he figures he's headed. Recreational vehicles and compact cars, maps splayed out on the dashboard, fast food drinks snug in plastic popout holders, antiradar devices plugged into cigarette lighters and bouncing invisible waves off ranges and peaks. A red Range Rover speeds by, trailing multicolored kids' balloons that are whipped and impelled by velocity. The mountain is in front of him. Maybe it is Big Bend. He thinks about what it must have been like before the road made it just another hill, to look at it and think, I'm going through this mountain. Then this line of thought evaporates and he half wishes he had a beer.

*We're going with dimwit one word. One word dimwit. Call if there's a problem.*

Under the word heroic draw a line and list all the meanings. He doesn't have a single one in him.

It is odd because it is just him and L'il Bob working the tunnel. John Henry and his partner always work with a second team. It keeps the productivity up. Two pairs of men boring twin holes into the mountain and singing to their work. The sound of the hammer is percussion, each blow a footfall into the mountain to the other side. But today he does not know why they are alone in the darkness and why they do not sing. He cannot see L'il Bob's face and cannot move his mouth to talk to him. To find out what is happening. It is as if neither can stop. Their labor pulls them like a stream and it is all they can do to stay afloat. It seems they have been at this hole forever. He cannot seem to get the bit deeper. The mountain has grown harder. They have hit the mountain's heart and the mountain is using all of its ancient will to prevent their violence against its self. It works against them. Then with one blow John Henry feels something give and with the next blow the bit sinks in deep, deeper than he has ever driven before. John Henry thinks, we've hit the western cut. The two ends of the tunnel have met. He is about to cheer. They have won Captain Johnson's bonus. Then the blood comes.

The blood is black until the candlelight hits it and it turns deep red. He can see then that it is blood. It should have been light from the western cut that came through the hole but it is blood. The black then red spray erupts from around the drill. He steps back. He still cannot speak. He looks at L'il Bob and sees his partner's head turn. L'il Bob blinks through the blood on his face and then he grins. John Henry cannot stop him from what he is about to do. L'il Bob's fingers open and the bit flies from the hole and the spray of blood becomes a geyser. The force of the blood pushes John Henry backward. He falls on the timber planks and when he wipes his eyes free L'il Bob is gone. The blood of the mountain pours into the cut. Out east. He thinks the planks are bobbing in it beneath him, and then he looks and sees that the rock around him is now flesh. The red shale glistens like animal meat. Ridges formed by the blasting are now tracings of sinew. Veins and arteries. It is a living breathing mountain and he is in its angry guts. The heart of the mountain pours itself over him. The blood is up to his neck. Then the blood spray blinds him again and he is awake.

When he wakened he was grateful for a moment and then he realized it was still dark. He had traveled through a series of fever dreams all night. They were coupled together like train cars. He knew that the caboose contained morning and each time he fell asleep he hoped that this time he would step into it. But he opened the door to the next car and stepped again into nightmare. He did not know what time it was. The camp was quiet. Every one else slept off their labor. He had lost two days' wages laid up in bed. It was all he could do to crawl to the outhouse and the outhouse stank with his stink. He shivered and his blanket was damp with fever sweat. John Henry could not get warm no matter what he did and the blanket chilled him even more. He was laid up with fever. It was the longest night he could remember. He prayed for morning.

He wakened to the bustle of the other men getting ready to go back into the mountain. L'il Bob came into his shanty looking worried. He carried a bucket of water and his blanket for John Henry to use while he was working. L'il Bob asked his friend was he coming back to work that day and John Henry tried to sit up. His head exploded with worms and he was too dizzy, he fell back to the bed like a felled tree. L'il Bob put the blanket on his friend and told him that he'd tell the boss John Henry is sick again. The shaker complained about Jesse, John Henry's replacement. He's slow and stupid, L'il Bob told his friend. You're twice as fast as him, he said. John Henry closed his eyes and his eyes rolled beneath their lids and when he woke up again he could tell from the sunlight it was about noon. He was grateful he did not dream again.

He got sick the day after Tommy died. The sun had just slipped behind the mountain. The smoke from the latest blasting had stopped sneaking out the tunnel and it was time to go back in to see how much the blast had advanced the heading. John Henry sat on a crate and rubbed tallow into the handle of his sledge. He waited for the sheen that said he had put enough oil in. That morning he had felt the blows travel up his arms and rock his shoulders and knew that the handle was getting stiff. He had to limber it up or else he'd be sore when he sat down that night, the pain would creep on him like floodwater over a bank. When Tommy said he was heading back in to start mucking out the rock from the blast, John Henry looked down at the handle of his hammer. He had not finished and Tommy went ahead. John Henry saw his friend walk into the heading and felt the first chill of his fever. The old man led a mule cart into the tunnel and that was the last John Henry saw of him alive. He rubbed the sheep fat into the wood while both the mule and the man were killed by the loose, falling rock. When John Henry went inside to see where it happened, he was not surprised to see that it was near the crag that haunted him. The beak of shale was still there, snickering, telling him something. They buried Tommy and the mule together in the fill of the eastern cut. That night after midnight John Henry's chill had become a fever.

He was sick and afraid. The fever will pass but the mountain will not. He pulled the blankets over his head. John Henry heard the clink of hammers on drills, he was too far away from them to hear them for real but he heard them anyway. Sometimes the clinking matched the beat of his heart for a whole minute and then they fell away from each other. The rhythms met again when he least expected it and it was like he was one with the labor. The doctor came in and said Captain Johnson wanted him to check on John Henry. The doctor opened a packet and dropped the white dust into water and gave it to the fevered man. The doctor said, you should be able to work tomorrow. The company can't afford to keep on men who won't work, he said. Then he disappeared into the afternoon light. John Henry's big body shivered.

He knew the mountain was going to kill him the first time he saw it. The railroad put out word it needed men to dig a tunnel and hitched a flatcar for Negro workers to a westbound train. The men filed into the old car and sat on seats fashioned from nail kegs. In the Negro workers' car the men sized each other up and talked about the ride. It was the first time any of them had been on a train. They spat tobacco to the floor. The train took them as far as the tracks went and a wagon took them the rest of the way to the mountain. The wagon arrived at the grading camp and John Henry saw the mountain heaped up to Heaven and knew right then that he had lied. He had told Abby that when he returned they would get married. John Henry would save his wages and come back a rich man. Or rich enough to start a life with her. He had carried water in the mines when he was a slave. The mining company leased him from Reynolds when he reached the age of six. By that time a slaveowner could not get insurance on his slaves any more because too many died in the mines and the insurance companies were no longer going to insure slaves. Reynolds didn't want to lose his investment so he only leased children to the mining company, with the order that his slaves were not allowed to do anything dangerous. They could carry water or learn a blacksmith's trade but no more. John Henry carried water to miners before the Proclamation and when he heard about the work on the tunnel he knew he was going. He knew about being inside mountains, the coolness inside rock. But that first day, he saw the mountain and knew that this one was different. It will kill him.

He fell asleep again and woke again. He might have slept for two minutes or two hours. If his hammer had not needed some tallow he would have walked in with Tommy. They would have stood side by side and John Henry would have been killed too. Tommy's death was a message. God was telling him to prepare. The mountain will take him. Sooner or later. Tomorrow he would go back to work.

After the shift L'il Bob came to see John Henry. He brought food and water. For the first time since Tommy died he felt like eating and he wolfed it down. L'il Bob complained about Jesse. The fool nearly hit him today. Not once but twice. L'il Bob had to tell him to watch what he was doing. John Henry said he'd be back in the mountain again tomorrow and not to worry about Jesse no more. L'il Bob said this city man in city clothes came into Captain Johnson's office today. They talked for a long time and then the city man left. L'il Bob said he was from a mechanical company trying to sell Captain Johnson on one of their steam drills. One of the bosses said them steam drills can do the work of a whole team of drivers and they're cheaper too. The steam drill is better and faster and cheaper. Pretty soon they're going to replace all the men, L'il Bob said, do you believe that? Do you think Captain Johnson is going to get one of those things? L'il Bob asked.

PART FOUR

# THE STEEL-DRIVING THEORY OF LIFE

❖

They come out of cars. Out of vehicles hot from sunlight and conveying engines. The hoods tick cool. Parking is a hassle. Nose to nose. On weeds, almost in ditches, on crumbling terraces of asphalt unstable because rainwater has swept the dirt from under. Passengers are reminded by other passengers to roll up the windows. The father surveys and orders the son to put the camera under the seat. Locks are locked, are doublechecked, sometimes by remote control with beeps. Somebody forgot something in the car, sunglasses nestle over ears snug on the scalp. Mud flaps. The cars move slowly, there are too many people on the road, little kids not looking where they're going, and it's a creeping progress. Those who have found parking spaces view these drivers with a certain superiority. Then they take a few steps and get lost in the fair.

Portable equipment has been hauled to the grounds. One look at the line for the portosans and you reconsider your need. The line for the mens is always shorter, discernible from the line for the womens and inspiration for many identical observations about biological equipment repeated over the course of the day by many different people. Some men sneak off into the woods. By the bandstand, toward the middle of the grounds, a generator rattles. The amps have already been tested. A man was sent to fetch tape to tape down orange industrial cable where a child might trip or an old lady break a hip. Along the sides of the bandstand black sheeting is taped up to keep people from seeing the fragile-looking scaffolding. Some kids will sneak in there when no one is looking and peek through at the people. A quarter mile of steel fencing separates the tracks from the grounds, and several guards patrol the space between all day, per the agreement with the railroad. No one wants a regrettable incident.

The day before, the registered vendors match lot numbers with marked territory and learn the pecking order. Of course some favoritism is to be expected and those who registered late are penalized with less than optimum placement. Those with plum spots feel something that draws itself up to contentment. Some try to come up with ways to beat the system. It is quite a thing to stand there the day before the fair and see the land sectioned off like that by strings and stakes, in three long rows. They can hardly believe the day is almost here. The people who will come the next day will move from booth to booth. It is important to have a flashy sign to draw them in and the next day some of the vendors will return with paint on the flesh that has resisted turpentine. Many of the vendors have never met before and extend greetings while checking out their neighbor's wares. No one wants to be next to a booth that will be a turnoff. Put all that effort in and then something like that happens out of your control. One booth will have some kind of trick to draw people over and the neighbors think, why didn't I think of that. Mostly friendly but then it's dog eat dog on some level.

There's almost a fistfight. Cooler heads prevail. A man argues with his wife over who had the keys last, they're in his back pocket where he never puts them. The baby won't fall asleep and that little song that always works isn't today. They take turns throwing dirt bombs. Children have too much sugar and get cranky suddenly. One after the other children run out of money and try to find their parents. Children manipulate tubes of fluorescent colors. The effect is not as striking in the daytime. Children express character traits that will turn out to be lifelong. One eats her candy slowly so it won't run out and discovers later she still has some to put under her pillow. Another has forgotten that rides employing the principle of centrifugal force make him ill and he leaves the metal steps slick for later thrillseekers. The Tilt-a-Whirl employs a system of red tickets that are exchanged for cash. The operators of the ride are down to one roll and improvise by reusing the tickets. At the end of the day the cardboard is gummy and bent, as if contorting the tickets would force the machine to slow.

The secretary and deputy undersecretary of the women's auxiliary smile above cookies and biscuits. They mix the more unfortunate batches around with the good ones for cover. A small gang of suspects dally by the kegs. Overflow from cups moistens the dirt. Hijinks by the helium canisters, a chorus of castrati. You watch a balloon slide up serpentine until it disappears. Ends up three states over, exhausted. Big weekend for the local distributor of miniature American flags. Shoddy work, translucent fabric, but the weekend's take eventually gets kicked up to the manufacturer and there are no repercussions. Fanny packs hoard valuables, identification. The scratching of Velcro vies for attention with distant crickets. Somewhere out of sight many voices cry out in surprise and people hustle to see what they are missing. Or maintain speed, confident the display will continue. He comments to his girlfriend and when she doesn't answer discovers a stranger beside him. She has exact change, but her hands are too sweaty, her pants too tight to get at it. An insurance salesman wipes his brow over fine print, over his wobbly-legged foldup table. It's a tough sell but he has a gimmick: monogrammed pens biding time to leakage. Everyone is prey.

Hangnails sun themselves atop flip-flops. First one cup then another cup is dropped on the ground. By the end of the day the rows will be filled with dashed paper cups. Ants find the red punch appealing and spread the word. The trash cans, there are never enough trash cans, spill over. People arrange their trash delicately on overflowing receptacles and hope to make a clean getaway before it tumbles off. The paper cups can be traced back to certain more popular vendors. Undone shoelaces trail in muck. There is no bank nearby and some despair. People are hungry and can't decide what to eat. They disdain worthy choices, stroll on, cherishing this rare chance to snob, find themselves too hungry to go farther and settle for third rate, something dead on a skewer. The grill of the Italian sausage stand resembles the floor of a garage. Mustard obscures clots of grease. Mustard bedevils the mustachioed. No instructions from a helpful second party, no matter how succinct, can lead the napkin to the spot.

Abstract horror for the fast walkers when they fall behind dawdlers. Invective, calumny. Finally maneuvering around to find the agent of delay is infirm, disabled, acquitted. They split up. They are left waiting at the meeting place and despise their companions. Excuses are tendered up and down the rows. You see that man hold something you want and wonder where he got it, what booth. She wants him to hold her hand and he keeps finding reasons to withdraw it, to look for change, check his watch. Out here all exposed. A mother disciplines her child and bystanders pronounce it abuse, but what can they do. Put that down, come over here, don't bother the nice lady. The soda is undercarbonated. Stingy, bubble-wise. You should have gone yourself, you ask for a Coke and they come back with orange drink. No one understands the martyrdom of the volunteers for the trip to food concession. Suspicions are raised as to the intentions of next person, do they intend to cut in front? When the vendor inquires who's next, people lie. Need a penny, take a penny, have a penny, leave a penny. The lonesome fathoms of the tip cup. Someone says, I just want to stop here for a second. By midafternoon certain vendors are sick of people who ask questions, lift objects, frown at the price tag, replace. People say they'll be back later to purchase, just stand there bold as day lying through their teeth. The vendors form a composite of this type and roll their eyes when one ambles up.

Look at that guy's T-shirt, it has a witty slogan. Desire coruscates. The woman in the red tank top leaves a wake. One woman thinks, if I could be single for just one day, absently sliding a finger across the scar of her C-section. Hey, wait up. Everybody's saying, hey, wait up. They skid along. At the information booth separated children are emotionally scarred. Cotton candy mollifies the more practical. Her boyfriend is very tall and easily spotted in the crowd when they get separated. Over time people memorize their companion's T-shirts so they know what to look for when they get separated. Mosey over there. You see that same guy over and over, you keep ending up at the same booths. At the ice cream stand parents commiserate through glances as their offspring demand below. Underage youths try to get beer, trade schemes. The tallest boy is always the one dispatched plus he has stubble. Teenage boys look at teenage girls. Vice versa too. His parents' friends walk up whenever he gets the nerve to talk to a girl. Happens every time. Grass stains on knees. One guy sells rocks he painted pastel colors. Temporary tattoos. One boy rolls a pack of candy cigarettes into his T-shirt sleeve and tries to look tough.

The cheap-looking raffle tickets always seem like part of some con job, don't they. Hot dogs 'n' hamburgers. The old lady fans herself with the brochure. She wishes he wouldn't drink so much beer. Older she gets the fatter she gets. People would be surprised how many people have the same unkind thoughts. People cast longer shadows than the angle of the sun can account for. His upper back is already sunburned, like that. Aloe is suggested. Arguments are fertilized for tonight's harvest. Never knowing whether or not to look at the guy with the facial scarring, which is worse. All agree it's criminal to pay so much for a bottle of water. He thought he was the only one with this kind of shirt but look around, everybody is wearing it. People encounter bad cover versions of their favorite people. More than one vendor miscalculates the amount of change the day requires and has to go around to competitors saying can you break a twenty. Contemplate the ride home. She's always buying that crap. She asks him to hold her purse for a minute and his face gets hot, what does he look like standing there with a purse. It's hot. In the dunking booth he makes remarks. They want to kill him but make do with dunking. They will all sleep a little easier tonight after they have dunked the insolent boy in the tank. He is a scapegoat with swimming goggles. He offers to take a picture of the couple but can't work the camera. One of those new Japanese jobs. There are too many buttons. The flash won't go off. He waits for people to clear out of the way but they walk into the frame as if instructed. Fleeting eye contact overanalyzed. Listen to me when I'm talking to you.

She reads palms, heck it's a living. People compliment her acumen. There's no place to wash your hands. Pebbles insinuate themselves into shoes like beings with a purpose. They hold no formal meetings but those who walk around with pebbles in their shoes and those who remove pebbles immediately form discrete groups with philosophies. It's his fault they collide but the other guy says excuse me. You try to pass each other but you both keep darting in the same direction, it happens three times and you chuckle sorry. In the middle of people the man bites his knuckle and mumbles over bone, if I could just beat this fever. Signs say homegrown and homemade. They keep kissing in public, shaming others into contrived gestures of affection. Where has the fire gone in their marriage. Smell of charcoal. The retired citizens organization has a booth where they all sit around with sun visors. Vendors take shifts, one leaves to see the fair and leaves the other behind. They come back with goods from other booths and to dissipate envy offer obscure directions to this or that distraction. There is a strange oompa-oompa and they stand aside for the high school marching band. Take photographs of this authentic local culture. The boy accidentally sprays a grownup with water when the other kid ducks. The time for the raffle nears, you can win a boat. The smoke from the firecracker drifts over when they are done being startled. They made fun of him for selling underwear and socks that people can get any old place but look at the till. The antacid is in the glove compartment. Someone has to go back to the car to get something. He takes a moment to himself and has a smoke. Everyone stays too long. It's a fair.

Don't find a lot of white men on the South Side of Chicago at night so when he sees the white man leaning on the bar Moses thinks he's out sneaking on his wife, head downtown to spend a sweet night with a colored girl. The bartender seems to know the man, or at least likes his tips, so Moses figures the guy is a regular in Rudy's, every weekend he comes down here for a little pussy and music. Then halfway through the set he notices the guy taking notes. Not even trying to talk to any of the ladies but writing down stuff on a piece a paper. Thin brown hair soaked with sweat and snake eyes squinting through wire-frame glasses. No jacket on, sleeves rolled up, the guy's not dressed up to talk to women. He's after something else.

He isn't that odd a sight, but Moses loses his concentration and forgets to tell the joke about the mule, not a show-killing mistake but he likes the joke and the city audiences love it. He knows half of them, shit most of them are only two soles from bare feet; they remember the country, remember every day why they moved North but they like to be reminded from time to time of where they came from. They can put on their airs, pretend to be city and take the El just like white folks but deep down they're still country. Rudy's is the great leveler, could be a Mississippi jook if you didn't look outside the front door and see the tenement rows across the street. And overlooked the absence of sawdust on the floor—Rudy likes to think this is a class joint. Moses will play the blues and draw these folks back home. That's what they pay for. He's sky and unimpeded sky, hilltop brush tickling blue and a sun.

He starts into "Queen of Spades" and sizes up the couples. It's his first night in Chicago and he falls to custom and looks for the ugliest woman in the room. There's rarely any difficulty in finding her: the ugliest woman in a room stands out, like the tallest tree or the biggest rock. She makes a stark jagged outline against the rest of her sex, a landmark of homeliness. In small towns he sings and looks around the establishment (a timber concoction rotting on stilts over a swamp, a tin-walled jook joint shivering on lonely road) for flaw until he finds rickety teeth, all-gum smiles, lazy eyes, or hair like a spiderweb. He'll make eye contact with the woman (her lazy eye makes him cock his head, which the audience takes for some performance tic) and sings the next song, "Sweet-Hearted Woman," to her, tossing each word to her like roses. Thorns flicked off one by one. Everyone else in the room recedes until she understands—first in mad glee, then incredulously, finally in rapture—that it is just her and him, he's singing about her sweet heart. No man has ever loved her as he does now (those goddamned honey eyes of his, he knows how to make his eyes goddamned and honey), and when the song ends she fears that it is the dim light in the saloon that has saved her, created a spell over him that will dissolve once the set is over and he sees her close up. She has developed techniques over the years to mask nature's imperfections: urged by stares and coarse comments she tends to look at the ground when someone addresses her, mumbles to prevent viewing of the teeth knocked out by her mother some years before, and is wholly and keenly aware when eyes flit over defect and then swiftly shift away. But the singer lifts her chin in his rough palm after the set and coos. His songs did not lie. He is a special human being and can see what the rest of the world cannot, that she is good and decent and has much love to give to the one who discovers her treasure.

A survival tactic for a far-roaming and rolling man like himself that suggested itself one night in Mississippi when his eyes sailed out into the audience and immediately wrecked on a reef of monstrous titties, titties of such abundant rightness that the botched face of the woman they were attached to did not perturb him. He couldn't get past the titties. He imagined her aureoles, counted each immaculate bump, they swirled and orbited around the nipple like faithful retainers. He didn't see her face at all and later that night when his mouth was pressed between her breasts and he could barely breathe he realized from her wetness and greed for him that she hadn't been laid in a long time. She was grateful. Conceiving in that moment his plan to find the ugliest woman in the audience. A simple matter of practicality. They were grateful and eager to please. They never had a man who was liable to cut him or send him running out the bedroom window with his drawers around his ankles. They always remembered when he came back to town and sat at a front table in a new red dress, with a new hairstyle, with all their scars and defects powdered into invisibility by an emergent confidence and the promise of a night with Moses. He has safe houses from here to Galveston maintained by ugly but worthy women no other man wants. They are good cooks, excellent cooks all of them, and sometimes when he recollects his time with them it is the food he remembers first. Maybe he does it for the food after all. For pig's feet like jelly.

This night Moses decides to change his repertoire. He's in Chicago for a week and he feels full of luck. There are so many beautiful women in the crowd tonight he thinks maybe he can do what he wants. Not play it safe. In the front row a young lady in a blue dress with a collar of white lace fans herself and he can see sweat slide out of the depression in her neck. He'll lick it dry, he thinks, and can't help grinning and gloating over that future taste. She's smiling too, back up at him, no man at her table, she's stepping out tonight with two sweet and wonderfully plump friends. All of them in a big bed together. What their asses will feel like with his guitar hands squeezing them. Knead them like dough. His eyes ramble on as he takes notes: Oh, that woman in the red dress leaning on the bar, the way her leg's cricked up on the rail, he can see the slope of her calf. It's a small sexy lump, obscured now by a patron dragging himself up for a drink, but it vibrates in his head and trembles with naughty notes. He'll talk to her, the ugly woman will have to fend for herself tonight. He's on the South Side of Chicago and he has one or two songs he's written that describe the devilment he'll get into tonight.

Calf or no calf it doesn't work out that way. He finishes his set, shakes a few hands and struts over to the bar to talk to the woman with the miraculous calf (such a tiny miracle must token other miracles hidden from view by the homemade dress, surely) but before he can get to her the white man intercepts him. Mr. Moses, he says, wiping his eyeglasses with a handkerchief and squinting, that was a powerful set. I wonder if I could talk to you for a minute about a business proposal. Moses, winded from his songs and his mind on his own business proposals thinks, I don't need any Bibles. He asks, can it wait? and the man says he's a scout for American Music and he'd like to make a recording of Moses's songs.

Down the bar within arm's reach and yet so far down the bar the woman in the red dress laughs and takes the arm of a sharp-faced man in a crisp pinstripe suit. He smiles back at her out of his blue-black face and notices Moses's stare, and the itinerant bluesman knows he's not getting any closer to that calf, in his dreams maybe but certainty not tonight. The white man now presses the handkerchief to his brow. It's hot in here but not that hot, Moses thinks, this guy's sweating like he's in the jungle. Ha Ha. At least he's not a detective about that other matter. My name is Andrew Goodman, he says, giving Moses his card. Have you ever been recorded before? Moses says no, even though Spier down in Jackson approached him on a street corner a year earlier (a dead afternoon, none of those country Negroes parting with coin for this songman, nuh-uh) with the same proposition. H. C. Spier, the guy that put Tommy Johnson and Ishmon Bracey on Columbia, and who he's heard just paid Charlie Patton fifty dollars a side. Spier sat him down, gave him some rye and recorded four demo songs. Moses never heard back from him, the songs didn't make it with the Columbia boys apparently so Moses says, no, never been recorded before. No use letting the guy know his business. He says he'll come tomorrow to the guy's shop and he forgets about it for a few hours.

Good old Rudy comes up and thanks Moses for coming, they clasp shared nights and time together with their hands, which leads to one drink and then a couple of drinks and a poker game in Rudy's back office. His woman thoughts for the night stepped on by the Chicago boy in the pinstripe suit, Moses finds gambling presents itself naturally as pastime for this night. Not that Rudy would let him beg off. He knows he can win back some if not all of Moses's pay. The other players joke, but not much: regulars in Rudy's game, they keep their eyes on the cards. Moses helps himself to rye whiskey and one of the guys asks, that's how you get your voice like that, huh? That and canned heat and antiseptic when he can't get his hands on anything else. Rudy wins back his money from the talent for the night. The cards are marked. Moses looks up at the stained ceiling; he hadn't noticed when the noise downstairs stopped. They play poker above an empty saloon. Come four in the morning Rudy's won half the next night's pay as well.

As Moses gets up to leave, he asks Rudy is that white guy on the level. Rudy says he's here whenever there's a blues act booked. Rudy buys his records at the man's store over on Forty-third. He's all right, Rudy says, a little quiet.

When he wakes, sun through slats striping his body, he doesn't know where he is. There's nobody next to him and he can see that the room is so small that he must be alone. Unless she's hiding under the bed. Spending his first night in Chicago by himself. He remembers losing his pay in a poker game and waking up the crotchety old hotel manager at dawn. Did he hit the man or just yell to get him to open the door (his keys glinting on the bureau where he left them before departing for his gig). There's his guitar along the wall, tilting and sure. He didn't lose that. He never loses that. It's like a curse. He drops his feet to the floor and looks at his hideous toes. Does he have anything, even a drop? There's a brown bottle from two towns ago in his scarred suitcase. It calms him down.

He's a mug. He has no money. But he feels better now and maybe he'll see that record man. Fifty dollars a side sounds more real after Rudy's okay of the man, after a night losing money in Rudy's back room. Nothing but a train stub in his pocket. He thinks back to how he never heard back from Spier; the lost opportunity made him feel like he does when he's playing music on a corner and just watching everybody walk on by, no one stops to put a dime in his guitar case. Like he's not even there. Cracker had a face like a handful of gravel. When he hears about Ish and Skip James selling records and people say, Moses, why don't you have one of those, he says, shit those crackers know better than to mess with a nigger like me. Tough, like he doesn't care. At a house party or a dance in a Delta mud town some fool with ashy elbows will ask him to play something he heard on somebody's record. You don't do someone else's stuff. Steal it, yeah, but you don't just do it like that because some burrheaded fool asks you to. Those guys have got something and it ain't nothing Moses ain't got. Sometimes. On a good night. With a good audience, fine women up front to look at and he hasn't been drinking too much. Spier didn't call him back so forget about him. Let's see what this Goodman has to say.

Goodman's Records is the store on the corner, and its windows are so clean compared to the rest of the establishments down the row that it seems to prop up the whole block, like a piece of wood steadying a wobbly chair. Moses burps, feels a finger of bile in his throat. He looks down at the black handle of the guitar case cut across his palm like a blood brother slash. Time to meet the man, he says and pushes in the door, waking bells.

He figures a lot of these people are in from the country, come into town on a Saturday afternoon to pick up what they need to make the neighbors jealous. Yards of fine new cloth, new pots like what they see only in the Sears catalog and maybe a new Bible. Dust in their cuffs and untamed hems, boots for the fields. No place to buy race records where they live, Goodman's is a telegraph wire to the rest of the Negro world. He's a smart little white boy: set up shop on the South Side where other white people are too scared to give the folks what they need. Where there's a clientele and a need. He sees four listening booths along the right wall and a skinny boy disappears into one, clutching some nasty tune under his arms. Generally he'll stay out of record stores; the names of his fellow songsmiths up there on the wall, or angled up in crates like a plot of wind-fret weeds, depress him. He sees the names of men he has played with, traded tunes with, shared women with. They have been recorded. A young woman, her face hidden by the drooping flaps of her hat, snatches a James record out of a bin; he recognizes the label: Paramount. Paramount and Decca and Lonely Moon. Lemon Jefferson has been dead for years but they don't want the public to know. They put out the backlog of recordings one after another so people will think he's still alive. He reads, *Paramount Records are recorded by the latest electrical process. Great volume, amazing clear tone. Always the best music—first on Paramount!* There's a little pip of a boy at the register but Moses doesn't see Goodman. Sweat pouring out of him. He tightens the fat knot of his tie and sees the instruments at the back of the store. Violins and banjos on little hooks on the wall like family pictures, sheet music in rows, folk ditties and Scott Joplin. He sees the guitars. Brand-new Stellas and Nationals for nine dollars and ninety-five cents. Rues his scratched-up old Stella that's almost as scratched up as him, and works the best as it can, like him. Have you seen the new Tri-Cone Nationals? Goodman asks, coming out of the back room. He nods up to something beautiful that Moses doesn't see; Moses sees a hundred-and-twenty-five-dollar price tag and strings popped on his old Stella. I'm glad you came down, Moses, Goodman says. The man nods to the stringy boy at the register and sends a stare that orders, don't let these people put anything in their coats.

Upstairs at Goodman's boxes and boxes of records are stacked to the ceiling and hide dusty windows. The air doesn't move up there. Walking up the steps makes him a little dizzy and red snakes writhe popping on his eyeballs. You can take that stool, Goodman says. Moses falls into the stool like a diver. I got the idea when I started doing vanity records for my customers, the white man says. For five dollars I put their songs down for them. "Happy Birthday, Annie," whatever they want. Then a man came in from American looking for some race records and we started talking. He was supposed to be in charge of the company's race music label and didn't know a thing about who's out there. Hadn't heard of anybody.

How much do I get for this?

I can offer you forty dollars a side.

I've heard people get sixty, seventy dollars a side for work like this.

Who's paying sixty?

That's what I heard.

Look, I don't even know if American is going to go for your stuff. Do you know how much they have to sell just to break even? Five hundred. I don't even know if what we get is going to be usable.

Do you have something to get me started?

What do you mean?

A little something.

Ah. That's right. Goodman considers how much whiskey to put in the tin cup, then pours a taste more in. Seems he was prepared, Moses thinks. He knows how to treat talent. Goodman opens an icebox in the back of the room and pulls out a platter of beeswax an inch thick. He says, The heat can ruin it so I have to keep the masters in there.

I've heard about that. (Seen it before.)

From that mike, your music will go from the microphone and through to the amplifying stylus and that will cut it into the wax. It's pretty straightforward.

Alcohol-sick and sick from the heat, Moses feels better after a little rye. Tin cup quivering in his hands. A minute ago he could have heaved his guts to the floor but now he's calm. Funny how his hands shake in the morning but never when he feels a string, pulls it to the fret and lets the arrow fly. Goodman wants the songs from Rudy's. Spier said play what you want to play. But Goodman stares at him when Moses leans to the microphone. He gives orders.

Let's do that one you sang about the old house.

"My Baby's House."

Let's do "My Baby's House," but this time don't do the "uh-huh" when you get to the chorus. Leave that out.

Can't leave out the "uh-huh." That's the whole song.

Just for this take. I'd like to hear how it sounds without it.

Goodman signals Moses to play. Goodman keeps telling the man his business. He'll nod at different parts in the songs, a quick jab, but he does it at parts that Moses doesn't think are important. Things Goodman hears in what he's doing that Moses doesn't even realize.

You changed the chorus. That's not how you did it last night. He waves his notes from the show last night at the man whose show it is no longer. Like he's in charge now.

I like to mix it up. Sometimes do this, and then some other time I'll do that. (It has a mind of its own.)

They do sixteen songs, two sides engraved into the disk while the hot air sucks sweat out of him and into his suit. Goodman says he wants him to come in tomorrow and Moses is so afraid he's fucked up his chance again that he says yeah, and doesn't even ask when he's getting paid. The man gives no sign as to if he liked it or didn't. Just—can you come back tomorrow at the same time?

Moses walks halfway to his hotel and stops. On the other side of the street an empty lot allows the sun to splash on him, blast of heat through that notch. He sets down his guitar case and starts playing a few songs. Six, seven songs in and no one drops coins in his guitar case in appreciation of his technique and mastery, his shaping of song. They sweat and walk past him, with their sagging bags or sweating bottles, hurry through that patch of sun and back into the shade. Then he realizes that he hasn't been playing at all, he's just been standing there panting, holding his guitar and staring off into sunlight.

He is fret.

He goes back to his hotel room and sweats out a few bad dreams before the gig.

Moses oversleeps and makes it to Rudy's just in time. The room is more packed than the first night. Word has spread. He hasn't eaten since yesterday. Rudy gives him a glass of whiskey and Moses sets it down next to his stool. Some nights it's all he can do to drag his ass from song to song, like tramping through ditches, just make it through the set. Then there are nights like this. The second night in Rudy's in the first song he accidentally repeats a verse—they don't notice of course—but it works. It makes the song better. The lines had to be said twice to get them in people's faces, to say you can't look away, look at me when I'm talking to you. The rest of the song benefits from the mistake, like it let off weight and now it can sail higher, above Rudy's and all the South Side. People in Canada look up and see it over the Great Lakes. And from there it only gets better.

An accident that's lucky. He brings them home.

He watches her all night and he goes to her table after he finishes the set. She sits with a couple, the odd woman out. He asks her, how did you like the show, and the man at the table, this big guy in a brown suit, says those sure were some good songs. Moses knew he liked them; fool jumped out of his seat half a dozen times and waved his hammy arms around. The woman has full red lips and a wide, solicitous mouth. Moses asks, can I join you, always like to ask the people who come what they think about the songs. The man says I'm Al and this is my wife Betty and this is Mabel. He says let me buy you a drink and Mabel says I liked that song about the woman with the sweet heart (the song he sang as he looked into her eyes). He tells her how he wrote it one brokenhearted evening when he was crying over a woman who was not half as pretty as her. Mabel, Mabel, he tells her, he has an aunt named Mabel and he always thought it was the prettiest name.

Al is a doctor. He and Betty have to get up early for church, Al says. Betty and Mabel consult. They'll see each other tomorrow in church, Mabel assures her friend. Mabel is a waitress at Clement's Luncheonette and no doubt can cook.

She has a clean room in a clean building a simple stroll away. Moses staggers a little on the stairs but he is behind her (ass for miles) and he doesn't think she notices. She lets him into her room and goes to use the bathroom down the hall, she'll be right back. Moses drops his jacket on a bedpost and leans his guitar against the wall. He walks over to the Victrola and sees a Lemon Jefferson record on the turntable. He looks at the silver nipple poking through the heart of the record and closes the lid. She has twenty records stacked between the wall and the Victrola's little stand; he sees this and retreats back into the center of the room. He's beat and sits on the bed. Loosens his tie some more.

Those are my nursing books, Mabel says on her return, pointing to the books he rests his hand on. He hadn't noticed; he thought his hand was on mattress. I'm studying to be a nurse.

Uh-huh.

Waitressing is nice but being a nurse, that's something. So I got those books out of the library. Al's a doctor and he said he'd put me in touch with some people who need a capable person.

He hears her erase her accent from time to time, it slips in, a leak into her city bluster before she puts her finger in it. He says, your parents still down South? Where did you say you were from?

They're down in Pacolet. In South Carolina. They keep thinking, oh, she'll be back soon enough. They're still of that same attitude, but I'm not going back except maybe for visits.

What made you leave? He removes his suspenders from his shoulders.

He watches her wince for a second in recollection or something else before she says, I got tired of working for those lintheads.

Lintheads?

They called them lintheads because it was a cotton mill and when they came out they were covered with it. They got seventeen cents an hour, poor as dirt, but they still had more money than us. They wasn't going to let no Negroes work in that mill. So they paid us to keep their houses and take care of their children. They worked from six in the morning until six in the afternoon so that's when we had to be there. My sisters, we all worked in the Liberty Street houses, all my cousins on my mother's side. You could stick your black hands, stick your black hands in their dough for bread, you could lay your black body in their beds to nap with the children, but you couldn't walk through the front door. I did that for going on almost two years and then I said I'm going to Chicago. They couldn't stop me. They tried but I was going to Chicago.

Sounds about right.

We had a colored school in my town. I knew how to read so I left.

I'm sure you have a lot of stuff up there in that pretty little head of yours.

She falls asleep after he shows her how people do it back where he comes from (verbatim, that), she snores on his arm and he thinks, what is it, what is it: he felt he had to bounce back from the afternoon's session. What is it: this could be his one chance. Fifty dollars a side, his name on the records on Goodman's wall, his name up there for all them to see. This night he nailed it. Like he was in competition with himself and he had to take each song higher. He was reaching for something all night and then he switched "Long Time Blues" with "John Henry" and that was what did it, he changed his mind, didn't know why, half a second before he chased the first chord out he knew that he had hit it. He starts falling asleep and thinks, he wasn't competing with himself, he wanted to beat the machine. The box on the second floor of Goodman's, the diamond needle cutting his fame into beeswax. People could buy him for seventy-five cents, after payday, and he's in rooms on layaway Victrolas, him and his guitar drifting through screen doors into the night air in Natchez and Meridian, some hot young girl listening to him, swaying in sweat and getting ideas.

When he wakes up she's gone and he doesn't know where he is. Then he remembers, remembers she said she had to go to church and would he still be here when she got back. He mumbled in his sleep and she put that mouth on his forehead and kissed him a kiss that stuffed him back down into sleep. He looks around and thinks, no breakfast. She didn't cook him no breakfast. What kind of women they raising up here? Waking up by himself—might as well have gone to bed by himself if that's what's going to happen. His temples pound like hammers when he lifts his head from the pillow. Good God. He rummages around her room and comes up with a small bottle quarter-full of a liquid that a sniff tells him is rum. He takes the bottle, leaves, and thinks she's lucky that's all he takes, shit. Next time, he's sticking with the ugly women. No way he could live up here. These are some people with some new ideas.

The pipsqueak kid at the register tells him to go on up, he's waiting for him.

Goodman unpacks records from a large box labeled *Columbia*. That new Patton record is really going fast, he says.

Let's do this, Moses says.

I'll be just a second.

Don't got all day.

Goodman frowns and prepares the equipment. Moses tells his fingers, I'm going to get it right this time.

Goodman says, how about we start with that John Henry thing you did last night?

You like that.

It had a nice mood.

Moses wouldn't call it nice. He'd call it something else. Most John Henry songs he's heard from people, they tend to talk about the race and the man's death. He sang a version like that a few times but it never sounded right to him. The words "nothing but a man" set him thinking on it: Moses felt the natural thing would be to sing about what the man felt waking up in his bed on the day of the race. Knowing what he had to do and knowing that it was his last sunrise. Last breakfast, last everything. Moses could relate to that, he figured most everyone could feel what that was like. Moses certainly understood: that little terror on waking, for half a second, am I going to die today. Am I already dead. When Moses woke every morning he had to think hard about where he was, what town and whose bed. But it was one thing to possess that fright for a moment, he thought, and another thing entire to know it for sure, that today is your last day. So he figured that was as good place as any for his song to start. What a dead man thinks.

He only sings it occasionally. He sings it in cities mostly. The people in the bigger cities respond to it better for some reason. He plays it second-to-last in a show, to make them think about the night that is passing and almost over, what they have shared and is closing, that loss, before going into "Little Snake Man," which really gets them stomping. Placing those two songs back to back like that he always gets a reaction. Like John Henry gets them thinking about the grave and then the adventures of the Snake Man make them say, fuck it, I'm going to have a good time. They pick up on it. John Henry gets on them slow, creeping up on them like a shadow and their heads begin to nod with the beat Moses keeps with his old shoes and his broken fingernails on the guitar's body, he beats it like a drum with his hand, and then their palms head for the tabletops, in time, to this slow and mortal beat. It spreads from table to table and that is the best part, when he knows the song has got them and they know that it is them he is singing about. Moses has done this thing. He's shut up the voices at the back of the room with their talk of wages or women, undone the low hands of lovers and forced them to the beat. His mother always said, James, you should have been a preacher.

He doesn't do requests but he agrees to Goodman's request and he does what he does for money: sings.

How do you fit all that in? At the monument finally after all these years, she's forced to erase the image suggested by her father's stories, forced to throw out what she draws from her hold of curdled perceptions. No one could possibly agree on what he looked like. He was everyman. Every freed slave, traveling under the most common freed slave name. He was a six-foot-tall bruiser, big as a barn, dark as chocolate, darker. He was a wiry trickster figure who lived by his wits, quite obviously had some white blood, gentle, mean. If the professors who came here to study the legend couldn't get people to agree on what he looked like, what chance did this sculptor? The artist was forced to rely on what the story worked on his brain. He looked at the footprint left in his psyche by the steeldriver's great strides and tried to reconstruct what such a man might look like. Everyone here is gathered for the fair, she considers, all those people below, and they all work from a different snapshot. All the people who have heard the song on radio or had the story read to them from a children's book, they all have their own John Henry. You summon him up from verses and he swings his hammer down with the arms you give him. Think he really lived and he's more human; deposit a smile on his face and beads of sweat or tears running down his cheek. Think he's legend and muscles slide under fantastic limbs, the mountain shudders and birds flee branches each time the hammer comes down. His death shudder is a trembling exhalation or an earthquake, take your pick. The artist who made this statue had a big job. She inches toward admiration. Thousands and millions of John Henrys driving steel in folk's minds, and his is the one that climbs up on this stone pedestal and gets the plaque, the concession stand right there. She looks up at the eyes of the statue and they shelter penumbra too deep to comprehend.

Really, how can you fit all that in? she thinks, shifting on her feet. Pamela studies the statue, slanted in self-conscious posture, as if she were in a museum and the portly guard hovering too near. Is he the same metal as the head of his hammer, the drill bits he struck, the tracks he advanced. The statue of

John Henry is black metal, pitted across the chest where bullets have struck. Bunch of guys in a pickup with guns and nothing to do on a Saturday night. Probably a rite of passage, take a few shots at the black man on the rock. He's much shorter than the image she had in her mind, a little more fireplug than she would have made him. Not that she is an artist. Perhaps there was a question of how much it would cost and they had to save on materials. Put in a bid and the most economical gets the commission. Chamber of Commerce cuts the check. She takes a step back and realizes that the statue is taller than she is, six and a half feet high, but maybe the chest is a little disproportionate to the legs or arms. The hard to define ratios sought by the eye when taking in someone new are off somewhere. She grants this might be an aesthetic choice. She's no artist. It makes him more brutish, puts a little of the animal in him.

She moves over because the white couple next to her wants to take a picture. The monument area bustles with people, baseball caps bruit esoteric slogans, they trickle in, jostle each other, drain down the road to enter the main part of the fair. Pamela thinks that with so many people around the right thing to do is to come over, pay some quick respects to the monument, mumble a dull observation, and then move off so others can get a proper glimpse. But she's just standing there. He looks like he's waiting for the gun to go off. It's the moment before the race. Or any working day for him, there's no difference, he's going to do what he has to do. In the way that happens in such situations she becomes suddenly aware of the noise of the crowd around her. Their exhalations and giddy utterances. They could be witnesses to the competition. Come from all over for the big day. He holds the sledge at a slight angle up from his waist, right hand gripping in a fist near the hammer's head, left a bit slack at the bottom of the handle. Legs apart, well balanced. His hammer is kind of like a dick, if you want to look at it at a certain way. He's a boxer, a confident contestant in this affair. But, Pamela wonders, is he about to strike or just finished. Sure of his next blow or pulling back from a swing, sure of the blow just dealt, gauging the disappearance of the drill into the rock. She can't fix him. He is open to interpretation. Talking out of both sides of his mouth. You hear what you want to hear. The shutter clicks and fixes this moment.

She catches herself. This is an artist's rendering. She is confusing the statue before her with the man, and the man with her conception of the man. His head is dipped slightly. He's not wearing a shirt. Too hot for that in the tunnel. His pants are loose, cut of no fine cloth, falling in static waves, and she thinks of slave clothes. She finds herself wondering about this artist's politics, exactly what agenda he is trying to get across here. A bird has paid its respects on John Henry's shoulder.

"They say he died with a hammer in his hand."

Pamela stares, drawn back to the world again. It's that guy J. in his silly Hawaiian shirt.

"Who's W.E.H.?" he says, nodding toward the bronze plaque, the inevitable bronze plaque, set resolutely, recently polished, in the body of the pedestal. Impossibly, she hasn't noticed it.

## JOHN HENRY

THIS STATUE WAS ERECTED IN 1972, BY A GROUP OF PEOPLE WITH THE SAME DETERMINATION AS THE ONE IT HONORS. THE TALCOTT RURITAN CLUB CHOSE THE MEMORIAL TO MARK A PAGE OF HISTORY, ONE HUNDRED (100) YEARS AFTER THE COMPLETION OF THE BIG BEND TUNNEL IN 1872.

JOHN HENRY DIED FROM A RACE WITH THE STEAM DRILL, DURING CONSTRUCTION OF THE TUNNEL FOR THE C. & O. RAILWAY CO.

MAY GOD GRANT THAT WE ALWAYS RESPECT THE GREAT AND THE STRONG AND BE OF SERVICE TO OTHERS.

BY W.E.H.

"I don't know," she shrugs.

"I thought you were the big expert."

"Are we on the record? This an official conversation?"

"I'm just a humble laborer doing an honest day's work. No John Henry but I break a sweat now and then."

"Here's a tidbit then. They call it the statue that Jim Beam built. Do you have a pen or what?"

"It's all up here, trust me."

"The centennial of the race was in 1972—"

"Hypothetical race," J. interjects.

"The completion of the tunnel then, and the, what's it say, Ruritan Club gets the idea for the statue, but they don't have any money. They need about fifteen thousand dollars. So Johnny Cash has this TV show at that point, a variety show, and he sings his John Henry song, which is a pretty good version, you should look around for it, but he misidentifies this place as Beckley, West Virginia, and not here. Most of the songs name Big Bend Tunnel, which is what we're standing on top of, but then some take the legend and put their own local spin on it. So the Ruritan people call him up and say, hey, you made a mistake and also we're trying to raise money for this John Henry statue. So he sends a check and that's some of the money. What's so funny?"

"Nothing. Keep going, please."

"Then Jim Beam calls up. The Ruritan people have copyrighted their model for the statue and Jim beam is doing a special John Henry bottle and they want to know if they can use it. So they're like sure, but we're trying to make this statue, can you kick in a little money. So that's where the rest of the money came from, and that's why they call it the statue that Jim Beam built."

"So you can drink John Henry whiskey."

"It was just a special thing they put out for a short time. But my dad has, had, a few bottles."

"These little telling details."

"And you see those dents on the statue? People come around and use it for target practice. One time they chained the statue to a pickup and dragged it off the pedestal down the road there. Then the statue fell off and they drove off so they found it next day just lying in the road."

"Probably not much to do here on a Saturday night."

"Hmm."

An energetic and determined clan moves in front them, driving them with gentle vulgarity away from the monument. While the matron wrestles her camera off her shoulder Pamela and J. withdraw into the parking lot. She asks him what he thinks.

"I thought it would be a lot bigger," he says. The monument land is a shelf on Big Bend, the lap of a squatting giant. Chain-link fence keeps the people with two left feet from the cliff edge. On a day like today it earns its keep; there are varied hordes around J. and Pamela in search of justifications for the day's drive over. Kids' heads dart between boiled hot dogs and soda cup straws. Galoots lumber about snapping photographs and announcing how many pictures they have left. Some have purchased John Henry T-shirts and put them on over what they drew from the laundry this morning, to fit in with celebration, to pledge fealty to the day in 50-50 cotton and polyester. Bound to be a few of the clumsy type, statistic-wise, and the fences gird and protect. Most of the folks congregate around the food stalls, attempting to connect things they might have eaten, or at least described to them from visitors to foreign lands, with the missing letters on the menu. They mill there or by the red caboose, underneath the sign that reads JOHN HENRY PARK below the virile swirl of the Coca-Cola logo. Not much of an assignment. "I'm not sure if they had to fly me down for this, expense-wise," J. says.

"This is just the monument," Pamela counters. "The fair is over there by the tunnel." She leads him to the fence and a vista of the fair, down there at ground level. The iron seam of the railroad tracks stretches directly below their feet, diving into the famous tunnel. Then there's a thin strip of bone-white gravel and fencing and the fair itself erupts, eager, full of moving creatures negotiating white tents and each other, amid rippling streamers sad in the heat despite their exuberant colors, pulsating movement in the sun. There's a nice turnout. The preparations have paid off. Between the three rows of booths and assorted attractions too small to make out from this vantage, where the people are, hundreds, it's all unruly delight, what kind of cold heart despises the sincerity of a county fair on a summer day. The grounds extend for a quarter mile to the east, a ragged-edged flow. The eye is drawn to the south where the river writhes, seized by its own turbulent movement, and the mind can't help connecting the two, the river of water and the river of people. Both move to their inevitable conclusions.

"Not bad," J. says.

"Let's see the caboose," Pamela suggests, sounding suddenly more peppy than J. has seen her.

They move three feet and are reintroduced to the rules of moving in crowds. The necks of the more mindful glisten with suntan lotion. They shuffle forward. The line to the food and the line to the caboose get confused at one point (they have evolved too far from ants to remember how to work in such an insect boil) until the problem is sorted out by the more aggressive and J. and Pamela are before the door of the train car. There's only one entrance, so as one or two exit blinking into the sunlight, they are replaced at the same rate. It doesn't look as if the caboose ever saw any service on those tracks below. It doesn't look sturdy at all, the wood planks more suitable for a backyard toolshed's walls than a train car hustling on grooves at multiple horsepower. Pamela can see why they want to buy her father's museum. Appropriately exhibited, the Street archive would fill a couple of these cars. A modest train. The *John Henry Express*. A young white couple from the city exit the caboose carrying a small figure. J. and Pamela enter the caboose.

Even if they were the only people inside, they'd still be climbing each other's backs. Some of the clutter can probably be blamed on the previous fair-goers, who pick something up, replace, never matching the fastidious arrangement of the proprietor. But it's still a haphazard assortment of wares. There are a stack of T-shirts in a soft slow topple along the right wall, and then a collection of figurines. The woman next to J. says, "This is cute," lifting a three-inch-tall John Henry. John Henry ranges in size from toy soldier to lawn jockey, in a range of poses that produce an animated strip of steeldriving. John Henry holds his hammer at present arms, lifts his hammer to dare a lightning strike, brings his hammer down to ruin rock. On shelves above the counter, postcards are for sale. More than a couple are well-framed shots of the monument and the caboose in which they stand, a few more black-and-white shots of demolished C&O structures, the construction of the dam, various bucolic-minded scenes from the length of the New River. Merchandise. The air does not circulate, the wares exhale something not quite breathable, a gas more fit for whatever ceramic planets these objects call home. On the other wall clutter items unrelated to John Henry. Confederate flags in different sizes, T-shirts with said symbol. Available for purchase are miniature license plates that say Talcott and Hinton, suitable only for fairyland vehicles. In a row await diecast metal train cars, some even with wheels that move, if reluctantly. Books published by publishers outside the known New York zip codes describe the history of the region, the Chessie railroad system, West Virginia mining strikes, slim volumes with big type. The busy hands of tourists touch these things to test their solidity. They try to envision where these items might go in their households, mantels are conjured, knickknack nooks reconsidered. Everyone has a limit to how many T-shirts they can own, the figure varies with the individual. And yet the days are fleeting or so mirrors argue and souvenirs provide unimpeachable proof. A sign suggests, WHILE IN HINTON BE SURE TO VISIT HERB'S.

Pamela says she'll meet J. outside. She leaves before he can respond. Outside she can breathe again. Trying to relax all day and almost there until she saw one of the John Henry's. It is identical to the one her father brought home twenty-five years before. The one that started it. It's in a box up in New York. If the museum is going to have a gift shop, it will be full of stuff like that in there. She has a smoke and J. returns with a souvenir under his arm. It's a mid-swing John Henry, of that vintage, two feet tall, and J. holds it like it's a toddler. "It was only fifteen bucks," he says.

"It's nice," Pamela murmurs. "Gonna carry that all day?"

"Hadn't thought of that."

"You want to head down there? I don't think there's much else to see here."

"What time is the taxi coming back?"

"We have to walk."

"All the way down there?"

"All the way down there with John Henry under your arm. And your fly is open."

They walk, he adjusts.

When the Sepia Ladies Club convenes in the downstairs parlor of the Sutter household Jennifer is conscripted into serving duty. Her mother fusses over her hair, pronounces it a bird's nest, then says there's my princess after taming brush. When the Sepia Ladies take the teacups from the serving platter in their white gloves, they tell Jennifer how pretty she looks. One by one down the crescent of soft chairs as they sip. The ribbons in her pigtails deserve no small portion of blame for these compliments, if their comments on how delightful they look are any indication. Her mother twists them a certain way. The women pinch her cheeks. Jennifer lingers in the doorway, scratching her right ankle with her left foot, as the Sepia Ladies go through the minutes and from time to time her mother tells her to fetch more crackers from the kitchen, where Jennifer sets them in mandallic arrangements on a silver platter. From what she can tell, they don't talk about anything. Nothing she cares about anyway. Mrs. Jackson (who could not attend this meeting) is acting all uppity because her husband bought that new emerald Cadillac, but it doesn't matter because Mrs. Greenley saw him outside the grocery store at noon and she swears she smelled liquor on his breath, it runs in the family, but we shouldn't talk about Mr. Jackson's father and the turpentine. Mrs. Barden (who has been attempting to join the Sepia Ladies Club for some time now but does not understand she has to earn her place and that bragging about her Creole blood is not going to do the trick) and her husband moved into the corner brownstone on 138th Street and have fixed it up all nice (from what they can see from the outside; Mrs. Barden has not graced these women with an invitation to her abode) with lace curtain ordered from an English catalog, but maybe she should be less worried about their nice lace and spend more time thinking about her young Angelique talking to the no-good shiftless Negroes who work at Hope's Garage, spend less time bragging about how her grandfather went to Harvard and the award he won for his speech about freedom in Haiti and more time thinking about their daughter's carrying-on.

The Sutter family lives on Strivers Row.

This afternoon the Sepia Ladies are holding their weekly summit at Mrs. Mason's house to set the procedures of the upcoming raffle in stone. Jennifer watches the atomizer, that deep purple gem, cajole liquid into essence. Mrs. Sutter checks to see how the sleeve of her yellow dress falls on her shoulder. She tweaks the shoulder pads. The dress is a slick yellow, her hat a satisfied gold that livens her face. Jennifer has always coveted her mother's pearl earrings, she longs for holes in her earlobes. Once she slept with the earrings under her pillow, her fist around them driving the pins into her flesh. Two days later her mother asked, "Jennifer, have you been in my jewelry box?" and that was the end of that. Except for the twin scars in her palm. Her mother sees her watching and asks, "Jennifer, what are you going to do today while I'm at my meeting?"

"RoseEllen can't play today," Jennifer says. She tells her mother the story of RoseEllen's sick grandmother in Maryland and how her family had to drive down there.

Her mother says, "That's terrible," and ponders her behind in the mirror and above that the oval of flesh on her back permitted to eyes by the cut of the dress, the brown pearl and its lone imperfection, a mole that required careful plucking by Dr. Sutter every fortnight. "This is a perfect opportunity to practice for your recital," Mrs. Sutter says, inspecting.

Jennifer Sutter demurs and after a little back and forth, mostly forth from Mrs. Sutter, who has little time for discussion as her Sepia Ladies Club mission draws near, who has paid good money to acquire the services of the best music tutor in Harlem, who will not be embarrassed by her daughter at the recital in front of the other women of the Sepia Ladies Club, who has gone to great lengths to provide the best for her daughter, Jennifer is left with a brand-new dime in her hand for candy, but then it's straight to the piano.

Jennifer pulls up her white socks and folds them over. She buckles her shoes.

They walk out into the neat hubbub of Strivers Row that afternoon together. The Strivers Row Property Association does not allow stickball on this street (they leave that to the other streets in the neighborhood, to Negroes who care less about noisy youth and their epithets, their window-smashing errant balls). Instead they dispatch their male sons with Mr. Harding to Morningside Heights for softball. Jennifer's brother Andrew is there now with Jackie, Garvey and the rest of his friends. While Jennifer has to stay in their stuffy house and feel Mr. Fuller's stare upon her even though he's not there (he's probably playing with that little rat mustache of his), feel his impatience at incorrectly-struck keys even when it's not her fault, her fingers just slipped. Mr. Fuller always makes it out to be her fault. He has a list memorized of things a proper musician does and does not do, he has a thing about posture and a back like a lamppost. Her mother tells her to make sure to lock the door and they diverge on their clean stoop, the elder Sutter east and the younger Sutter west.

The Candy Store is only a block and a half from her house but she's forbidden to enter the disreputable radius of the Tip Top Lounge so Jennifer has to cross the street, walk down the opposite side and then cross the street again like a good girl. This circuitousness a condition of her release. She looks over at the open door of the Tip Top but cannot see inside it. She passes four sewer grates on her journey and each time she glances down between their iron teeth but she does not see any musicians. Never has.

The store doesn't have a name on a sign anywhere. Grown-ups call it The Polish and the kids call it the Candy Store. There was a time when the first thing Jennifer did when she entered the store was pivot left and head for the comics rack. Superman routing Nazis, Sub-Mariner crashing U-boats, occasional mayhem in the Pacific theater. Captain America was a normal GI until the medical experiments and then he became a fighting machine. But the war comics disappeared. First the Nazis, then the Japs, and then the conflict moved to the home shores: her mother realized that the four-color confections belonged to her little girl and not her young man, and that put an end to the comic books. It wouldn't do for her baby girl to dirty her hands with that messy ink, the violent images. But Mr. Polaski still remembers those days, he has dossiers on his customers beneath the glass counter, and when she enters his establishment he says, "Just got the new Action Comics in."

Jennifer mumbles quickly, "No thank you." The avuncular proprietor, with his gray undomesticated thatch of hair and tidy red face, is a relieving sight. His wife, who works occasional shifts in the omnibus store (scissors, candy, newspapers and wrapping paper, round tins of tobacco for those taken with the habit, items every tenant has special drawers for, and dust) doesn't like Jennifer, or children, or Negroes, and does not have a pleasant manner at all by any measure. Twice she shortchanged Jennifer, but grown-ups are so adamant and sure about being correct in all things that Jennifer never protested. The old lady has a shrunken face like a rat and little rat paw hands that curl around coins as if they were treasured crumbs. But she isn't in the store today. Jennifer holds up her dime and says, "I'd like ten redhots and ten caramels, please." Always say please. She likes to alternate the feeling on her tongue. First the rocky redhots burning red into her tongue until she's able to smash them with her teeth, then the soothing gooey caramel that's like sweet gum for a few chews before she dissolves it. On hot days like this the red from the redhots and the goo from the caramel sticks on her hands. She remembers that she'll have to wash them before her mother gets home, but she doesn't remember that each time she has that much candy she always feels sick afterward. Little wonder, how fast she eats it, but she never remembers that fact about her routine, just the nice contrast of the alternating flavors and textures that she makes in her mouth.

"I'm afraid I'm all out today, friend," Mr. Polaski apologizes with smile. "Cleaned out by noon and I haven't got my new shipment in. They don't work on the Sabbath."

Sabbath must be how they say Saturday in Polish. She looks up at the empty jars behind the counter. The jars are empty and her heart falls.

"Still have plenty of gum," Mr. Polaski offers. "We have redhot gum and that's almost the same thing." His hand already dipping into the jar. But Jennifer's not allowed to eat gum even though everyone else is. Her father is a doctor and has explained the situation to her. Eating gum will give her big lips. It is very important for her to keep her mouth shut when not talking or forking food into her mouth, or else she will get big lips like so many of their race. If the mouth is allowed to remain open, the muscles in the face relax, and after a time the lips slowly begin to curl outward, exposing the pink inside, until they remain like that. It is important to learn to always breathe through the nose, the nostrils. That's why God put them there. When one chews gum, the natural urge is to chew with the mouth open, which in turn promotes *lippus maximus*. So gum was not allowed in the Sutter household on Strivers Row. Often when they walked in the neighborhood her father would point out those afflicted with *lippus maximus* and reiterate his professional advice.

No more suckers and only gum. RoseEllen, of course, can eat as much gum as she pleases. Chew it brazenly, blow bubbles, stick it on the undersides of furniture. Which was why Jennifer rued deeply her grandmother's sudden illness. Mrs. Turner keeps a bowl of rainbow gumballs on the mantel in the living room and Jennifer can help herself to as many as she likes. She crushes them, sucks on the candy shell until its all gum, defenseless against her violence, blows bubbles that she snaps like firecrackers. RoseEllen might say, "You're eating all my gum!" but only when she's already mad at something else. Jennifer almost considers buying the redhot gum, which probably mixes the tartness of the redhot with the pliability of the caramel, but just two Saturdays ago she forgot to spit out her gum before she got home and was sent to her room without dinner. The redhot gum jar used to have a picture of a firecracker exploding on it, but after they dropped the bomb on the Japs they renamed it A-Bomb Gum and now a mushroom cloud unfurls itself in redhot taste.

"No thank you," Jennifer says and nearly runs out. She stops a few stores down, her face hot. She has a dime. She could walk two blocks down to the Five and Dime but it seems so far. Jennifer looks up the street and sees the stained black awning of the Tip Top and immediately turns away to face the music store. Halfway between the Candy Store and the Tip Top, around the corner from her house and yet she's never seen this store before. Seen it from across the street of course but there's no name on the outside. From here, her face in the glass, she sees records taped up all across the window, so many that she can't see in the shop. She doesn't know any of the names on the records. Billie Holiday, Bessie Smith and W. C. Handy. The sun has faded the record covers so that they cling on the glass as blanched barnacles of what they had been. She has a dime. She doesn't know why, she pushes the door.

Jennifer smells air that at bottom is dusty and musty, and up top sweet and slightly acrid. The light allowed by the record covers in the window, all those sliver cracks, merges into a limp gray that is defeated only at the end of the room, where a naked bulb shines down over the counter. The room is narrow, and the aisles between the boxes of records and stacks of old, amber magazines remind her of the tramped spaces in the park, the beaten-down grass that through wordless agreement of all who pass makes a path. The two men at the counter stare at her interruption. The one behind the counter is a fat man in a striped red sweater whose palms are pressed down resolutely on the cluttered counter, as if it might levitate. His head is shaved and the sweat glistens on the short hairs, like dew impaled on grass. The man leaning against the register slouches with his shoulders forward in a bony landslide, his head ducking beneath a cloud of slow smoke. He's dressed in jeans and a denim shirt with one tail tucked in. He exhales out of the corner of his mouth, looking at Jennifer, sticks a toothpick between his lips and passes a tiny cigarette to the man behind the counter, who secrets it out of sight.

Jennifer turns her face to the record crate nearest her and starts fingering the heavy 78s, trying to be obscure. W. C. Handy spreads his hands wide on the cover of the first, his band behind him poised at their instruments. She flips quickly through them for a few moments to kill time. What is she going to do with a dime and a Victrola at home she's not even allowed to touch? The phonograph sits in the parlor, polished to gleam. Not that she could do anything with it anyway, since her parents don't own any records. It's like a vase, or the candlesticks in the downstairs hallway, something that roosts in the Sutter brownstone in its designated place. For show. She hears the men on the other side of the room begin to murmur to each other. They've gotten over her intrusion here. She smells the strange air in the place and remembers that her mother told her to practice for her recital and thinks she should go home. Her mother won't like it if she messes up in the middle of Jacques Wolfe's "Shortnin' Bread" while Jimmy Mason and Sojourner Gardiner, with their flute and recorder and snotty attitudes, get through their songs fine. Scandalized by her pretty little girl in front of the Sepia Ladies Club. She's about to leave the store when it occurs to her: she can buy sheet music. Then she has an excuse to be here in this store her mother would obviously not approve of, with its dirt and shiftless-looking clientele, just two doors down from the Tip Top. She glances over at the counter. The two men face her, heads tipped together and saying something she can't hear. The man with the toothpick pulls it out of his mouth like tugging a weed, looks down at it and replaces it on the other side of his mouth.

She makes her way between the piles of newspapers, steps over a broom currently enjoying an indefinite period of unemployment and deeper into the sweet cigarette smell at the back of the store. She looks up at the owner and waits for him to say, "Can I help you?" be friendly like Mr. Polaski, but he continues talking, obviously seeing her there but not saying anything. He has twin moles on each cheek waxing over his bushy black goatee.

"Do you sell sheet music?" Jennifer asks.

The owner's head rolls on his neck and he stares down at her. "I got sheet music over there, I got sheet music all over the floor over there, what kind of stuff you looking for?" His tone like she's been asking him questions all day. His eyes shift over quickly to his friend in message, then return to Jennifer. "I got Hit Parade shit, jazz, I got New Orleans, what do you want?"

"Do you have anything for ten cents, please?"

"Ten cents? Ten cents won't get you a dime in here. I'm just a man trying to make a living here," he says, opening the cash drawer with a button and a smart chime, and then slamming it shut again to underscore his point.

"Why don't you give her a break, man?" asks the man with the toothpick.

The owner squints at his Saturday afternoon companion. "What did you say?"

"Give her a break, man"—clearing his throat with a gush—"she's a little girl." He smiles down at Jennifer, parting lips to promenade gums and three loyal teeth.

"You got other places to be, right? I know you got other places to be." The toothpick man shrugs and looks down at his feet. The owner looks down at Jennifer again, grimacing. "I'll tell you what," he says, "I have some old stuff in the back that I can't get rid of. Why don't you wait a minute and then you can see what you see." He condemns his friend with a stare and disappears behind dusty green curtains into the back before Jennifer can say thank you.

The man reaches behind the counter and retrieves the cigarette. "Little crotchety," he says to Jennifer as he lights the end. He removes the toothpick and holds it straight up in his fist as if there were a balloon at the tip of it. Jennifer watches him inhale with dedication and then he adds, without letting smoke escape, "He's crazy." He nods to himself, agreeing anew with what he just said. Jennifer spies an autographed photo on the counter of the owner with his arms around a big woman in a black dress. She can't make out the signature or the dedication. In the photograph, the owner is much slimmer and wears a smart pinstripe suit and a homburg hat. His slim mustache then is now somewhere in his overgrown goatee. Hearing movement in the back room, the man exhales quickly and returns the slim cigarette behind the counter. Toothpick back in his lips.

"Here we are," the owner says. As he parts the curtain with the corners of the Coca-Cola crate, he sniffs, nostrils flapping like bellows, and he frowns at his friend. "Pipes burst in the basement and soaked all this through," he says, setting it down on the floor. "Some of it—you can see for yourself. That's all I got for ten cents."

"Thank you," Jennifer says.

While the owner starts berating his friend in a low voice, Jennifer kneels before the crate. A strong gust of cellar hits her from the water-ruffled paper. There's grit on her fingers as soon as she touches the first one, "Hallelujah, I'm a Bum" by Jack Waite. Black clumps of mold bloom in some spots on the wrinkled pages, and each page she touches releases more of the musty smell. She's going to have to wash her hands as soon as she gets home. She hears a match struck. She doesn't recognize any of the composers or the songs. Mr.

Fuller doesn't teach her songs like these. "Abdul Abulbul Amir" by Frank Crumit, "Swingin' Down the Lane" by Isham James. They're really old, these songs, over twenty years old, from 1928 and 1920 and 1923. She looks at the dust on her fingers, looks down to make sure her dress isn't touching the floor. She can't find anything she wants, and her mother would take one look at whatever came from this box and put in it the fireplace. It's dirty. But she doesn't feel she can just walk out without buying something because the crotchety owner went all the way downstairs, so she grabs the next piece of music, "The Ballad of John Henry" by Jake Rose, and rises from the box.

"Let's see what you got here," the owner says, trying to touch as little of the sheet music as possible.

"Look at that shit," the man with the toothpick says, "Why don't you just let her have it for free, man?"

The owner barks, "Is this your store or is this my store? If someone wanted to kick some lazy, hanging around all day doing nothing but smoking other people's stuff never has any on himself out of here, would that be you or me?"

The man shrugs and shifts his toothpick from the left corner of his mouth to the right.

"Here's ten cents," Jennifer says.

"That is indeed a dime," he says, opening the register and dropping the coin into a clinkless hollow. "Knock yourself out."

The sun is twice as bright once she leaves the store, until her eyes adjust again to this average world. She almost walks past the Tip Top, then doubles back, takes her usual long route around the prohibited saloon. At each sewer grate she looks down, below the street, but does not see what she thinks one day she will see.

She feels that the piano has been waiting for her whole life, on its sculpted paws, and before that. Her mother and father do not know how to play, and her brother Andrew prefers his models and sports. Her parents bought the baby grand for Jennifer alone, it seems, for the day she would take her place in the scheme, setting the piano in the corner of the parlor room where the sun attends for whole hours in the late afternoon, the light charging facets of the crystal vase atop it as the star heads west. All for show, for years, until Mrs. Sutter retained Mr. Fuller, the piano instructor, said to be the best in all of Harlem, a bit expensive but well worth it, and Jennifer learned how to play. "It's never too early for a little girl to get herself cultured," her mother informed her, and her free time retreated before the advance of lessons and practice, half an hour of practice a day and now an hour. After school, on weekends. The old piano had a use now beyond decoration, and Jennifer attended to her instruction. The first thing Mr. Fuller does each lesson is to remove the vase from above the piano with a tsk-tsk-tsk, and Mrs. Sutter replaces it after every lesson.

Jennifer hears some kids laughing outside and closes the window. Above the music it reads, "Another fine musical composition by Yellen & Company Music under the auspices of Dr. Simon Ramrod's Patent Medicines." On the back is an advertisement for Dr. Ramrod's Essential Tincture of Gridiron, Otherwise Known as Nature's Grand Restorative, in which a contented gentleman dozes against the bark of a weeping willow, in supreme repose, anodyne lulled. She places the music over the oppressively familiar staffs of "Shortnin' Bread." She knows that piece as well as she is ever going to, even though her mother shakes her certitude at every opportunity. There was no way, Mrs. Sutter reminded her daughter, that she would stand to be humiliated at the club's recital next week, when the Sepia children, or at least the ones blessed with the gift of music, will perform familiar ditties from the Hit Parade while their parents sip tea and clap dainty hands together. She pays Mr. Fuller good money and will not stand to be disappointed.

"The Ballad of John Henry" by Jake Rose hides the music for "Shortnin' Bread," which Mr. Fuller has decided will best showcase Jennifer's facility with the pianoforte. Mean Mr. Fuller, whose skin reeks of a sharp cologne, who breathes loudly through his nostrils as she tries to concentrate on her finger drills, who reminds her to turn the thumb under the hand and not over. There's a notion forming in Jennifer's head, not yet articulated but understood: if it's in another language, it must be culture. Mr. Fuller knows many languages. He says, "Music is a tonal art, but we must always remember the words of Liszt when he first heard Henselt—'*Ah, j'aurais pu aussi me donner ces pattes de velours*'—'I, too, could have given myself these velvet paws.' Tone is the means, not the purpose." Which means nothing to Jennifer. He says things like, "We must strive to embody Michelangelo's words, '*La mano che ubbidisce al intellecto*,' to be the hand which obeys the intellect." Which means nothing to Jennifer except a few moment's respite from her next attempt at middle C. Whenever Jennifer tries a new composition, the words of Mr. Fuller and her mother shout: he tries to remind her of what to look for in the piece; she tries to remind Jennifer of the importance of being a lady. The melody of "The Ballad of John Henry" is not complicated. But this time she does not hear any of the usual voices as she starts the piece. As she looks down at the yellow and stained paper, she hears something Mr. Fuller said once, a few months before at the end of a lesson. She can't recall the German words or the name of the man who said it, but she remembers this: you think you push but you are being pushed. Her first round through the song is remarkably easy. It speeds by, like a walk down a street she has been down a thousand times before, something seen but not seen, gone in a blink but navigated without mishap as she thought of something else. She tries it again, top of the wilted page, and this time is even easier, there's something sad about the song, but what she feels most is—pushed. The song pushes her. There is something in this song that does not exist in the music that Mr. Fuller brings, it quickens inside her. It doesn't go to church and cusses, wears what it wants. For a second she thinks, this is what I should play next week at the recital, not that other song. But she knows that won't happen. The afternoon light glides along the dark wood of the baby grand, reminding her of sunlight on the Hudson River, something here in her vision for a little time before it goes into the ocean, joins a larger thing. The last note withers in the empty brownstone, down the hall and up the stairs into empty rooms, and this time she decides she'll sing the words. She's in a heat right now. She sings lyrics that tell a story of a man born with a hammer in his hand and a mountain that will be the death of him: you think you push but you are being pushed. She sings it again and is so pushed that she doesn't hear her mother come in the front door, only hears her mother yell, "Do you think your father works ten hours a day walking up and down the neighborhood treating sick people so that he can come home and listen to his little girl play gutter music?"

Unexpected accompaniment. Jennifer jumps off the piano bench, fingers recoiling from the keys. "No, ma'am!" she says. Gutter music. Gutter music always conjured in her head the image of an orchestra in a sewer, neatly dressed gentlemen in tuxedos, their tails dragging in the muck beneath the city. She used to always look down into sewer grates to see if she would see them playing, sneaking a peak surreptitiously, but all she ever saw was glinting liquid and she does this less frequently now. Today she did, because she has always wondered: what music do they play?

Her mother drops her shopping bags in the doorway and strides over to the piano. She rips away "The Ballad of John Henry" and shakes it in the air, the cheerful stanzas of "Shortnin' Bread" restored to vision and dignity. "Where did you get this?" she demands, her hat slanting off her hair.

Jennifer looks down, cracks her foot and grinds her shoe tip into the new carpet, which is a self-satisfied regiment of whorl much admired by the good soldiers of the Sepia Ladies Club, expensive, alluding to the European.

"Where did you get the money for this, Jennifer Sutter? You used that dime I gave you for candy, didn't you?"

"Yes, ma'am." Jennifer settles into this dressing down by her mother, winded, still trembling a little from being pushed. She hadn't thought she was doing anything wrong, but apparently the sheet music was part of a larger transgression that she had never considered. When she was older, she thought, she'd know where everything lay.

"Look at me when I'm talking to you, young lady." Her mother takes her daughter's chin in her hand. "This afternoon when I left for my club meeting you said you wanted a dime for candy because I always try to do the best for my only daughter. Don't your father and I always try to do the best for you and your brother?"

"Yes, ma'am." Often when their parents walked them down the street their clothing was tight and constrictive compared with that of other children their age, whose parents were not as cognizant of the role appearance played in social standing, whose parents did not know that people will talk. These other children invariably looked more comfortable.

"Does this look like candy to you?"

"No, ma'am." If the sheet music was that much more horrible than candy, it must truly be horrible. Of such low social standing.

"When we walk to church on Sunday morning down Broadway," her mother said, cheeks red in her light brown skin, "you see the dirty men with their shirts all out their pants, drinking the devil's liquor and stinking to high heaven when good people are going to church. Do you know what they've been doing all night?"

"No, ma'am." She did know, because now this discipline had wound its way down the hills away from the music and into a familiar body, and Jennifer was well acquainted with its currents and undertow. She knew all about the good-for-nothing niggers who passed bottles back and forth and were an eyesore. But it seemed best to feign ignorance.

"Staying up all night drinking and listening to music like this!" her mother screeched. "Because they are good-for-nothing niggers who don't care about making a better life for themselves. They want to stay up all night and carry on and pretend that just because they don't have to pick cotton they have no more duties to attend to. We can't do anything about good-for-nothing niggers who don't want to take their place in America, but we can watch ourselves. This is Strivers Row. Do you know what striving means?"

"It means that we will do our best," Jennifer recites.

"It means that we will survive. Now I want you to promise me that you will never play that music again. Will you promise me that?"

"I promise, Mother."

"That's the girl I raised," her mother says, this tempest now just draining damp. "Now I'm going to put my bags away," she says, reassuring herself, "and I want to hear that song that Mr. Fuller has been teaching you so you can be ready for your recital."

It's always *that song*. Her mother doesn't know any of the names of the composers. They're just nice things to her, more nice things to have in the house. Her mother disappears with the groceries and leaves Jennifer alone in the room. Her eyes fix on the good and pleasant notes of Jacques Wolfe's "Shortnin' Bread." She hears the instructions of Mr. Fuller and her mother's explanation of why it is important to be a lady. She thinks as she starts to play: no, it wasn't candy but it sure was sweet.

The citizens practice their aim. Some shoot BBs at tin cutouts of fowl, which are dragged in ellipses by iron chains and tip back ninety degrees when hit. Some shoot water pistols into the mouths of clowns to fill a balloon, and others toss baseballs into cupped targets. This is good old American know-how. It's all rigged. The prizes for excellent marksmanship hang on hooks, dingy teddy menageries. Alphonse quiets the temptation to engage in a little target practice. It would be a little perverse in light of his plans for the next afternoon, and besides, he's already put in his time at the range over the last few months. Plus there's nothing more ridiculous than a man hauling a gigantic miniature green elephant.

Tiny hollows, pits, and chips pock here and there the skin of the tin ducks, and these depredations prove them kin to the John Henry statue on the hill above. The targets take the shots and persist. His fingers fall over his purple fanny pack; through the thin plastic he can trace the barrel. It would be perverse to take a shot at the ducks or the clown, he thinks, but it sure would be a nice piece of color for a journalist. Trace back the steps of Mr. Miggs of Silver Spring, Md. over the days leading up. One of them might ask Eleanor if her husband often attended stamp-related events. Would she remember? He rarely goes to expos or conventions outside the D.C. area. Then they might ask her, why do you think he did what he did in Talcott? What they should ask, Miggs thinks, is why the mountain chose him.

He can't decide if he should walk faster or slower. There's more to see that he might miss and so much he cannot savor if he speeds. He allows his legs to take him, sniffing the fair into him, receiving a gutter bouquet of popcorn, beer, children's vomit. There's a table full of stuff no one wants in tableaux of disappointment, silk wraps, tin rings, family heirlooms offered up after debate to help out with the mortgage. That woman there selling her bad paintings—he recognizes them as paint by number specials, produced in a factory for people to fill in. She's chosen some bizarre colors—residence in her mentality for one second would be too long—but at least she's stayed in the lines. (More than he can say for himself.) He overhears conversations he doesn't want to overhear and wants to sprint past them but he can't. This is all so important. He might miss something. Alphonse looks around for something to dissuade him but nothing he sees offers argument or counterpoint, not the couple in romance sharing a public private smile, nothing in all the human connections he magnifies through the lens of his disquiet into infinite love. Of course these people don't know he is seeking something from them. Of course no matter how hard he tries to avoid looking at the mountain, he knows it is still there with its unavoidable message. The twin tunnels are like eyes.

If he keeps his eyes on ground level maybe he can avoid it for a while. A little redheaded girl in overalls holds a goldfish in a plastic bag. She slides her left hand across the bottom of the bag and raises it and for a few moments the poor fish doesn't know what to do. It can choose one half of the bag or the other. By a casual gesture its world has been halved into inevitabilities. He watches as the girl disappears to catch up with her mother. Alphonse thinks the fish will be lucky if it makes it back to her home alive. Asphyxiation. Drowning in water, invisible plenty. They never had children. It bugs him only occasionally, generally at times like this when he sees families and families out together. He has small hands but he could take a smaller hand into his own and lead. He has things he could pass on to someone, a message to communicate beyond tomorrow's dispatch. What would it sound like if he heard it aloud, he wonders, and heard it for once outside his head. He could scream in this crowd and no one would hear him because of all the happy noise.

The announcer says, "Lost child Kevin Graham is at the information booth. Lost child Kevin Graham is at the information booth. His mother's name is Carol." Alphonse looks around—no woman runs through the crowd toward the information booth with tears of relief on her face. He spots the man whose life he saved last night, over near the kegs with some of his journalist pals. The man seems none the worse for wear. Alphonse waves—for a second there it looked like the black man was looking in his direction. But he doesn't see him and there's no way Alphonse is going to go over there. To say what, I saved your life last night, remember me? If he had done nothing, he would be no less a stranger to that man. Alphonse could be another one of the man's readers, anyone in this crowd.

He turns around and finds himself in front of soft stacks of John Henry T-shirts. He recognizes the design as a black-and-white copy of the stamp.

The image is a little hard to make out because it has not been well reproduced, the grays aren't that forceful, and John Henry is very black, like a smudge almost. He can almost make out the mouth and chin, but for the most part the face is just dark. What expression is there is anyone's guess. Past the right shoulder of John Henry a locomotive speeds into futurity. The business end of his sledge rests on his shoulder. Alphonse thinks the hammer looks in pretty good condition, pristine, as if it's never been used.

Everybody's wearing one. They sell like hotcakes. The owner's young son handles all the transactions while his father chats with a crony and the boy is meticulous with the change, counting aloud.

Alphonse puts the T-shirt on over his red polo shirt, tugging the collar out over the neck of the T-shirt. The black church sells plates piled heavy from heated aluminum trays. Do they still call it soul food, or have they changed that too, Alphonse wonders. In the sensitivity seminar at work the consultant they hired said that any word out of the mouth can be a ticking timebomb. He hears, "Lost child Kevin Graham is at the information booth. Lost child Kevin Graham is at the information booth. His mother's name is Carol." Then the siren blows and everyone stops in their tracks. The train is coming.

The fairgrounds are adjacent to the tracks, separated from the fair by steel fencing and frowning rent-a-cops. It might be a special day for the town of Talcott, but the business of CXS Transportation must continue. Alphonse, denizen of middle management, understands this. The crowd charges over to the railward part of the grounds to jockey and jostle by the fence. There's a slim space between there and the last row of booths, and the people squeeze in. Alphonse finds a place in the second row, behind a father balancing a daughter on his shoulder. The guards tell everyone to take it easy, hold on, don't lean on the fence. Most of them are teenagers and wish they had a gun to go with the uniform. Instead they have to rely on tough guy stares honed over time in convenience store parking lots. Everyone looks away from the mountain. East toward the coming, crawling train.

Hey.

The general readership magazine that recommended stamp collection as a worthwhile hobby advised that choosing one kind of stamp, a specialty, might add shape and purpose. Before he caught on Alphonse collected only those stamps that arrived on his correspondence. He cut out the corner of the envelope and soaked it in warm water. Once the stamp loosed, he removed it gingerly with the tongs that came in the mail order stamp collecting kit, and dried it overnight in a paper towel. The next day he slid the stamp in the hinge and deliberated, directed by personal symmetry, over its place in the album. After a few months he had many stamps, to be sure, an index of received confidences and dull immediacies, but there was no order to them. It was a collection of randomness he had preserved there, and looking over what he had assembled depressed him. Surely this was not what a hobby was supposed to be. Hobbies made the days easier, what, they knocked down imposing hours into moments that stretch. Then he went to his first stamp fair, at the convention center. He walked up and down the rows. Everyone was so serious and seemed to know what they were doing. Even the little kids knew what they were looking for, going up to dealers to ask if they had NASA space stamps or reptiles. He tried to look busy; everyone knew he didn't belong there, surely, he felt it on his neck in pore-squeezed sweat. He busied himself in a dealer's penny box, where they put all the dregs that no one wants, that have no value, where everything goes for a penny no matter what the postage declares. He picked through Thomas Edison, Dutch tulips, a number of South American military dictators. Sweat stained his collar; everyone was looking at him. Then he found his first railroad stamp.

It was a commemorative for the first trip of the *Atlanta Zephyr*. Was he supposed to recognize the *Atlanta Zephyr*? Was it famous and he was out of the loop or was the line something lost and his ignorance the common and most appropriate response to the name of the old Georgia train? A nibble off the top left edge was missing, and half the perforations were gone. But—he couldn't stop his finger from running over its rough skin. He could feel the speed. The image fell into what he would later discover to be the standard portrayal of trains on stamps: a locomotive and a car or two speeding off the right edge with a little puff of steam, foreshortened to suggest departure from an old world and speed across the border into the new. It was not a picture of a vase or a cat. The train, tinted blue, was a notion of possibility. Human beings had made these trains, men like him, and if to outsiders a stamp was no kind of monument to a grand idea, for Alphonse this was true craftsmanship. With a few simple strokes, with a few anonymous cars and one noble locomotive, the artist had composed the definition of dreaming. Anything could be in those cars, anything he wanted. Off the border, nameless destinations that all who boarded knew as Paradise. Inside, special people bound for safety, the saved and the blessed, and what kind of freight in the boxy cars? Gold or the smart man's invention or penicillin for the epidemic. News of the peace treaty. Once his collection started in earnest, he'd spend hours with a magnifying glass trying to discern human faces in the passenger cars, with such en- thusiasm his posture degraded to its present stoop. He placed his face behind those sooted windows and willed himself safe passage.

Now he can log on the internet and trade information through his phone line, but in those early days he haunted catalogs and newsletters, discovering that every specialty had its society, and they communicated through a secret language. He mailed a five-dollar money order and received a F/VF com- memorative of the Gold Rush Centennial, sent another for six seventy-five and got General Motors' Train of Tomorrow, with its optimistic jet age an- gles. Sometimes when the illustrations were uninteresting, falling into the standard locomotive/car profile, the titles were enough to trigger enthusiasm. The *Florida Sunbeam* Is Coming Back—he didn't know the history, what tragedy had befallen the Florida line that made its return such a glorious event, but his blood rushed. The First Winter Run of the *Georgia Mercury*, M condition. He read the words Alaska Railroad, 25 Years of Progress (F/G) and saw crews hacking ice in the tundra, a few sled dogs dozing by the fire and a new settlement just over the next hill that needed supplies by rail. Progress, progress in limited issues, warmed him and justified his days. The Inaugural Daily Service Chi-LA *El Capitan* (NM) described to him a nation learning to run; daily service across half the country was civilization. Even the mundane issues—the solemn Helsinki Railway Station (VG), the humble First Diesel (G) in Bangladesh, Bulgaria's Unloading Mail Car (F), the commemorative for unsung hero Andel Pinto, Railway Builder (NM) of Brazil—were like press releases from the office of the twentieth century, from his basement view, informing the citizens of the world that each new peak bested was mere appetizer to the next novel summit just now in view. He filled albums and al- bums with stamps from around the world. Every place on the globe was linked by the invention of the railroad, it crossed oceans and cultures.

He didn't notice when he started collecting the stamps of dead places. The Last Run of the Sante Fe Motor (P), Commemorating the End of Old Erie (G), Old Brighton Terminal (NM). They issued stamps for dead lines, defunct lines, extinct depots. Routes that had become obsolete, replaced by superhighways or snipped short by politics. Towns failed, everybody moved away and the terminal shut its doors in anticipation of vandalism, became a stamp. Small independent lines were bought up and swallowed by larger ones. Tracks uprooted to be melted down into arms for the revolution, or left to weed over. Impractical lines laid out of vanity that never justified the plan- ning of the right of way. Top of the line locomotives made inefficient by technical advances. What remained of the ultimate in human achievement was a stamp. It was all obsolete and preserved in adhesive elegies, limited-issue testament. He collected it all.

The engineer blows the horn and they all cheer. The train departs the Talcott depot and advances on the crowd, sliding coyly across the rails. The locomotive isn't sexy at all, just a utilitarian snout prodding ahead to shift its freight to safe berth. Nothing like anything in his albums, this is the new machine. It moves slowly, Alphonse notes, to ensure that no one from the fair gets hurt. They can't cancel the shipment, John Henry Days or no John Henry Days, because there are timetables and money involved. What's in there? he wonders. CXS hauling aluminum. The fair-goers cheer ore, or a stack of struts. Rolls of fiber-optic cable—that's where the true lines of communication are these days—fiber-optic cable. That's the way people get the stuff they need these days. The engineer blows the horn again and waves out the window. People whip American flags or balloons, whatever they have in their hands, in response. Then they can make out the banner draped along the black metal of the first car: CXS TRANSPORTATION SALUTES JOHN HENRY DAYS AND TALCOTT, WEST VIRGINIA. They probably kicked in a little money for today's celebration, that's good p.r., Alphonse thinks. People around him applaud the sign; those with items in one hand bring their hands together feebly to make a show of applause. He watches the locomotive pass, and he turns to face the mountain. The train will slither into the tunnel, the new tunnel that replaced the one John Henry dug a few yards over. John Henry's tunnel didn't stand the test of time, the roof gave in, and they built the new tunnel adjacent, according to modern specifications. Obsolete.

He can't help it; he looks up at the mountain and finally gets his confirmation of his fate.

S oon after her father died the temp agency farmed her out to a content-driven interactive information provider. She was a temporary. She went where they sent her. This particular job was for a rapidly expanding company in the rapidly expanding industry called the internet. They needed bodies. They were set to launch in six weeks and needed all the bodies they could get as they ramped up for launch.

At orientation the first day, Pamela sat in a room with the other new hires and the parameters of the job were explained by a teenager dressed in faded jeans and a faded T-shirt. She discovered later he was pretty high up in the company, a bigwig in Implementation. He laid out the scene after they signed nondisclosure agreements; reams of nondisclosure agreements sat in piles along one pockmarked plaster wall, just in case. The company was going to launch a new portal in a few weeks. The internet was growing by leaps and bounds every day and every day people were getting on without knowing where to go. Their portal would be an on-ramp to the information super-highway, although, he added, information superhighway was not a word they liked to use around the office because it was really more of an old media term. This was the new media.

Your job, he told the new hires, is ontology. With millions of websites out there, a newbie will need a reliable source to tip them on where to go. Where they can find things that might interest them, discount diaper retailers or aluminum pliers. The ontologists classify websites into root categories such as Entertainment, News, and Health, categories recognizable to many from the real world, and write descriptions of no more than thirty-five words. The database also allowed them to rate the sites from one to five stars.

Then he explained about the Tool. There was a new data-entry interface on the way called the Tool. Technology Services had been scheduled to de-liver it a few weeks before, but there had been some glitches. These things happen. Until the glitches were worked out, the company needed extra hands. The present database was fine for the average business but not for a new media company such as theirs. It was cumbersome. It was obsolete, dodo bird in this new world. Awkward fields, counterintuitive commands. All that would be eradicated by the healing balm of the Tool. The Tool is HTML-based, he said, and will publish their ontology directly on the web, saving the extra step of having to export and convert information from the old database. The Tool is being specifically designed for the needs of ontology. The Tool will possess data-entry fields specifically designed for the ontologists, fields for URLs, fields for site descriptions that automatically cut off if they get too wordy, handy pull-down windows for marking one to five starts. It will cut the ontologists' workday in half, he said. They will need half as many ontologists once the database is web-friendly. The Tool.

But until Technology delivered the new Tool, he continued, abruptly dispelling this magnificent dream with a strategic conjunction, they would need all the bodies they could get. Have fun with it, he added, and left the room, sneakers squeaking on the new tile. The new hands picked up slim cardboard rectangles from the stack by the door. The writing on them read, Office in a Box. The box contained tape, scissors, scratch paper and pens. Anything a person might possibly need.

Instead of the modular Ls and Ts and Us of cubicle labyrinth she had expected, her workspace was an open room. In an industry that chose its terminology with an astounding lack of irony, the nickname for the room was refreshing. With people, for example, when they talked of visitors who might come to the site instead of human beings they talked about the hits, the eyeballs, the clicks. It sounded like a bill of bad garage bands. But her room was simply called the Box. Ten workstations lined the walls, leaving the center of the room open for hypothetical pacing, which remained hypothetical for they generally remained in their ergonomic chairs. The ten members of the team faced the walls. There was ample space between each workstation and available wall space for items or totems of personal significance one might tape up or tack up, but no one had essayed such a thing.

Once the people on her team got their morning coffee, they sat at their workstations and put on their headphones and started their workday. Everyone had CDs they brought to work. They put them in the CPU's CD-ROM drives and listened to them through headphones. They all listened to different kinds of music, which seeped out of the cheap earpads of the office-issue headphones and overlapped. She was forced to bring some music from home because if she didn't all day she felt as if she was lost between stations.

No one talked in the Box. If you wanted to borrow your neighbor's stapler, you sent them an email and waited. They sent you back an email in the positive or negative. Only then did you reach over to the next workstation for the stapler or whatever. In this system, by design perhaps, there was little eye contact, and the rest of the team was almost as anonymous as the people whose web pages they wrote up. Who knew what those people looked like out there. If it said Herbert's Pet Rock Shrine, Herbert could be a pseudonym, a nom de web, and the pet rock fanatic is really a Bob or an Orville. It took some getting used to. Occasionally the ergonomic consultants laid hands on her, tilting her limbs, modifying.

Anticipation of stock splits trembled the premises, tremors became tumultuous expansion. The company leased two and half floors, and then leased another two, and then the half floor, which had been shared with a law office, was also leased after a long negotiation. Now they had five floors, and periodically the construction caused problems. This server or that server might go down for a few hours while they rewired, and no one on the team could work for a while. It was a handsome prewar building and everything had to be ripped apart for the new power requirements and the T1 lines. The voice mail system went crazy. Sometimes she would see the red light on her voice mail go on even though the phone had not rung. She would check the message and it would be someone she didn't know trying to reach someone she didn't know, a person who was not on the new, frequently updated phone list and there was no record. The messages dated back weeks. Sometimes they were urgent but she had no other recourse but to delete them. I'm at the airport and where are you? Mom's sick, you should give her a call but don't say I said anything. The people were gone. The red lights winked out. Maybe they were temporary like her.

While she had never been on the internet before coming to work there, it did not take her long to familiarize herself. For such a big thing, it was actually pretty small once you spent an hour or two on it. The websites they were supposed to write up appeared in her email each morning, delivered by bots. The bots were lines of code that prowled the internet at night searching for keywords of interest to each team's area of ontology, night owls. Then other specialized lines of code randomly assigned the new websites to each team member. If you ran out of sites to cover halfway through the afternoon, the bot could send you new ones to work on. The bot worked in the daytime, too. Day and night. It did not tire like people. How could one not admire a bot?

Pamela didn't know why everyone got excited the morning the wipeboards appeared over the desk of each computer, but once she saw how the rest of the team hurried to write in red or green or blue their to-do lists, she realized that a void had been filled. The wipeboards were like a little bubble of hope inside each person that they had been unaware of. They made charts on the wipeboards, some people just lists, and when an item had been achieved, it was crossed out or wiped away. In some ways these to-do lists were the only outward markers of the progress made each day. Everything else was held tight by the database in cells, rows, columns.

For lunch she went to overpriced salad bars in search of the unwilted. No matter how far she walked, everything was overpriced. Because of all the renovations the elevators were slow and filled with the mysterious remains of heavy moved things, bits of plastic or insulation, and the delays cut into her lunch hour. Once she was past the doors of the building, she never ran into anyone she recognized from the office. They all went somewhere else for lunch. The midtown lunch hour streets were a welter of trundling dry cleaning.

Around the coffee machine people talked about who was going to be laid off once the Tool arrived. Since the office was anonymous, you could offer your own contribution without fear. They could have been standing in line in the bank discussing why aren't there more tellers on duty or at the departure gate of a delayed flight in communal bitch about the fucking airlines. The kind of honest and fleeting camaraderie you only get with strangers. One guy said half the ontology team would get the pink slip once the Tool arrived—that was how efficient the Tool was. Another said it wouldn't happen all at once—that was how insidious the Tool was. Some people would be kept on to keep things running smoothly during launch week, to look out for glitches. But most people understood that some people were going to be let go. A lot of this talk didn't interest her because she knew she would move on, Tool or no. That was the nature of being temporary.

A negative article appeared on one of the internet news sites, dubious as to the viability of their venture. No one liked it when financial analysts were quoted. There was the stock to think about. Most of the staff had enrolled in the stock plan and they checked the stock market throughout the day searching for dips. The goddamned dips. Plus the investors. An email with a link to the article was in her inbox when she booted up that morning. By noon a dozen interoffice counter-emails had joined the negative email, disputing some of the points in the piece. The Project Manager promised a pizza party. This cheered everyone up a bit.

One night, just before she left for home, she got an email saying that due to shifting priorities and the great flood of new hires, her team was going to be relocated to a more strategic location in the building. She put on her coat and left the building for the day. The next morning when she walked into the Box, it was filled with people she had never seen before. This was an entirely new collection of bad posture. Where the skinny skater-type had been, a beer-bellied former athlete hunched. The aerobics addict had been replaced by a teenager with braces, and so on. The email had not informed them that the move was going to happen overnight. She noticed a sign on the door offering directions. When she walked into the new Box, which was just next door to the old Box, all the members of her team were at their workstations. The workstations were in the same configuration, in the same order along the walls, but now there was a window. She turned her computer on and it was the same one she had used for the last few weeks. They'd moved it all overnight, like that. Even the wipeboards. She sat and attacked the next item on her to-do list. The window looked out on corporate slabs.

The worst thing was when the bot sent her to a place that didn't exist. She would cut and paste the URL from the bot's list, but when she got there the site would be gone. The browser could not find the page. It had been taken down, or abandoned, who knew what. It happened pretty frequently. Someone said, that's the information age for you. Here today and gone tomorrow. And indeed one day she came in and was informed that the Tool had arrived. It worked to specifications and that was her last day there. She was only temporary.

The old connections re-form, and Lucien is reminded of how to eat an ice cream cone on a hot day. "Mmm, this is really good," Lucien says, extending a cold tongue to newly minted double scoop. "This is Rocky Road, right? This is really good," he says, tilting the cone to catch with his tongue a cascade. The old skills come back. The smell of cotton candy, the cheers swirling out in a tornado of joy and fear from the Tilt-a-Whirl, these particulars remind him of the mechanics of ice cream. It's the day, he can't help himself. Everything is unironic, sincere, even. Canned preserves! He read an article about the magical process in a lifestyle magazine recently. The photospread for the piece featured color-saturated shots of a runway model with tight pigtails, dressed in a blue pinafore. She made the apples into jelly and rendered them airtight, bent provocatively with dripping fingers. It must have cost twenty, thirty thousand dollars to produce. Drop in the bucket of their art budget. He could have given that preserve lady back there a dollar and gotten change back.

Lucien and the ice cream melt in the heat at deviating rates. He could have gone incognito in jeans and a T-shirt, perhaps a ribbed T-shirt of combed cotton, opted instead for his usual attire. His undershirt sops and he regrets his decision but not out of discomfort. He regrets his suit because he looks at the people around him and feels envy. He has a theory of course. He is accustomed by the necessities of his job to think of civilians as a herd to be shepherded by those of his elite. There is no real way to do his job if he thinks of these people as peers. Peers know what you're up to, understand if not the specifics then the generalities of your schemes, the clients and press and p.r. men are in on the joke. Even the damned caterers will give you a wink now and then at an event. But every so often an Olympian must gaze down through clouds at mortal pastures and see his face in those faces and envy their simple bliss. They can enjoy. They can wear a T-shirt and a baseball cap and not consider it an ironic gesture. They can mess up their hair without dashing for the spritzer. The little things in life.

Lucien feels dampness between his fingers. He unbandages the bottom of the cone and sucks out the melted ice cream through the hole. Lawrence watches this as if apprenticing to an alchemist: rapt and respectful and calculating the years to the coup. The conjure ends with a flourish as Lucien pops the cone into his mouth and crunches. He instructs Lawrence to ask the ice cream stand who their distributor is, and to make arrangements for a tub to be sent up to the New York office.

Free of his familiar, Lucien relaxes and takes in the beautiful crowd. Normal folks, what they call families, kids and the like. They're all dressed naturally, like they picked out their favorite clothes and stepped into them, like that. Even the USPS men have relaxed for the occasion, Lucien notices. They wear navy-colored polo shirts of the same manufacture, possess the same Middle American faces as the majority of the fair-goers. In their identical khaki pants with sure pleats, they resemble undercover police in this crowd, but they look comfortable. Lucien spies Parker Smith, their leader, by the dunking booth, weathering the taunts of the insolent drenched lad, and he waves. Parker catches this, volleys a greeting at Lucien and then a baseball at the bull's-eye. His theatrical windup is justified. The boy falls into the water to applause.

Parker's underlings clap him on the back and launch hands to high five. Parker has his platoon here, and Lucien has his. Lucien imagines a war room away from the front where they moved colored pins over a satellite map of Summers County but of course all the planning for the operation had been conducted over the phone, Parker's long distance charges paid for by taxpayers and Lucien's tucked neatly into the overhead. It had all been Parker's doing. The start of it. Lucien had been recommended to Parker by a friend in the judicial branch whom Lucien had flattered once. Parker described the unique dimensions of the event with the honesty of a professional, much to Lucien's appreciation. It was a weird gig, no doubt about it, a new paradigm. Public relations were only a small part of the USPS's goals. Target Marketing, he explained, had decided that community events such as this, tied into popular innovations like limited, commemorative stamp series, were a small but significant means of getting the people involved with their government again. Tepid, downright embarrassing voter turnout was only one example of a widespread public disaffection with the national apparatus. He had the figures right in front of him; through the speakerphone Lucien heard a tapping noise. Like surly teenagers, the people of the country holed up brooding, bedroom doors shut against the invitations and entreaties of national life.

But ever since they opened the selection process for commemoratives to the public, the number of responses had astounded. Post Office statisticians tabulated and correlated the numbers on government-issue ledgers and hypothesized. It went far beyond the stamp collectors. The Post Office announced the category and the people voted. All types of people. A jumbo crayon box of ethnicity. They voted for flowers. Everyone had a favorite flower, maybe it was a gift once from a true love or something worried over in the back garden that finally blossomed for two days before the slugs got to it, but everyone had a favorite flower and they voted. They voted for the dead in order to see their faces on stamps. As if the particular dead celebrity on the stamp watched over the passage of the letter to its recipient, blessing the correspondence, the top right-hand corner of the letter a perch in heaven. In some ways it was an exploration of the American psyche, and keep it under your hat, Parker whispered, but they've been getting calls from the CIA. They think the data can be useful somehow. Parker explained this to Lucien. The kind of power a red convertible had on the people, hands down the favorite in the classic car commemorative. Sometimes the artist responsible for the image received fan letters whose freight had been paid by his particular creation. That was the funny thing: they used stamps to mail in their choices, like it had all been planned in some boiler room pyramid scheme. These commemoratives had a hold on the people. Combine it with local events such as this and you had an important experiment in progress with implications.

Lucien inspected his fingernails while Parker erupted from the speakerphone.

And Talcott, Parker elaborated on the phone that day, Talcott is the perfect partner. An event like John Henry Days is a slice of Americana. It is a window into true lives that men like Parker and Lucien never get to see. Sure there had been some bellyaching when Talcott contacted them and demanded that they hold the stamp ceremony in their little town. Fact-finding had already occurred in Pittsburgh. The home of steel. Foundries already scouted out for photo ops and overtures made. Nothing signed but an inconvenience nonetheless. Then—a small town! Someone proposed a motion to table irritation for the moment and raise the issue of serendipity. It was seconded and many said aye. Talcott was planning an annual festival whose inaguration would coincide with the release of the John Henry commemorative. The timing was perfect. It was almost a scheme, it might appear as a scheme to the cynical observer, fast food cups tied to the big summer blockbuster, something concocted by men who neither ate fast food or patronized big summer blockbusters. One of the Quality boys pointed out that this kind of event was the type of thing they had set out to accomplish from the beginning of their late public relations push. Synergy. One mind, one people. If no one got excited about presidential candidates anymore, they certainly came out in droves to support their beloved heroes and artifacts. On stamps. If Talcott wanted some funding to help publicize their festival (for how does something exist without decent publicity) how could the Post Office not oblige? There were all sorts of different kinds of disbursement forms at the ready, in reserve, for such eventualities.

Lucien had never done a town before. Worked with the government, sure, Democratic fund-raiser for the education candidate one week and a Republican fund-raiser for the tax-cut candidate the next. Remarkable how many people were at both events. Same band, same caterer, same signatures at the bottom of the checks. He doesn't think of himself as political. What others see as politics he perceives as momentary breezes. But he'd never done a town before. As Lucien considered the assignment, it occurred to him that maybe the trick about doing a small town is making the thing into the idea. Which raised the question of the chicken and the egg. This question dogged him as he got to work—he couldn't figure out which came first, the stamp or the festival. Is the stamp a merchandising tie-in for festival, or the festival a press conference for the stamp? Looking around today, he's still confounded. There are canned preserves and men walking around in old conductor uniforms. Is this really homey or is it constructed in some way. Is their sincerity actually the hapless grasping after something they believed their fathers possessed. There's a safe deposit box containing their heritage, but they don't possess the right documentation. Lucien suspects he is falling for a deception that beguiles the con artist and the mark in equal measure.

Lucien laces his fingers behind his back and walks, chest thrust out, dictator among the banana fields. The people moving, the flags ripping, the sound checks, are all interconnected gears set into motion by the idea of John Henry, every thing and person here grinds into another to keep this mad happy machine operating. He is cog, too, set to purpose and function. Lucien passes one table where a furtive young man hawks primitive masks he's carved of wood, his own private mythology laid out on his table for converts, sixth grade math teachers, proxied bullies, assorted nemeses. Then kids erupt around Lucien's hips, their faces daubed rainbow colors. Strawberry-flavored blood drips from these bloodsuckers' mouths, raccoon circles blacken their eyes. Slim black whiskers bow over cheeks. Lucien traces these mini demons to a table where a matron asks the kids what kind of monster they want to be before she administers fright makeup. A long line of children await transmogrification. And what kind of monster would Lucien choose to be?

Another one of these characters in a railroad engineer's outfit has attracted a ring of boys and girls around him. Lucien inches closer and hears the man say, "From that first day he appeared at the C&O camp, John Henry proved himself to be the strongest, fastest steeldriver they had ever seen. He swung the hammer down and the whole world jumped." Not all of these kids are local, Lucien figures. Maybe they're hearing this story for the first time. Truth be told, Lucien had no idea who John Henry was when Parker contacted him; first thing when he got off the phone he dispatched Lawrence to do some research. When he returned with a children's book, Lucien frowned, squinted and asked Lawrence to do a summary. Later that night, as he read his assistant's notes, he began to remember the story. It was familiar, but he couldn't place where he'd first heard it. It was one of those stories that seems like it has always been a part of you. Like the stork story about the pebbles in the water glass, or however that story went. The fox and the grapes. Maybe some of these children squatting on the grass are getting the story for the first time. How many of their parents remembered the story? How many have heard of Talcott before today? He is proud of himself.

"Lucien? It's Apple Valley Brand Rocky Road. I got their contact number." This is the dull announcement of Lawrence's return. He had dispatched his assistant on a mission in order to have a few moments to himself, lose the bottom beneath his feet at each new swell of the fair and here comes Lawrence back too soon. As long as he doesn't start talking about the animals again. Lawrence whined that when they returned from the airport, there were all these paw prints in his bathtub and since then he can't stop talking about bears mauling him in his sleep. Just the prints in the tub, nothing else was touched. What did he think, a bunch of cubs let themselves in with a key? Lawrence probably thinks he's roughing it down here.

In the end they don't really have to be here, on this flattened grass, hundreds of miles from his new leather chair. (Certainly that is one ill-planned aspect of this expedition; never get a new leather chair delivered just minutes before you have to hop on a plane. There are breaking-in rituals to be performed, imprinting to be executed.) Apart from the novelty of doing a town, the quiet audacity of such an idea, in the end Lucien hasn't done more than tailor his methods to the needs of the client, as always. His people gave these folks a few tips on how to write a decent press release. He alerted the appropriate travel guides to get the event included in 1997 editions, called upon old New York colleagues who had fled the metropolitan turmoil and put themselves out to pasture in small Southern dailies. Small advance items appeared here and there. He called upon the List.

The List still amazed him. Cell phone signals probably turned to mist in these mountains but the List penetrated. He had put this weekend down out of habit, but never expected this kind of turnout. Five junketeers. In Talcott! The food is terrible, the only celebrities around are high school football greats yakking about that one big game, and the atmosphere is what climate control switches are meant to eradicate. He doesn't know what surprises him more: the efficiency of the List or the desperation of its subjects.

A convenience that started as an experiment. As Lucien's private game, not so long ago, a chin tuck ago. He noticed that the same people dragged themselves out for his events, for his competitors' events, for whatever trough was laid out that night. Glossy writers, daily writers, beat reporters, scrabbling freelancers of mixed pedigree. (Not counting the true hangers-on of course, the blue-haired Park Avenue freaks, bony spouse hunters, and other assorted night fiends they haven't invented pesticides for.) The writers were like day workers who crowded the farmer's truck every morning for penny-work. They ate and drank, migrant workers, wiping maw on sleeve, and sometimes they got out the word like they were supposed to. There had to be a better system than this mooching free-for-all, it seemed to him. He took note of the names and faces, linked them to later bylines. A good number of them, it appeared, did the work. Sure they leeched, but a certain kind of creature maintained a more-or-less stable ratio of coverage to freeloading. He decided to add another database to his shifting A-list and B-list invitees, one devoted to this overlooked species of freelancer. He monitored their progress through the nights. How many drinks they poured down their gullets, how long they lingered after the food disappeared into lonesome garnish, how many bylines sprouted in the aftermath.

Soon he had a hand-picked crew who could be depended upon in times of need to fulfill a quota of coverage. Gossip columnists, music writers with Coke-bottle glasses, airline magazine habitués scheming passage to the next cabana, home electronic experts who sold review products to pawnshops, the eager and ambitious and just furloughed from internships. They were dependable, and he watched them. Surveying slime trails from above, patterns emerged, and he discovered a ratio he liked. When he was ready he mailed them anonymously. He didn't mind including his rivals in his commu-

niqués—the more experienced these select became with the rules of the contract, the more healthy the entire industry would become. He added names,
scouted out rookies and journeymen, subtracted slackers. There were few
complaints; there was no one to complain to. They were fed, through them
the public fed, and they filed pieces that paid the rent and subsidized their
habits. Everybody won and the List flourished.

"Lucien?" Lawrence intrudes.

"Yes, Lawrence."

"I saw the boys, sir. Dave and Tiny and the rest. They're over by the beer
garden. Do you think it's time we glad-handed?"

"Lawrence, I think it's a perfect time for glad-handing." Who came
down? He remembers he hooked Dave Brown up with Milt Chamber from
*West Virginia Life*—Milt, formerly a Condé Nast regular, had fled back home
after rehab to start a new life. Tiny is probably here for the food, Frenchie,
he can't remember at the moment, but there might be a travel magazine involved, knowing his predilections. Is One Eye doing anything? One Eye has
been giving Lucien evil looks lately, but he is used to One Eye's periodic fits
of pique. And J. is here, from all accounts continuing his attempt at the
record, poor guy. That way lies madness. Might have to have a talk with the
boy at some point if he keeps it up. At least J. followed up on that website lead
and is doing some coverage. Two out of five of them down here working.
That makes forty percent. Well within the acceptable range.

Lucien takes one last look at the children. The storyteller's face is a stone
engraving and the children lean forward, drawn by suspense. He's not doing
too bad a job, probably trying to remember how his father or grandfather
told him the story decades ago. At the booth adjacent they're taking dona-
tions for the museum. The parents of the kids dig out a few bills while they
wait for John Henry to win his race. Yes, it is a nice day. They're taking do-
nations for the construction of John Henry Museum. Throw in the museum
thing and this is almost an artsy-type gig. He always feels good after an artsy-
type gig.

"Let's go, Lawrence," he says, "and review the troops."

At the all-night bodega of souls the crackheads promenade, jigger and shimmy, trade palsies in fitful games of one-upmanship, count coins beneath the corrugated tin of the yellow canopy. The bodega never closes. At midnight the night man removes the brick from the front door and transactions proceed through bulletproof plastic. He takes requests. He strains to hear the crackheads. When he withdraws into the recesses of his mercantile domain to retrieve malt liquor and potato chips of anonymous manufacture, protein shakes if that's all the customer can keep down, the crackheads etch nonsense slogans and their names into the plastic with keys or dimes, half-hearted dispatches from underground. They look over their shoulders for 5-0; if they pooled their resources they could come up with two dozen warrants and summonses among them, surely. They taunt the night man for no reason, reason enough. They deprecate his sensory apparatus. Yo, you deaf? I wanted one St. Ides and two O.E.s, motherfucker, not two St. Ides, shit. I wanted those Lays chips you got right there, not that plantain shit, shit, you blind? They talk through the bulletproof plastic about the state of the economy. What you want another ten cent? Day before yesterday it was a dollar ninety-five, now you trying to tell me it's another ten cent? My boy was down here two hours ago, nigger, he got the same shit and it wasn't no ten cent more. You Dominican niggers try to rip a nigger off. If the night man is too tired to grant this impromptu haggling session the attention it deserves, he'll let the guy off the hook and hear his name cursed by the man to the other crackheads down the line. If he feels like standing his ground, he'll turn the revolving bulletproof box around so that the man sees his insufficient coin there on the yellowed plastic, a museum exhibit on ghetto commerce. He can come up with that dime or he can leave. Cigarettes and condoms may be purchased singly. The new demand for Phillies cigars is accounted for. The night man runs back and forth. Even a request for simple orange juice from this crowd, at this time of night, gathers licentious aspect. These people take ordinary items from his uncle's shelves and convert them into criminal accessories. The same faces night after night. Crackheads and drug dealers and here's that guy for three Coronas.

J. Sutter on deadline queues up with crackheads in the sinister A.M. His fingers hurt from late employment at the tiny buttons of J.'s microcassette recorder, where they teased shrill idiocy from metallic spools. On the tape the actor and pinup expounded on Tantric sex and the Dalai Lama, from a white table poolside at a hotel in Los Angeles. That day, a year ago, J. sipped a margarita and squinted at his notes in the bleaching sunlight. He felt himself getting soft and overripe in the sunlight just like everything else in the state, his brain splitting and spilling juices. Brody Mills had just finished a stint at a court-appointed substance abuse rehabilitation facility. "Four weeks of seriously getting my head together," as he described it that day, and a year later in J.'s apartment through diminutive technology. He tapped ash on the coarse tile of the hotel Sun Deck Lounge, eschewing for reasons of his own the elegant ashtray proximate his hand. "I'm clean for the first time in years and it feels so great," he said, while eyeing and coveting J.'s frothy blue margarita like a Bedlam fiend.

Brody Mills dispensed rehearsed penance as the viscount of the studio publicity mechanism nodded and smiled and tapped Brody's tanned forearm when he wandered too close to the demilitarized zone between their agreed-upon orchestrations and the facts themselves. His implosion had announced itself for months, first as nameless ectoplasm in blind items of gossip pages, then as bold-faced and named instigator in a brawl at a Manhattan after-hours club, finally no longer omen but event itself, as Brody Mills was cast against type in a hooded sweatshirt and detectives led him into the precinct at the top of the nightly news. On every channel. He was Wednesday's scandal, he took a wrong turn after an afternoon spent with his surgeon-sculpted proboscis deep in cocaine anthill, slapped his longtime model girlfriend around, and bit the arresting officer on the ass when he came to investigate the noise complaint delivered to 911 by fellow residents of the upscale downtown co-op. The judge gave the actor and heartthrob probation and ordered a mandatory stay in rehab. J. was one of ten journalists scheduled for poolside chats that day, one of pop's own parole review board. Brody certainly looked better than in his now infamous mugshot: the goatee shreds in a Beverly Hills sink; the black halos around his eyes trod away by step after step (numbering twelve in total) of self-awakening. J. was there to force the man to his mark, the X of tape where the public wanted him to stand, centered beneath the cleansing spotlight of contrition. Brody moved obediently. "Fame came so quickly," he conceded, "I never had a chance to grow up."

When J. got to that part of the tape, a few days later, when he was back in the civilized regions of Brooklyn, that quotation insisted on itself as an obvious and natural segue for a recap of Brody's early career. He grew up before the public's eyes but the child remained inside him. It was obvious, blunt, and ready for copy.

The magazine called him up, asked J. if he wanted to fly to L.A. to interview the actor and idol on his release from rehabilitation. J. flew out, interviewed this nipple-pierced Lazarus and filed the piece on time. But Fellini died. The great director Federico Fellini was dead in Italy and the managing editor wanted to run a package on the man's demise: capsule reviews of his key movies rated by one to four stars for video store convenience; brief statements by leading American directors (no one too art housey) who were influenced by his work; and an essay on his impact on the world of film, the peculiar economy of postwar Italian life and how it produced idiosyncratic and beautiful art, this essay prepared months before when the man first checked into the hospital, just in case. There's a protocol for such things. J.'s piece on the Confessions of Brody Mills, Actor and Superstar, was pushed back a week to make room for the package, and then another week, and then no one cared and a kill fee (full) arrived in the mail. That was a year ago.

Then this morning J. got a call rousing him from a dream, one of the agitated type that he gets only when the noon light gushes full and accusatory on his face through the bedroom window. Brody was in trouble again, falling naturally to mischief just as he did in the show that made him famous, the Fox television program *Quaker's Dozen*, a situation comedy concerning twelve orphans of different ethnic backgrounds and the hip preacher who is their guardian. (When one of the child actors wanted to leave the show, or was eliminated by the producers' caprices, they were "adopted" at the end of the season, a truly successful adaptation in the Darwinian jungle hell of modern entertainment, rarely a dry eye in the house when this stunt was performed, and seismic, Neilsen-wise.) Brody arrested yet again, and on the eve of the premiere of his new action film, yet. Will neighbors ever refrain from calling the police over loud noises that disturb the early morning metropolitan calm? When the constables arrived at the Paramount Hotel this morning and knocked down the door, Brody Mills was as naked as a babe (or the famous bare-ass scene in *Ten Miles*, the first film he made after he was adopted from the hip priest's orphanage) and arguing with invisible critics and studio executives (for the unseen goblins he harangued must have surely been critics and studio executives) while the paraphernalia of narcotics abuse lay in plain sight and the hotel reservoir of pay-per-view pornography inundated the well-appointed suite at high volume. "It took half a dozen of New York's Finest to restrain him," the magazine editor related to J. from the AP wire, and would J. mind fixing up his piece from last year, two thousand words if possible, buck a word and by tomorrow noon?

J. put down the phone and went back to sleep. Paid twice for basically the same thing: he slept unperturbed by hectoring afternoon light, tranquilized by the thought of taking money off the troubled celeb. He woke and mulled over, guzzling coffee, the talk show disaster on his TV screen. At five he strolled to Fort Greene Park for what he reckoned might be a pleasant hour of meditation but he bored quickly with the pavement and pitbulls and wilted condoms and beat it home after five minutes. His thoughts did not touch on the assignment for more than a few moments through the evening. Pop a few details into the original fifteen-hundred-word piece, no sweat, snatching lollipops from a baby, the tikes have no grip yet, he could get up early and do that easy. He ordered Chinese food and watched television until eleven o'clock, when the faint angel of professionalism perched on his shoulder, implored in a whisper, and he went to check the file. Place the X rays up to the light and see exactly where the fractures were, what needed mending tomorrow so to speak. When he called up the file he found gibberish, a glyphic conspiracy of pixelated symbols he didn't even know how to muster from his keys, it was a language from a cranky sect deep within the motherboard. He couldn't explain it. He had fifteen hundred words of shit when he called up the file *B. Mills Repentance Spiel*.

But he still had the interview tape in his income tax receipt drawer, and he had coffee beans. J. knocked back a pot of coffee and transcribed once again the actor and teen scream's confessional peregrinations. J. fastforwarded past his own voice; he loathed the sound of his voice through the tiny speaker, it was amplified and remastered by the machine so that it contained a quality of earnestness and sincerity that he did not truly possess. Since Brody Mills never answered any of his questions, preferring instead a dada discourse, it did not matter that J. did not hear his questions. But two and a half hours into his reconstructions, J.'s fingers were rebellious from rewinding and fastforwarding, and his stomach and heart convulsed with the coffee bean's harassment. He was so jazzed up that he needed to calm down if he was going to get, what, two hours sleep maybe and be fresh for the morning's foray to the happy hunting grounds of hackery. And that meant an expedition to the only establishment open at this time of night. He must make his descent.

There was a time that whenever he suited up for a late night bodega run, J. would take the necessary bills and leave his wallet behind. Crackheads begging for change, knuckleheads out on the prowl: best to make a strategic withdrawal. But nothing ever happened and he stopped. More dreadful than becoming a participant in the city's most popular street theater (the mugging on darkened corner, a spectacle tourists from all over the globe line up to get to see, easier to get than Broadway tickets) are the black windows in all the buildings. Surely, he thinks when he sees them, he cannot be the only one awake at this hour, he is not alone. But in all the buildings and brownstones the neighbors sleep. The decent folk forsake these hours. Blue TV flicker in some windows tells him there are a few like him awake at this time, not many. Always the same windows too, he's noticed, scattered and well dispersed from block to block so as to adumbrate this nocturnal isolation to best effect. He waves at one blue dancer. No response. It's a four-block walk to the trading post with only two sketchy parts: the blind turn from Carlton to Lafayette (who knows what kind of scene he'll stumble into rounding that building's blade); and that block where streetlights stare blindly, handicapped by vandalism and city neglect, where shadows confab to trade samizdat decrying illumination. But nothing has ever happened on the walk. Two blocks down he sees the huddled messes group outside the bodega. He takes a deep breath and sallies forth.

The freaks come out at night.

He gets in line behind the crackhead who sometime dons a subway worker's reflective orange vest, a souvenir he picked up somewhere in the tunnels. This character likes to tell passersby he needs a token to get home, the orange vest intended to provide evidence of solid citizenship; why he'd need a token if he worked for the Metropolitan Transit Authority has apparently never occurred to the man. J. sizes up the group before him, they are travelers who have come a long way, certainly troubadours finally come to this neck of the woods: The most popular entertainment troupe in all of ShabbyLand, the Freebase Players. Yayo the Clown, his face rouged by dried blood and nose swollen after a recent third fracture, stands in his gay gray attire—he prefers to play the dignified gentleman raconteur down on his luck, happy to share a comedic tale of woe for some change. Those dynamic men on the flying trapeze, Gordy and Morty, who zoom on leave from gravity through alkaloid extracted from cocoa leaves, death defying, without a net worth, falling to earth only at dawn, when this team is too exhausted to perform any trick except attempting sleep while wired to the limits of human endurance. And of course the elders, Ma and Pa, married for twenty years, half that on the pipe, God bless 'em, keeping vigil over the dirty garbage bags containing the cherished props of their act, deposit bottles and broken toasters. And at the fringes of this group, mingling with the celebrities, are assorted teenagers just ducking around the corner for supplies, some malt liquor and Newports, identifiable by their baggy jeans and beepers and youthful joie de vivre, so refreshing beneath the timer-controlled beam of the streetlight.

The line progresses slowly. Tonight everybody hassles the night man, they denounce the service at this establishment. But there are no questionable characters hanging around who fall outside the usual disrepute of the crowd, so J. starts thinking about the article, he leaves this corner and is conveyed to its double on Grub Street. Then J. sees him.

J. sees him zigzagging down the street, stymieing any snipers of euthanasiac bent who might be roosting on the Brooklyn rooftops, an out-of-control prop plane in for an uneasy landing. Tony darts here to finger the coin slot of a pay phone, diddling around in luckless pursuit of change, scrambles there to see if that glint (bottle top) is a dime or *mirabile dictu* a quarter. J. sees Tony, the ghoul's fingers wiggling in the air like crab's legs over wharf bottom detritus. Tony lopes down the avenue, scanning and panning, and J. knows that with Yayo the Clown's meticulous and agonized counting of pennies (always that same deficient sum, the limited number of pockets in which to search), there is no way J. will get clear before Tony lands at the bodega.

J. is the only mark in the ragged assembly on the corner; Tony will not approach the malt liquor boys, contusions have taught him better, and the crackheads are his comrade connoisseurs of the pipe and competitors for change, outside the game. During the day the street has enough traffic that J. is not always discovered as the object of Tony's salvage operation. During the day Tony is a puppy; at night he's a damned barnacle, strung out on an odyssey for the next piece of rock and there's no shaking him. J. and Tony have a relationship at this point, going back to when J. first moved to Brooklyn and had a pocket full of change. Tony looked more craving than hungry, but he needed the change more than J., fuck it, J. was in a good mood. Tony smiled and memorized the sucker's stupid face. The act wed them as mark and con man, till zip code do you part. That first contribution was a binding contract (everyone at the bodega now would attest to its legality) although J. hadn't bothered to read all those subclauses, the fine print he couldn't see in the bright and easy light of that aimless afternoon. They have a relationship, with rules. During the day "Sorry, man," will dispatch Tony to the next mark down the street, that bohemian homesteader of these Brooklyn badlands, the goofy white dude with the goatee. Plenty of marks on the afternoon street, such is the bounty of the neighborhood. Another rule: Tony won't beg for change if J.'s escorting a lady; he'll tip a nonexistent hat, but that's it. At night, though, times are tough, and tonight J.'s the only sap around.

Tony's evidently having a bad night. All sorts of tectonic mayhem afoot in Tony's face this eve: his troubled visage bursts with subcutaneous lumps of calcified ooze and porous eruptions trickling a clear fluid. The hair he managed to grow last week and was quite proud of (they talked about it while J. walked briskly for the subway, forbidden turf for the shambling man; the subway cops had beat him up once, or so Tony claimed), has evacuated in patches, exposing old and angry scabby flesh. Tony arrives just after J. asks the man behind the bulletproof glass for three Coronas. He assumes his hovering remora position and says, "Hey, Mickey Mouse man, you having a good night?"

"All right," J. responds, glancing at Tony and then staring dead into the store. J. was wearing a freebie T-shirt from Disney that first day Tony hit him up for cash. Remembering and filing his clients' distinguishing characteristics helps the crackhead keep his various pitches in order.

"That's good, that's good," Tony says, nodding to comrades down the line, who pantomime back things seen. "Say, listen, listen, could you spare a few dollars for some food? I haven't eaten all day, man, and I'm hungry." Holding his stomach urchinwise.

"We'll see," J. says. This is one night he should have left his wallet behind. In a few moments J. will open his wallet and Tony will take a big thirsty peek at the cash. Can't really say he doesn't have any cash when there's a sheaf of twenties in there.

"Sure am hungry," Tony says, nonchalant.

"Maybe," J. says. He withdraws a five, holding his wallet close. He thinks of soldiers in trenches cupping their cigarette tips so that the Kaiser's goons won't see the flame and draw a bead. The night man returns with three Coronas and rings it up, cue now for J. to slide the money into the bulletproof box and spin it around for approval. The night man slips his agile fingers into the register and drops the change and the bottles into the box, slides it around, transaction complete.

Tony bobs happily next to him. J. stuffs the dollar twenty-five into his jeans and withdraws from the crackhead bazaar. "Hey, brotherman, how about that change?" Tony murmurs.

"Sorry, man," J. says. Cradles beer to his chest and strides.

Tony's head rocks back and forth and he pulls up next to J. "But you said so."

Semantics now. "I said maybe. Can't help you out tonight." He just got two checks in yesterday, so giving the man a quarter is no big deal. Tony can have the change and smoke himself to death, no big deal, it's spare change. But J. has that article due, he's been transcribing word for word a Hollywood junkie's incoherent speeches and he's had enough of junkies tonight. Coffee curdling in him, deadline creeping: he's in servitude to one druggie tonight and that leaves him with empty pockets for this neighborhood nuisance. "See ya later," J. says.

They're the same age, J. found out one day. Tony trotted next to him, like he is now, halfheartedly rapping about needing some Similac for his baby, a ploy Tony used the first few months after their original meeting but eventually dropped when he realized that he didn't come off as a dutiful daddy (no one glows that maniacally with the joys of paternity). Tony said, "How old do you think I am?" and J. guessed forty-five. Tony grinned broken teeth and giggled, "I'm twenty-nine! Twenty-nine years old! Today's my birthday!" And with that he cackled away down the block.

Tony is not giving up so easily tonight. He's hurting for a little something. Tony says, stepping closer than J. would like, "You want some LPs? 'Cause I know a Guy that got some. You like that old funk? I could hook you up." Switching tactics tonight. He knows a Guy, a Guy who J. has learned is a truly enterprising individual. Over the years this Guy, with Tony as the middle man, has been able to furnish stereos ("Real cheap!"), VCRs of the finest Japanese craftsmanship ("Videos too! You like porno?"), sticky weed ("I saw you walking with that dread last week. Maybe he wants some smoke."), and women ("The night guy at the old people home pays me five bucks to get a woman for him—I could hook you up!"). The Guy Tony knew was a true entrepreneur. Perhaps one day J. will ask if the Guy has a line on devices that make receipts, but not tonight. Nor is he interested in a bunch of old records that the Guy robbed from someone's house.

"No thanks," J. says.

"I haven't eaten all day, man, please."

"No."

"What do you mean no? I see you every day, motherfucker, and now you can't even help a nigger out with some money to eat. That's terrible." A boil splits on Tony's face and drips. "Can't even help a nigger out with a sandwich. I saw you got plenty of money on you."

"No." They're on the block of broken streetlights. Tony's mother lives on this block. Tony's pointed it out to J. before; it's a nice old brownstone in the middle of the block. Family discord: Tony lives a few streets away in a vacant lot shack. Or he used to. The habitation burned down a few weeks ago and Tony pointed to a glistening pink burn on his arm for proof. A problem with the wiring no doubt.

"You got money for alcohol but I can't eat," Tony says. As if this suppurating shade wanted the money for food, strung out like he was. No one on the street but them and all the windows dark. Tony takes the advantage of his opponent and leans up and whispers, "I'm so hungry I might have to take it then, I'm so hungry," and the threat sits there in J.'s ear. There was that night when J. was heading for the subway to make it to a book party in Manhattan and he saw Tony prowling around, cussing. His clothes were inside out and blood seeped from a gash above his eye. When he saw J. he asked him if he'd seen these three knuckleheads walking around anywhere. J. replied he hadn't and Tony said that he got into a beef with them and they beat him up and made him take off his clothes and put them on inside out. Or maybe they made him put his clothes on inside out and then beat him up. At any rate, he was looking for them and he had something: he pulled up his shirt and pointed to the long carving knife tucked into his belt. He was going to cut them when he found them. J. told him to calm down and get himself cleaned up. He wasn't going to cut anybody. Tony considered this possibility, nodded and agreed. He pulled his shirt down over the knife. Then he asked J. for some change.

J. doesn't respond to the threat. They walk in silence for a few feet, and they leave the threat on the pavement behind them. They move into the next streetlight's circle and Tony says, "Hey, you know I wouldn't do that. I ain't like those other crazy niggers they got up in here. But I gotta eat. What do you want me to do?"

"Can't help you, man." If he gave into the crackhead now, it would look as if he was giving in to the threat, even with Tony's withdrawal of it. A principle involved: he doesn't want to be punked out. There's one more block before he gets to his house and he doesn't want Tony there when he gets to his front door.

"You want me to sing for my supper?" Tony asks. "You want me to sing for my supper? I'll sing for my supper." He spits a gremlin of phlegm to the pavement and scratches his foot across the sidewalk like a pitcher taming his mound for a pitch. Then he jumps up and down and sings from his singed throat, "This old hammer killed John Henry but it won't kill me! This old hammer killed John Henry but it won't kill me!" J. looks back at the crackhead. Tony's eyes bulge out with the strain of producing that gross racket. "This old hammer killed John Henry but it won't kill me!" And here, J. thinks, this is the essential difference between this neighborhood and those of Brody Mills's orbit. No one here will call the police about the noise. They hear gunshots and arguments in the middle of the night and they might creep to the window to see what's going on but they won't call the police. They'll pray they don't hear a rape, something that will force them to get involved, or consider getting involved, but the people behind the black windows will not call the police at this. "This old hammer killed John Henry but it won't kill me!" It's up to J. He has no more resistance. He pulls out the change from the five dollars and gives it to the crackhead. Without touching the man's palm. Who knows what the guy wipes his ass with.

"You like that song?" Tony asks.

"You won," J. responds. Yards between them now, the distance between the mark and the expert con.

J. hears Tony yell, "Hey, brotherman, brotherman, wait a minute!"

J. turns, knowing from the volume of the man's voice that there are distances, old distances, between them. Tony jabs his finger at him and says, "You're a solid brother, Mickey Mouse, you're a solid citizen." He bows and scampers away in the direction of a building without a door, a building with secret steps and codes.

At his desk J. sips his first Corona and looks down at his notes. He calculates what he'll get done before he's dampened enough to fall asleep. He considers how much sleep he'll get and through the calculus of doggerel arrives at how many words per hour he has to produce by noon. He presses a button and listens to the lying junkie. Only variety of junkie awake at this hour.

The biggest spud in Summers County is a mean-looking son of a bitch, whole cubic feet of lumpy resentment, a bad-ass tuber from the bowels of Hell. Last year's winner, enthroned on a table across the aisle and encased in a top of the line plastic sheath to preserve its nefarious glory for generations to come. The proud father, a grizzled farmer garroted by a bolo tie, stands behind junior pointing to the sign at its swollen base that invites the passersby to touch it. Just an exhibit, not for sale. J.'s almost bored enough to walk over and see what kind of tater miracle will be performed on him, but he's not there yet. It's comfortable on the beer garden bench, even if he's not drinking, and the boys are doing well enough by themselves, rapidly exhausting the roll of drink tickets the city fathers, via the taxi driver, gave them when they arrived at the fair. J. can't keep his eyes off that spud, though. It's a Paul Bunyan potato, a John Henry snack.

The boys sprawl across the benches, bending elbows and killing time. Flies alight on their faces for brief disappointed moments.

"I think they should give us free T-shirts. I want a free T-shirt."

"Don't think they carry your size, my man."

"For my mother."

"How old do you think she is?"

"She's seventy-four. That why I want to get it, for her birthday."

"Not your toothless ma, that woman there in the red tanktop."

"Those guys over there keep drinking out these jars, man, been watching them. It's moonshine."

"Ever tell you about the time I was interviewing Lynrd Sknyrd and we drank from their still? Drinking a bucket of nails."

"What time is this steeldriving thing? It's like some kind of monster truck thing, right?"

"I say we go over there and buy some of that shine."

"I gotta dig that steeldriving event. Maybe I can squeeze a *GQ* thing out it. Mano-a-mano is really big right now."

From time to time, J. sneaks a peak at the next bench over, where some locals have bivouacked for similar purposes. So far J. has cataloged one "get a load of these guys" thumb gesture, three different rounds of chortles at his friends' expense, and assorted steel-eyed squints of challenge. Only he has noticed. There's not a fight brewing, but one or two lessons to be taught to the rude outsiders are being debated under their baseball caps, drawn from fisticuff curricula.

"Still pissed?" One Eye taps on his shoulder.

Ever since their embarrassing internment in Lawrence's bathroom, One Eye has avoided him. J. figured his friend was probably busy with caper preparation: diagrams of heating vents, timing with a stopwatch the length of time it took to get to Lucien's room from his, counting and recounting paces, calculating lines of sight. *At 12:05 on the dot every night the security guard leaves his post for a bathroom break.* Now here he is with a white cotton candy cone picked bare except for a few tufts of pink fur, as if he's been picking meat off a dead cartoon animal.

J. says, "Forget it. Just don't mention it again."

"It's up to you, my friend," One Eye says, ripping remnants of pink, "But I'm hitting Stage Two tonight, with or without you. Lucien's having dinner with some of the local muckety-mucks and I'm going to hit him them."

"Enjoy."

"I'll take you off too if you want . . . Oh, look, here comes Captain Johnson now."

Lucien and his herald try to make an elegant stride over to the beer garden as gawking tourists and hyperactive children divert them into constant course corrections, pausing here, dodging left or right. Dressed in the only Angelo Marini suits for a hundred miles probably. Lawrence follows behind his master conjugating *to irritate* with every step (he irritates, has irritated, will irritate). "Hello, friends," Lucien says as the final obstacle jets across to the giant spud and clears the way. "There is a truly exemplary ice cream stand on the other side a little farther up."

"Just between you and me," Lawrence says in a Dow Jones whisper, "the Rocky Road is your best bet."

As they greet the group, J. looks over their shoulders to see if he can spy Pamela. She ditched him once they made their way down the hill. He had a bit of trouble maneuvering around this lady's double stroller, asked, "Do you want to go this way or down there?" and she was gone. He stood there with John Henry under his arm and correctly reckoned he'd find Dave Brown,

Tiny, Frenchie and One Eye near the most convenient beer station. He doesn't see her.

"Glad to see you're all enjoying yourselves," Lucien smiles. "Not the usual, eh?" J. has to agree. The sun is a pleasant kind of irritation on his back. Out here in the open, under unpillaged blue, it's a nice rest stop, it breaks things up as he goes for the record. Monday he's back in cities again, taking his usual train routes to the standard event locales, taking his usual cab routes home after the standard event closings. "Off the beaten track to be sure," the p.r. man continues, "so you know I appreciate the effort you men have put in."

"Ours is not to wonder why, Lucien," One Eye growls.

"Dave," Lucien turns, "how is old Milt Chamber? You're covering this for *West Virginia Life*, correct?"

"Nice guy," Dave hiccups, "we've only talked on the phone, but didn't he used to be at the *Times*? I think I met him a few years ago. Had some kind of breakdown, right?"

"Dehydration, I think, was the explanation I heard. One of those new fad diets. J.—heard you talked to InterTravel. It sounds like it's going to be one hell of a site when they launch. Apparently you can just click on any city and you'll be able to get restaurants and hotels. The local attractions. Isn't this world wide web marvelous? The head of content there is a dear friend."

"Yeah."

"He's really smart. You guys should get together once you get your piece in. I think they're looking for good writers, and with Time Warner behind them, they should pay quite well."

"Sounds great." Lunch, let's do lunch, let's meet for drinks, here's my card, that's the office number and I'll put my cell number on the back.

Lawrence points. "What is that?"

"That's J.'s," Dave Brown says, tapping the John Henry statue. "His little buddy."

"He's really got the spirit."

"The merchandise isn't too garish," Lucien says. "I'm quite surprised. They've shown remarkable restraint."

"I would have gone for an action figure at least," Lawrence twitters. "Margins on action figures these days are not to be believed. Board games, any number of directions they could have gone in. There's not even any sweatshirts. Everybody makes sweatshirts these days."

"Why don't you write them a memo, Larry?" Frenchie asks, winking to comrades.

"Oh, J." Lucien interrupts, "I have something that might interest you. Lawrence?"

Lawrence fumbles with his leather briefcase and hands J. a newspaper. "We thought you might get a kick out it," he says.

"The *Hinton Owl*," Tiny says, "All the News That's Fit to Hoot."

It is the special John Henry Days edition, a slim four-sheeter. J.'s seen stacks of it lying on tables. But what's it got to do with him? JOHN HENRY DAYS ARRIVES! with a picture of Mayor Cliff standing beneath the monument on the hill. This is real breaking news.

"Below the fold," Lawrence offers, smiling thinly.

J. flips the paper. TRAGEDY AVERTED AT OPENING NIGHT GALA—VISITING JOURNALIST SAVED BY HEROIC LOCAL DOCTOR. There's a crime scene photo of J. on the ground, his arms spread out, while onlookers—he recognizes Frenchie's coif—bend over him. Jesus Christ.

Tiny snatches the paper from his hand, roaring, " 'A near fatal accident was averted last night when J. Sutter of New York City almost choked to death during the opening ceremonies of the John Henry Days . . .'—catchy lede, I'll say that. Blah blah—'local talent Bobby Martin sang the famous "Ballad of John Henry" '—blah blah—'only inches from death'—yeah yeah— 'if not for the expertise of respected physician Dr. William Stephenson, Mr. Sutter surely would have expired. A piece of roast beef is the suspected culprit.' Wow, J., you got your name on the front page!"

"Better put out an APB on that roast beef before he strikes again!"

"It's written by that guy who was hanging around, Honnicut or whatever. Gotta give that guy credit for having a nose for a story."

"Guess you never know when you'll make the news."

Lucien smiles. "Thought you might want to have that for your clip file. Keep it."

Tiny says, "It's a good omen. Could've been an obit—misadventure by buffet."

"Thanks for the paper, Lucien." J. knows One Eye has some kind remark or squint-related communiqué, so J. refuses to look in his direction. He gives Tiny his drink tickets and tells them he's going to check out the fair.

He's a few yards in when Dave Brown says, "Hey, Bobby Figgis—aren't you forgetting something?"

J. turns around. His John Henry statue rests on the picnic table, presiding over a fief of half-filled beer cups.

He's in. He walks past pastel menageries of balloon fauna with knot navels, is enticed to linger over rows of pies. This isn't the Aryan Nation re-cruitment rally he thought it would be from what he saw last night and this morning. More black people than he expected; he's doing a lot of the old afro-nod, the hello you give to folks when you get out of the city and into friendlier climes. He notices quite a few teenage couples, dressed in the hip-hop gear he'd see on any Brooklyn ave; there are even one or two hardrocks around, fronting. Cable allows every teenager, no matter how country, to cat-walk into the latest styles. And maybe looking at these woods forces them to reach for what they see on TV as ghetto realness, and they cling to it. A life raft in this cracker wilderness. So they know who they are even when mow-ing the lawn. Hell, the circulation of the people he works for reaches every-where, so he's helped it along in his small way. Wrote about the new sneakers the rap crowd decided on this spring, interviewed Down Ready Crew just a month ago to abet the push for their first major label release. Even the white kids have a little flavor. There are older bourgie couples with small kids, the Range Rover crowd out for a weekend excursion. Of course we're here, he thinks, but his New York prejudices still urge him to surprise.

The next trash can he comes to is full, overfull, topped with the last un-eaten nubs of hot dog buns and crenellated paper plates with Rorschach ketchup smears, so he rolls up the *Hinton Owl* and stuffs it in his back pocket. Christ. He's seen his name in the paper plenty of times, that's his trade, mi-grating to where the work is and getting a byline at the end of the day, but he's never been *in* the paper. He felt so good he'd almost forgotten about last night. And with his picture like that, stretched out like a KO'd heavyweight. The closest he's ever come to being in print was when one of his college friends imagined himself as his generation's Proust and stuck J. in under a pseudonym as a talented fellow who'd allowed himself to betray his talent. His pal denied the character was based on J.—after all, his name was name Ray, wasn't it?

Sniveling Lawrence handing him the paper like that, and Dave Brown's Bobby Figgis crack. In this anonymous fair, surrounded by the motley, he felt out in the open. Out here all exposed.

John Henry is too heavy. He feels like he's been lugging him around for years. He wasn't that heavy up in the caboose, but he started to get heavy as J. walked down the hill to the fair, and now he's heavier than ever. Slighted anonymous muscles in his hand grumble. There's no place to put him. He thinks, I got John Henry here in fine condition! Get your authentic John Henry here! How much would you like to bid, sir? No one else has one.

They've stuck to T-shirts, some kids have green foam sledgehammers, but he's the only jackass walking around in spy sunglasses and Hawaiian shirt with a John Henry under his arm.

So where would Pamela be?

Not in the moonwalk. The moonwalk is a machine that takes children into its input and has three settings: jump, tumble and headrush. Once they have been output the children have been altered, possessing a new appreciation of solid ground. But the true heart of the lesson, J. thinks as he watches the gamboling and careening kids, is that reality is always waiting. Solid ground will rush up to meet you after your momentary escape. The Enchanted Castle has seen better days in more blessed kingdoms; gray patches cover puncture wounds in the plastic, half the turrets on top wiggle in asphyxiation, they sag, wobble at every pratfall of the children inside. Blue smoke chugs out of the gasoline engine pushing air inside. Perhaps a steam engine would be more eco-friendly.

His arm is tired; he readjusts his grip on the statue and John Henry dangles upside down as J.'s fingers curl around his leg. Not a dignified pose for a legend, but . . . On the bandstand the bluegrass trio who performed during his last pass has been replaced by O'Leary the One-Man Band. Cymbals collide tinnily between his knees, he wheezes into a harmonica that's hooked onto his face like emergency room apparatus, his banjo writhes, and an extra hand comes out of nowhere periodically to squeeze the tiny black horn at his hip. Is he singing John Henry? This is an instrumental, and the kinetic extravaganza before his eyes distracts his ears, he can't make out the song. He moves through the bottleneck of O'Leary fans, soldiers past a stall of tie-dyed wall hangings and finds her.

He finds her in a wedged-in booth, an illegal space probably off the official map of vendors, between a tableau of assorted shriveled jerkies and a booth offering photographs of dead celebrities in glamorous poses. Pamela is having her palm read by an old white lady perched on a green-and-white plaid lawn chair. The fortuneteller is skinny as barbed wire, rusted as such, just as bent. She smokes a brand of cigarettes J. has never seen before, discounted tobacco calibrated to the region's economic profile, an off-brand with on-target carcinogens. The weatherbeaten oracle notices J. and cuts off her prognostications, folds Pamela's palm into her mottled hands and drinks deep from the seeker's eyes. A might theatrical, J. thinks, but what can you expect from a lawn chair psychic?

Pamela notices J. as well and turns to ask the woman, "You're not going to tell me how it turns out?"

She lights a cigarette with another cigarette and says, "What do you expect for two bucks?" leaning back into the soft slats of her throne.

"How's the future looking these days?" J. asks as they retreat into people.

"She was just reminding me of something." The muscles in her face unratchet. "Where did you go?" she asks.

"I was right behind you," he says, "I thought you ditched me." She denies convincingly. They stroll.

Into his hand is thrust a flyer for auto repair, a few seconds later a flyer for soul repair; mechanics and Christians alike work the crowd. He thinks, we are officially hanging out now, but what does that mean. Nothing. They've merely been thrown together at an odd occasion and talking and walking together is easier than being alone in a crowd. She doesn't say anything. He feels like an ass. His eyes follow the barricade that runs along the tracks and he can make out half the arch of the new tunnel. Right now the one John Henry dug is hidden by a tent, but Pamela has steered them in that direction, so he'll soon see the famous place. What all the hubbub is about. He knows the fair isn't that big, but all this aimless cutting across the rows makes it seem like it goes on forever. His sneakers scud across crushed paper cups and they stroll through the fair.

"My father would have loved this," Pamela says.

"Have you decided about the museum?"

"Not all this junk they're selling, but the idea behind it." She finally looks at J. "He would have loved it."

"John Henry!" rolls the voice across the field. "I'm looking for John Henry! Are you out there?" Before J. can suggest they check out this next petty spectacle, Pamela charges ahead toward the shouting, where a small huddle has assembled around a contraption. The worn sign at its base urges, TEST YOUR STRENGTH, and a sheet of paper taped up for this occasion offers as postscript, JOHN HENRY CONTEST. J.'s eyes skitter up the length of the wooden totem, to the bell at the crest. At intervals along the way, obscuring the usual designations, newly taped-up shreds of paper read, WATER BOY, APPRENTICE, SHAKER, STEELDRIVER, and at the top, JOHN HENRY. "Looking for John Henry, paging Mr. John Q. Henry," shouts the barker. In a worn green suit, beneath the rim of a dusty brown bowler hat, he says, "Take a chance, take a chance, every swing might be your last."

J. slides in next to Pamela. She says, "I'm not sure what I thought this would be."

Three teenagers in U of WV football shirts perform calculations in their heads, make charts with Risk, Ballsiness and Ridicule Potential headers. While they ponder and cogitate, their date rape stares ease into squints of scholarly contemplation. Two arrive at a figure in unison and shove their slower comrade toward the barker, spilling beer over rims.

"All right, citizens, looks like we have a contestant!" the barker yelps, grabbing the redheaded conscript's arm before he can squirm back to his friends. "Listen here, Red," steering him toward the contraption, "this ain't hauling kegs up the frat house steps. This is serious business." He shoves a scraped-up wooden mallet into the frat boy's hand. "You don't want your friends there telling Lisa Ann that her beau doesn't have what it takes, do you?"

Red can't back out now, so he hams it up for his pals and the crowd, hoping to shape this incident into a flattering anecdote his friends will recount for years to come, preferably when he is trying to get laid. He flexes Atlas-style, does two pushups and spits into his palms while his chums hand over the two bucks.

"Just hit the target, Red, and try not to break anything," the barker advises, less solicitous now that he's roped one in. He directs Red's attention to the padded plug at the base of the device. Red takes one last look at his cronies, unleashes a rebel yell and brings the mallet down on the target, whereupon rudimentary kinetic energy transfer systems are initiated and the red ball shoots up the center groove of the totem. It jets up; he's no WATER BOY or APPRENTICE, but SHAKER, and the red ball, having judged and designated, delivering in quivering apex summary judgment, falls back down. Red does not ring the bell, sound in clear summer air his legend. His friends shout "Shaker! Shaker!" and slap the man on his back.

The barker says, "Too many shakers and not enough men around here, been like this all day." Back at the crowd now, ushering this last contestant back into the crowd and searching for rubes. "Who's next? Two dollars an affirmation, who's next, who's next? Two dollars to see if you have that steeldriving stuff. Take a swing, every day may be your last." Spittle off his lips clear in the sun. "Think you got what it takes?" Judging the crowd in advance of his machine. "You, in the sunglasses, come on up and take a swing, son."

It becomes evident to J. that the man is addressing him. "No, thanks," he says, taking a step back.

"Why don't you go ahead?" Pamela asks. Perhaps a mischievous expression roosting there in those oxbow eyebrows, wide pupils.

"No thanks," J. repeats.

"I understand, my man," the barker says, drawing disappointment from the well of his face. "Don't want to look bad in front of your girlfriend, but performance anxiety is nothing to worry about. Happens to a lot of men, I hear."

"Here's two dollars," Pamela says, handing him the cash. She looks back at J., hands on her hips as if he's been standing there for hours. "Come on, J., take a swing."

"I'm not sure if your friend has taken his Geritol today," the barker offers, "perhaps that's what's bothering him. You take your Geritol today, son?" He extends the mallet to J.

Can't escape without pushing past the crowd behind his back. He doesn't have any choice, really, does he? He steps up to meet his fate.

"You gonna let go of that?" the barker asks.

He has the statue under his arm.

"I'll hold that for you," his new enemy Pamela offers, and an exchange is performed whereby he trades the statue for the mallet.

"Where are you from, son?" the barker inquires, mock friendly. Up this close his face is all pores. He's going to have a little fun with J. before he lets him take a swing.

"Brooklyn," J. mumbles.

"Big Apple," nodding, scratching beneath his bowler. "I was in New York once when I was in the navy. Hung out in Times Square with all the lights. Caught a dose so bad it still hurts to—sorry, ma'am. Wouldn't go back there if you paid me. Let's see—do you work out? This muscle tone, what are you, a construction worker?"

"Writer. I'm ready to go if you'd just step aside."

"College boy, huh? Well, we don't discriminate here. Why don't you take your shot. Wait a minute, hold it like this. It ain't a bunch of daisies. Hold it like you want to drive steel, son."

J. spreads his legs apart, trying to insinuate his slack limbs into a pose of classic athleticism. A statue a museum would be proud to acquire. Wouldn't mind giving Pamela a little knock on the head, to tell the truth. Ignore everybody; he attempts to do so, but he can feel their eyes on his neck, and sweat torrents from ducts. He feels like he felt at dinner last night, all the crackers around him watching his troubles. The mallet is a little heavier than he thought it would be. He makes a note to himself to give the swing a little oomph when he brings the head over his shoulder. Makes a note to have good aim and hit the mashed plug square. He will not falter and damn Pamela and damn all them behind him.

WATER BOY.

Out of the crowd whitecaps of swelling laughter, which collapse into a splashy foam of chortle and chuckle. A few cheer out of honed politeness. The mad barker at the end of the world nods exaggeratedly in commiseration, hat in his hands over his belly. He takes the mallet from J. and says, "Noble profession, Water Boy. Some of my best friends are Water Boys. No shame in a trade like that," then he quickly pivots and faces the crowd, hectoring, on to the next victim, "Hit the bell and make it ding ding ding, make it sing that old John Henry song!"

"Come on, Water Boy," Pamela says, sliding her arm into his.

J. is startled by the heat of her arm, but still too pissed to take in the full implications. "What did you have to do that for?" he sputters, but he doesn't take his arm away.

She pats his hand with warm fingers. "Don't worry about it. You were just a little too smug. It's all in good fun."

"Those things are rigged," he halfheartedly fumes. "See how he was leaning on the post? Has a switch back there where he can adjust if he doesn't like someone. That college boy crack . . ."

At their backs they hear, "Think you're John Henry? You ain't no John Henry, I'll tell you that."

"I still haven't seen the tunnel up close yet," he says. He can't think of anything else to say.

"That's where we're going."

### GENUINE STEEL-DRIVING EXHIBITION—4 P.M.
### MATT HENDRICKS OF HINTON
#### vs.
### TONY LESLIE OF TALCOTT

The biggest rock in Summers County sits on a wooden stage, bulging eight feet high, one side sheared off into an almost level surface. Red, white and blue streamers dangle from posts, patient for wind that will marshal and inspire them into patriotic ruffle. Two ruddy white men, shirts off, take practice swings with sledgehammers; they stretch muscles and suckle water bottles. J. and Pamela force themselves into the biggest clot of people yet. It's almost four o'clock and time for the show.

"The steeldriving exhibition," Pamela says. "I don't know how they plan to do it," pointing up at the flat front of the rock. "See those two holes there? I think they drilled a little ways in to start them off, and then the two of them will hit into the holes and see how far they get into the rock in a set amount of time."

"Gambling allowed in West Virginia?"

"They need someone to hold the bits straight—they need shakers."

"Water boys, too, Ah reckon."

"And the shakers better hold those bits straight or else they're going to lose a hand."

He looks up at the two white guys up there warming up. They live for this. They wink at confederates. Nothing life or death here, just a chance to show off for the crowd. Buy each other beers after the match and the loser has to endure jokes until next year's rematch. What is at stake here? he wonders, looking over the well-scrubbed faces of the crowd, drawn here across miles, to the main event after an afternoon of sugar-rich foreplay. Their steps get smaller as they approach; they press together, dropping individual fancy for group delectation. An unkind part of him says *mob* but he knows they are not bloodthirsty. What will happen will be entertainment. A few pictures on a roll of twenty-four that will be picked up at the drugstore on Tuesday. And what would it have been like that day in 1872? On that ghost day. Who did they root for before legend and meaning accreted around the competition between the man and the device. Progress or the black man. A wife or girlfriend rubs the latest sunblock into the arms of one of the steeldrivers. This is where they stood, after all, right? On mashed grass like this. Waiting outside the tunnel for news of the competition. Today it is entertainment. Gift from the bounty of pop. They can see for themselves, the way they always do nowadays. Real-time, and they can almost touch it, all participants in this competition, this spectacle.

It will be a fun time, pay per view.

"There's still time to see the tunnel," Pamela says, and they squirm through; she leads him with a warm touch, batting back balloons held by tiny sticky hands.

At the edge of the fair, finally, he sees the tunnel for the first time. He thought it would be bigger. This is the John Henry tunnel, not the one over there that has replaced it. The functional tunnel draws in the modern freight, the John Henry tunnel old wives' tales. Rain and dirt have sullied the dignity of the entrance but the cut and arranged stones announce a tamed mountain. The message out of the black mouth is not that of conquest but shrugged failure. The county has recently repainted the words GREAT BEND TUNNEL in smart white paint, an effort at renovation that merely forces the weather's violence to stand out in relief. He looks right, over at the new tunnel, past the barricade. An electrical cable glides into its mouth, steel tracks shiver along the ground into it, testifying to utility. What does John Henry's tunnel have on that? The sun just dips over the mountain and a fantail of shade sets the tunnel into obscurity. Whatever crowd gawked here earlier has decamped to the steeldriving exhibition; in their wake popcorn boxes and cups lay scattered like abandoned tools. A trickle of water from above scratches its way down and into the face of the tunnel. Slow work, but it gets the job done, melting stone and the arrogance of men. Repair the damage, what human beings have done, and the mountain will close its wound.

They move up on vague feet to the wide black mouth. Five haphazard and ineffectual slabs of concrete have been lugged over to block entry, just for show, really, satisfying some city council subordinance on keeping the kids away from the town treasure. Five teeth for this maw. A cool cemetery gust scrubs their faces as they get close. He looks up when he gets directly beneath the tunnel's mouth, eyes tracing the irregular black stone of the arch and then the burst of dirt and greenery advancing on the tunnel entrance from above, the sky beyond the mountain; it is a vista of scorched land and the renewed, regenerating growth inching up on it. They don't have to discuss it; he clambers up on the top slab and extends a hand to Pamela's warm hand and they jump inside.

He feels sleepy and calm. The ground is muddy with pooling water, confused by where to go, why this tunnel is here where familiar rock should be. It hasn't sunk in. He looks up at the arching of the tunnel above them and can make out only darkness from which crags and broken pieces occasionally emerge, breaking the surface of the ocean darkness like scattered atolls. His eyes need to adjust.

"What do you think it looked like to him," Pamela's voice, "before he was an inch in, before he started. He had a big mountain in front of him."

He hugs the statue closer to him, for comfort, for an anchor in this novel gloom. It smells like every dank basement he has ever been in. He remembers the stories of accidents from the p.r. packet, where the miners were caught by cave-ins, crushed or trapped by rock and left to asphyxiate. He read about a train that got stuck in this tunnel during a cave-in or mechanical fail-ure and people suffocated on the engine smoke. After last night he can imag-ine suffocating in here, choking on soot. This feeling seeps into him and resounds against his bones, where he can feel the angry tonnage of the moun-tain pressing down on his body, as if he has the mountain on his shoulders. Or he is in its fist, and it is squeezing. A touch of claustrophobia? No previ-ous indications of this condition so no, more than that.

"Standing in here now, I thought I would never be here because I hated it all. Listening to the same stories out of his mouth every day. John Henry, John Henry. But being here now."

Toes cold. His shoes are soaked through from the water. The puddles are deeper than he thought or else he's sinking. Like he has ghouls grasping his ankles to pull him beneath. Puddles, dejected bits of rock that continue to rain from above, but no tracks. They've been melted down or relaid in the re-placement tunnel. No respect for the obsolete. Air from outside is pulled in here and wrung of all good things by diseased alveolae, converted into pesti-lential exhalation, pushed out of this mountain's diseased lungs. But this place is not diseased, or evil, or anything more than rock. Surely. An echo rises from unidentified critter or natural event and in him surges almost an im-pulse to run, quickly stifled by reason. This is merely a tunnel and a few yards away the real world spins at its normal rate. As his eyes adjust he cannot make out any graffiti. No looping declarations of love or lust, the name of the lo-cal football team in fuzzy exclamations, the latest band rules. Kids dare each other to step inside but no one gets very far in or stays too long. How does the song go? *Big Bend Tunnel will be the death of me, Lord, Lord, Big Bend Tun-nel will be the death of me.* Why didn't they wall it up. They need something from it. Need their ghosts. And what else?

"Of course they say if you listen hard you can hear his hammer and it's a bad omen. Can you hear it? Why don't you say anything?"

He has half a mind to set the statue down on the floor of the tunnel, make a puppet show of this scene. Diorama of the big day, the John Henry minia-ture making literal the scale of his competition. So small beneath this grand arching and the infinite tons crouching above him considering pounce and collapse. That's how he feels now—small. Step in here and you leave it all be-hind, the bills, the hustle, the Record, all that is receipts bleaching back there under the sun. What if this were your work? To best the mountain. Come to work every day, two, three years of work, into this death and murk, each day your progress measured by the extent to which you extend the darkness. How deep you dig your grave. He wins the contest. He defeats the Record. This place confounds devices, the steam drill and all that follows. This place defeats the frequencies that are the currency of his life. Email and pagers, cell phones, step in here and fall away from the information age, into the mountain, breathe in soot. Unsettling but calming, too. The daily battles that have lost meaning are clearly drawn again, the opponents and objectives named and understood. The true differences between you and them. And it. He presses a hand to the cool blasted wall. There are no rough edges to the stone; they have been smoothed away by falling water, decades of healing and forgetting. How long does it take to forget a hole in your self. He wins the contest but then what?

"If I asked you to help me do something tomorrow, would you do it?"

She has been squeezing his hand for some time now but he hadn't noticed. Some time ago this became a silent movie. They are in the seats, shifting thighs, as the outside world and those other people from the fair unspool on the parabola screen of the tunnel mouth. The competition is about to begin, all the characters have been set up. The bit players move through the fair, staring past each other, waiting for cues; they have spent their whole lives rehearsing. All that rehearsing is cutting-room floor discard, the outtakes from the perfect American movie no one will ever see. In the middle rows are J. and Pamela. If they did what the audience never does and turned in their seats, they would see the light of the projector, the white flickering projector that is the light at the other end of the tunnel. A dream projecting itself from the west.

He says, sure.

Out of the mouth of the tunnel, on that screen, it is time for the main event. They are all there.

They were all there, from the eminently fuckable to the differently attractive, the not conventionally handsome and the walking airbrushed in complimentary pairs, the critics' darling and the promising newcomer milled about. Miracles abounded in that room. The recovering nicely thank you and the unknowingly metastatic discussed a summer share. The shy and awkward essayed the latest dance. The junior professors dismissed their dread over the upcoming tenure review and the last to know were informed by the gatekeepers of scandal while teetotalers guzzled and juicers sipped fizzy water. The Wall Street warriors in their surreptitious girdles felt secure. The easily startled possessed a beatific calm later unrecallable. The muscle boys did tricks with their pecs and the feeble were happy in their own bodies. The lipstick lesbians and the baldheaded butches traded stock tips and the rhinoplasty specialist chuckled on meeting a performance artist named the Nose, an individual renowned for spectacular inhalations. The secret diarist took notes. The shortlisted for the position and the recently eliminated shook hands, unaware of their fates. It was the main event. They were all there. And it was only nine o'clock.

J. was there. He alone was not carefree, this night he was a chap of heavy heart, unswayed by ambient and intrusive cheer. He had read about a death in the newspaper just that very afternoon. It weighed on him.

The devout danced with the dissolute and they traded numbers they would never call. The chairman of the board stooped to tie his shoe and the boy from the mail room attending tonight via intercepted invitation later splurged for a taxi home. A faint smell of jasmine filled the room. The coat check girl needed a fix. The bathroom attendant hovered over a stack of white towels.

J. had never met the dead man. He encountered the obit on the jump page of an article describing a Hollywood actress's new animal rescue charity. The obit ran down the dead man's greatest hits, his days as a student protester on the steps of Berkeley and his strut over to the Oakland offices of the Black

Panthers. The day he changed his name to Toure Nkumreh. The shoot-out with police and his flight to Cuba, where he drove Russian cars under palm trees, and his return to America. The dismissal of the murder charges after his lawyers convinced a jury that the police raid had been in fact a contract hit, his two years in prison for the lesser charge of weapons possession. That was it, until he was found dead in Tallahassee, of unknown causes, an autopsy would reveal all. Dead in his apartment for five days before the neighbors noticed the stench. That was it for the obit except for the cool archival photograph of Nkumreh in his Black Panther gear, black leather jacket, sunglasses, the tilted arrogant beret, automatic rifle pointing up at the photograph above, at the abused puppy who had found a new home thanks to the actress's good efforts.

The spinach dumplings deposited a green rot on the incisors of all who consumed them and everyone was too polite and malevolent to remark upon it.

They had gathered in a club called Glasnost to partake of the spread, the panoply of bite-sized widgets laid out by the publisher of Godfrey Frank's *A Chiropodist in Pangea*, a fifteen-hundred-page grimoire of mysterious content that would debut in a few days on the *New York Times* best-seller list. There was some question as to whether it would be categorized as fiction or nonfiction. Someone had to finish it first. It might debut sandwiched between the memoir of the man who got lost in the ice and the volume of the Akita's wisdom as collected by his enterprising owner, or between the novel about the magical patriarch and the one about the CIA cryptographer who gets caught up in a conspiracy. Waitresses dressed in the red uniforms of the Czar's honor guard distributed victuals and refreshments from platters to open hands. The party was cosponsored by a vodka manufacturer that had rethought its advertising campaign a few months prior. The guests walked and chatted while a large painting of Lenin's angular visage frowned at them.

They discussed the book.

The lapsed Catholic said, "It's about the environment."

The socially liberal but fiscally conservative said, "But it's not hit you over the head with it, from what I hear. It's a philosophical treatise in the form of a prose poem."

J. was a sophomore in college when the lonesome monks of the Afro-Am Department retrieved Toure Nkumreh and hired him as a visiting lecturer for a semester. None of the students had heard of him before, but on the announcement of his arrival all were sure they had heard of him, and they cackled excitedly. One student claimed that his father had marched with the man;

another recognized the name from a documentary. The school newspaper conveniently recounted his biography, and the excitement trebled now that they had something concrete about the man to discuss. The turnout the first day was so big that they had to move the class to a bigger lecture hall, displacing the Classicists.

The reluctantly sober since waking offered, "It's a roman à clef about the publishing world. Apparently there's a lecherous haberdasher who's really the head of Condé Nast."

The voted most likely to succeed by her high school class insisted, "But I thought it was a history of the twentieth century as seen through a bunion."

Gray insurrection beset Nkumreh's quaint, sculptured afro and gnarled goatee. He no longer wore that black leather jacket and black turtleneck, favoring instead brown corduroy blazer and beige turtleneck, as if his old gear had faded, bleached by circumstance and striding history. He spoke in a deep, bedrock voice and the students took notes. Black Power doodles writhed, marginalia, clenched fists detailed by disposable pens. "I'm the last member of the Black Power Traveling All-Stars," he joked, and the lecture hall filled with laughter. The students believed they had been embraced as intimates. He recounted trucking through Texas in the middle of the night with a trunk full of pistols and cruising the streets of Oakland on a food drive, and each tale was equally suspenseful.

The smiling politely said, "It's a postmodern retelling of the Midas story—you know, capitalism."

The natural storyteller declared, "No, it's a memoir."

The morning person asked, "What, is he in A.A.?"

The voice of the disenfranchised responded, "No, but he had a funny uncle. That's what I heard, anyway."

Graduate students from the History Department were bused in to teach the weekly sections. There wasn't an Afro-Am graduate program at the university, but there were always students in other disciplines who needed the extra cash. Lean times as they crawled over dunes toward dissertations. They conducted tours of primary sources that Nkumreh mentioned in passing, to give the students a better picture of the period in question. Nkumreh had written a book of poetry in 1969 called *Whitey Counting Missiles While Cities Burn*, but it was out of print so they made do with Xerox copies that dangled on their staples in dorm rooms. The teaching assistants placed Nkumreh's bad poetry in context, declaiming on the oral tradition and revolutionary consciousness.

The spokesman of his generation said with authority, "It's about two war-ring groups of chiropodists. One group does it the natural way, looking for fungus and corns, and the other—"

The nymphet interrupted, "What about the bunion?"

The rock promoter said, "Society is the bunion. The bunion is us. That's what I heard."

The hooker with a heart of gold added, "The chiropodists are just the prologue. The rest of the book is a social history, according to the *New Yorker*."

And the don't swing that way said, "Oh."

J. liked the class. While he had to admit that the man didn't look that good some mornings and tended to repeat anecdotes, often changing the ending depending on what was in the news that week, the class was held at 1 P.M. in a building close to the dining hall, and thus spectacularly convenient. That April J. enlisted in the takeover of the Dean's Office to protest the lack of funds for the Afro-Am Department. It was an annual event, as much a to-ken of spring as the cadre of fertilizer sprayers who roamed the Quad grass in plastic masks. The students filed a permit to take over the Dean's Office, and the Dean took a few days off to go fishing until the university sent the customary "let's open talks" letter to the students inside, who were pretty sick of each other after three days of sundry privation. Three or five days, depending on whether the takeover fell on a weekend. Fired up by Nkum-reh's tales of revolution, the front lines, the failed prison breakouts, that year's sit-in was well attended and J. was sure he'd get laid. Beneath the Dean's desk, or behind a filing cabinet filled with musky and aphrodisiac transcripts, surely he'd get laid, perhaps by one of the freshman girls who brought in soggy McDonald's every couple of hours. All he got were back pains from sleeping in the hallway; the precious square feet of carpet space had already been claimed by the dashiki-clad upperclassmen, who had taken over the Dean's Office the year before and prioritized. He was glad when he got to sleep in his bunk bed again, and drifted to slumber with the ease of the righteous.

The prodigal son said, "I read how the second person voice hasn't been used this effectively since the mid-eighties."

The Jew for Jesus uttered, "I thought it was nonfiction."

The postfeminist countered, "It's a nonfiction novel."

And the twelve-stepper said, "Oh."

In the first class after the takeover of the Dean's Office, they expected

Nkumreh to praise their protest. To welcome them as comrades in the struggle. But he did not mention it. He talked about his maroon days in Cuba, and
the Marxists he broke bread with, he discussed Pan-African consciousness
and unity across borders. He began to miss a lecture here and there, and the
head of Afro-Am Department, a German who had written books about
Nietzsche and the natal alienation of the slave, filled in for him. Technically,
Nkumreh had office hours, but when J. tried to go to them the man's office
was always dark, the receptionist no help. After lectures, Nkumreh picked up
his satchel and scurried away and after a time the students learned that it was
impossible to snag his attention despite their famous parents.

The sex columnist pronounced, "In a weird way it's a reinterpretation of
*Hamlet*."

The analyst said, "And Joycean in its use of language."

The analysand said, "It's a masterpiece."

The triskaidekaphobic added five and eight without unease. The substituting *big black guy* when really meaning to say *nigger* related a tale about a
misunderstanding at an ATM. A man crouched on all fours and barked like a
dog when the drugs hit.

The man of the hour, Godfrey Frank, was popular on talk shows, he left
his deep tread in popular magazines and sent the junketeers scurrying for
cover. It Came from Academia: Frank shambled through the media like a
creature from a science fiction film, a monster whose mutant gigantism he
could doubtless locate in nuclear-age anxiety, cold war terror. He could write
about anything it seemed, from baseball to hip-hop to weapons manufacturers, hold forth on historicized interpretations of ladies underwear while
sprinkling in obscure double entendres for the Medievalists in the cheap
seats. Articles written by the man (or cooed into microcassette and then later
transcribed by a succession of Women's Studies majors who all shared a
prominent body part adored by the cultural studies demiurge) sometimes appeared a few pages distant from articles about the man, profiles that included
photographs of Frank perched pensive on Le Corbusier furniture, legs
crossed, eyes fixed simultaneously on the high and the low. He quoted French
theorists who liked to inflate helpless nouns with rhetorical gases until they
burst into italics, and did some inflating of his own. The nouns were never
the same after that. *A Chiropodist in Pangea* was said to be his breakout book,
his release from the university press ghetto. That was the word in publishing
circles. It was getting raves everywhere.

A cover girl dared to eat a peach and another vomited in the little girls' room. The groupies and the hangers-on equipped with strategic filofaxes giggled among themselves for a moment before trolling for the famous.

No, the junketeers were not fond of Godfrey Frank. He was an outsider who had connived his way into their world of free events as if he were a celebrity. But he was not: he was an academic. Despite their hatred of him, the junketeers came here tonight because it was the best party going in Schadenfreude City, and they wheeled and dipped, ripping sinew from this carcass lately thrown up on their feeding grounds: top shelf, fat olive, chicken saté. Uptown at the Waldorf, the great-great-granddaughter of a wealthy nineteenth-century industrialist who still had plenty of money after the trust-busters robbed him of his empire announced her new charity, but there was no open bar, according to the word around town, and the junketeers stayed away. Downtown in a gallery, a painter who specialized in the whimsical desecration of corporate logos in order to make a point about consumer society and to extend the brittle dominion of irony held a party for his latest show, but his publicity firm had a reputation for thin white wine and supermarket cheese, and the junketeers stayed away. They came here.

The priapic stroked themselves to swift release under the tables and wiped themselves with cocktail napkins. The trust fund babies invited the rough trade back to the apartment papa bought for them, got more than they reckoned for and bled on catalog sheets before falling asleep with a smile.

A publicist he recognized from stress-born nightmares and events like this grabbed his hand. Short moussed spines erupted from her scalp to repel predators and a ring of metal in her left nostril helped the behaviorists track her movements through glittery habitat. He couldn't hear what she said for the music and he couldn't remember her name for the inebriation associated with her every appearance in his life. She smiled, withdrew a promotional CD from her expensive and artificially distressed messenger bag and deposited it in his hand. It was warm and moist. Then she scampered off to spread the rest of her spoor around her territory, until her bag was completely evacuated.

The recently liposucked found their palms falling farther than usual to pat new and improved thighs and at this sensation their eyes widened in astonishment, which was taken for animated interest by the food critic, who continued to describe Chef Jean-Phillipe's cassoulet. Those who longed for the days of the Algonquin round table could think of nothing witty to say because they were not witty people.

J. made his way through densities. He stepped on the high-heeled hoof of a woman whose face was a fright mask that did not change as he caused her injury. He accidentally and without realizing dislodged a gimlet from a man's hand, but the man did not protest because he was afraid of black people and in a subfloor of his consciousness thought perhaps he deserved it because he had made a killing that day while others shambled through the metropolis without cappuccino machines, sans arugula, pestoless. J. joined a human tributary that had eroded a course between canyons of the standing still, he trusted that the waif in front of him would not dawdle or stop. He gave himself to the current, the sure freckles on the back of the waif in front of him and the jostling idiot behind him who nibbled at the back of his shoes. J. put his hands in the air and looked at them as they grasped at the cardboard mobiles, the glossy vodka bottles blossoming on invisible wire, he looked as he spread his fingers wide in the air. No one noticed, and he did not expect them to. The diva shrieked through the sound system, addling the neighbors once again, and the waif took him to the altar, fellow traveler, fellow pilgrim, guided by the same instinct now hectoring J. They stood before the open bar.

The hip-hop artist in heavy rotation on the video music channel lost his clip-on gold tooth in the hummus. The man with no name accidentally revealed it after his third martini: Melvin. The rock star who just got clean fell off the wagon, or on the spike as the case may be.

At the bar J. beached on a khaki shoal that turned out to be Dave Brown. Dave Brown had both his elbows bracketed into the bar to keep himself steady. The old-timer's arm moved in a slim arc, like a robot on a production line; when he wanted to sip his drink, it pivoted on the knob of his elbow. This technique kept the shakes at bay. The junketeers nodded at each other, sopping but safe for a moment from the vengeful tides behind them. Dave Brown introduced J. to a woman on his left, a woman whose eyes shimmered beneath scythe eyebrows. Dave Brown tendered her name and credentials, she was an editor at woman's magazine, and J. had heard her name damned from this man's lips at an event two days ago, an event much like this. She smiled as Dave Brown offered J.'s credentials, the slim capillaries in her pink nostrils dilating as if she were taking this information into her very bloodstream, and then she turned around to talk to another darling.

"Can you believe this?" Dave Brown asked. The junketeer's head panned across the room. "All this for him. Criminy. I have to get my act together." His arm arced over to his drink. "You see anyone else out there?"

J. said, "I think I saw One Eye and Jimmy the Turk on the other side of the room."

"The rest'll be here soon," Dave Brown decided. "Not much else going on tonight." He looked down at J.'s palm. "What do you think of the song?" he asked.

J. tried to make out the song coming from the speakers, but the ponderous beat effaced it whenever he identified a note or two. "Don't know, what is it?" he asked.

"Not that song—that," Dave Brown said, pointing at the CD. J. still had it in his hand and he held it up to the purple light emanating from behind the bottles in the bar. The name of the song was "Awestruck Post-Struct Superstar," and the performing artist was billed as Godfrey Frank with Fire Drill and the Orderly Fashions.

"What's this?"

"That's the CD that comes with every copy of the book. He's singing now." Dave Brown shook his head. "I really have to get my act together."

It occurred to J. that Dave Brown had been around, he had forded shifting and treacherous trends, a hobo of pop, and had seen many things. J. asked his comrade if he'd heard about Nkumreh's death. Dave Brown plucked the lemon twist out of his martini and sucked it, gnawed it. He said he used to party with him in Bob Rafelson's house in the early seventies. The Panthers, he said, always had the best coke. Then something shifted on the far end of the room eventually but inevitably triggering a local effect: a sudden eddy that whisked Dave Brown to another corner, to a mellow grotto where there were couches and the media mercenary could rest for a few minutes and drink in peace. J. was left alone at the bar holding the CD. He leaned over and tried to get the bartender's attention.

The social climbers clambered unimpeded. The walking wounded realized that time heals all wounds after spying a new object of obsession. The spoken word artist skipped his inner beat and everything he said came out wrong, lyrical and classically cadenced.

J. had seen them perform once, some time ago at record release party: Fire Drill and the Orderly Fashions, a pop group in moribund drag. A few years before, bands from their hometown had made it big by fomenting a new sound that critics and record company executives believed would save rock and roll from the gloomy tyranny of European drone and inner-city armageddon. The bands from that hometown were an angry bunch who had converted their pain into a dread palatable for mainstream radio, a zippy melancholy, and Fire Drill and the Orderly Fashions played the game by se-

creting their sweet pop in thrashing and deadly arrangements. A wah-wah
pedal helped exceedingly. A record company signed them on the basis of their
place of origin and their willingness to adapt to the new flavor of pop. But
things did not go as planned. After two years, the children tired of the new
sound. Even the parents were no longer afraid and found themselves humming minor chords while driving to work, signing contracts, closing the deal.
The bands of the new sound broke up, or went into rehab, or put out records
that were perceived to have betrayed their early promise. Fire Drill and the
Orderly Fashions, the epigonic poseurs, found themselves in a difficult position when the big record label dropped them after an even newer sound appeared on the scene, antidote to and savior from, according to the arbiters of
taste, the last new sound.

The just last week stomach stapled felt something give. The fond of comparing every civic discomfort to the days of Nazi Germany complained about
alternate side of the street parking. The hypocritical said they would never do
such a thing.

Until the band was saved by Godfrey Frank. In a long and heavily foot-
noted article in a popular music magazine, Godfrey Frank smeared away the
muck to reveal the bubblegum underneath. He situated them in a lineage of
the Dionysian going back centuries, he located their Thanatotic flourishes as
a necessary guise in the final days of a self-conscious century, he outed them
as a canny pop band just in time for the demise of the new sound and rescued
them from the bargain bins. Critics, insecure about their lack of academic
grounding and ignorance of music history before the dusty advent of the
blues, reversed themselves; radio station programmers placed the band's next
single in strategic slots. Fire Drill and the Orderly Fashions befriended Frank
and hired him as a consultant on their new video. And this was the final miracle. He went after the adults without pretense. The video's conceit dispatched the formerly shabby rockers into the re-created sets of a television
show popular when the older demographic was young, and the sight of Fire
Drill and the Orderly Fashions attired in the bright and lively gear of the
television characters they had loved in their youth tickled them, on repeated
viewings warmed them inexplicably, reminding them perhaps of easier times,
loosening the intractable fear that seized them every minute of the day. Fire
Drill and the Orderly Fashions, skinning knees in sitcom mischief to a merry
tune, comforted them, more than hedge funds and acupuncture, and made
them whole.

J. read on the CD, This song is a special limited edition companion single available only with the purchase of *A Chiropodist in Pangea* by Godfrey Frank.

The so happy they could bust a gut did so, and the content with their lot in life grew more comfortable with their self-definition. The op-ed columnist had no op on Ed, the rent boy with a line for every occasion, but particularly ones like this, particularly for women like her.

J. had spent the afternoon filing a piece for a consumer electronics magazine. The manufacturer of a digital video playback device had sent him a model of the machine, gratis, and the film companies mailed him free copies of movies formatted for the device. But something was amiss. It was a gloomy occasion. This particular gadget had debuted at the same time as another with identical capabilities, and even though this evil sibling was more expensive and less efficient, the public had chosen, had spoken, had decided that this other device was the one they wanted for digital playback of their favorite classic films and recent box office smashes. The device J. was assigned to write about had already been discontinued, and the film companies were no longer going to produce disks for the machine. But all concerned had a backlog of product they wanted to get rid of, they gave incentives to retail salesmen, the men on the floor, to move the stuff off the shelves and to lie to the hopefully uninformed, who wanted and needed a new digital playback device and might invest in the hapless superannuated boxes. The vested companies advertised heavily in the consumer electronic magazine. J. had an article to write.

The biracial who adopted a superficial militancy to overcompensate for light skin discussed the perfidy of ice people with the gangster rapper ashamed of a placid upbringing in a middle-class suburb. The queasy at the sight of blood and the weak of stomach found new fortitude.

It was a tale of doomed technology and ruined hopes, an old oft-told story. Star-crossed since the implementation of its marketing scheme lo those many months before, the device never had a chance. Years from now white dudes with goatees who had never been loved in high school and so channeled their sexuality into the fringe and obscure would rescue the device from a dusty nook in a hip trash store and revive the machine, deify it in the name of kitsch. Name a zine after it. But the travails of this future pop sect did J. no good. He had a job to do and described resolution, picture quality, packaging. He used the word pixel. It was unrecognized by the spellchecker of his word processing program. His profession usually called for him to justify to the people out there the indispensability of this or that artifact to their lifestyles. Now he was trying to praise an object that would not exist in a few months to those who had already voted with their electronics store credit cards against its usefulness. The device did not increase their self-esteem, it did not percolate joy in their blank hearts, it did not gather and glue the potsherds of their fragile psyches. He wrote the piece about the dead machine, faxed it in to a number that answered shrilly, and then he read about the dead man in the newspaper he purchased at the corner bodega.

A urinal filled with vomit and the antiseptic puck bobbed in that horrible sea. The newspaper's crusader of truth held his tongue when he spied the party boy's sweet nipples and this was one less truth he related to his public.

They came here. They came because their empty and periodically disinfected apartments slurred threats at them, malevolent tides seeped from tight carpet moss or between wooden floorboards, and the original wood at that. They came because they had heard good things, there was a good buzz, and it was the worst thing they could imagine to be shut out, to be one of the anonymous shapeless out there banging on the castle walls. They came because it kept the hate away, but most of all they checked out their chipped bodies in mirrors, inspected the bits that had fallen away and came here because they thought tonight might be the night of the transfiguration, that sidereal maneuverings up above might allow that thing in the center of the universe to see them for the first time and it might love them, unclip the bowing velvet rope and accept them into itself. But it wasn't going to happen.

A social disease would induct novitiates by dawn. The beard of the closeted actress turned out to be that someone in the kitchen with Dinah, the scullery maid who later sold the photos to a national gossip magazine with sure distribution in supermarkets.

In the last class of the semester, Nkumreh talked about some of his former comrades in the struggle. Some were dead by bullets or drugs. One was a congressman on the Republican ticket who appeared on talk shows as the voice of black reason to denounce all he had believed in the fever of youth, talking of quotas and bemoaning the popularity of male-bashing black female writers, and another sold a barbecue sauce whose label featured the infamous curling panther, this one poised to strike tongues with vinegar and hot pepper. The condiment did a healthy business in soul food restaurants across the Midwest. It was the last class. The bell rang to signal the end of class and Nkumreh leaned into the microphone and said, staring up into the institutional rows, "In five years you will have forgotten everything I've said." He stared straight ahead into the dead heart of the room and yet more than one person felt he was staring into their eyes, and these shuddered. He exited the room with his customary speed and that was the last J. ever saw of him. Instead of a final exam, they had to hand in a term paper, which the graduate students in the History Department graded with circumspection.

The actress in the sequined dress lost a sequin and through mysterious repercussion never worked in a film again unless she bared her breasts, which were exuberant and strained against fabric, culpable in the final analysis for the lost sequin.

Sometimes he ran into people he went to college with. At a party, say, in a neighborhood he rarely had cause to visit. All sorts of things happen when you leave your stomping grounds, all sorts of ghosts pop up. They saw each other and looked away, down into the plastic cup cool with cocktail, suddenly interested in the words of the entity they'd been thrown up against at this party, next to the bookcase filled with unread books. They avoided each other until their guards slipped and they found themselves face to face, waiting in line for the bathroom or after making a wrong turn in search of a friend. The other people in Nkumreh's class, the righteous brothers and sisters who had memorized the Panther's Ten Point Plan, thought it quaint that he wrote for magazines, scribbling little pieces, and J. thought it obvious that they worked downtown, beetles chittering in the shadows of skyscrapers. They had nothing to say to each other, made plans to hang out, chuckled at the news of some classmate's misfortune. They made excuses and departed, to look for a friend, to piss, just getting my coat, great seeing you. Each secure about the path they had taken, smug and fondling the keys to the city. Toodle-oo, toodle-oo.

The marginally talented but well connected mentally decapitated their betters and those gifted with second sight were frightened by all the bloody heads on the floor.

He had never talked to the man. He had known people who had died, and what he felt on those occasions was nothing like he felt now. He didn't even feel like he did when a famous person died, when he suddenly realized what a large role they had played in his pop life, whether the deceased was the expert songsmith unavoidable on the radio or the crag-faced character actor, the bit player who soldiered on through Hollywood decades always double-crossing the hero, reliable that way. This thing in him now was peculiar and he couldn't figure it out.

The lately upgraded to homo erectus slouched anew, as was their lot.

The rock critic pontificated about the latest sound from the latest town, and found few cared.

J.'s body slipped into another current in the room, he fell into a pattern that nature had imposed on this crowd, and after a time his drink was empty and that very moment he found himself deposited at the bar again. This time One Eye was there, dressed in a blue prom tuxedo, with an eye patch of the same blue covering his signature wound. He was trying to get the bartender's attention. "J., J., my man, do you know what time the open bar closes?" he asked.

"I don't know," J. responded.

"Maybe I should get two drinks then, just in case." He leaned over the bar and whistled. No one could hear him for the sound system.

"What's that getup for?" J. asked. The texture of One Eye's tuxedo seemed to the dance under his gaze, an ancient magic living in polyblended fabric.

One Eye, the gentleman junketeer, without a care, hoarding drink tickets, said, "What, this old thing?" He smiled and then noticed J.'s expression. "Why so glum, chum?"

J. related his confused feelings over Nkumreh's death while behind One Eye's shoulder, the bartender came to take his order and then departed in response to One Eye's inattention.

"You're upset that the dude's dead," One Eye said. "That's natural."

J. said that wasn't quite it; he felt something new. He described some of the symptoms as One Eye looked back after the bartender, who had repaired to the other end of the bar to flirt with the underage. J. talked about the class he had taken in college and the fact that the man had died alone in Tallahassee. Tallahassee wasn't on his map, and if the man died in Tallahassee he died in another world apart from the one J. lived in.

"I know what's wrong with you," One Eye appraised, apparently listening despite the evidence to the contrary. He turned, rocking his head back and forth to the DJ's latest selection, a tawdry thing whose refrain was a looped simulated orgasm. "You're not upset that the guy's dead," he said. "You're upset that you don't care that the guy is dead. That you should be feeling something that good people feel when someone dies."

J. exhaled something and felt lighter.

One Eye clapped his hand on the shoulder of his fellow junketeer. "I envy you your youth, my friend," he began, hazarding a quick glance after the mercurial bartender, a man of untold transactions. "Hold on to these days. You still care that you don't care. The time will come when you don't care that you don't care, and on that day you will become a man. If you want I can arrange some sort of ceremony to mark the occasion, tasteful but symbolic, you know what I mean. Rent a donkey, something along those lines."

The music stopped, a giant lifted the roof off the club: a sudden shift in the barometric. The sound system cut out in the middle of a song that had shrieked for so long that it had come to seem the sound of their bodily processes, enzymatic reaction, mitotic doubling, a siren deep within the guests that made them go. Dazed, unable to account for this alien silence, the people in the room looked at each other, blinking, they looked at the sky to confirm that the shelling had stopped. Lights choreographed by computer, tilting on gyroscopes, burst in frenzied illumination, in a welter of patterns. This was a new effect to the night, novel sensory vandalism in an evening of myriad crimes. More than one among them wondered what they were in for next.

Along one innocent wall perpendicular to the bar, nondescript and overlooked all night, a curtain began to rise, a prehistoric red eyelid. Behind the curtain was a stage. The roving lights converged upon it, became one light.

The falling starlet contemplated a stick of celery and realized in its rectitude the fact of her wilted career. The polymorphously perverse and those repressed in that area hit it off like old army buddies until it came to the deed, where they parted ways.

Godfrey Frank took the stage and the four boys from Fire Drill and the Orderly Fashions trailed behind him, seizing guitars, a gold bass. One crawled into the drum kit. Godfrey Frank stood on bright green platform shoes. He had squeezed his sausage legs into black leather pants above which damp chest hair weaseled through a red mesh T-shirt. His long brown curly hair, glistening with a relaxing fluid, poured down his shoulders. He grabbed the microphone between his hands as if wrestling a rattler and screamed, "New York—are you ready to 'rock'?" The deficiently jaded in the crowd assented and he repeated, "I said, New York—are you ready to 'rock'!" The lights fled from each other again, seeking every inch of the room for a millisecond and roaming farther, and the guitarist pummeled the first chord of "Awestruck Post-Struct Superstar," the song that would haunt all of them for months, on the radio, on the television, in the listless aisles of supermarkets and gourmet delicatessens while shopping carts skidded on hobbled wheels.

J. couldn't make out the words. He looked back into the crowd, daring the replacement of his every cell with salt, and saw heads tilted in angles of strict attention, eyes split wide in hunger and mouths tastefully ajar as the ravenous lights licked their faces, savoring and considering who will be the first to go. He turned back to the stage. It was not that they liked the music or didn't like the man they had come here to celebrate, he thought, but that something was happening they could talk about later, and talk was important, it filled minutes, it flattered the speaker when delivered with the correct wise and knowing intonation. Information the last currency in this town. The act onstage was conversation tomorrow morning, an anecdote at next week's dinner party. The audience that night thought about the next audience and watched.

The editor of the magazine that published the finest literary fiction found that no one had ever heard of him, the publication, or those he published, and he longed for the days of Fitzgerald. The ne'er-do-well daughter of the famous actor and the tycoon's son got along swimmingly because they both lived off another's name.

J. couldn't hear the words, but when Godfrey Frank got to the chorus a tech man flicked a switch and the words were projected on the face of Lenin, that old Russkie hustler, which had been painted on the far wall of the stage:

> *Roland Barthes got hit by a truck*
> *That's a signifier you can't duck*
> *Life's an open text*
> *From cradle to death*

Some people sang along, some merely pretended to.

The best man and the groom kissed for the first time and the wedding was off. The architect to the fabulously stupendous misplaced all sense of the perpendicular that night, and turned to igloos. The hot, the tarty and the downright slutty traded notes with the well endowed, the flaccid, and those who just liked to watch, and come morning destiny's inscrutable hand had transformed all of them forever.

PART FIVE

# ADDING VERSES

❖

Even this late in the performance, there is still one more member of the ensemble yet to make an appearance. Standing patiently in the wings, resisting the temptation for one last smoke before the big scene, the steam drill, the heavy in this particular drama, waits for the cue. What's a hero without a villain?

Much maligned, much vilified, few songs celebrate the struggle of the steam drill. The hand-shy childhood, the ups and downs in the early days of implementation, the sad defeat on the proving grounds. "Ballad of Jo Jo the Steam Drill" is no chart-topper, virtually unhummable by human mouths, and you can't dance to it besides. Things looked so promising, too, for the Burleigh steam drill, with that sexy new drilling bar. Replacing all the luminaries of mechanical drilldom up to that point, the Brunton Wind Hammer, the Couch Drill, the Fowle, the Fontainmoreau. 240 pounds, 200 blows a minute, nifty pneumatic action. Until the Ingersoll came along, and Charles Burleigh's baby was just another bunch of obsolete scrap. This is the way the world works.

Progress may be imagined as a railroad line, its right-of-way surveyed through rough plains of trial and error, deep gullies of botched innovation, until the terminus of perfection is reached, the last cross-tie firmed into earth with one final spike. One day's bustling depot, current pinnacle of human invention, is tomorrow's skipped-over station, glimpsed in staccato through grimy windows and swiftly banished from consciousness. The Burleigh steam drill is the terminus of a series of inevitabilities, but only terminus until the line is extended, the rails laid farther into frontier, until the next model replaces and advances the heading. The new timetables say that the locomotive stops there only sometimes, at odd hours, and never the express. It's not like it used to be. Few talk of the Burleigh much anymore, and the ticket window accumulates dust and no one bothers to repaint what the weather has kissed away.

No one writes the songs, no one remembers. Perhaps a quote from the engine itself might shed some light on the situation, explain the events of that day in Big Bend Tunnel, lend some perspective. Let the other side speak.

Steam drill, can we get a soundbite? Silence only greets that quiver of jabbing microphones. No comment, no comment, sweatshirt hood cinched tight for anonymity on the perpwalk. Even if its lawyers hadn't given strict instructions, it is just a device, it cannot answer. It is only a machine, and it keeps its own counsel.

The purpose of the blackout curtains utilized by hotels and motels throughout the land is to engineer various mental states in the guest. When a guest opens her eyes in a completely dark environment, the first sensation generated is often one of anxious dislocation, which may escalate to modulated panic if the guest is slow to situate, find a landmark, reconstruct the journey to this darkness. Once the guest has oriented herself, reassuring notions introduce themselves. In the case of the guest in room 14 of the Talcott Motor Lodge, for example, after the digital display of the bedside alarm clock firmly tethers her to reality, she is relieved that life seems to continue pretty much the way it always does even if one has temporarily been removed from engaged participation by an overlong nap. It is this feeling of relief or reassurance, not the blockade of irritating sunshine, or the excitation of the fear impulse, that is the final aim of the blackout curtain; it is hoped that this feeling of comfort will be permanently associated with the particular place of lodging or chain of establishments, and encourage return visits. For we need our safe places in this world, there are far too few.

When Pamela Street wakes there is nothing beyond her skin but darkness. Deep inside the Talcott Motor Lodge and Sensory Deprivation Tank. She is not the first to be saved from madness by the soothing red numbers of an alarm clock. The cord of the alarm clock, trailing into the wall socket, is a lifeline to a verified world, power plants, standardized time, civilization. She knows where she is, disquiet exhaled. Retracing the events is no problem. Once the taxi dropped her from the fair, she stumbled on the bed, pratfalled into a deep sleep, and now she recovers, sensation by sensation. It is eight-thirty. Men talk in the parking lot. The circulation in her foot is ransomed where the blanket has kidnapped her sneaker. By the time she turns on the light she has forgotten her first thought on waking. She thought J. was lying beside her and something had happened.

She's not hungry right now. Had plenty to eat at the festival, a periodic table full of concocted nitrates and artificially colored beverages. She'll be hungry at some inappropriate time in the future, she figures, a couple of hours from now when the entire county has retreated behind screen doors, and her only choice will be stale pretzels from the vending machine. That will have to do. This time tomorrow she'll be back in New York, coated in a city summer sweat, but currently she's still in between towns on musty sheets. A big breakfast in the morning will have to sustain her for all she has to accomplish before she escapes on the plane.

Half an hour later she's smoked the room into an advertisement for cancer (the Compulsive's Council and League of Lonely Folks perhaps chipping in for this particular media campaign) so she slides back the blackout curtains and shoves the window across its grooves. The breeze wants into room 14 as much as the smoke wants out, and they negotiate border crossings. By the pool the journalists explore a case of the local discount pisswater beer, jiving it up with mosquitoes. J.'s out there, too. He raises a glass and they all toast to something. Did she actually grab his hand in the tunnel. Do anything else out of character. They stood in the tunnel she had heard about for so many years, and the poison that the stories had put in her blood drained from her, leaving her veins frigid and depleted as that stuff disappeared into puddles the earth drank. She felt like saying, my how you've grown, as if the rock were a gawky cousin not seen for a long time and now matured into his own person with quirks. Pools of gray water for a floor, an emphysematous gurgle for breath. Everybody else was outside watching the steeldriving contest, Pamela and J. missed the steeldriving contest and don't know who won. Not that she knows one of those crackers from another, to tell the truth. They heard the cheers, far away in the fairgrounds, but didn't leave the tunnel until the main event was over and the victor was at the microphone, thanking an extensive genealogical tree for their support. She grabbed his hand and asked if he'd come with her tomorrow. There, that was the dumb part; not holding his hand but asking him to come along. She didn't know if it was worse that she asked him or that he said yes. He'll think she's crazy when she opens up the box. Even from the bed she can make out that laugh of his. It hitches a ride on the breeze.

On the plane she took the box as her carry-on. A white guy in pinstripe pants and power tie came up the aisle when he spied her wiggling the box into the overhead; he didn't want her to mess up his suit jacket, wrinkle or otherwise mar it. The box fit, tilted a bit, and the latch shut without fret. She rode through the air with the box directly over her head; it perched, corrugated gargoyle, above the air nozzle and light, and this set childish tremors of unease inside her until the landing gear groaned open. At the arrival gate the driver's spotted hand went for her bag but she thrust the box at him instead. As they drifted down the escalator, with him in front carrying the box, she felt like a fake billionaire, the scruffy taxi driver her chauffeur chained to the briefcase full of bearer bonds. But it didn't contain bearer bonds. He put the box in the trunk, tilted again, this time over the spare tire and a couple of girlie mags, and when the trunk closed she was able to shut the box from her mind. On the ride to Talcott the mountains claimed her attention. When she unlocked room 14 she put the box in the closet, where it remains. Or the closet area, more properly: there is a clothes rack and handcuffed hangers and a shelf, but no door. She managed not to look at it nonetheless.

On the sides of the box, in the style of a design aesthetic long extinct, the Diego Grapefruit Company falsely describes the contents. That box hasn't held fruit for a long time. Along the corners of the box silver duct tape pinches, a discontinued brand drawn from the shelves of her father's hardware store. Miracle it still sticks. Some of her father's suppliers specialized more in indictments than quality merchandise. The white cardboard has been blackened by a hundred reconsidered situations. Move it over there, make room over there for it, put this in it and take that out.

The first time she saw it was fifteen years ago. She had made plans to go to the movies with Angela; the teenage guys who sat on the right side of the theater smoked cheeba and if she asked they'd give her a hit and she'd hope it wasn't laced with something and when the credits started she'd have to run out or else they thought they had the right to rap to her. That had been her plan until her father told her she'd have to wait for the package. He was expecting a package from one of his John Henry dealers; he'd wait for it himself but her mother wasn't letting him off the hook, not this time. It was her club's Christmas dance and he'd skipped too many. Her mother said Pamela was old enough to take care of something like that, she was big enough, so there was no way he wasn't going to be her escort. Walk in there without her man on her arm. She hadn't made a special trip to get his suit dry cleaned so he could back out for John Henry. She knew how to make him behave, sometimes, when she really wanted to. Back then, for a time. He'll be here in time for you to make your movie, her father said as he put on his fur hat. He better, Pamela said to herself.

When the room was suddenly rocked by a swell of gamey romance, via the title theme of *The Love Boat*, she knew she wasn't going to make it out that night. The theme of *The Love Boat*, in her history, meant that she was staying in for the night. Usually her father met his John Henry pushers at the store and Pamela never witnessed their ridiculous transactions. Just saw the crap when he brought it home, beaming, dying to show it to her as if she gave a shit. Already cluttering the house would be a dozen identical John Henry statues, a gang of shellacked gremlins, and he'd hoist in another one that was exactly the same and try to get them excited about this new piece of garbage. The house brimmed with John Henry. Not that she cared about her childhood toys at that point, but when her father discovered a box of her old toys in a closet one day he made her throw them out so there'd be room for more John Henry. There was no room in which John Henry did not hunch, no wall across which John Henry did not heave and toil and die in paint and ink and charcoal, no tables where smaller memorabilia, diecast and ceramic figurines, did not pose in martyrdom. (She didn't have friends over because that meant explaining. She met them downstairs when they buzzed.) He made it out like it had been excavated from King Tut's tomb. He usually got the stuff at the store, and the few times he conducted John Henry business at their home, Pamela beat it upstairs and turned her boombox on real loud, until the latest batch of weirdos got the hell out of their house with their smelly-ass selves.

Her friend Angela called from a pay phone and Pamela told her she wouldn't be coming out. The street noise made it sound like Angela was in the middle of a big party Pamela was missing. The second she put the phone down the buzzer rang. On *The Love Boat*, the bumbling white people set a course for adventure, their minds on a new romance. Pamela hustled to the intercom, and it took three tries before the weirdo employed the talk button correctly and she heard clearly, "Mr. Mails." She rolled her eyes, buttoned the top two buttons on her shirt and buzzed him up.

He looked nasty. Loitering there on their doormat, in his stained tan overcoat, with those fogged-up, big-ass glasses on his face, he looked like a bag lady. Looked like her biology teacher, who was from Yugoslavia, and when he talked about "the genitalia" everybody had to laugh because he sounded like he was talking about his girlfriend. He was the inspiration for vulgar caricatures that bore no resemblance to him yet incited giggles as they passed furtively row to row in sneaky gestures. This man, Mr. Mails, could have been his cousin. Mr. Mails scraped his boots on the doormat too many times, as if it was the first time in years he has been invited indoors. She had no intention of letting him inside. Hell no. She grabbed for the Diego Grape-fruit Company box, the envelope tucked into her right hand for implicit handoff. Give him the money, grab the box and with subway luck she could still rendezvous with Angela and the big party at the other end of the pay phone. "My father said to give you this," she blurted, curt, in undisguised revulsion. They traded goods, but before Pamela could slam the door, Mr. Mails said, "May I use your facilities?"

He could be a rapist. The *facilities*, the *genitalia*; now he was her biology teacher's brother. It would be her father's fault if he was a rapist. He should have done this himself. From hypothetical stench her nostrils reared. She led him down the hallway, gestured to the room where pink tile shone through the half-open door. He shuffled. The rain had swept the back of his black hair into a duck's butt. His head swiveled left and right, registering, cataloging her father's collection of John Henry memorabilia. It was not yet a museum, if it ever was, it was junk on the wall. He paused only at the sledgehammer, which rested on the wall across nails that lacked resolve; periodically they'd leap out of the walls, inevitably when the family was asleep, and the hammer would hammer on the floor. He started to comment but seeing Pamela's expression, that potent concoction of adolescent contempt, he decided against it.

At least the pervert ran the faucet to cover whatever nasty thing he was doing in there. Luckily under the sink all manner of industrial cleaner, shiftless offbrands that sometimes wandered into Street Hardware, dropped off by shady distributors, were on call. One time a pigeon flew into the bathroom window and shat and hopped and spat on everything in the bathroom for who knows how long. Her mother chased it out with a broom. It was Pamela's chore to clean up, and for the first time she attacked a household task with meticulous zeal. Every surface could have a cootie on it, so she scrubbed, sacrificing an army of sponges in this tactical engagement. Not that she would tell him to, but her father should repeat that cleansing when he got home. The *facilities*. This pervert, she didn't want to think about it.

He wasn't a rapist, at least not this night. With that overcoat, though, he probably had some flashing to do. As she closed the front door, he said through pink lips, "Tell your father I might have some new stuff coming in next week that might interest him." She put the chain on, just so he could hear her do it and know what she thought of him. It was too late to meet Angela.

The other thing she did that night was the result of less easily elaborated motives. Revisiting it, she wishes the motel covers didn't smell so wretchedly; she'd pull them over her head. She doesn't know why she did it. She slit open the box and pulled out fists of newspaper. The figure wasn't that heavy, she'd moved figurines like it many times, to sweep away the grit they attracted. It seemed identical to others her father had dragged into the house, a ceramic statue of John Henry with his loyal hammer. It had lost paint in different places than its brothers, and when her father came home he'd explain the minute differences as if she cared, point out that this was from a company out of Alabama in the fifties that specialized in railroad items and had once been owned by a country and western singer, or this was from a small West Virginia house that produced only ten John Henrys before they reconsidered and this was the first of the series, look at the crosshatching on John Henry's cutoff pants. The statues circulated from room to room in their house. Periodically her father hit upon a new organizing scheme, and rusted drill bits replaced the framed sheet music above the couch, and the Johnny Cash album cover went into the storage room of the store for a time. These were her father's planets and their interminable trajectories through her space. It took a few tries to break it into pieces. First couple of times it just bounced on the floor. Then she figured out how to break it. The upper body, the arms, were susceptible. She put them back in the box, delicate now as she arranged the pieces in the newspaper, mama bird to baby chicks. Swept up the white dust of its blood.

Her father cursing out Mr. Mails woke her up. Two in the morning. He cursed him out for quite a few minutes; she kept her eyes closed. When he was emptied, she heard him open the door to her bedroom. She didn't move an inch, the door closed and that was the last time she picked up John Henry stuff for him. He never mentioned it.

A couple of days before she came down here, Pamela looked through the storage space for an appropriate box. She recognized the Diego Grapefruit Company box after all that time. The latest tenants, she saw, were piano rolls. She remembered the day her father got those things. He explained the process to her while she plotted an escape from his vicinity. He ran his fingers along the tiny perforations in the white paper scrolls and told her that when set into a compatible player piano they would tinkle out a version of "The Ballad of John Henry." Out of the music machine would come the familiar melody, this was before the days of stereos and that's how they listened to music in the olden days. Now they were obsolete. She said, how do you know it's the real thing? How are you going to test it out? He didn't have an answer for that. She put the scrolls in a shopping bag and locked up the storage facility.

Pamela pulls back the blackout curtains. She lifts the box onto the bed and checks her special delivery. None of her father's ashes have spilled from the urn.

"When we finally got the dishwasher, my mother said, you can't fight progress." This is Dave Brown as he implodes an empty beer can. "She liked putting her hands in the suds and scrubbing. She said it had dignity, you make a mess you should clean up after yourself. But everybody on the block had one at that point, so what choice did she have? Every magazine, they had an ad for an automatic dishwasher. What was she, the neighborhood fool? Were we a family of fools? So she said, you can't fight progress."

"A woman of quiet defiance," J. offers.

"Did she have a race with the dishwasher and keel over after beating Final Rinse?"

"Rinse Cycle's gonna be the death of me, Lord, Lord, rinse cycle's going to be the death of me."

In slumping assembly around the pool, the junketeers loiter and loll. Occasionally they extract beer from a styrofoam cooler and readjust the ice around the dwindling bounty. It is night, above them stars appear fixed yet career imperceptibly, correlative to a certain member of the junketeers, who reclines in apparent sloth while machinations comet through the deep black stuff of his mind.

Crickets on the stump campaign in the near woods.

"Tabling the whole hubris thing here for a moment," Tiny starts after a volcanic belch, "maybe Johnny's real problem was a congenital heart defect. You know the religious edicts against eating pig—because if you didn't cook it long enough you'd get trichinosis. The bearded community fathers gotta come up with some holy reason to get people not to eat pig. So it's like that. Creating a fable to explain something natural but they don't have the science yet. Genetics. Johnny knows from childhood Big Bend is going to be the death of him because he has heart trouble. It runs in the family. High blood pressure—you know black people have higher blood pressure than white people. What does he expect to happen with all that hard work? They didn't know about this kind of stuff back then. Might as well be mainlining pastrami sandwiches."

"Black people and fat people—high blood pressure," J. says.

"Good point. Hey, can you pass me some of those chips over there?"

"I'm all into the prophecy thing, you understand," Frenchie grunts, his arms splayed in a gesture of Gallic expansiveness. "I respect it, I'm a Sagittarius, have been since the day I was born. What I don't get is, if you read the horoscope and the experts tell you to be careful about financial transactions or look out for Tauruses, what do you do? You keep the purse strings tight and look out for those horns. John Henry has a premonition that Big Bend is going to be the death of him. So you avoid Big Bend Tunnel. Meet a guy named Benjamin Tounelle, he's a big guy, you avoid him too. He could have avoided the whole situation if he'd listened to his horoscope."

"There goes Frenchie again, bringing the topic around to fate versus free will."

"Everything's a think piece to this guy."

"Think he had a choice?"

"We all have choices. Look at that atrocious shirt you're wearing, J.—that's a choice."

"Pass me one of those beers, will you, son?"

"I was born with a caul on my face."

"A what?"

"A caul. On my face."

"He means afterbirth. He had afterbirth stuck on his face when he was born."

"It means you have special gifts."

"It's true—it's not everyone who gets to be a contributing writer to six different tax shelter magazines."

"This is my impression of a contributing writer."

As the next cricket candidate described his platform, it was the only sound to be heard among the junketeers. After an appropriate time had passed, the junketeers chuckled at the joke.

"Okay, okay. This is my impression of a contributing editor."

After another interval of silence, shorter this time, as the joke settled amiably into its promising future as an in-joke among their number, the junketeers chuckled.

"Who won the race?"

"John Henry."

"The steam drill, dummy."

"Steam drill always wins in the end."

"I meant at the thing today."

"That's right—you were in the tunnel of love."

"The local boy won."

"They were both local boys."

"Exactly."

"I think it might make a nice article. Pretty butch stuff, it might make a good pitch for one of those new men's mags starting up. Man against machine becomes man against man, how the times change the nature of the contest."

"Beer for you, J., or are you still on the wagon?"

"I'm cool."

"You know the hard thing about being on the wagon?"

"What?"

"So many hours in the day."

"What time is the grand coronation tomorrow?"

"I think the stamp ceremony is at one o'clock. In the town square. My flight is taking off at five."

"Mine, too. J.—you going to that paperweight thing next week?"

"Yeah. You?"

"No. Just wondering."

"He's trying to protect his investment. Frenchie thinks you're going to beat the record. Has a hundred bucks on you."

"You're betting?"

"Of course we're betting. We haven't had this much fun since, well, since Bobby Figgis. In total disclosure, I don't think you're going to make it. No offense. I just don't think you're in shape."

"He can do it. Look in his eyes. He's halfway there."

"One Eye has spoken, glimpsing into the mysteries of the human spirit. So what kind of party you want to have when you beat the record? I think we should rent out something appropriate to the occasion, like a dive bar downtown. Lock up the place for a couple of hours and have festivities."

"When it gets to that I'll tell you. Frenchie—why don't you tell us a story? What about that incident in Caracas?"

Beset by such idiots, One Eye buttons himself up in smug resentment, a finely tailored item of apparel, every seam stiletto, each stitch bitter. He is beset by idiots, he can see this clearly; his depth perception may have been affected by his wound, but not his moral acuity. Setting his half-full swill to the concrete he takes leave of his comrades without a word. He's put off this mission for too long, distracted by a game that had occurred to him: to see how many times his comrades could repeat the lines they have said so many times before. Their troupe improvises, of course, each locality has its customs to incorporate, but they respect the spirit of the text. The run of their show is completely booked, far in advance, and there are obligations. Dropping out of the show is no simple matter. Bracing himself he ticks his tongue against his teeth and squares his shoulders.

His progress up to the second floor of the Talcott Motor Lodge is to him a gallows shuffle up stairs to destiny's waiting instrument. The mechanism up there. Such is the cast of his recent hallucination, extreme, melodramatic. He remembers in Brazil, in Rio on an airline magazine's dime to help repair crime's erosion of the tourist trade, he noted the faces of the blinded as he walked the streets. All his far-flung kin. No one wore eye patches. Their wounds were on display, darkened sockets pooling dread from passersby. One Eye covers his wound as much for himself as other people.

From his adventure this afternoon, One Eye finds the key easily. He takes one last look to see if his fellow dogfaces have noticed his disappearance— maybe J. has changed his mind and is halfway up the stairs—but no one sees him. What is he trying to prove exactly? Ridiculous times call for ridiculous measures, and that is enough, he is inside Lucien's room with a hundred keys in his hand like clanking alms-coins.

Two things register first. The first is parcel of this weekend. Instead of the maudlin drawing of railroad tracks that hangs above the bed in his room, Lucien's room features a drawing of John Henry. It's a headshot of the man of the hour, familiar to him from all the hours at the fair: the postage stamp. This version is full color, blown up, bordered by drawn-in perforations for effect. Along the bottom it reads, First Annual John Henry Days July 13, 1996. What strikes him is the fact of today's date fixed under glass. It implies a series and a division: this day and what has come before from all those fairs to come. Big weekend for the town, of course, that's why he's here, to help bring it into being. The little dispatches of his kind contribute. Next year's guests see the poster and feel part of a ready-made tradition. Seeing the date up there, even on flimsy hooks drilled into cheap plaster, it is monumentalized. Glory attends even to this small affair in the mountains. He takes it as an omen, for today is also the date of his manumission. It is the day he exits the List.

The second thing he notices is that Lucien's computer is on.

Lucien's laptop is open in a sleek black L on the desk. References cycle through his brain: L for List; Venus stepping from her big clam. One Eye glances at the bathroom, maybe he's in there, but no, One Eye saw Lucien and his party leave the parking lot with his own eye, half an hour before, and the p.r. man's dinner with the local burghers will leave him with more than enough time for the caper. Time enough for a few simple keystrokes. Tap tap. Sliding into the chair, fingers fluttering like a pianist minutes from performance, he notices the screen saver's joke. A dollar bill roves and glides across the passive matrix screen, arrogantly ricocheting off edges with impunity. Hmm. It's kind of a bald joke for Lucien, distant from his usual wit; surely the novelty would have worn off after a few days. But maybe it's not meant for Lucien's amusement.

There's no sound outside the door, no detectives to nab the prey of the intricate sting operation. He taps a key, the dollar bill disappears into the machine's billfold, and he finds himself looking at the List. The file open on the computer is the List.

If Lawrence knew One Eye and J. were in the bathroom when he returned from picking up his boss, why didn't he say anything? The flunky's not cool enough a customer to have kept his mouth shut, not by any stretch. If he knew there was someone in his room he'd have shrieked like a tot with a rat in its crib. It's possible One Eye left the file open when they made their hasty retreat to the bathroom, but he clearly remembers the window closing. Maybe they missed something when they put the room back together. At any rate, Lucien knows someone is on to him, and perhaps he even knew it at the fair, when he and Lawrence strolled up to them. He knows.

What's a one-eyed man to do in such a predicament. He's being dared to tamper with it. Delete it, take his name off, take any one's name off. He scrolls. The names are all of them reduced to vitals, names and addresses and affiliations, tics and predilections. He clicks and clicks and the names march across the information plain, toward ordained engagement, implacable and resolute.

A trap and a test. Lucien doesn't care one way or the other. And why should he? It's just a little bit of data. After all One Eye's scheming and sneaking and extravagant declarations, it's just a little bit of data.

He spends twenty minutes prowling across the dingy carpet; it only takes him a minute to accept his weakness and defeat in this contest but the expenditure of a few extra minutes of ersatz deliberation makes him feel better.

He can't do it. Finally he writes a little note for Lucien and deposits it on the keyboard. A two-word message, a verb-noun combo understood across the globe. He shuts the door gently behind him.

It has cooled off considerably from the afternoon. As he hits the stairs his hand absently latches onto the guardrail and slides. Down in the foxhole the junketeers drink and bullshit one another. His chair is probably still warm, it is all the same, nothing has changed. He rubs his eye patch, scraping the stitching across his palm. Frenchie mutters something ribald and they all laugh and their chairs creak. This is all the same. Sitting among his comrades again, he adjusts his eyepatch. It's itchy under there. No one remarks on his absence. Dave Brown asks if they remember the time at that party. He had the eye patch made special for him in Spain. The slim leather band attaches to the black heart of the patch. It's a smart little number. Tiny says he knows a trick that allows you to get as much stuff as you want out of a vending machine. He often gets comments on the pattern across the front, an elegant arabesque that approaches a shape, but declines disclosure at the last second. It draws the gaze, draws attention to his accident. J. says he's going to get a ginger ale. Of course the average person must wonder exactly what is under there. The answer is, the eye patch secrets his fear. He settles in. It will always be the same.

The day in the mountain was almost done. The blood in his arms kept time better than any clock. The stacks of lead in his arms kept track of his labor better than the wheels inside a watch or the foreman's whistle. It was almost time to lay down his hammer when one of the runners came in telling all of them to come outside and see. The runner clasped his palms to his knees and panted, pushing each word up out of his body. John Henry and L'il Bob and the other team assumed there had been another accident and another death. The work had gone too peacefully for too long and they were due for grief. His partner tossed his bit to the dirt and John Henry slung his sledge over his shoulder and they walked across the planks toward the sun. John Henry was near the mouth of the tunnel when he heard laughter behind him. He twisted his body and saw only the crag of rock behind him, craning down from roof. He had never before seen that the blasting had opened two shiny stones in the crag's rock face. The stones glinted like cruel eyes. As he stepped out into the thick dusk he knew it would never again taunt him. It had delivered its message.

The bosses and the crews and Captain Johnson stood around a long cart. The planks of the cart were fresh-cut wood and the tarp had seen little rain. Everything the railroad brought to the site aged fast. Years of calluses formed in days, newborn aches immediately felt ancient and lifelong. This thing that had gathered the men was new. The horses were well-fed and handsomely groomed. Not mules. They had never hauled exploded and blasted rock, the insides of mountains. The white tarp draped over a shape that was unfamiliar. It propped up fabric and bulged beneath the tarp but its true shape was impossible to tell. A man talked while his fingers snapped in the air like sparks. He wore the clothes of a city man, a carpetbagger, and was so clean shaven his face glowed like bleached bones. One of the men next to John Henry said it was a man from Burleigh company come to sell the Captain on a steam drill. The steeldriver and his partner shouldered up to the front to hear what he had to say. L'il Bob said, I told you it was coming. I told you it was coming.

The steam drill had been the talk of the work camp for the last few days. After dinner one night, before the men dispersed into gambling or sleep, one of the graders, a red-skinned man named Jefferson, said he knew of one of those things. He had seen it with his own eyes. He had been a blacksmith on the Hoosac Tunnel job in Massachusetts before coming down here to this mountain. Before the steam drill, he said, they could not find purchase in the rock. The work was slow. But then the bosses brought in one of them Burlee machines and the rock was more like sand once that machine got on it. It was powered by steam and it drank more water than a man but it didn't need food and worked twice as fast as a man. L'il Bob said Jefferson was one ignorant nigger, talking about that rickety thing like he looked up to it. But over the days and nights the talk returned again and again to the steam drill and many of the men were curious. Their speculations swarmed in the air like gnats at twilight. John Henry kept silent with his back to the mountain that was always there.

The salesman talked of tunnels up and down this line. He spread his arms as if he held all between the oceans between his palms. He talked of tunnels up and down railroad lines all across the country. Then he tucked his thumbs into his vest pockets and strummed his chest with thin fingers like spider legs. Captain Johnson reached for his pocket watch when the salesman from Burleigh started talking about feet per day, pennies per inch and advancing the heading. Most of this talk went in one ear and out the other ear of the men but they understood the meaning. They had all dealt with the doubletalk of merchants before. L'il Bob said I told you it was coming. All around them the work had stopped before this talk and even some of the men from the western cut had made their way around to see. Boss and water boy, black man and white man came to see the invention.

The salesman pulled back the tarp to reveal the thing he had ferried there. From the city to the country over those long roads. It was a strange creature. The trunk of it was the engine, and it stood on four slim steel struts. Sticking out the side of it like a broken rib was a handle where a man could control what happened inside. Black hoses like tails came out of the rear end and connected to a big, round boiler. And the snout of the thing, that was the drill. It gleamed. The men shifted on their feet. They did not sigh or gasp in astonishment. It was a curious sight and it kept their mouths shut. In their minds they put it inside the mountain, up against the rock. The salesman hopped onto the cart and rubbed the flank of the engine. He said it was eight horsepower. A device like this made quick work of the Hoosac, he said. A mountain like this will fall just as easily before it. He had been in camps on every line you have heard of and when they saw what the machine could do, they marveled, he said. He talked about the machine as a man would talk about a great man. One who had accomplished great things. Captain Johnson stared up at the steam drill and nodded. Then he looked at John Henry as if he expected the steeldriver to open his mouth and speak.

John Henry looked at the dirt and then back at the thing in the cart. It had steel that was stronger than his muscles and bones. The blood in his heart was nothing compared to the steam of the boiler. It had the power of eight horses. He felt the men around him turn toward him and look at him. He kept his eyes on the thing in the cart. Lord, he had not thought that it would be so soon. But he had known it would come. He looked at the thing in the cart and saw tomorrows. Tomorrows and all the tomorrows after all those tomorrows because he understood as he had always understood that that was what this machine was going to take away from him. He saw the future, the very thing the machine would steal from him. Just as he stole from the mountain every day with his steel that which made the mountain what it was. The three of them were linked like brothers.

The salesman asked Captain Johnson if he wanted a demonstration of the steam drill for him and his men. It's a simple operation to set up a demonstration, he said. He withdrew a kerchief and wiped his brow. His men can watch him use the machine and learn how to work it, he said. Then Captain Johnson can see for himself what a boon the machine will be in fulfillment of his contract with the railroad and his obligations to the timetable. L'il Bob made a sound from his gut.

John Henry let the head of his hammer fall to the ground softly, easily, like it was the first leaf of autumn. Like it was only the first of many to fall and gliding down on sorrow. In that moment a cloud moved across the sky, taking the mountain into its shadow and in the same moment John Henry's heart as well. He nudged the man in front of him and walked up to the cart. The head of the hammer carved a line in the dirt behind him. All the men followed him with their eyes. He stood before Captain Johnson and the salesman and all the men and made a challenge. Then he hoisted his hammer onto his shoulder and stared into their faces. He was sure that no one could see him tremble but the mountain.

That spring there were pipebombs and pipebombs. They detonated in the parking lots of abortion clinics, behind the dumpsters of fast food restaurants, outside venerable banking establishments. Some were duds, but others injured or killed people, escalating insurance premiums. Near-victims described to news cameras how if they had only happened by the scene of the crime a few minutes later, it would have been them on the stretcher, while in the background the broken windows gaped, the drywall lay shredded. It was possible to download from the internet the instructions of how to make a pipebomb. During sweeps a newscaster demonstrated how easy it was by having a fifth grader log on to an anarchist website from the computer in his elementary school library. So easy a child could do it. Some of the bombs were twisted pranks but others clearly had a terrorist intent. They were supposed to send a message.

That spring also the disgruntled haunted public places and pulled the triggers of their guns.

That spring Alphonse Miggs ran cable down into the basement and brought the TV down, too. When he wasn't at work, or at his stamps, he lay on the pullout sofa with his chin against his palm and he watched the twenty-four-hour cable news outlets, waiting. He heard Eleanor walk above, in her new shoes. If he watched prime-time shows he waited for the white scroll along the bottom of the screen that informed viewers something terrible had occurred. Mostly the white scroll related a severe weather warning for his or neighboring counties, or a flood warning. But sometimes something terrible occurred and after the white lettering scrolled along the bottom of the screen, the network cut to a special report on the breaking news. Spectacular and unexpected news. An explosion, a hostage situation. Sudden catastrophe in the middle of regularly scheduled programming. It was what he was waiting for, but he didn't get through to the switchboard until June.

That summer, in June specifically, he noticed that in America the killers were usually lone psychos, but overseas the killers were generally part of a group with an ideology. In America when someone started shooting in a crowded public square, they were mad at their domestic or work situation, or maybe both. Disgruntled types. Overseas when someone started shooting in a crowded public square, they were mad at the government and specific policies. In the case of overseas catastrophes, after the news network cut to the scene of the tragedy, they would run a brief story on those who had claimed responsibility, describe their grievances and rerun the now-familiar footage of their previous terrorist act. Their violence placed in context. In America, they showed the killer's high school yearbook picture, which in hindsight invariably portrayed dementia in a bad haircut, no matter how normal they looked. In fact the more normal they looked, the more crazy they seemed, for normalcy is to be distrusted these days. Overseas, the killers lived on to tell the world why they had done such a thing. In America, the killers were taken out by police sharpshooters, or, surrounded by the authorities and spent, they killed themselves. Instead of articulated manifestos, the messages these men gave to the world were small sadnesses.

When the white scroll crept across the screen, or the networks cut to the special news report, Alphonse Miggs leapt for the phone. He had a phone down there and he dialed the numbers he had gathered. In the midst of preparations he had looked up the numbers of the news stations and the major networks. Each time stymied. The switchboard was jammed, or he was put on hold until the moment had passed.

He finally got the message out when a plane went down over water. In the middle of the workplace sitcom, the screen changed to *Special Report*, interrupting pratfall. He dived for the phone. The newscaster shared what little he knew, the destination of the plane, its departure time, the airport of origin. How swiftly the flight number passed into shorthand for doom. Witnesses on the ground reported seeing a flash or a bright orange light in the sky, and air-traffic control told of a distressingly swift disappearance from radar. Then the newscaster put two fingers to his earpiece and said, hold on a second. He said there has been an unconfirmed report that a group known as the AMLF has claimed responsibility for the explosion on board the plane. He repeated, an unconfirmed report that a terrorist group known as the AMLF has claimed responsibility for the downing of the flight. In the studio, they scrambled to find information on these extremists, these Muslims or militiamen. They found no graphic, no footage. Over the hours, this lead was replaced by deeper, more perfect mysteries, dismissed as a prank and forgotten, but nonetheless the message had been heard and in the basement Alphonse Miggs, founding member and main theorist of the Alphonse Miggs Liberation Front, briefly smiled.

Upstairs, Eleanor passed out hors d'oeuvres to the guests.

Every Sunday morning is a blessing from God. Josie prays, elbows on the windowsill, knees bunching nightgown, hands interlaced so tightly her fingernails slit half-moons between her knuckles. Her bedroom looks out on the river. Through her eyes, the world is charged this morning, livened to an almost audible crackle. The current hustles a little more swiftly, urging the soil of the bank to defect to its movement, as recent converts—serrated leaves, twigs, brainwashed rafts of moss—tumble on the surface committing to memory aquatic slogans of fidelity. The arms of the poplars grope from the shore more aggressively than usual, their daily attempts at embracing the water feverish now, desperate, and perhaps even under roots eyeless insects burrow with a passionate sense of adventure. The mountains still hold greedily to the sun, keeping the treasure to their bosoms for as long as possible, but in an hour that water will be livid with amber shards, full of sunlight that has been shattered and banished downstream. The best time of day. So why the long face? She prays this bountiful day will continue on its gorgeous course and nothing bad will happen.

The enchantment outside her window is what the towns have conjured this weekend. After all the months of arguments, preparations, parleys across red-checked tablecloths, they have brought the new thing into being. It has been a natural progression, first the popularity of the New River, then the motels, the opening of resorts like Pipestem, but this is entirely new. In town the day before, she strolled the streets of the only place she has ever called home and it was like her honeymoon night; every curve and shallow of her love's face reinvented. It was a new town. Who were the strangers and why were they here. They were here for John Henry, for Hinton and Talcott, for her and all who lived here. Last night Benny, before he passed out mid-sentence with one final hops-soaked wheeze, told her about everything that had gone on at the fair. People he hadn't seen in years had rallied themselves from whatever side road cranny they called home and said hello, ten years older but still wearing the same clothes. Children clutched the legs of men and women he recognized from here and there and suddenly these people had whole histories, families, descendants. Some of them had booths, so he could see, finally, what they were all about, this guy works at the plant nursery or that guy is a Ruritan secretary. Benny related a joke Freddy had told but he forgot the punchline; Josie stroked his head and patiently waited until he got it right. Matt's and Tony's steeldriving contest, and how Matt accused Tony of jumping the gun, so they should do it over. It was a success all around, he said, his voice drifting into a rasp, and they'll do it again next year for sure, and the year after that. The whole town was there, he said, except for you, why didn't you come, sweetie?

She didn't have to stay at the motel; all the guests were going to the fair, they were fully booked, and anyone who did stop by could be placated by a note taped to the office window. She stayed because while the county had planned everything meticulously, they had left something out. Things don't just happen because you tell them to. They happen because something has been paid. Their motel, for example. The materials had been supplied by the contractors, the mortgage by the bank. But the principal, the guarantee, had been provided by the insurance company. Benny's mother's life insurance had given them this place, the room in which she and her husband sleep. Pain is a down payment on happiness. You pay for happiness with grief in this world. This annual fair, the John Henry Museum when they complete it, will bring the world to their town, to the Talcott Motor Lodge. It is a new beginning but by her sights, it hasn't been paid for yet. There's some blood to be paid. John Henry spilled his, for the railroad, for his fellow workers, for Talcott and Hinton. Where will this weekend's come from?

She's a witch looking into bubbling murk: the land is full of the ghosts of dead men who sacrificed themselves to give this region life. They tremble in every tree, inhabit the wind and dwell in the soil. Surely they have opinions on this weekend's events.

The pills don't help much.

When the last taxi departed for the festival Josie started her rounds. She cleaned the rooms, of course, did her duty. But she wasn't looking for sheets and towels to replace. She was looking for the ghost. She pushed her cart down the rows. It took longer than usual because they were at full vacancy. Room after room, she found no trace, and she grew more anxious. In her hands keys trembled at each new lock, the clacking tumblers shorthand for suspense—what was behind the door? The usual disarray, the usual unre-markable clumps of balled-up socks and tilted area guides on nightstands.

When she couldn't take the waiting anymore, she ditched her disguise, abandoned the cart and went directly to the black man's room. Beneath that musty bouquet, particular fragrance of this establishment, she could smell the ghost. It had indeed been in this room. Nothing unfortunate had happened; she saw Mr. Sutter depart that morning without any outward signs of damage. She gave him directions to Herb's. But the ghost had been there, perhaps just standing over the man as he slept, or whispering into the man's deaf ears. She fetched her supplies and tidied up the room; in returning the room to its natural state she attempted to put things right, dispel.

She resumed her circuit through the rooms, relieved at the ghost's mercy. The cars on their way to the fairgrounds pounded down the route; children's faces smeared up against the windows of air-conditioned vehicles, observing her. There was still time to make it over to Talcott, to the tunnel, but she felt content to swab and tuck. Someone had to take care of the practical matters. Josie was fine until she came to room 12; she had almost put the ghost out of her mind as she retrieved undershirts from their indignant poses on the bathroom floor and folded the edges of toilet paper rolls into triangle points. But when she opened the door to room 12 she knew that the ghost had been there as well. She dropped the new towels to the carpet. There was no evidence that something bad had occurred, but this was terrible news.

Josie ran back to check the register, knocking aside the cleaning cart, dispatching it on a skid that continued for as long as its cockeyed wheels allowed, blue disinfectant sloshing. The guest's name was Alphonse Miggs, Silver Spring, Maryland, LN# RHU 349. Two nights. She remembered the man; he had been one of the first guests to arrive. A quiet little fellow, and very polite. She had seen him leave for the fair in the last taxi. Didn't seem out of sorts or otherwise terrorized from a brush with the supernatural. She didn't know what to make of it. What it meant. But she didn't have a good feeling about it. She shut the door of room 12 and spent the rest of the day in her bedroom. She didn't want to know. She took a green and a red from her stash; she has a chemist's array of pharmaceuticals guests have left behind and each day she mixes and matches. The green-red combo blows a pleasant creeping fog across her fields. When Benny came home and slurred nothing but good news to her, she finally eased into sleep.

Every Sunday morning is a blessing from God but Benny's snores are a liturgy of obscenity. As she prays before the window they blaspheme, insinuate, warn. She has done all she can. Whatever will happen will happen. Whatever the connection between the men, she has done all she can. Perhaps the ghost doomed both of them, embracing them into its dark territory, or blessed both of them and they would be saved, or perhaps the ghost blessed one of the men and cursed the other. A train enters Big Bend Tunnel; she hears the sound of the whistle as the engineer begs safe passage from John Henry. She trudges slippers into the kitchen to fiddle with Mr. Coffee. As she hovers over the tap filling the coffeepot, she glances through the window and sees five chairs dragged around the pool, empty chip bags that have skittered across the parking lot through the night, empty beer cans in tottering cairns. First thing after her coffee she's going to have to clean all that up. Then she sees the black couple walk across the parking lot and into the road, headed toward Talcott. It's that Mr. Sutter and Mrs., no, Ms. Street. Where on earth are they going and why are they holding that box?

The same night as the shooting in Hinton, West Virginia, a beloved star of stage and screen, whom most people believed had died years before, succumbed after a long illness and the story of the tragedy was bumped from the front pages. Nonetheless segments of the public engaged in lively discussions about the John Henry celebration and its tragic denouement. Stamp collectors, for example, speculated about possible besmirchment. War correspondents drew analogies from their own experience. And at a bar on M Street in Washington, D.C., an inquisitive patron could have overheard this conversation between two postal employees:

POSTAL EMPLOYEE #1:

*(cupping his hands)*
I was on the ground in a compact, defensive position because I knew what to do. I took that class, remember?

POSTAL EMPLOYEE #2:
Maybe I should take that class.

POSTAL EMPLOYEE #1:

*(nodding to himself)*
It wasn't cheap but it was worth it. The Don't Be a Hero Urban Readiness and Preparedness Seminar—covers everything from road rage to hostage situations. Bank robbery *and* airplane. It's a one-day thing, I'll get you the info.

POSTAL EMPLOYEE #2:
So he pulls out the gun.

POSTAL EMPLOYEE #1:
The mayor was up on the podium and then blam blam like that and I look over and the guy's standing up just shooting into the air.

POSTAL EMPLOYEE #2:

How far away was he?

POSTAL EMPLOYEE #1:

He was right there! In the second row. Me and the guys were up in the front row, and the guys who got shot, the newspaper guys, were sitting right in front of him. It could have been us right there.

POSTAL EMPLOYEE #2:

Dag. Just started shooting?

POSTAL EMPLOYEE #1:

Didn't even say a word. Hear this blam blam then I look over and see the gun but I see that and boom, I'm recumbent in a compact, defensive position. Drop, Tuck and Roll. So I didn't see the cop shoot him or the two guys, I just heard it.

POSTAL EMPLOYEE #2:

*(sipping)*
Dag.

POSTAL EMPLOYEE #1:

*(demonstrating)*
Everybody screaming. See that? Somebody stepped on my hand.

POSTAL EMPLOYEE #2:

Little vitamin E will prevent a scar.

POSTAL EMPLOYEE #1:

*(nodding)*
I been rubbing it on.

POSTAL EMPLOYEE #2:

Didn't leave a note or anything.

POSTAL EMPLOYEE #1:

Had his wife on the news today. He didn't leave a note or a clue. She said nothing seemed out of the ordinary.

POSTAL EMPLOYEE #2:

Some kind of stamp collector.

POSTAL EMPLOYEE #1:

Collected railroad stamps.

POSTAL EMPLOYEE #2:

Christ.

POSTAL EMPLOYEE #1:

You said it, brother.

POSTAL EMPLOYEE #2:

*(eyebrows raised)*

What, was he trying to raise the value of the John Henry stamp through notoriety?

POSTAL EMPLOYEE #1:

Could have picked a better way—how's he going to profit from machinations if he's a goner?

POSTAL EMPLOYEE #2:

Doesn't it smell fishy? Papers say the guy didn't have a history of mental illness. Job's okay, still poking the wife it sounds like. No dismembered heads in the basement. Nothing.

POSTAL EMPLOYEE #1:

Quiet fellow, kept to himself. That's what the neighbors say.

POSTAL EMPLOYEE #2:

And regardless of what we think, stamp collecting to most of the world is a perfectly innocent pastime. Maybe this will increase awareness.

POSTAL EMPLOYEE #1:

So what makes him do it?

POSTAL EMPLOYEE #2:

Did he say anything?

POSTAL EMPLOYEE #1:

*(turning on the bar stool)*

His famous last words?—"I wasn't going to shoot you."

POSTAL EMPLOYEE #2:

What, he just wanted your attention? Pulling out a gun. Easier ways of getting people's attention. No stamp collecting manifesto in his coat pocket?

POSTAL EMPLOYEE #1:

Who knows what he was trying to do?

POSTAL EMPLOYEE #2:

We must ask ourselves, who stands to profit? Any jump in the orders of the John Henry stamp since then?

POSTAL EMPLOYEE #1:

I'll ask Jimmy. Say you hear about Jimmy and that new secretary in Quality? The redhead?

POSTAL EMPLOYEE #2:

Maybe it's nothing complicated at all. Maybe it's nothing. Maybe he just snapped. It happens. "He just snapped."

POSTAL EMPLOYEE #1:

Leaving behind this message to the world.

POSTAL EMPLOYEE #2:

Leaving behind a challenge.

POSTAL EMPLOYEE #1:

People just snap all the time these days.

POSTAL EMPLOYEE #2:

We peer into the inexplicable.

POSTAL EMPLOYEE #1:

And every day are confronted with the unknowable.

POSTAL EMPLOYEE #2:

Least he wasn't one of ours. The first reports said he was one of us. Randy looks like he could snap at any moment now that he's trying to grow that mustache.

POSTAL EMPLOYEE #1:

I was sitting right next to Randy! Post Office executives—they'd have a field day with that. Now it's not just the rank and file but the top brass going—

POSTAL EMPLOYEE #2:

Don't say it!

POSTAL EMPLOYEE #1:

I wasn't going to say that, I was going to say, going to give us a bad name. Two dead and one wounded, did you hear that? The second guy died today.

POSTAL EMPLOYEE #2:

Shame. They bringing the cop up on charges?

POSTAL EMPLOYEE #1:

Just doing his job, really. Taking out the homicidal madman. Sure he hits two bystanders but that's his job. Sucks that they're members of the media, for his sake, but he got the guy before he could hurt somebody. Preserving the peace.

POSTAL EMPLOYEE #2:

Gonna sue like crazy. The journalists' families. Cop kills two bystanders while trying to get one guy? Gonna sue the town like crazy. *(noticing empty glass)*
Damned shame. You want another beer?

POSTAL EMPLOYEE #1:

*(signaling the barkeep)*
Sure.

POSTAL EMPLOYEE #2:

So tell me about this seminar.

She wore blue. The song said never wear black, wear blue so she wore blue and they had a map. They walked down the road.

AFTER THEY HAD walked a bit, he offered to carry the box for a while. But she refused, shook her head. A mile on he repeated his offer and this time she let him take it from her hands. It was heavier than he thought it would be. The weight was the urn and not his ashes. Probably the ashes did not weigh that much; the main part of him was smoke. They took turns after that, passing the box between them, juggling across arrangements of purchase, cradling it like this and holding it like that against their chests. The cardboard heaved and sank.

THE ROAD WAS a lazy black line after all the busyness of the previous day, slouching and shirking between the mountains under a martinet sun. He wasn't that surprised when she told him what was in the box and her plan. When she knocked on his door he was already awake. He'd had a strange dream and had been up awhile, already dressed and wishing the motel had one of those mini coffeemakers. They hadn't clarified their plans after their interlude in the tunnel so he was surprised when she knocked on the door that early. He'd entertained scenarios, most of them ridiculous, about what her favor might be, but none of them held up to scrutiny for more than a few minutes. When he opened the door, he noticed she was dressed all in blue, in blue jeans, in a blue blouse, but he didn't connect it to the song until she explained it to him.

THERE WAS A lot of time for explanations on the walk up there. East, reversing the trajectory of laid steel and time. It was two or three or four miles, she wasn't entirely sure. Her father's map didn't have a legend or niceties like that. He'd sketched it out on his last trip down here, judging from the box she'd found it in. The box containing the map held, in crumbling strata, copies of the Hinton newspaper from a few years back, awkwardly folded roadmaps of the area, some receipts, and those helped to date the map. He came down here a couple of times over the years, always alone, on his inscrutable itineraries, but the neighboring items in the box clinched it. She told him that when she was in the storage facility a man walked in, opened his space, and in there he had a little living room, with a big armchair, a coffee table. Also a random assortment of stuff, three toasters, a big army bag of clothes, watercolors of canals hung on the cement walls. He sat in the chair, crossed his legs and read the daily paper. It didn't look like the guy was going anywhere. When she left she asked the manager about it and he said the guy slept nights in a shelter but hung out in his storage room all day. It's where he kept his clothes and things, and he was a nice guy, weird of course to live like that, but he wasn't dangerous or anything. The guy basically lived in there, in the storage space. After she finished the story, he made a joke about the size of the average New York apartment. How we all live in boxes.

SHE ASKED HIM if he felt uncomfortable about her request, and he said no. He wasn't going to have to do anything particularly, just accompany her up to the place, and he didn't feel uncomfortable at all. He was in his life comfortable with the role of passenger, and he did not mind that today he was a passenger on a tour, as she guided him through this John Henry territory. It was only once he felt the weight of the box that he started to grow a little uncomfortable about this enterprise, her mission. The weight made it more real.

TO END A silent quarter of a mile he told her about the record and the List as a prelude to a description of his dream. So that she could understand the terms. His hands went for the box.

IN THE DREAM he was somewhere downtown and hip. Where old cobblestones broke through asphalt, enduring, resenting centuries, and wheatpasted posters and slogans shriveled on plywood in evanescent counterpoint to those cobblestones. Everything was closed. He was walking to a destination but possessed only a dim idea of where it might be. And what it might be. A voice called his name. He turned and it was Bobby Figgis, he of the record. In the waking world he had never met the man but in the dream he understood this to be the man's identity. Far from his imaginings of the man, this apparition of Bobby Figgis seemed healthy and happy. Well fed and well off. The old junketeer was garrulous and well dressed in a fine black suit. Bobby Figgis grabbed his hand and said they were all waiting for him inside, it was just down the alley. He knew then, in the lucent clarity of dreams, that this was where he was supposed to go. His final destination of the night. He followed Bobby Figgis down an alley that only exists in film, full of steam and jumping alley cats and slithering rats. His guide knocked on a beat-up metal door, above which a red light glowed. A bouncer opened the door and welcomed them with extravagant affection. He welcomed Bobby Figgis as one might welcome an old friend, and then welcomed him as well, as if he had been there many times before. Then he suddenly remembered that he had been there many times before, all the time in fact, every night, and for every night after. He went inside.

WHEN HE FINISHED relating his dream, he looked over at her. It didn't seem like she understood a word of what he was saying. Maybe he didn't, either. He passed her the box.

SHE SAID THERE are many versions of the song, as many versions as there are people who sing it. Passed between work gangs and families and friends in the old days of folk music, on record, on the radio. You could split the song into so-called official versions, her father used to say, the ones made by established singers and put on vinyl, cassette, and CD, and then there were the songs of the people, entirely different, the mis-sung versions, belted out by people who misremembered the lyrics and supplied their own haphazard verses. Like when you sing in the shower, she told him, and if you can't remember the right words you make up your own to fill in the gaps. Her father used to say that what you put in those gaps was you—what you inserted said a lot about you, what you grabbed from your personal dictionary and stuck in there was you. You mix it up, cut a verse or two and stick to the verses that you like or remember or mean something to you. Then you've assembled your own John Henry, and maybe it's only the chorus, or a single line, *C&O railroad's going to be the death of me* or *A man ain't nothing but a man* and you just sing that. That's all there is to the song for you.

IN SOME VARIANTS, she said, his wife Polly Ann is a big figure and gets the last word. She picks up John Henry's hammer and becomes a steeldriver herself. Polly Ann says, *I'm going where my man fell dead*, and then she picks up his hammer and goes, *I'm going to die with the hammer in my hand, I'm going to drive steel just like a man*, and it ends there. She picks up where he left off. In those ones, she usually wears a red dress, since red rhymes with dead and it fits. Then some versions end with John Henry's last words to her, *John Henry told his woman, Never wear black, wear blue. She said, John, don't never look back, For, honey, I've been good to you, Lord, Lord, For, honey, I've been good to you.* Blue and you. In some—probably made up by the more family values–minded of the singers—John Henry has a daughter. It goes, *John Henry had a little daughter, The dress she wore was blue, She followed him to the graveyard sayin', John Henry I'll be true to you, Lawd, Lawd, John Henry I'll be true to you.* In the ones where he has a son, it goes, *John Henry had a little son, Sittin' in the palm of his hand, He hugged an' kissed him and bid him farewell, Oh, son, do the best you can, Lawd Lawd, Oh, son, do the best you can.* In the silence of the road and the morning she was suddenly startled at how loud she sang. Each time she sang a new bit of lyrics it was louder than the time before. Her throat and heart knew more than she did about this enterprise. She looked away from him. He took the box from her hands.

She said her father had come down here three times. She and her mother were not invited along, nor did they wish to accompany him. He took a train and was gone for almost a week. He came back with lots and lots of stuff for his collection, of course. He said the place was beautiful, and of course it was. He said Talcott was nothing like he thought it would be, it was tiny, no real stores but just residents, an unincorporated town. And Hinton was a neat little outpost wedged in between the big river and the mountains. It was like on one side of the mountain people were living scattered all around and then once they got to the other side there was a whole town, so that on the one hand you had nothing and once the mountain was beat you got into a civilization. You had achieved a society. He brought back a lot of pictures and old railroad equipment and a jar full of soil.

THE SECOND TIME he went he said he wanted to interview the residents to see what he could come up with. Neither she nor her mother probed this statement. They were past caring. Who could he talk to. They were all dead, anyone who could have provided insight or tidbit. What little there was to be found had been gathered by other researchers over seventy years before. The second time he did not stay too long, and when he came back, he didn't really go into what he found here.

———

THE THIRD TIME he went she and her mother were gone. Her mother had moved to Arizona to live near her sister's family. They weren't divorced, but they had half a country between them and a lot more. As for herself, she was living on her own in her first apartment in the city and saw her father only on holidays, and she did not stay long. She visited him on his birthday one year and he told her he had gone down to Talcott one more time, to find the grave. She didn't ask if he'd found it, and left as soon as she could. It smelled bad in there.

WHEN THEY GOT to the monument the place was empty. The food stand was closed up and the door of the caboose was locked. All the people were gone.

INSTEAD OF PROCEEDING down the hill to the tunnel as they had the day before, they turned in the opposite direction up the mountain. She consulted her father's map, interpreting his lines. She found the road. It was overgrown but people had parked there the day before, reassured by the ratchet grind of the parking brake, and wheels had chewed the weeds to the ground. Snapped back slim branches, exposed white marrow and bits of chewing gum foil gleamed like quartz among the ruined green shoots. A black fly dogged them for yards. They left the asphalt and walked up the slope of the jagged road until the mashed-down section stopped being mashed and wildness took over. The road was unpopular, overlooked to wallflower, and seeds and spores had sidled in to seduce the dirt. In tire grooves, yellowish weeds stunted by periodic molestation streamed in parallel lines, between which lithe grass dipped and curtsied, only occasionally assaulted by undercarriage. Then the road simply ceased. He said it's always funny when you go walking in the woods following a path and then it just stops. You wonder who made it, and why, because there's never any destination, it just stops. She looked at the map, strode over to an unremarkable pine and moved the branches aside. There was a little footpath. She stood there with her hands on her hips and tilted her head. He was holding the box at this point.

THE BRANCHES OF pine trees flailed at them with delicate points. He said he was glad he was wearing sunglasses. The path maundered and feinted, avoiding inclines and whole clans of rock. It hopped over prostrate trunks and the footing argued for better shoes.

SHE FOLDED THE map and slipped it in the back pocket of her jeans. What she called the graveyard was a clearing of level ground. When they stepped out of the gloom of the woods into the tall, wild grass the susurrations of the insects ceased. He had expected tombstones, but there were none. She said this is where the black workers buried the men who died. The company would tell them to bury them in the fill and then at night the men would exhume them and carry them up the mountain and give them stone markers and proper dispatches. The legend had it this is where John Henry was buried. That's what her father had been looking for the last time he came down here. But they did not see any graves. They waded into the field, into the green and brown lagoon. They found nothing but burrs and then he tripped. He spread apart the thin blades and crouched. He had tripped over a long flat rock with initials carved into it and he realized he was standing on a grave. With a fingernail he scraped out the dirt so he could read the intials. She came over to see this.

THEY FOUND A dozen graves scattered across the field. None of them bore the initials J.H. It was possible they missed it, in all probability they missed more graves. The grass and weeds were too high, the field too large for them to cover completely. It might have been a minefield for the care of their steps. Anything might erupt from there. When one of them discovered a marker, the other would scramble over and they would kneel down among the brambles and the hardscrabble flowers and scrape the dirt off the dead man's marker. After that even dozen, she said there was no telling how many men were buried there. The map did not indicate the locations of graves and did not mention John Henry. Just the rough line to this place. They might as well get on with it, she said. Her choice of words, the timbre of her voice, startled him. But he decided he was in no position to judge her after all.

THE URN WAS not handsome, coming up into the sunlight from the box. The brass grabbed the sunlight and turned it into a greasy sheen along the simple curves of the urn. He asked a question about how she wanted to spread the ashes, after wondering for a time on how to phrase it, and she told him she didn't want to spread them she wanted to bury it, the whole urn, in the ground. She hadn't spoken to her father about it and he hadn't left any instructions. It wasn't his idea, this assignment. After the funeral she put the urn in storage with his collection and turned out the light and locked the door. He might have preferred that his ashes were scattered, she didn't know, it just made sense to her once they got up there to bury it. She walked out into the middle of the field and without an overlong consideration of where the perfect place would be she stopped and said, Here.

FIRST THEY TUGGED weeds and grasses, there was always this resistance and then the roots gave in, soil dripping from their whiskers. When he realized they didn't have anything to dig with he thought it was going to take forever and he hadn't eaten yet. At least he wasn't hungover. She said, now's your chance to move up to pick-and-shovel man. He grunted. On their knees trying to figure out how to make that hole.

AT LEAST IT wasn't a whole body, he thought. She told him that the mayor or his staff had left the plans for the museum at the motel the afternoon before and she had passed hours looking over them. They had obviously spent a lot of time on it and put their hearts into it. She explained about the inventory she had sent them, and they had even marked on the proposed plans where some of her father's things might go. He had the biggest collection of John Henry in the world, and there was no reason why the town shouldn't have it. She had tried to find other people, colleges, who might have wanted it, but had no luck. And then something had happened where it seemed like the worst thing to give it away and she couldn't bring herself to get rid of it. And then last night after all this resistance she gave in.

HE FOUND A slim rock to stab at the dirt with and that helped. She continued to talk. He would hear a crack in her voice and expect to see her weeping, but it was just a series of cracks. The dirt crawled under their fingernails and pained but they made progress. She said whenever she went to visit him he was so disheveled. He had sold his store to devote all his time to the museum, which no one ever visited. Who would go up to some creepy stranger's apartment. He always wore the same clothes, he'd had them for years, and on this one pair of pants the fly was broken and he walked around with his fly open, not caring. You couldn't see anything, so it wasn't a spectacle, but she was embarrassed by him. On Father's Day they'd go around the corner to a restaurant and there would be all these families in their best clothes, and her father would be this shambling homeless man.

IT WAS STRANGE to sit there in the dirt. Their hands moved and moved. He was tired out from this one simple task, and in the same dirt he was feebly scratching into lay dead men who did more back-breaking work in a day than he had done in his whole life. And the legendary John Henry, nearby or not nearby in the ground. He tried to think of what the modern equivalent would be for his story, his martyrdom. But he lived in different times and he could not think of it. He dug some more.

SHE SAID SOFTLY, *And when she got to where John Henry fell dead, She fell down on her knees, And kissed him on the cheek, and these are the words she said, Lord, there is one more good man done fell dead* and her voice got that crack in it again.

SHE SAID THERE was another interesting thing about the song. Before it came into ballad form, the men used to sing it as a work song, to keep the rhythm of their strokes. And in those early songs, they'd sing, *This old hammer, killed John Henry, Can't kill me, Lord, Can't kill me.* They sang it like a song of resistance. They wouldn't go out like John Henry. But maybe they were condemning him instead of lamenting him. His fight was foolish because the cost was too high. Are they saying they're not as arrogant as John Henry, or are they twice as arrogant for thinking themselves safe from his fate. You could look at it both ways. You could look at it and think the fight continued, that you could resist and fight the forces and you could win and it would not cost you your life because he had given his life for you. His sacrifice enables you to endure without having to give your life to your struggle, whatever name you gave to it.

SHE ASKED HIM if he had to die to bring this weekend into being. All his life he wanted something like this weekend, a celebration of John Henry. His collection would have been a star attraction, he could have made speeches. Get the key to the Presidential Suite at the Talcott Motor Lodge. The crowds finally would have come to his museum. She asked him, would this have still happened, the fair, the museum, if he was still alive. Or did he have to give up himself for this to happen. The price of progress. The way John Henry had to give himself up to bring something new into the world.

THEY FILLED UP the hole and scratched his initials into a gray stone. She scratched them, he found the stone. They stood over it and it seemed enough.

———

FROM THE MOUTH of the path, they could not see where they buried him. The brown tips of the dry grass left no sign, huddling back to cover the brief paths they had made. There was no sign to mark any of the dead men in that field. It was an accidental clearing on a mountain that ridged upward. He hooked fingers into the empty box and they started back down the mountain.

As he did every morning to prepare for crowds, he turned the sign in the window from closed to open. The landlord had refused his appeal to hang a larger sign, something more grand and appropriate to the venture, for what he had assembled behind that sooty unassuming brick. The landlord was trying to spruce up the brownstone, people were returning to Harlem, new vigor in the streets of Harlem, and the schemes of the tenant ran counter to the schemes of the landlord. If the landlord had been less busy, he'd have looked up zoning regulations re the legality of running a so-called museum out of a residence. Surely there were laws. But he never got around to it. For now he let the old man put the sign in the window, and figured it was only a matter of time before the old man died and plaster and drywall split the first-floor apartment into two rental units.

At the head of the crimson stoop, up those steps, next to buzzer number one, he had replaced the name of his family with *THE JOHN HENRY MUSEUM*. The modesty of the sign in the window and the southern exposure's shower across the panes of that window conspired to dispatch the sign to obscurity. Alternately the sign hid in glare and shadows. Over time the sun drained the lettering, leaving it to specter. Seasons of rain fostered layers of black particulate on the panes. Only from certain angles at certain times of day was the sign completely visible to passersby and its message observable. Thousands walked by the sign, which sat patiently in its roost on the sill of the center window, tilted against the glass for leverage. The vagaries of peripheral vision sorted the people into categories. Percentages did not notice the sign and progressed to corners; smaller percentages noticed the sign and tossed it in mental bins to join the rest of the city's non sequiturs. A smaller percentage wondered for brief seconds what the sign might mean, but did not stop, progressing to corners and other streets.

In the front hallway on a small table the pen lay aslant, tumbling through the perfect white void of the guest book. There were the names of no one in there. Admission was free but a slim blue dish accepted contributions. He left a dollar bill in the dish to indicate procedure to crowds. On occasion he needed the dollar bill for an errand, leaving the blue dish empty for hours until he replaced it. One day he used the dollar and never returned it. For a while each time he passed the table he felt a pang but as the months passed the pang disappeared. Sometimes the doorbell rang and taking it for crowds come at last he opened his doors discovering a man or woman looking for someplace else.

Depending on the time of day the music for crowds came from one of many sources. In the morning he played the earliest recorded versions of the song on a tape deck. These songs were distinguishable by the faraway cast of the singing and strumming, emanating as if from deep within a pit or tunnel. Music historians had recorded the songs on primitive equipment while they sat on porches, in backyards, in parlors, in country regions, and indeed he had on his excursions recorded some himself, from old men he had sought out. Around noon he switched to heavy 78s, sliding them carefully from yellow flaking sleeves. He cranked up the Victrola and let the needle etch the songs into the air. And so on, through a short history of home music technology, a 33 rpm turntable, an eight-track tape player for the novelty of the gawky machine, more cassette tapes and CDs on their respective playback machines. Through the rooms of the museum work songs, folk songs and the blues resounded, dead voices pinioned across an array of instruments.

It had been his original scheme to present the song to the crowds in concordance with how it shambled through the decades, hopping off a boxcar in this place and reappearing with new boots in that place, but of course it was impossible. Some of the oldest versions in his possession existed only on cassette, throwing off the chronology. A few specialty houses had released versions of compilations of regional folk music, and these he was forced to play on his CD player. He didn't have a piano, let alone a player piano, and thus could not represent the contributions of sheet music and music machines to the transmission of the ballad except as pieces of paper behind glass. The replacement of one form of technology by a superior form was an exhibit in itself, and he wished he could have presented it to crowds in a better way. Over time as he waited for crowds the accumulation of aches in his body put an end to his daily hustle from switch to switch, machine to machine, and he recorded a master tape that simply and conveniently played the songs in chronological order. He lined up the music devices in a row, with little tented slips describing their impact on the dissemination of the John Henry legend, displaying the stillborn e's of his typewriter as a subexhibit. In his speech he could elaborate on the theme of the march of technology and the march of progress and the prices paid. In the end what was important was not the machine but the man.

The speech slept in his mouth. He had composed the speech over many years, for each new item required a deep caption to situate it in the collection. Each time his hand touched the new acquisition, a railroad implement, a photograph of the tunnel's inauguration, the speech extended its heading. Extolling, explicating, making gentle asides. He practiced hand motions and gestures, where his arms swept across exhibits, the panorama of his accumulations, and perfected the timing of puns. In the speech he presumed no prior knowledge in the crowds. He started at the beginning. He would walk from room to room as he delivered the speech and the disposition of each room colored the words of the speech. In the music room, among the exuberant plenitude of the song, as if among all the men and women who had sung it, the ragged American chorus, the speech transformed into a declaration on the power of the legend to draw so much from so many and find in so many souls one name. In the document room the brittle assortment of materials, from old C&O requisition lists to blueprints of the Burleigh steam engine to out-of-print scholarly researches, withered the speech in kind, the ink grew faint, the truth of the tale distant, scattered by contradiction and time, words drifting through the air as mere echoes of something greater. In the art room, over here, where children's books lay on stands there and there, have a look, pages open for perusal of larger-than-life adventure, the sign says you're allowed to touch them, the walls have disappeared into thin white lines for all the paintings and posters of martyrdom, triumph and sadness crammed together, see how you can barely see an inch of the walls, the speech trembling with new comprehension, all those artists lending feverish strength to the words, feeding the speech with their labors, all those elemental forces flooding through the aperture of this room. In the statue room, in here, among the figures, some as small as children and others as large as giants, the music now far away in the distance, the speech receded into sighs, into deep aphasiac awe, urging on the crowds' contemplation of the man and this moment, seeing him for the first time in a way, in this final room after all those previous rooms, palpable, with dimensions, looming, with solid and unimpeachable weight. The speech trickled away as crowds consider John Henry in his infinite masks.

In some ways it was less of a speech and more of a story.

In the long days one after the other he pictured the crowds. The long lines of crowds, announced first by the doorbell and then the shadows of their feet beyond the door. He had seen some of them before, they had passed by his windows, or their parents had passed by his windows, their families and friends, they had patronized his store when he still had the store and he had sold them things, passed them on the street, sat next to them in public places. But if they had been in his store, he had never presented to them such indispensable items as those he had finally gathered in his museum. Those were material items and this was so much more. It had cost him so much and the crowds had finally come, a jostling hungry throng, whole neighborhoods and clans ready to receive John Henry, dawdling before the favorite exhibits that made them return again and again, alone or leading treasured friends by the hand to share revelation. Beautiful children with round faces and wide eyes who were hearing of the legendary steeldriver for the first time and learning possibility, teenagers slouching and cracking jokes to hide what they see in the man but cannot admit, adults, men and women pushed here for so many reasons, getting reacquainted with the story they first heard as children and now connecting it to every one of their hard mornings, these strivers, and the old ones, old as him, who had seen the same things he had, lingering before photographs respectful feet away, understanding the legend as he did now, as a lesson that had finally been learned at great cost, moving from room to room in recognition and resignation, all of them a family he had lost at last returned to him.

Every day he stood like that, with his arms crossed, as he listened to John Henry, and he waited for crowds.

John Henry stood in the work camp with his sledge in his hands. He grasped it as a drowning man might cling to a branch in the currents of the spring thaw. No one saw him. Most of the men had gone on ahead. The camp was nearly empty. It was time to work but this was not an ordinary workday on the mountain. No one stalked the tunnels. The men were not grading or mucking or pounding spikes. They waited for the contest. They gathered at the mouth of the eastern cut to see the truth of the challenge. This afternoon the timetable did not matter, neither the seconds nor the inches, for the line had to be stalled before it could go on. Everything stopped before the words John Henry had said. Tools lay untouched and the horses' tails whipped lazily in the sun. No hands covered ears to keep out the sound of blasting, the ground did not shake with the violence they made inside the mountain. It was still, and it was time.

As he lay in his bed on his last night he heard the words of the men coming through the walls of his shanty. If John Henry wanted he could have put faces to the voices but he did not try. He knew all the men. Some were friends. Some were enemies. It did not matter where they stood with him as their talk swirled into one talk about the contest. They laid bets on whether a man could beat a machine. All of their wagers on John Henry before this time were rehearsals for this day. One voice came to him saying it was impossible. Another voice said John Henry was no kind of man like you and me but a demon and no machine was going to stop him. One voice laid down odds. The voice said, step right up and make your bet, men. He heard voices raised in anger and then the scrambling sound of men in the dirt fighting. There was more than money on the line. Each wager was a glimpse into the man who made it. There was more than wages on the line in this contest.

On his last night John Henry did not allow L'il Bob to see him. His friend was hurt by the words John Henry spoke to him, one foot on the dirt floor within and one foot on the dirt ground without, and he did not understand why his partner had forsaken him. But I have a plan, L'il Bob said. I can fix that machine so it won't do nothing but shake and squawk, he said. No plans are going to help me tomorrow, John Henry said. He told his partner to get Adams and L'il Bob asked why but John Henry would not tell him. Just get the man, he said. When the door closed he heard his friend's voice crying for Adams, Adams. It was not fair to his friend but he could find no other course in himself.

John Henry had wages saved. Even as he collected them through the long months to give to Abby he knew he would never present them to her in person, standing in front of her after so long, to show her what all the time away had brought them. He had lied about his return and the bills he stuffed into his hiding place were hope against the mountain. He did not drink. He did not gamble with money. When he gambled he put himself up as his winnings and in the long time in this place he had saved more money than any of his friends knew. He was the highest-paid steeldriver for what he could do with his arms. Captain Johnson gave him bonuses for steeldriving contests that he won with his arms. He trusted L'il Bob to send it on to her.

Adams could make letters and write. His hands had been chewed up from his labor on the tunnel but he could still write. He was the one the colored men came to when they wanted something written. He put on paper the stories and the lies they posted to their families and their women. When Adams showed up John Henry told him he wanted to write a letter, and the man departed to get his materials. In that time he composed again the words and in the middle of it he remembered that Adams had come to the mountain in the same car as he had. John Henry had first seen the man in the workers' car, across from him on the journey up here, as they sat on the nail kegs that were their seats and they all wondered what was waiting for them up here. Now John Henry knew. But none of that was going to go into the letter. L'il Bob could give her the details of the contest but he wanted to put other things in the letter. He warned Adams to keep his mouth shut about why he had called him there. When he looked into the man's eyes he knew he would not say anything. Adams was not one of the stupid and shiftless men the railroad company attracted. He had sense. When Adams left John Henry put the voices out of his mind and wept. With the salt in his mouth he said, never wear black wear blue, never wear black wear blue.

It was almost time. When he ate his breakfast that morning all the men he had worked alongside for so long looked at him over tin plates as they ate. His stare told them not to talk to him so they just looked at him, taking measure of him with their eyes. They wanted to know what was in him that was not in them. One man said that all the people from all around were coming down to the eastern cut to see the contest. The word had traveled beyond the work camps, beyond the hearths of the bosses, and everyone wanted to come and see the contest between the man and the machine. Another man said they were going to charge tickets to see. This was bigger than the black man against the white man and they were drawn by these new stakes. It was once in a lifetime. In this talk some of the men looked at John Henry and changed their wagers. Beating another man, beating twenty men was one thing and this was another. L'il Bob came over to John Henry, scraping food off his plate to give to his partner. He had a ridge of bruises along the right side of his face and John Henry knew it was because of him. L'il Bob had fought someone for saying John Henry would lose. The bruises did not need to be explained, them or anything else except the letter and the money he had saved. L'il Bob would follow his wishes and get it to her. When he finished eating he went back to his bed and waited for the sounds of the men to die out, to drift over to the tunnel.

John Henry stood in the camp with the sun on him. It was almost time. Down there they all waited. He spat at the ground and rolled back his shoulders. He looked up at the top of the mountain, where the treetops stretched with their little points, like a million fingers grasping at Heaven. The mountain was so tall and John Henry was so small. He drew a hand across his brow to put the sun out of his eyes and he looked up at the mountain, past the leaves and down the trunks and into the soil and into the rock heart of the mountain, he looked and addressed. There was no one to hear him but himself. He walked down the road with his hammer in his hand.

J. Sutter stands in the parking lot of the Talcott Motor Lodge. His stomach is empty. It does not bother him. Even after all the walking and all he did up there on the mountain, he still is not hungry. It is as if he struck into his body and found a secret reservoir within his self. He watches his hands in the sun. He has tiny scratches along the tips of his fingers and dirt hiding under his fingernails. There is a little bit of fire in his legs from the walk and fire in his hands from the digging but it does not bother him. He closes his eyes and the sun falls across him.

She asked him on the way down if he got his story. J. Sutter said yes. He has a story but it is not the one he planned. Before he had been kidding about the story in order to get close to the woman. He had put on paper some of the things she had said the day before but now he thought what happened today was the real story. It is not the kind of thing he usually writes. It is not puff. It is not for the website. He does not know who would take it. The dirt had not given him any receipts to be reimbursed. He does not even know if it is a story. He only knows it is worth telling.

Above cooking tar the air shimmers. It is as if snakes of heat dance on their tails. The sweat on his clothes chills him. After all that walking he stands without moving, coming back into himself. There is still time to take a shower. In an hour or two it will be time for the stamp ceremony and the weekend here will be over. He has time enough to shower and to put his things in his bags. Then it will be time for today's event, tomorrow's event and the ones after. They loom over him and he is in their shadow. He has a decision to make in the parking lot. Pamela had stood before him and said to him, I'm leaving before the ceremony. When they reached the motel she said, I think I've done everything I needed to do. She looked into his face. The town can have it all and I'm going to take an earlier plane and go home, she said. You could leave, too, she said.

The night before J. Sutter had been in the parking lot with the other men. In the day it is different. In the night they talked and drank to keep away the darkness, the vastness outside the streetlight. The mountain and all that it meant. The talk was the only defense they possessed against the great rock within themselves. The talk shored them up like braces. When the talk finally stopped, J. Sutter went to his room and lay awake for hours. He thought about the challenge he had made to himself. Through the back window he could hear the river and its dark course through the land. Frantic, pushing across distance until it broke free of land and found release. But it is a long course downriver. His sleep when it came did not comfort for the dreams it brought. He lay in his bed and shook. It was only when they were walking up the road to the graveyard that his discomfort eased. In the graveyard, with his hands in the dirt.

Behind him he hears the creaking of a door and he twists his body. J. Sutter sees the crag face of the stamp collector as the man walks out of the room, hunched down as if he carries a mule load on his back. They meet eyes. J. Sutter walks over to the man. He says, I wanted to thank you for the other night. For saving my life, he says. He extends his hand to the other man's hand. The man's hand is cold in his and J. Sutter shrivels. He does not mean to but he shrivels as the coldness goes through his palm and enters his blood. The man mumbles something that J. Sutter does not hear. It is like he has stones in his mouth. The eyes of the man squirm away like white bugs under a rock that has been picked up. As if they have been suddenly exposed and are afraid of being seen. He asks the stamp collector his name and the man tells him. The man quickly shrinks away and scuttles back to his room, abandoning his errand. He does not have another chance to thank the man for saving him from choking.

The yellow paint that had divided the asphalt into parking spaces has been scratched away. There are no dividers anymore. Just open space out on the black tar. J. Sutter stands in the open lot trying to decide. If he catches an earlier flight out he will miss the event and fail in his attempt to go for the record. He has been at it a long time, he has put a lot of labor into advancing the unbroken line of events. Each day he makes progress and goes deeper in and the line is advanced. He tucks his thumbs into his jeans and the fabric chafes against the cuts on his fingers. It pains him. His comrades have laid odds on his chance of success. They will joke and trade their wages if he skips the event in town. The winner will hold out his palm and say pay up. J. Sutter will no longer be the man going for the record.

The other men are already in town, eating food and preparing for the ceremony. Lucien will be there too, checking his watch to preserve the timetable. J. Sutter will not get to say good-bye if he leaves early. He and Pamela are on the same airline. It is a simple matter to get on an earlier flight. He knows about airports. The man behind the ticket counter can work his machine and seat them together. He will get the rest of the story, the parts she has not given him yet. Over time he will get the rest of the story. He already knows the ending. He witnessed it with his own eyes. But there is more. When he gets it all it will be done and there is no telling where he will be then. If he does not stay.

Cars round the corner of the mountain. They come more frequently as he stands there deciding. The cars come from the east. It is the final event of John Henry Days and it is what they have all been waiting for. All the people from all around are coming to celebrate the old contest. They have heard about it and they want to be up front when it happens. It is a once in a lifetime thing. It will become part of the legend of this place. One car comes from the east but it does not keep going. The car slows off the road, grinding across dirt and then asphalt, and comes to rest a few feet from him. The sound of the horn is loud above the sound of the river and the occasional cry of birds. It is a taxi. Pamela opens the door of her room. She looks first at the taxi and then she looks at J. Sutter. She waves a hand at the taxi driver. She looks at J. Sutter and cocks her head for a moment. Then she pulls the door a little, leaving him a bit of wall to see inside her room. There is still time. It will not take him long to get his little things together. They will wait if he asks. He stands there with the sun on his face deciding, as if choices are possible.

She asked one last thing when they came down the mountain. When they came down the mountain she asked, what's the J. stand for? He told her.